I0523788

Hans Christian Andersen

Stories and Fairy Tales

Vol. 1

Hans Christian Andersen

Stories and Fairy Tales
Vol. 1

ISBN/EAN: 9783337245849

Printed in Europe, USA, Canada, Australia, Japan

Cover: Foto ©Andreas Hilbeck / pixelio.de

More available books at **www.hansebooks.com**

ANDERSEN'S
STORIES & FAIRY TALES

Her tears fell upon the jasmine bough,
and day by day, in the same measure as she grew paler, the bough
became fresher and greener; one
shoot after another sprang up;" †
A 36

STORIES & FAIRY TALES BY HANS CHRISTIAN ANDERSEN

TRANSLATED BY H. OSKAR SOMMER. Ph.D. WITH 100 PICTURES BY ARTHUR . J . GASKIN.

VOLUME 1

"ROCK A BY BABY ON THE TREE TOP."

PUBLISHED BY GEORGE ALLEN
LONDON & ORPINGTON. M·D·CCC·XC·III

BALLANTYNE PRESS
LONDON & EDINBURGH

CONTENTS

CONTENTS

The Nightingale

IN China, as you know, the emperor is a China-man, and all those he has about him are Chinamen too. The following story happened many years ago, but that is just why it is worth hearing before it is forgotten. The em-peror's castle was the most beautiful in the world and was entirely of fine porcelain ; it was very costly, but so brittle and delicate to touch, that one had to be very careful. In the garden were seen the most won-derful flowers, to the finest of which tinkling silver bells were tied, lest people should pass without noticing them. Indeed, everything in the emperor's garden was well thought out, and it was such a large one that the gardener himself did not know where it ended. If you kept on walking you came to a noble forest with high trees and deep lakes. The forest sloped straight down to the deep blue sea, and large ships could sail right up under the branches of the trees. In one of these trees there lived a nightingale who sang so beautifully that even the poor fishermen, who had plenty of other things to do, would stop and listen when, on going out at night to spread their nets, they heard it sing. "Heavens! how beautiful that is," they would say; but they had to attend to their work and forget the bird. So if it sang again next night, and the fishermen came that way, they would again exclaim, "How beautifully that bird sings!"

Travellers came from every country in the world to the emperor's city, which they admired very much, as well as the castle and the garden. But when they heard the nightingale, they would exclaim, "That is the best of all!" And when the travellers returned home they told of these things, and the learned ones wrote many books about the town, the castle and the garden. Neither did they forget the nightingale: that was praised most of all, and those who could write poetry wrote most beautiful poems about the nightingale in the wood by the deep sea.

These books travelled all over the world, and some of them came into the hands of the emperor. He sat in his golden chair reading and reading on; every moment he nodded his head, for it pleased him to find the beautiful descriptions of the city, the castle and the garden. Then he came to the words:

"But the nightingale is the best of all!"

"What is this?" said he. "I don't know the nightingale at all. Is there such a bird in my empire, and even in my garden? I have never heard of it. Fancy learning such a thing for the first time from a book!"

Hereupon he called his chamberlain, who was so important that when any one of lower rank than himself dared to speak to him or to ask him anything, he would only answer, "Pooh!" and that meant nothing.

"There is said to be a most remarkable bird here, called the nightingale," said the emperor. "They say it is the finest thing in my great empire. Why have I never been told about it?"

"I have never heard it mentioned before," said the chamberlain. "It has never been presented at court."

"I wish it to come and sing before me this evening," said the emperor. "The whole world knows what I possess, while I myself do not."

"I have never heard it mentioned before," said the chamberlain; "but I shall look for it and I shall find it."

But where was it to be found? The chamberlain ran up and down all the stairs, through halls and corridors, but not one of those whom he met had heard of the nightingale. So he ran back to the emperor, and said that it must certainly be an invention of those people who wrote books.

"Your Imperial Majesty will scarcely believe," said he, "what things are written in books. It is all fiction and something that is called the black art."

"But the book in which I have read this," said the emperor, "has been sent to me by the high and mighty Emperor of Japan, and there cannot therefore be anything untrue in it. I will hear the nightingale! It must be here this evening! It has my highest favour, and if it does not come, the whole court shall be trampled upon after supper."

"Tsing pe!" said the chamberlain, and ran up and down all the stairs again, and through all the halls and corridors; and half the court ran with him, for they were not at all desirous of being trampled upon. Then there was a great inquiry after the remarkable nightingale which was known to all the world except to the people at court.

At last they came upon a poor little girl in the kitchen, who said, "Dear me, I know the nightingale well, and it can sing too! Every evening I have leave to take home to my poor sick mother the scraps from the table; she lives down by the seashore, and when I am tired I sit down to rest in the wood as I come back, and then I hear the nightingale sing. It makes the tears come into my eyes, and I feel just as if my mother were kissing me."

"Little maid," said the chamberlain, "I will get you an appointment in the kitchen, and permission to see the emperor dine, if you will lead us to the nightingale, for it has been commanded to appear this evening."

So they all went out into the wood, where the nightingale was wont to sing; half the court was there. When they were well on their way a cow began to low. "Oh," said the courtiers, "now we've got it! What wonderful power in such a small creature! I have certainly heard it before."

"No, those are cows lowing," said the little maid; "we are a long way from the place yet."

Some frogs then began to croak in the marsh.

"Beautiful!" said the Chinese court chaplain. "Now I hear it; it sounds exactly like little church bells."

"No," said the little maid, "those are frogs. But I think we shall soon hear it now." And then the nightingale began to sing.

"That's it!" said the little girl. "Hark, hark; there it sits!" And she pointed out a little grey bird up in the branches.

"Is it possible?" said the chamberlain. "I should never have imagined it like that. How simple it looks! I suppose it has lost its colour at seeing so many grand people around it."

"Little nightingale," the little maid called out in a loud tone, "our most gracious emperor wishes you to sing to him."

"With the greatest pleasure," said the nightingale, and sang so nicely that it was a pleasure to hear it.

"It sounds exactly like glass bells," said the chamberlain. "And look at its little throat, how it works. It is remarkable that we never heard it before; it will be a great success at court."

"Shall I sing before the emperor again?" asked the nightingale, believing that the emperor was also present.

"My excellent little nightingale," said the chamberlain, "I have great pleasure in inviting you to a court festival this evening, when you will bewitch His Imperial Majesty with your charming song."

"That is best heard in the woods," said the nightingale; but still it came willingly when it heard the emperor wished it.

The castle had been elegantly decorated. The walls and the floors, which were of porcelain, glittered in the light of many thousands of golden lamps; the most beautiful flowers, which tinkled merrily, stood in the corridors. In fact, what with the running to and fro and the draught, the bells tinkled so loudly that you could not hear yourself speak.

In the centre of the great hall in which the emperor sat, a golden perch had been fixed for the nightingale. The whole court was present, and the little kitchen-maid, having now received the title of a real court cook, had obtained permission to stand behind the door. All were dressed in their very best, and all had their eyes on the little grey bird, to whom the emperor nodded.

The nightingale sang so beautifully that tears came into the emperor's eyes and ran down his cheeks, and when the bird sang still more beautifully it went straight to one's heart. The emperor was so pleased that he said the nightingale should have his golden slipper to wear round its neck. But the nightingale declined with thanks, saying that it had already received sufficient reward.

"I have seen tears in the emperor's eyes, and that is the greatest treasure for me. An emperor's tears have a wonderful power. Heaven knows, I have been sufficiently rewarded." Thereupon she again sang in her beautiful, sweet voice.

"That is the sweetest coquetry that we know," said the ladies who were standing round, and then took water in their mouths to make them cluck when any one spoke to them. This made them think they were nightingales too. Even the footmen and the chambermaids allowed themselves to express their satisfaction— that is saying a good deal, for they are the hardest to please. In a word, the nightingale was a great success.

It was now to remain at court, have its own cage, and liberty to go out twice a day and once during the night. It was then accompanied by twelve servants, each of whom held it fast by a silken string attached to its leg. There was by no means any pleasure in such flying.

The whole city talked about the wonderful bird, and if two

people met, one would say to the other "Nightin," and the other would answer "gale." And then they sighed and understood each other. Eleven pedlars' children had even been named after the bird, though not one of them could sing a note.

One day the emperor received a large parcel, on which was written : "The nightingale."

"Here we have a new book about our celebrated bird," said the emperor. It was no book, however, but a small work of art, which lay in a casket : an artificial nightingale, supposed to look like the living one, but covered all over with diamonds, rubies and sapphires. As soon as the imitation bird had been wound up, it could sing one of the pieces that the real bird sang, and then it would move its tail up and down, all glittering with silver and gold. Round its neck hung a little ribbon on which was written : "The Emperor of Japan's nightingale is poor compared with that of the Emperor of China."

" How beautiful ! " they all cried ; and he who had brought the artificial bird immediately received the title of Imperial Nightingale-bringer-in-chief.

" Now they must sing together ; what a lovely duet that will be ! "

And so they had to sing together ; but it did not go very well, for the real bird sang in its own way, and the imitation one sang only waltzes.

" That is not the new one's fault," said the music-master ; " it sings in perfect time, and quite according to my method." So the imitation bird had to sing alone. It had quite as great a success as the real one ; besides, it was much prettier to look at glittering like bracelets and breast-pins.

Thirty-three times it sang one and the same tune and still was not tired.

The courtiers would like to have heard it all over again, but the emperor thought that the live nightingale ought now to sing something as well. But where was it ? No one had noticed it flying out of the window back to its green woods.

" But how is that ? " said the emperor. And all the courtiers blamed the nightingale, and thought it a most ungrateful creature. " In any way, we have the best bird," they said ; and so the imitation one had to sing again, which made the thirty-fourth' time that they had heard the same tune. Even then they did not know it by heart, for it was much too difficult. The music-master praised the bird exceedingly; indeed, he assured them that it was better than a nightingale, not only in its dress and the number of beautiful diamonds, but also in its inside.

"For, see, your gracious majesty and my lords, with a real nightingale we never know what is coming next, but with the artificial one everything is arranged. You can open it, you can explain it, and make people understand how the waltzes lie, how they work, and why one note follows the other."

"That is just what we think too," they all said; and the music-master received permission to show the bird to the people on the following Sunday. The emperor commanded that they should also hear it sing. When they did so, they were as pleased as if they had all got drunk on tea, which is a Chinese fashion; and they all said "Oh!" and held up their first fingers and nodded. But the poor fishermen, who had heard the real nightingale, said, "It sounds pretty enough, the tunes are all like too, but there is something wanting—I don't know what."

The real nightingale was banished from the country and the empire. The imitation bird had its place on a silk cushion close to the emperor's bed; and all the presents which it had received lay around it, and it had been promoted to the rank of Number One on the Left, with the title of Grand Imperial Toilet-table Singer. The emperor considered the left side, on which the heart lies, as the most noble, and an emperor has his heart on the left just like other people. The music-master, too, wrote a work of twenty-five volumes about the artificial bird; it was so learned and so long, so full of the most difficult Chinese words, that all the people said they had read it and understood it, or otherwise they would have been thought stupid and had their bodies trampled upon.

For a whole year it went on like that. The emperor, the court, and all the other Chinamen knew every turn in the artificial bird's song by heart, and that was just why it pleased them now more than ever. They could sing with it, and often did so, too. The street boys sang "Tseetseetsee! Cluck, cluck, cluck!" and the emperor did just the same. It was really most beautiful.

One evening, when the artificial bird was singing its best and the emperor was lying in bed and listening to it, something inside the bird snapped with a bang. All the wheels ran round with a "whirr-r-r," and then the music stopped.

The emperor immediately jumped out of bed and sent for his physician; but what could he do? Then they fetched the watchmaker, and, after a good deal of talking and examining, he got the bird into something like order; but he said that it must not be used too much, as the barrels were worn out, and it was impossible to put in new ones with any certainty of the music going right. Now there was great sorrow; the imitation bird could only be allowed to sing once a year, and even that was almost too much. On these occasions the music-master would make a little speech full of big words, and say that the singing was just as good as ever; and after that of course the court were as well pleased as before.

Five years had now passed, and a great sorrow fell upon the land. The Chinese were all really very fond of their emperor, and now he was ill and could not live long, they said. A new emperor had already been chosen, and the people stood out in the street and asked the chamberlain how their old emperor was.

"Pooh!" he said, and shook his head.

Cold and pale lay the emperor in his great, splendid bed; the whole court thought he was dead, and every one ran away to greet the new emperor. The pages ran out to gossip about it, and the maids-of-honour had a grand tea-party. Cloth had been laid down in all the halls and corridors, so that no footstep should be heard, and it was therefore very, very quiet. But the emperor was not dead yet; stiff and pale he lay on the splendid bed with the long velvet curtains and the heavy gold tassels, and high up a window stood open, and the moon shone in upon him and the artificial bird.

The poor emperor could hardly breathe; he felt as though

something were sitting on his chest. He opened his eyes and saw that it was Death who was sitting there ; he had put on the emperor's golden crown, and held his golden sword in one hand, and his beautiful flag in the other.

All around, strange heads peeped out from the folds of the large velvet bed-curtains: some were hideous, others were sweet and gentle.

These were all the emperor's bad and good deeds, which were staring at him now that Death was sitting on his heart.

" Do you remember this ? " they whispered one after another. "Do you recollect that ? " And then they told him of so much that the perspiration ran down from his brow.

"That I did not know," cried the emperor. "Music ! music ! the great Chinese drum !" he shouted ; "so that I may not have to hear what they say."

But they went on, and Death nodded like a Chinaman to all that was said.

" Music ! music !" shrieked the emperor. " You precious little golden bird ! Sing, do sing ! I have given you gold and jewels, I have hung even my gold slipper round your neck. Sing, I say, sing ! "

But the bird was silent ; it could not sing without being wound up, and there was no one to do it. Death continued to stare at the emperor with his large, hollow eyes, and all was still, terribly still. Suddenly from the window came the sound of sweetest singing ; it was the real little nightingale sitting on a bough outside. It had heard how the emperor was suffering, and had therefore come to console him and bring him hope by its singing. And as it sang, the ghostly heads grew paler and paler, the blood began to flow faster and faster through the emperor's weak limbs and even Death listened and said: "Go on, little nightingale, go on."

"Yes, but will you give me the beautiful golden sword? Will you give me the rich banner? Will you give me the emperor' rich crown ? "

And Death gave up each of these treasures for a song, whilst the nightingale still went on singing. It sang of the quiet churchyard where the white roses grow, where the elder tree scents the air, and where the fresh grass is moistened by the tears of those who are left behind. Then Death longed to be in his garden, and floated out through the window like a cold white mist.

"Thanks, thanks," said the emperor. "You heavenly little bird! I know you well. It was you that I drove out of my country and my empire. And still you have charmed away the evil faces from my bed, and removed Death from my heart. How can I reward you?"

"You have rewarded me," said the nightingale. "I drew tears from your eyes when for the first time I sang to you; that I shall never forget. They are jewels that gladden the heart of a singer. But sleep now and get well and strong again. I will sing you something."

And as it sang the emperor fell into a sweet slumber. Oh, how mild and refreshing was that sleep! The sun shone in upon him through the window when he awoke strong and well. None of his servants had yet returned, for they believed he was dead; only the nightingale was still sitting by him singing.

"You must always stay with me," said the emperor. "You shall now sing only when you like, and I shall smash the imitation bird into a thousand pieces."

"Don't do that," said the nightingale. "It did its best, as long as it could. Keep it, as before. I cannot build my nest and live in the castle; but let me come just when I like. In the evening I will sit on that bough near your window and sing something to you, so that you shall be joyful and pensive at the same time. I will sing of those who are happy and of those who suffer. I will sing of the good and of the bad that are hidden all around you. The little singing bird flies far away, to the poor fisherman, to the peasant's cottage, to all who are far removed from you and your court. I love your heart more than your crown, and yet the crown has almost a halo of holiness around it. I will come and I will sing to you. But you must promise me one thing."

"Everything," said the emperor, and standing there in his imperial robes, which he had himself put on, he pressed his sword, all heavy with gold, to his heart.

"I only ask one thing. Let no one know that you have a little bird that tells you everything ; it will be for the best."

Saying this the nightingale flew away.

The servants came in to look after their dead emperor. When they saw him they stood aghast, and the emperor said, "Good morning !"

The Rose-Elf

N the midst of a garden grew a rose-tree ; upon it were many, many roses ; in one of them, the most beautiful of all, lived an elf. He was so very small that no human eye could perceive him. Behind every petal of the rose he had a bedroom. No child could have been more beautifully formed than he was ; he had wings that reached from his shoulders down to his feet. All his rooms were so sweet and fragrant, the walls were so bright and beautiful, for they consisted of the pink rose-petals.

All day long the elf enjoyed himself in the warm sunshine, flying from flower to flower, and dancing on the wings of the fluttering butterfly. One day he measured how many steps he would have to take in order to pass through all the roads and paths which were on a single leaf of the lime-tree. These were what we call the veins of the leaf; to him they seemed to be endless roads. Before he had finished the sun set ; he had begun his task too late. It became very cold, dew fell and the wind was blowing ; at this time he would have been best at home. He hastened as much as he could, but his rose was closed up, he could not enter, and not a single rose was open. The poor little elf was very frightened. He had never before been out of doors at night ; as he had always sweetly slumbered behind the warm rose-petals, this would mean certain death to him !

The elf knew that at the other end of the garden stood a summer-house, covered all over with beautiful honeysuckle ; the blossoms looked like large painted horns ; in one of them, he thought, he might enter and sleep until the next morning   Thither he flew.

But hush ! Two people were sitting in the summer-house : a handsome young man and a beautiful girl. They sat side by side and wished that they need never part. They loved one another so much—much more indeed than the best child would love his father or mother.

"Alas ! we must part," said the young man. " Your brother dislikes me, and that is why he sends me on an errand so far away over mountains and seas. Farewell, my own dear love, for that you will always be to me."

Then they kissed each other, and the girl cried and gave him a rose. But before she gave it to him she so ardently pressed it to her lips that the flower opened.

Now the little elf flew into it and rested his head against the fine fragrant walls ; there he could hear very well how they bade farewell to each other ! He felt that the young man placed the rose on his breast. Oh, how his heart was beating ! The little elf could not fall asleep, it throbbed so much.

The rose did not long remain undisturbed on his breast. The young man, while walking alone through the dark forest, took it out, and kissed it so often and so passionately that the little elf was almost crushed. He could feel through the leaf how hot the young man's lips were ; and the rose had opened its petals as if the strongest midday sun were shining upon it.

Then came another man, sullen and wicked; he was the malicious brother of the beautiful girl. He drew out a dagger, and while the other fondly kissed the rose, stabbed him to death ; then he cut off the head from the body, and buried both in the soft ground under a lime-tree.

"Now he's gone and forgotten," thought the murderer ; " he will never return again. He was to set out on a long journey, over mountains and across the sea ; on such an expedition a man might easily lose his life, and he has lost it. He will never come back, and my sister dare not ask me what has become of him."

Thus thinking, he scraped dry leaves together with his foot, heaped them on the soft mould, and went home in the darkness

f the night. But he was not alone, as he imagined, for the little
lf was with him. He had seated himself in a dry, rolled-up leaf
f the lime-tree, which had fallen on the wicked man's hair while
e was digging the grave. He had put his hat on now; it was
ery dark inside the hat, and the elf was trembling with horror
nd indignation at the evil deed.

In the dawn of the morning the murderer reached home; he
ook off his hat, and entered his sister's bedroom. There the
eautiful girl, with rosy cheeks, was sleeping and dreaming of him
hom she loved so dearly, and whom she supposed now to travel
ver mountains and across the sea.

The unnatural brother bent over the girl, and laughed hideously,
s only evil demons can laugh. The dry leaf dropped out of his
air on her counterpane, but he did not notice it, and went out of
he room to have a little sleep in the early morning hours. The
lf left his resting-place and slipped into the ear of the sleeping
irl, and told her, as in a dream, the horrible deed; he described
he spot where her lover was stabbed and where his body was
nterred; he told her of the blooming lime-tree standing close by,
nd said: "That you should not think all I told you is only a
ream, you will find on your bed on awaking a dry leaf." And
hen she awoke she really found it. Then she cried bitterly.
he window was open all day long; the little elf might easily have
eturned to the roses and to the other flowers in the garden, but
e had not the heart to leave the unfortunate girl.

On the window-sill stood a little bunch of monthly roses in a
ower-pot; in one of its blooms the elf sat down and looked at the
oor girl. Her brother came several times into the room, and in
pite of his crime seemed quite cheerful, and she had not the
ourage to say a word about her grief.

No sooner had the night come than she stole out of the house
nd went into the wood, to the spot where the lime-tree stood;
he removed the dry leaves from the ground, turned the earth up
nd found her murdered sweetheart. And she wept bitterly. She
rayed God that she might also die.

She would have gladly taken the body home with her, but that
as impossible. So she took up the pale-faced head with the

closed eyes, kissed the cold lips and shook the earth out of the beautiful curls. "I will at least keep this," she said. When she had replaced the mould and the dry leaves on the body, she took the head and a little bough of a jasmine-bush growing near the spot where the body was buried, and returned home. Upon

reaching her room she took the largest flower-pot she could find, put the head into it, covered it over with mould, and planted therein the jasmine bough.

"Farewell, farewell," whispered the little elf, being unable to witness any longer her grief and pain. He then returned to his rose in the garden; but the rose was faded, only a few withered petals were still clinging to the green stalk. "Oh, how soon all that is beautiful and good vanishes," sighed the little elf.

At last he found a new rose and made it his home; under the shelter of its tender and fragrant petals he could abide in safety. Every morning he flew to the window of the poor girl, and every morning he found her crying by the flower-pot. Her tears fell

upon the jasmine-bough, and day by day, in the same measure as
she grew paler, the bough became fresher and greener; one shoot
after another sprang up; many little white buds burst forth, and
she kissed them. The heartless brother scolded her and asked
her if she had lost her senses; for he did not like to see her crying
over the flower-pot, and he could not make out why she did it.
He had no idea whose closed eyes, whose red lips were decaying
in the flower-pot.

One day the little rose-elf found her slumbering and resting with
her head on the flower-pot. He slipped again into her ear, and
told her of the evening in the summer-house, of the sweet smell of
the rose, and of the love of rose-elves. She dreamt so sweetly, and
with her dream her life passed away; she died a calm and peaceful
death. She had gone to heaven to him whom she loved.

And the jasmine unfolded its buds into large white flowers, and
filled the air with its peculiarly sweet fragrance, it could not otherwise give vent to its grief for the dead girl.

The wicked brother took the beautiful jasmine bush as his inheritance, carried it into his bedroom and placed it close by his
bed; for it was delightful to look at, and its fragrance was very
pleasant. The little rose-elf followed; he flew from flower to
flower—for in each of them lived a little elf—and told them of the
murdered young man whose head was decaying beneath the mould,
and of the wicked brother and the poor sister.

"We know all about it," replied the little elves, "we know it, for
have we not sprung forth from the eyes and lips of the dead man's
face? We know," they repeated, nodding their heads in a strange
manner.

The rose-elf could not understand why they remained so calm;
he flew out to the bees, which were gathering honey, and told them
the story of the wicked brother. The bees told their queen, and
the queen ordered that they should all go on the next morning to
kill the murderer. But when it was night—the first night after
his sister's death—while the brother was sleeping close by the
fragrant jasmine-bush in his bed, all its flowers opened and all the
little invisible elves came out, armed with venomous spears, and
seated themselves in his ears and told him terrible dreams; then

they flew on to his lips and stabbed his tongue with their poisonous weapons. "Now we have avenged the dead," they said, and returned to their white flowers.

When, on the next morning, the window of the bedroom was opened, the rose-elf and the whole swarm of the bees with their queen entered to carry out their revenge. But he was already dead. People standing around the bed, said: "The smell of the jasmine has killed him."

The rose-elf understood the revenge of the flowers and told the queen of the bees about it, who with her whole swarm was humming round the flower-pot. The bees could not be driven away from it, and when at last a man took up the pot a bee stung him in the hand, so that he dropped it, and it broke to pieces. Then all saw the bleached skull and understood that the dead man in the bed was a murderer.

The queen of the bees hummed and sang of the revenge of the flowers and of the rose-elf, and said that behind the smallest leaf dwells *one* who can disclose evil deeds and revenge them.

The Emperor's New Suit

MANY, many years ago lived an emperor, who thought so much of new clothes that he spent all his money in order to obtain them; his only ambition was to be always well dressed. He did not care for his soldiers, and the theatre did not amuse him; the only thing, in fact, he thought anything of was to drive out and show a new suit of clothes. He had a coat for every hour of the day; and as one would say of a king "He is in his cabinet," so one could say of him, "The emperor is in his dressing-room."

The great city where he resided was very gay; every day many strangers from all parts of the globe arrived. One day two swindlers came to this city; they made people believe

at they were weavers, and declared they could manufacture
e finest cloth to be imagined. Their colours and patterns,
ey said, were not only exceptionally beautiful, but the clothes
ade of their material possessed the wonderful quality of being
visible to any man who was unfit for his office or unpardonably
upid.

"That must be wonderful cloth," thought the emperor. "If
were to be dressed in a suit made of this cloth I should be
le to find out which men in my empire were unfit for their
aces, and I could distinguish the clever from the stupid. I
ust have this cloth woven for me without delay." And he
ve a large sum of money to the swindlers, in advance, that
ey should set to work without any loss of time. They set up
·o looms, and pretended to be very hard at work, but
ey did nothing whatever on the looms. They asked for
e finest silk and the most precious gold-cloth; all they got
ey did away with, and worked at the empty looms till late
 night.

"I should very much like to know how they are getting on
th the cloth," thought the emperor. But he felt rather un-
sy when he remembered that he who was not fit for his office
uld not see it. Personally, he was of opinion that he had
thing to fear, yet he thought it advisable to send somebody else
st to see how matters stood. Everybody in the town knew what
remarkable quality the stuff possessed, and all were anxious to
e how bad or stupid their neighbours were.

"I shall send my honest old minister to the weavers,"
ought the emperor. "He can judge best how the stuff looks,
r he is intelligent, and nobody understands his office better
an he."

The good old minister went into the room where the swindlers
t before the empty looms. "Heaven preserve us!" he thought,
d opened his eyes wide, "I cannot see anything at all," but he
d not say so. Both swindlers requested him to come near, and
ked him if he did not admire the exquisite pattern and the beau-
ul colours, pointing to the empty looms. The poor old minister
ed his very best, but he could see nothing, for there was nothing

to be seen. "Oh dear," he thought, "can I be so stupid? I should never have thought so, and nobody must know it! Is it possible that I am not fit for my office? No, no, I cannot say that I was unable to see the cloth."

"Now, have you got nothing to say?" said one of the swindlers, while he pretended to be busily weaving.

"Oh, it is very pretty, exceedingly beautiful," replied the old minister looking through his glasses. "What a beautiful pattern, what brilliant colours! I shall tell the emperor that I like the cloth very much."

"We are pleased to hear that," said the two weavers, and described to him the colours and explained the curious pattern. The old minister listened attentively, that he might relate to the emperor what they said; and so he did.

Now the swindlers asked for more money, silk and gold-cloth, which they required for weaving. They kept everything for themselves, and not a thread came near the loom, but they continued, as hitherto, to work at the empty looms.

Soon afterwards the emperor sent another honest courtier to the weavers to see how they were getting on, and if the cloth was nearly finished. Like the old minister, he looked and looked but could see nothing, as there was nothing to be seen.

"Is it not a beautiful piece of cloth?" asked the two swindlers, showing and explaining the magnificent pattern, which, however, did not exist.

"I am not stupid," said the man, "it is therefore my good appointment for which I am not fit. It is very strange, but I must not let any one know it;" and he praised the cloth, which he did not see, and expressed his joy at the beautiful colours and the fine pattern. "It is very excellent," he said to the emperor.

Everybody in the whole town talked about the precious cloth. At last the emperor wished to see it himself, while it was still on the loom. With a number of courtiers, including the two who had already been there, he went to the two clever swindlers, who now worked as hard as they could, but without using any thread.

"Is it not magnificent?" said the two old statesmen who had

been there before. "Your Majesty must admire the colours and the pattern." And then they pointed to the empty looms, for they imagined the others could see the cloth.

"What is this?" thought the emperor, "I do not see anything at all. That is terrible! Am I stupid? Am I unfit to be

THE EMPERORS NEW SUIT.   A]G.

emperor? That would indeed be the most dreadful thing that could happen to me."

"Really," he said, turning to the weavers, "your cloth has our most gracious approval;" and nodding contentedly he looked at the empty loom, for he did not like to say that he saw nothing. All his attendants, who were with him, looked and looked, and although they could not see anything more than the others, they said, like the emperor, "It is very beautiful." And all advised him to wear the new magnificent clothes at a great procession which was soon to take place. "It is magnificent, beautiful, excellent," one heard them say; everybody seemed to be delighted, and the emperor appointed the two swindlers "Imperial Court weavers."

The whole night previous to the day on which the procession

was to take place, the swindlers pretended to work, and burned more than sixteen candles. People should see that they were busy to finish the emperor's new suit. They pretended to take the cloth from the loom, and worked about in the air with big scissors, and sewed with needles without thread, and said at last: "The emperor's new suit is ready now."

The emperor and all his barons then came to the hall; the swindlers held their arms up as if they held something in their hands and said: "These are the trousers!" "This is the coat!" and "Here is the cloak!" and so on. "They are all as light as a cobweb, and one must feel as if one had nothing at all upon the body; but that is just the beauty of them."

"Indeed!" said all the courtiers; but they could not see anything, for there was nothing to be seen.

"Does it please your Majesty now to graciously undress," said the swindlers, "that we may assist your Majesty in putting on the new suit before the large looking-glass?"

The emperor undressed, and the swindlers pretended to put the new suit upon him, one piece after another; and the emperor looked at himself in the glass from every side.

"How well they look! How well they fit!" said all. "What a beautiful pattern! What fine colours! That is a magnificent suit of clothes!"

The master of the ceremonies announced that the bearers of the canopy, which was to be carried in the procession, were ready.

"I am ready," said the emperor. "Does not my suit fit me marvellously?" Then he turned once more to the looking-glass, that people should think he admired his garments.

The chamberlains, who were to carry the train, stretched their hands to the ground as if they lifted up a train, and pretended to hold something in their hands; they did not like people to know that they could not see anything.

The emperor marched in the procession under the beautiful canopy, and all who saw him in the street and out of the windows exclaimed: "Indeed, the emperor's new suit is incomparable! What a long train he has! How well it fits him!" Nobody wished to let others know that he saw nothing, for then he would have been unfit for his office or too stupid. Never emperor's clothes were more admired.

"But he has nothing on at all," said a little child at last. "Good heavens! listen to the voice of an innocent child," said the father, and one whispered to the other what the child had said. "But he has nothing on at all," cried at last the whole people. That made a deep impression upon the emperor, for it seemed to him that they were right, but he thought to himself, "Now I must bear up to the end." And the chamberlains walked with still greater dignity, as if they carried the train which did not exist.

The Storks

N the roof of the last house in a little village was a stork's nest; a mother-stork sat in it, and four young ones were stretching forth their little heads with the pointed black beaks, which had not yet turned red like those of the old birds. At a little distance the father-stork stood upright and almost immovable on the ridge of the roof; he had drawn up one leg, in order not to be quite idle, while he was watching over his nest like a sentry. He stood so still that one might have thought he was carved in wood. "Surely, it must look very important, that my wife has a sentry before her nest," he thought. "Nobody knows that I am her husband. People will think that I am commanded to stand here. That looks so distinguished." And he continued to stand on one leg.

A crowd of children were playing below in the street; no sooner had they noticed the storks than one of the pluckiest boys began to sing an old ditty to tease them; soon all his playmates joined in; but they only repeated what he could remember of it:

> "Fly away, stork, fly away!
> Stand not on one leg all day,
> While your dear wife in the nest
> Gently rocks her babes to rest.

> *" The first little stork they will hang,*
> *The second will fry by the fire,*
> *The third will be shot with a bang,*
> *The fourth will be roast for the squire."*

" Do you hear what those boys are singing?" said the young storks, "they say we shall be hanged and roasted."

"Never mind what they say," replied the mother-stork; "if you do not listen to them, they can do you no harm."

The boys went on singing, and pointed at the storks with their fingers; only one of them, named Peter, said that it was wrong of them to tease the birds, and did not join them. The mother-stork comforted her children. " You must not pay attention to them; look at your father, how quietly he stands there on one leg !"

" Oh, we are so frightened," said the young ones, and then they hid their heads in the nest.

On the following day, when the children had come out to play and saw the storks, they sang again the song :

> *" The third will be shot with a bang,*
> *The fourth will be roast for the squire."*

"Shall we really be hanged and roasted?" asked the young storks.

"Certainly not," replied the mother, "you will learn how to fly ; I shall teach you myself. Then we shall fly into the meadows and go to see the frogs, who will bow to us in the water and cry : 'Croak, croak'; and then we shall eat them up. That will be delightful."

" And then ?" asked the young ones.

"Then," continued the mother-stork, "all the storks of this country will come together, and the great autumn manœuvre will be gone through ; every stork must be able to fly well, for that is of great importance. All those who cannot fly the general kills with his beak. Therefore you must take great pains to learn it well, when the drilling begins."

" Why, then we shall be stabbed after all as the boys sing ; listen, they are singing it again."

"Only listen to me, and not to them," said the mother-stork.

"After the great autumn manœuvre we shall fly away from here to warmer countries, far away over mountains and woods. We shall fly to Egypt, where you shall see three-cornered stone houses, the pointed tops of which almost touch the clouds; people call them Pyramids, and they are much older than a stork can imagine. There is a river in that country which rises every year over its banks, covering the whole land with mud. We shall walk about in the mud and eat frogs."

"Oh, how charming," cried the young ones.

"Yes, indeed, that country is very pleasant; we shall do nothing there but eat all day long; and while we shall be so comfortable there, they will not have a single leaf on the trees in this country, and it will be so cold that the clouds will freeze, and fall down on the ground in little white rags." She meant, of course, the snow, but she could not otherwise explain it.

"Will the naughty boys also freeze to pieces?" asked the young storks.

"No," answered the mother, "they will not freeze to pieces, but they will not be very far from it. They will have to stay all day long in-doors, in the gloomy room; whereas you will fly about in foreign lands, where the warm sun shines and many flowers are blooming."

After some time the young ones had grown so tall that they could stand upright in the nest and look about into the neighbourhood; the father-stork returned every day with frogs and little snakes and all sorts of stork-dainties which he had picked up. Oh, it was so funny to see him perform tricks for their amusement; he used to place his head quite back on his tail and clatter with his beak as if it had been a rattle; and then he used to tell them stories about the marsh-land.

"Come along," the stork-mother said one day, "now you must learn to fly." The four young storks had to come out of the nest on to the ridge of the roof. At first they tottered about a good deal, and although they balanced themselves with their wings, they nearly fell down.

" You have only to look at me," said the mother. " You must hold your heads like this, and place your feet thus : one, two, one, two—that's right ; that is what will enable you to get on in the world." Then she flew a short distance away from them, and the young ones made a little jump, but they fell down with a thud, for their bodies were still too heavy.

" I do not wish to fly," said one of the young ones, and crept back into the nest ; " I do not care to go to warm countries."

" Would you prefer to freeze to death here, when the winter comes ; or shall the boys come to hang and roast you? I will call them."

" Oh no, no, dear mother," said the young stork, hopping out on the roof again to the others. On the third day they could already fly a little, and now they thought they would be able to soar in the air like their parents. They tried to do so, but they tumbled down, and had quickly to move their wings again. The boys in the street began to sing again :

> " *Fly away, stork, fly away,*
> *Stand not on one leg all day*," &c.

" Shall we fly down and pick their eyes out? " asked the young storks.

" No," said the mother ; " do not mind them. Only listen to me, that is far more important. One, two, three, now we turn to the right ; one, two, three, to the left ; now round the chimney-top. That was very good indeed ! The last clap with the wings was so correctly and well done that I shall let you come to-morrow with me to the marshes. There you will see several respectable storks with their families ; you must let them see that my children are the prettiest and best-behaved. You must proudly stride about ; that will look well, and by this you will gain respect "

" But shall we not punish those wicked boys? " asked the young storks.

" Let them cry as much as they like ; you will rise high into the clouds and fly away to the country of the pyramids while they are freezing, and have not a single green leaf nor a sweet apple."

"We shall take our revenge upon them," whispered the little ones, and went on practising.

Of all the boys in the street none was more bent upon singing the song than the one who had first started it, and he was quite a mite and not more than six years old. The young storks thought he was more than a hundred years old, because he was so much taller than their father and mother, and what did they know about the age of children and grown-up people? They made up their minds to take their revenge upon this boy, because he was the first to sing the song and was never tired of going on with it. The young storks were very angry with him, and the older they became the less they would suffer it; at last the mother had to give them the promise that they should be revenged, but not until the day before their departure.

"We must first see how you will behave at the great manœuvre. If you do badly, so that the general has to thrust his beak through you, the boys will be right, at least in a way. But let us see."

"You shall see," said the young ones, and took still greater pains; they practised every day, and soon they could fly so well that it was a pleasure to see them.

Autumn came at last: all the storks began to assemble and to set out for the warm countries, to pass the winter. That was a great manœuvre! They had to fly over woods and villages, only to see what they could do, for their journey was a very long one. They acquitted themselves so well that they passed the review excellently, and received frogs and snakes as a reward. That was the best certificate, and they could eat the frogs and the snakes, which was better still.

"Now we shall take our revenge," they said.

"Certainly," cried the mother-stork. "I have already thought of the best way. I know where the pond is in which all the little children are lying until the storks come and take them to their parents. The pretty little babies sleep there and dream so sweetly, much more sweetly than they will dream ever after. All the parents wish for such a little child, and the children wish for a brother or a sister. Now we shall go to the pond and fetch one for every child who has not sung that wicked song to tease the storks."

"But what shall we do to the bad boy who began to sing the song?"

"In the pond lies a little dead baby that has dreamt itself to death, that we will take to him; then he will cry, because we have brought him a dead little brother.   But the good boy—I hope you have not forgotten him, who said that it was wrong to tease animals—we will bring him a brother as well as a sister. And as this boy's name was Peter, you shall all henceforth be called Peter."

And so it was done, and all the storks are called Peter to the present day.

The Daisy

NOW listen! In the country, close by the high road, stood a farmhouse; perhaps you have passed by and seen it yourself. There was a little flower garden with painted wooden palings in front of it; close by was a ditch, on its fresh green bank grew a little daisy; the sun shone as warmly and brightly upon it as on the magnificent garden flowers, and therefore it thrived well One morning it had quite opened, and its little snow-white petals stood round the yellow centre, like the rays of the sun It did not mind that nobody saw it in the grass, and that it was a poor despised flower; on the contrary, it was quite happy and turned towards the sun, looking upward and listening to the song of the lark high up in the air.

The little daisy was as happy as if the day had been a great holiday, but it was only Monday. All the children were at school, and while they were sitting on the forms and learning their lessons, it sat on its thin green stalk and learnt from the sun and from its surroundings how kind God is, and it rejoiced

THE STORY
OF THE DAISY.

hat the song of the little lark expressed so sweetly and distinctly
ts own feelings. With a sort of reverence the daisy looked up
o the bird that could fly and sing, but it did not feel envious.
'I can see and hear," it thought; "the sun shines upon me,
ind the forest kisses me. How rich I am!"

In the garden close by grew many large and magnificent
lowers, and, strange to say, the less fragrance they had the
iaughtier and prouder they were. The peonies puffed them-
ielves up in order to be larger than the roses, but size is
iot everything! The tulips had the finest colours, and they
:new it well, too, for they were standing bolt upright like candles,
hat one might see them the better. In their pride they did not
ee the little daisy, which looked over to them and thought,
'How rich and beautiful they are! I am sure the pretty
iird will fly down and call upon them. Thank God, that I
tand so near and can at least see all the splendour." And while
he daisy was still thinking, the lark came flying down, crying
'Tweet," but not to the peonies and tulips—no, into the grass to
he poor daisy. Its joy was so great that it did not know what to
hink. The little bird hopped round it and sang, "How beauti-
ully soft the grass is, and what a lovely little flower with its golden
ieart and silver dress is growing here." The yellow centre in
he daisy did indeed look like gold, while the little petals shone as
irightly as silver.

How happy the daisy was! No one has the least idea. The
iird kissed it with its beak, sang to it, and then rose again up
o the blue sky. It was certainly more than a quarter of an
iour before the daisy recovered its senses. Half ashamed, yet
lad at heart, it looked over to the other flowers in the garden;
urely they had witnessed its pleasure and the honour that had
ieen done to it; they understood its joy. But the tulips stood
iore stiffly than ever, their faces were pointed and red, because
hey were vexed. The peonies were sulky; it was well that they
ould not speak, otherwise they would have given the daisy a
ood lecture. The little flower could very well see that they were
l at ease, and pitied them sincerely.

Shortly after this a girl came into the garden, with a large sharp knife. She went to the tulips and began cutting them off, one after another. " Ugh !" sighed the daisy, " that is terrible ; now they are done for."

The girl carried the tulips away. The daisy was glad that it was outside, and only a small flower—it felt very grateful. At sunset it folded its petals, and fell asleep, and dreamt all night of the sun and the little bird.

On the following morning, when the flower once more stretched forth its tender petals, like little arms, towards the air and light, the daisy recognised the bird's voice, but what it sang sounded so sad. Indeed the poor bird had good reason to be sad, for it had been caught and put into a cage close by the open window. It sang of the happy days when it could merrily fly about, of fresh green corn in the fields, and of the time when it could soar almost up to the clouds. The poor lark was most unhappy as a prisoner in a cage. The little daisy would have liked so much to help it, but what could be done ? Indeed, that was very difficult for such a small flower to find out. It entirely forgot how beautiful everything around it was, how warmly the sun was shining, and how splendidly white its own petals were. It could only think of the poor captive bird, for which it could do nothing. Then two little boys came out of the garden ; one of them had a large sharp knife, like that with which the girl had cut the tulips. They came straight towards the little daisy, which could not understand what they wanted.

" Here is a fine piece of turf for the lark," said one of the boys, and began to cut out a square round the daisy, so that it remained in the centre of the grass.

"Pluck the flower off," said the other boy, and the daisy trembled for fear, for to be pulled off meant death to it ; and it wished so much to live, as it was to go with the square of turf into the poor captive lark's cage.

" No, let it stay," said the other boy, " it looks so pretty."

And so it stayed, and was brought into the lark's cage. The poor bird was lamenting its lost liberty, and beating its wings against the wires ; and the little daisy could not speak or utter a consoling word, much as it would have liked to do so. So the forenoon passed.

" I have no water," said the captive lark, "they have all gone out, and forgotten to give me anything to drink. My throat is dry and burning. I feel as if I had fire and ice within me, and the air is so oppressive. Alas! I must die, and part with the warm sunshine, the fresh green meadows, and all the beauty that God has created." And it thrust its beak into the piece of grass, to refresh itself a little. Then it noticed the little daisy, and nodded to it, and kissed it with its beak and said: " You must also fade in here, poor little flower. You and the piece of grass are all they have given me in exchange for the whole world, which I enjoyed outside. Each little blade of grass shall be a green tree for me, each of your white petals a fragrant flower. Alas! you only remind me of what I have lost."

" I wish I could console the poor lark," thought the daisy. It could not move one of its leaves, but the fragrance of its delicate petals streamed forth, and was much stronger than such flowers usually have : the bird noticed it, although it was dying with thirst, and in its pain tore up the green blades of grass, but did not touch the flower.

The evening came, and nobody appeared to bring the poor bird a drop of water; it opened its beautiful wings, and fluttered about in its anguish; a faint and mournful " Tweet, tweet," was all it could utter, then it bent its little head towards the flower, and its heart broke for want and longing. The flower could not, as on the previous evening, fold up its petals and sleep; it drooped sorrowfully. The boys only came the next morning; when they saw the dead bird, they began to cry bitterly, dug a nice grave for it, and adorned it with flowers. The bird's body was placed in a pretty red box; they wished to bury it with royal honours. While it was alive and sang they forgot it, and let it suffer want in the cage; now, they cried over it and covered it with flowers The piece of turf, with the little daisy in it, was thrown out on the dusty highway. Nobody thought of the flower which had felt so much for the bird and had so greatly desired to comfort it.

The Steadfast Tin-Soldier

HERE were once twenty-five tin soldiers, who were all brothers, as they were cast from an old tin spoon. They all carried a gun in their left arm and looked straight forward; their uniform was red and blue. The first words which they heard upon seeing the light of day, when the lid was taken off the box in which they were packed, were, "Tin soldiers!" These words were uttered by a little boy who had received them as a birthday present, and clapped his hands for joy; he then put them in rank and file on the table. One soldier looked exactly like the other: only one, who had been cast last of all, when there was not enough tin, was not like his brothers, for he had only one leg; nevertheless, he stood just as firmly on his one leg as the others on two; and he was the one who became remarkable.

On the table on which they were placed were many other toys; but what caught the eye most of all was a pretty little castle of cardboard. Through its small windows one could look into the rooms. Before the castle stood little trees surrounding a clear lake, which was formed by a small looking-glass. Swans made of wax were swimming on it and were reflected by it. All this was very pretty, but the prettiest of all was a little lady who stood in the open door of the castle; she was cut out of paper, but she had a frock of the whitest muslin on, and a piece of narrow blue ribbon was fixed on her shoulders like a bodice, on it was fixed a glittering tinsel rose, as large as her whole face. The little lady stretched out both arms, for she was a dancer; and as she had lifted one leg high up, so that the tin soldier could not see it, he thought she had only one leg like himself.

"That is a wife for me," he thought; "but she is very grand; she lives in a castle, while I have only a box, which I share with twenty-four; that is not a place for her. But I must make her acquaintance." And then he laid himself at full length behind snuff-box which was on the table; from his place he could see the little well-dressed lady, who continued to stand on one leg without losing her balance.

At night the tin soldiers were put back into their box and the people of the house went to bed. Now the toys began to play, to pay visits, to make war, and to go to balls. The tin soldiers rattled in their box, for they wished to take part in the games, but they could not raise the lid. The nutcrackers made somersaults, the slate-pencil enjoyed itself on the slate; they made so much noise that the canary woke up, and began to talk, and that in verse. The tin soldier and the dancer were the only ones who remained in their places. She was standing on tiptoe with her arm stretched out; he stood firmly on his one leg, never taking his eyes away from her for a moment. When the clock struck twelve, suddenly the lid of the snuff-box was flung open; there was no snuff in it, but a small black Jack-in-the-box, who had performed his trick.

"Tin soldier," said the Jack, "don't covet things that do not belong to you."

The tin soldier pretended not to hear anything.

"All right; wait till to-morrow," said the Jack.

When the morning had come and the children were up, the tin soldier was placed on the window-sill; all at once, whether through draught or through the Jack, the window flew open and the soldier fell headlong down into the street from the third storey. That was a terrible fall! His one leg high up in the air, he stood on his helmet, while his bayonet entered into the ground between the paving stones. The servant and the little boy came at once down to look for him; but although they were so close to him that they almost trod upon him, they did not find him. If the tin soldier had cried: "Here I am," they would surely have found him; but he did not consider it proper to cry aloud, because he was in uniform.

Now it began to rain, first very little, but soon more, till it became a heavy shower. When the rain had ceased two boys passed by the soldier.

"Look, there is a tin soldier," said one of them, "let us make a boat for him."

They then made a boat out of a piece of newspaper, put the tin soldier in it, and let him float down the gutter; both ran by the side and clapped their hands for pleasure. Heaven preserve us! there were large waves in the gutter, and a strong current, too, for the rain had been pouring down in torrents. The paper boat was rocking up and down; sometimes it turned round so quickly that the tin soldier trembled; but he remained firm, he did not move a muscle, and looked straight forward, holding the gun in his arm. Suddenly the boat was driven under a large bridge which was over the gutter, and there it became as dark as in the tin soldier's box.

"Where am I going to?" he thought. "That is the fault of the black Jack-in-the-box. I wish the little lady were here with me in the boat, then I should not mind how dark it was."

Then came a big water-rat which lived under the bridge.

"Have you a passport?" asked the rat. "Give it up at once."

But the tin soldier was silent and held his gun tighter than before. The boat was rushing forward; the rat followed, gnashing its teeth, and crying out to the chips of wood and straws: "Stop him, stop him! He has paid no toll, and has not shown his passport!"

The current became stronger and stronger; the tin soldier could already see the light of day where the bridge ended; but he also heard a roaring noise, strong enough to frighten a brave man. Just think: the gutter ran there, where the bridge ended, into a canal, that was for him as dangerous as for us to cross a big water fall. He was already so close to it that stopping was impossible. The boat drifted on, the poor tin soldier held himself as stiff as he could; nobody could say of him that he had blinked an eye. The boat rapidly whirled round three or four times, and was filled with water to the very brim; he must sink down. The tin soldier stood up to his neck in the water; deeper and deeper sank the boat, more and more the paper became wet and limp, then the water closed over his head. He thought of the sweet little dancer which he should never see again, and it sounded into his ear:

> " *Farewell, soldier, true and brave,*
> *Nothing now thy life can save.*"

Then the paper-boat fell to pieces, and the tin soldier, sinking into the water, was swallowed up by a large fish.

It was indeed very dark inside the fish, much darker than under the bridge over the gutter, and, in addition, it was awfully narrow, but the tin soldier remained firm, and lay down at full length, holding his gun tightly in his arm.

The fish was swimming about and made most extraordinary movements; at last it became quiet; it seemed as if a flash of lightning passed through it, the broad daylight appeared, and a voice said, "Hallo! there is the tin soldier." The fish had been caught and taken to market; there it had been sold and brought to the kitchen, where the cook was just cutting it open. With two fingers she took the tin soldier round the waist, carried him into the room, to show everybody the wonderful man who had been travelling about in a fish's stomach; but the tin soldier was not proud. They put him on the table, and there—what strange things occur in this world!—he was in the same place where he had been before; he saw the same children, and the same toys were on the table; there was also the pretty castle with the dear little dancer. She stood still on one leg and held the other high up in the air: she too was steadfast. The tin soldier was very much touched, and he nearly shed tin tears, but that was not becoming for a soldier. He looked at her but said nothing. Suddenly one of the little boys took up the tin soldier and threw him into the stove, without giving any reason for this strange conduct; surely it was again the fault of the Jack-in-the-box. The tin soldier stood there in the strong light and felt an unbearable heat, but whether this heat was caused by the real fire or by love, he did not know. His colours had vanished, but nobody could say if that happened during his journey, or if heart grief was the cause of it. He looked at the little lady and she looked at him, and he felt that he was melting, but still he stood upright with his gun in his arm. All at once a door flew open, the wind seized the dancer, she flew like a sylph into the stove to the tin soldier, where she was burnt and gone in a moment. The tin soldier melted down into a lump, and when the servant cleared out the cinders on the next morning, she found it in the shape of

a little tin heart.   Of the little dancer only the tinsel rose was left
which had become as black as coal.

The Buckwheat

HEN you pass by a field of buckwheat afte
a thunderstorm you will often find it lookin
blackened and singed, as if a flame of fir
had swept over it.   Peasants say : " Th
lightning has caused this."   But why did th
lightning blacken the buckwheat?   I wi
tell you what I heard from the sparrow, wh
was told by an old willow-tree standing near a field of buckwhea
It was a large imposing old willow-tree, although somewhat cripple
by old age, and split in the middle ; grass and a bramble-bus
grew in the cleft ; the tree was bending down its branches so tha
they nearly touched the ground, hanging down like long gree
hair.   On all the neighbouring fields grew corn, not only rye an
barley, but also oats—splendid oats indeed, which look, when the
are ripe, like many little yellow canary-birds on a branch.   Th
corn was lovely to look at, and the fuller the ears were the lowe
they were hanging down, as if in godly humility.   Close by, righ
opposite to the old willow-tree, was also a field of buckwhea
The buckwheat did not bend down like the other corn, but stoo
proudly and stiffly upright.

"I am certainly as well off as the corn," it said, ." I am i
addition to this much better-looking ; my flowers are as beautifu
as the blossoms of the apple-tree ; it must be a pleasure to loo
at me and my companions.   Do you know anything more magn
ficent than we are, old willow-tree ? "

The willow-tree nodded its head, as if it wished to say : " Ye
certainly, I do."   The buckwheat spread, full of pride, its leave
and said : " This stupid old tree !   It is so old that grass is grov
ing out of its trunk."

Soon a heavy thunder-storm arose ; all the flowers in the fiel

lded their leaves or bowed their little heads down, while the
orm passed over them; but the buckwheat remained proudly
anding upright.

"Bend your head, as we do," said the flowers.

"Why should I?" asked the buckwheat.

"Bend your head, as we do," said the corn. "The angel of
e storm is approaching; his wings reach from the clouds down
the ground; he will cut you in two, ere you can cry for mercy."

"But I refuse to bend my head," said the buckwheat.

"Close up your flowers and bend down your leaves," cried the
d willow-tree. "Do not look up at the lightning when it tears
e clouds; even mankind can't do that, for while a flash of
ghtning lasts one can look into heaven, and that dazzles even
ankind; what would then happen to us, the plants of the earth,
hich are so greatly inferior to men, if we dared do so?"

"Why greatly inferior?" said the buckwheat. "If you cannot
ve a better reason, I will look up into heaven." And in its
oundless pride and presumption it did look up. Suddenly came
flash of lightning, that was so strong that it seemed for a
oment as if the whole world was in flames.

When the storm had abated, the flowers and the corn stood
freshed by the rain in the pure, still air; but the buckwheat was
irnt by the lightning, and had become a dead, useless weed.

The wind moved the branches of the old willow-tree, so that
rge drops of water fell down from its green leaves, as if the tree
as weeping; and the sparrows asked it, "Why do you cry?
lessings are showered upon us all; look how the sun shines, and
ow the clouds sail on! Do you not smell the sweet fragrance of
owers and bushes? Why do you cry, old willow-tree?"

Then the willow-tree told them of the pride of the buckwheat,
its presumption, and of the punishment which it had to suffer.
who have told you this story have heard it from the sparrows;
ey related it to me one night when I had asked them for a tale.

The Swineherd

NCE upon a time lived a poor prince; his kingdom was very small, but it was large enough to enable him to marry, and marry he would. It was rather bold of him that he went and asked the emperor's daughter: "Will you marry me?" but he ventured to do so, for his name was known far and wide, and there were hundreds of princesses who would have gladly accepted him, but would she do so? Now we shall see.

On the grave of the prince's father grew a rose-tree, the most beautiful of its kind. It bloomed only once in five years, and then it had only one single rose upon it, but what a rose! It had such a sweet scent that one instantly forgot all sorrow and grief when one smelt it. He had also a nightingale, which could sing as if every sweet melody was in its throat. This rose and the nightingale he wished to give to the princess; and therefore both were put into big silver cases and sent to her.

The emperor ordered them to be carried into the great hall where the princess was just playing "Visitors are coming" with her ladies-in-waiting; when she saw the large cases with the presents therein, she clapped her hands for joy.

"I wish it were a little pussy cat," she said. But then the rose-tree with the beautiful rose was unpacked.

"Oh, how nicely it is made," exclaimed the ladies.

"It is more than nice," said the emperor, "it is charming."

The princess touched it and nearly began to cry.

"For shame, pa," she said, "it is not artificial, it is natural!"

"For shame, it is natural,' repeated all her ladies.

"Let us first see what the other case contains before we are angry," said the emperor; then the nightingale was taken out, and it sang so beautifully that no one could possibly say anything unkind about it.

"*Superbe, charmant,*" said the ladies of the court, for they all prattled French, one worse than the other.

"How much the bird reminds me of the musical box of the late lamented empress," said an old courtier, "it has exactly the same tone, the same execution."

"You are right," said the emperor, and began to cry like a little child.

"I hope it is not natural," said the princess.

"Yes, certainly it is natural," replied those who had brought the presents.

"Then let it fly," said the princess, and refused to see the prince.

But the prince was not discouraged. He painted his face, put on common clothes, pulled his cap over his forehead, and came back.

"Good day, emperor," he said, "could you not give me some employment at the court?"

"There are so many," replied the emperor, "who apply for places, "that for the present I have no vacancy, but I will remember you. But wait a moment; it just comes into my mind, I require somebody to look after my pigs, for I have a great many."

Thus the prince was appointed imperial swineherd, and as such he lived in a wretchedly small room near the pigsty; there he worked all day long, and when it was night he had made a pretty little pot. There were little bells round the rim, and when the water began to boil in it, the bells began to play the old tune:

> "*A jolly old sow once lived in a sty,*
> *Three little piggies had she,*" &c.

But what was more wonderful was that, when one put a finger into the steam rising from the pot, one could at once smell what meals they were preparing on every fire in the whole town. That was indeed much more remarkable than the rose. When the princess with her ladies passed by and heard the tune, she stopped and looked quite pleased, for she also could play it—in fact, it was the only tune she could play, and she played it with one finger.

"That is the tune I know," she exclaimed. "He must be a

well-educated swineherd. Go and ask him how much the instrument is."

One of the ladies had to go and ask; but she put on pattens.

"What will you take for your pot?" asked the lady.

"I will have ten kisses from the princess," said the swineherd.

"God forbid," said the lady.

"Well, I cannot sell it for less," replied the swineherd.

"What did he say?" said the princess.

"I really cannot tell you," replied the lady.

"You can whisper it into my ear."

"It is very naughty," said the princess, and walked off.

But when she had gone a little distance, the bells rang again so sweetly:

> "A jolly old sow once lived in a sty,
> Three little piggies had she," &c.

"Ask him," said the princess, "if he will be satisfied with ten kisses from one of my ladies."

"No, thank you," said the swineherd: "ten kisses from the princess, or I keep my pot."

"That is tiresome," said the princess. "But you must stand before me, so that nobody can see it."

The ladies placed themselves in front of her and spread out their dresses, and she gave the swineherd ten kisses and received the pot.

That was a pleasure! Day and night the water in the pot was

boiling; there was not a single fire in the whole town of which they did not know what was preparing on it, the chamberlain's as well as the shoemaker's. The ladies danced and clapped their hands for joy.

"We know who will eat soup and pancakes; we know who will eat porridge and cutlets; oh, how interesting!"

"Very interesting, indeed," said the mistress of the household. "But you must not betray me, for I am the emperor's daughter."

"Of course not," they all said.

The swineherd—that is to say, the prince—but they did not know otherwise than that he was a real swineherd—did not waste a single day without doing something; he made a rattle, which, when turned quickly round, played all the waltzes, galops, and polkas known since the creation of the world.

"But that is *superbe*," said the princess passing by. "I have never heard a more beautiful composition. Go down and ask him what the instrument costs; but I shall not kiss him again."

"He will have a hundred kisses from the princess," said the lady, who had gone down to ask him.

"I believe he is mad," said the princess, and walked off, but soon she stopped. "One must encourage art," she said. "I am the emperor's daughter! Tell him I will give him ten kisses, as I did the other day; the remainder one of my ladies can give him."

"But we do not like to kiss him," said the ladies.

"That is nonsense," said the princess; "if I can kiss him, you can also do it. Remember that I give you food and employment." And the lady had to go down once more.

"A hundred kisses from the princess," said the swineherd, "or everybody keeps his own."

"Place yourselves before me," said the princess then. They did as they were bidden, and the princess kissed him.

"I wonder what that crowd near the pigsty means!" said the emperor, who had just come out on his balcony. He rubbed his eyes and put his spectacles on.

"The ladies of the court are up to some mischief, I think. I shall have to go down and see." He pulled up his shoes, for they were down at the heels, and he was very quick about it. When he had come down into the courtyard he walked quite softly, and the ladies were so busily engaged in counting the kisses, that all should be fair, that they did not notice the emperor. He raised himself on tiptoe.

"What does this mean?" he said, when he saw that his daughter was kissing the swineherd, and then hit their heads with his shoe just as the swineherd received the sixty-eighth kiss.

"Go out of my sight," said the emperor, for he was very angry; and both the princess and the swineherd were banished from the empire. There she stood and cried, the swineherd scolded her, and the rain came down in torrents.

"Alas, unfortunate creature that I am!" said the princess, "I wish I had accepted the prince. Oh, how wretched I am!"

The swineherd went behind a tree, wiped his face, threw off his poor attire and stepped forth in his princely garments; he looked so beautiful that the princess could not help bowing to him.

"I have now learnt to despise you," he said. "You refused an honest prince; you did not appreciate the rose and the nightingale; but you did not mind kissing a swineherd for his toys; you have no one but yourself to blame!"

And then he returned into his kingdom and left her behind. She could now sing at her leisure:

> "*A jolly old sow once lived in a sty,*
> *Three little piggies had she*," &c.

The Elfin Hill

OME large lizards were nimbly running about in the clefts of an old tree; they understood one another very well, for they all spoke the lizard language.

"I wonder what is rumbling and rattling in yon old elfin hill," said the first lizard. "I have been unable to shut an eye for the last two nights, so great was the noise; it was just as bad as toothache, for that also prevents me from sleeping."

"I am sure there is something on," said another lizard; "they had the top of the hill propped up on four red pillars until the cock crowed this morning; it must be well aired; the elfin girls have also learnt new dances. Surely, there is something on."

"Yes," said a third lizard, "I have seen an earthworm of my acquaintance, just when it came out of the hill where it had been groping about in the ground day and night. It has heard a good deal; the unfortunate animal cannot see, but knows well enough how to wriggle about and listen. They expect visitors in the elfin hill, and very distinguished ones too; but whom the earthworm was unwilling or unable to tell me. All the will-o'-the wisps are ordered to take part in a torchlight procession, as it is called; the silver and gold, of which there is plenty in the hill, is polished and placed out in the moonlight."

"Who may these visitors be?" asked all the lizards. "What are they doing? Listen, how it hums and rumbles!" No sooner had they said this than the elfin hill opened and an old elfin girl, hollow at the back,* came tripping out; she was the housekeeper of the old elfin king, and being distantly connected with the family, she wore an amber heart on her forehead. Her feet moved so nimbly—trip, trip. Good gracious! how she could trip— she went straight down to the sea to the night-raven.†

"I have to invite you to the elfin hill for to-night," she said; "but you would do us a great favour if you would undertake the invitations. You ought to do something, as you do not entertain yourself. We expect some very distinguished friends, sorcerers, who can tell us something; that is why the old king of the elves wishes to show off."

"Who is to be invited?" asked the night-raven.

---

* Elfin girls are, according to the popular superstition, to be looked at only from one side, as they are supposed to be hollow, like a mask.

† When in former days a ghost appeared the priest banished it into the earth; on the spot where this had happened they drove a stake into the ground. At midnight there was suddenly a cry heard: "Let me go." The stake was then removed, and the banished ghost escaped in the shape of a raven with a hole in his left wing. This ghostly bird was called the night-raven.

" All the world may attend the grand ball, even human beings, if they can talk in their sleep or know anything of the like which is according to our ways. But for the feast the company has to be strictly select: we only wish to have tiptop society. I have had an argument with the king, for in my opinion not even ghosts ought to be admitted. The merman and his daughters have to be invited first of all. Perhaps they may not like to come to the dry land, but we shall provide them with wet stones to sit on, or with something still better; and under these circumstances I think they will not refuse this time. All the old demons of the first class, with tails such as the goblins, we must invite, of course; further, I think, we must not forget the grave-pig,* the death-horse, nor the church dwarf; they belong, it is true, to the clergy, who are not of our class, but that is only their vocation; they are our near relatives, and frequently call upon us."

" Croak," said the night-raven, and flew off at once to invite the people.

The elfin girls were already dancing on the hill, they were wrapped in shawls made of mist and moonshine, which look very pretty to people who like things of this kind. The large hall in the centre of the elfin hill was beautifully adorned; the floor had been washed with moonshine, while the walls had been polished with a salve prepared by witches, so that they shone like tulip-leaves in the light. In the kitchen they were very busy; frogs were roasting on the spit, dishes of snail-skins with children's fingers and salads of mushroom-seed, hemlock and mouse noses were preparing; there was beer of the marshwoman's make, sparkling wine of saltpetre from the grave vaults: all was very substantial food; the dessert consisted of rusty nails and glass from church windows. The old king of the elves had his golden crown polished with crushed slate-pencil; it was the same as used by the first form, and indeed it is difficult for an elf king to obtain such slate-pencils. In the bedroom, curtains were hung up and

* In Denmark, superstitious people believe that under every church a living horse or pig is buried. It is supposed that the ghost of the horse limps on three legs every night to some house where somebody is going to die.

fastened with snail-slime. There was a running, rumbling and jostling everywhere.

"Now let us perfume the place by burning horse-hair and pig's bristles, and then, I think, I have done all I can," said the old elfin girl.

"Father, dear," said the youngest daughter, "may I now know who our distinguished guests will be?"

"Well, I suppose I may tell you now," he said. "Two of my daughters must be prepared for marriage; for two will certainly be married. The old goblin of Norway, who lives in the old Dovre-mountains and possesses many strong castles built on the cliffs and a gold mine, which is much better than people think, will come down with his two sons, who are both looking out for a wife. The old goblin is as genuine and honest an old chap as Norway ever brought forth; he is merry and straightforward too. I have known him a very long time, we used to drink together to our good friendship; he was last here to fetch his wife, she is dead now; she was a daughter of the king of the chalk-hills near Moen. He took his wife on tick, as people say. Oh, how I am longing for the dear old goblin again! They say his sons are somewhat naughty and forward, but people may do them wrong by supposing that, and I think they will be all right when they grow older. Let me see that you can teach them good manners."

" When are they coming?" asked one of the daughters.

" That depends on wind and weather," replied the king of the elves. "They travel economically. They will come when they have the chance to go by ship. I wished them to come through Sweden, but that was not to the old man's liking. He does not advance with time, and I do not like that at all."

Just then two will-o'-the-wisps came leaping in, the one much quicker than the other, and therefore one arrived first.

" They are coming, they are coming," they cried.

" Give me my crown, and let me stand in the moonshine," said the elf king.

The daughters raised their shawls and bowed to the ground. There stood the old goblin from Dovre; he wore a crown of hardened ice and polished fir-cones; he was wrapt in a bear-skin and had large warm boots on; his sons, on the contrary, had nothing round their necks and no braces on their trousers, for they were strong men.

" Is that a hill?" asked the youngest of the boys, pointing to the elfin hill. " We should call it a hole, in Norway."

" Boys," said the old man, "you ought to know better, a hole goes in, a hill stands out; have you no eyes in your heads?"

The only thing that struck them, they said, was that they were able to understand the language without any difficulty.

" Don't be so foolish," said the old goblin; "people might think you are still unfledged."

Then they all went into the elfin hill, where the distinguished visitors had assembled, and so quickly, that it seemed as if the wind had blown them together. But every one was nicely and well accommodated. The sea folks sat at dinner in big water-tubs; they said they felt quite at home. All showed very good breeding except the two young goblins of the north, who put their legs on the table, for they imagined that they might take such liberties.

" Take your feet off the table," said the old goblin; and they obeyed, though reluctantly. They tickled their fair neighbours at table with fir-cones which they brought in their pockets; they took their boots off, in order to be at ease, and gave them to the ladies to hold. But their father, the old Dovre goblin, was quite different; he talked so well about the stately Norwegian rocks, and of the waterfalls which rushed down with a noise like thunder and the sound of an organ, forming white foam; he told of the salmon which leap against the rushing water when the Reck begins to play on the golden harp; he spoke of the fine moonlight winter nights, when the sledge-bells are ringing and the young men skate with burning torches in their hands over the ice, which is so clear and transparent that they frighten the fishes under their feet. He could talk so well that those who listened to him saw all in reality; it was just as if the sawmills were going, and as if servants and maids were singing and dancing; suddenly the old goblin gave the old elfin girl a kiss, and it was a real kiss, and yet they were almost strangers to each other.

After this the elfin girls had to perform their dances, first in the ordinary way, and then with stamping of their feet, and it looked very well; afterwards came the artistic and solo dance. Good gracious! how they threw their legs up; nobody knew where they began or where they ended, nor which were the legs and which the arms; all were flying about like sawdust, and they turned so quickly round that the death-horse and the grave-pig became unwell and had to leave the room.

"Hallo!" cried the old goblin, "that is a strange way of working about with the legs! But what do they know besides dancing, stretching the legs, and producing a whirlwind?"

"That you shall soon see," said the elf king, and called the youngest of his daughters. She was as nimble and bright as moonshine; she was indeed the finest-looking of all the sisters. She took a white chip of wood into her mouth, and disappeared instantly; that was her accomplishment. But the old goblin said he should not like his wife to possess such a power, and was sure his sons would be of the same opinion. The second could walk by her own side as if she had a shadow, while everybody knows that goblins never have a shadow. The third was quite different in her accomplishments; she had been apprenticed to the marsh-woman in the brewery, and knew well how to lard elder-tree logs with glow-worms.

"She will make a good housekeeper," said the old goblin,

drinking her health with his eyes, as he did not wish to take anything more.

Now came the fourth, with a large harp to play upon; no sooner had she struck the first chord than all lifted up the left leg —for the goblins are left-legged—and when she touched the strings again every one had to do what she wished.

"That is a dangerous person," said the old goblin; and his two sons went out of the hill, for now they had seen quite enough. "What does your next daughter know?" asked the old goblin.

"I have learnt to admire all that is Norwegian, and I shall never marry unless I can go to Norway."

But the smallest of the sisters whispered into the old man's ear: "That is only because she has heard in a Norwegian song that when the world is destroyed through water the Norwegian cliffs will remain standing like monuments; therefore she wishes to go there, because she is so much afraid of being drowned."

"Ho, ho!" said the old goblin; "is that really what she meant? But tell me, what can the seventh and last do?"

"The sixth comes before the seventh," said the elf king, for he could count; but the sixth was rather timid.

"I can only tell people the truth," she said at last. "Nobody cares for me, and I am sufficiently occupied in making my shroud."

Now came the seventh and last; what could she do? Why, she could tell fairy tales, and as many as ever she wished.

"Here are my five fingers," said the old goblin; "tell me one for each of them."

And she took him by the wrist, and he laughed so much that he was nearly choked; when she came to the ring-finger, which had a golden ring upon it, as if it was aware that a betrothal should take place, the old goblin said, "Hold fast what you have; this hand is yours; I shall marry you myself."

Then the elfin girl said that the tales of the ring-finger and that of Peter Playman had yet to be told.

"Those we shall hear in the winter," said the old goblin, "and also those of the birch-tree, of the ghosts' presents, and of the creaking frost. You shall relate all your stories, for nobody up there can tell stories well; and then we shall sit in the rooms of

tone where the pine logs are burning, and we shall drink mead
ut of the drinking-horns of the old Norwegian kings—Reck has
made me a present of a couple of them—and when we are sitting
here the mermaid will come to see us ; she will sing to you all the
ongs of the shepherd-girls in the mountains. We shall enjoy it
ery much. The salmon will leap up in the waterfalls against the
tone walls, but they cannot come in. Indeed, life is very pleasant
n dear old Norway. But where are my boys ? "

Where had they gone to? They were running about in the
elds and blowing out the will-o'-the-wisps who had so kindly
ome to march in the torchlight procession.

" What have you been doing ? " asked the old goblin. " I have
aken a new mother for you ; now you can each choose one of
he aunts."

But the boys declared that they preferred to make speeches
nd drink ; they had no wish to marry. And they began to
make speeches, drank to other people's health, and emptied
heir glasses to the dregs. Afterwards they took off their coats
nd placed themselves on the tables to sleep, for they did not
and on ceremonies. But the old goblin danced with his young
weetheart about the room, and exchanged boots with her, for
hat is more fashionable than exchanging rings.

" The cock is crowing," cried the old elfin girl that did the
ousekeeping ; " now we must close the shutters, lest the sun
urn us."

Then the hill was closed up. But outside, the lizards were
nning about in the cleft tree, and one said to the other: " I like
e old Norwegian goblin very much."

" I prefer the boys," said the earthworm ; but the unfortunate
nimal could not see.

The Fir-Tree

AR out in the forest grew a pretty little fir-tree. It had a favourable place; the sun shone brightly on it, and there was plenty of fresh air, while many taller comrades, both pines and firs, were thriving around it. The little fir-tree longingly desired to grow taller! It was indifferent to the warm sun and the fresh air, it took no notice of the peasant children, who ran about and chattered, when they had come out to gather strawberries and raspberries. Often they came with a basket full, and had threaded strawberries on a straw like beads; then they used to sit down near the little fir-tree and say: "What a pretty little tree this one is!" But this the tree did not like to hear at all.

In the following year it grew taller by a considerable shoot, and the year after by another one, for by the number of shoots which fir-trees have, we may discover how many years they have grown.

"Oh, that I were as tall a tree as the others!" sighed the little tree; "then I might spread out my branches far around, and look with my crown out into the wide world! The birds would build their nests in my boughs, and when the wind blew I could proudly nod, just like the others yonder!"

It took no delight in the sunshine, in the birds, nor in the red clouds which in the morning and evening passed over it. When the winter had come and the snow was lying white and sparkling on the ground, often a hare came running and jumped right over the little tree—oh, that annoyed it so much! But two winters passed, and in the third the little tree was already so high that the hare had to run round it. "To grow, to grow, to become tall and old, this is the most desirable thing in the world," thought the tree.

Every year in autumn woodcutters came and felled several of the biggest trees; the young tree, now well grown, shuddered, for the tall magnificent trees fell to the ground with a crash; and when their branches were hewn off, the trees looked so naked, long and slender, they were hardly to be recognised. Then they were placed upon carts, and horses drew them out of the wood. Whither were they going? What was to become of them? In spring, when the swallows and storks returned, the tree asked them: "Can you not tell me whither they have taken them? Have you not met them?"

The swallows knew nothing about them; but the stork looked pensive, nodded his head and said: "Yes, I think I know. When I left Egypt I passed by many new ships, and on the ships were splendid masts; I suppose these were the trees, for they smelt like fir-trees, and they looked very stately indeed!"

"I wish I were tall enough to go over the sea! I should like to know what the sea is. What does it look like?"

"To explain that," replied the stork, "would take me too long," and thus saying he flew away.

"Enjoy thy youth!" said the sunbeams; "take pleasure in thy vigorous growth, in the fresh life that is within thee."

The wind kissed the tree, and the dew shed tears over it; but the fir-tree did not understand them.

About Christmas-time people cut down many trees which were quite young and smaller than the fir-tree, which had no rest and always wished to be off. These young trees, the very best that could be found, kept all their branches; they were placed upon carts and drawn out of the wood by horses.

"What are they doing with them?" asked the fir-tree. "They are not taller than I am—nay, there was one much smaller! Why did they retain all their branches? Where are they conveying them to?"

"We can tell you; we know!" chirped the sparrows. "Down below in the town we have looked through the windows! We know where they are taken to! They come to the greatest splendour you can imagine! We have looked in at the windows and have seen them standing in the middle of a warm room covered with the most beautiful things: gilded apples, gingerbread, toys, and many, many wax-candles."

"And then," asked the fir-tree, trembling all over, "what happens after that?"

"Why, that is all we have seen! But that was very beautiful."

"I wonder whether I am destined to receive such great splendour," exclaimed the fir-tree merrily. "That is far better than crossing the sea! How much I am longing for the time! I wish Christmas had arrived! Now I am tall and have grown to a good length like the others which they took away last year! I wish I were already placed on the cart or in the warm room adorned with all the bright and beautiful things! And then there is something much better and brighter to come, or why would they decorate the trees so beautifully? Yes, indeed, there is something more splendid and grand to follow! But what can it be? Oh, how I suffer with longing; I hardly know how I feel."

"Enjoy our presence," said the air and the sunshine; "delight in thy young life here in the forest."

But the tree did not enjoy anything, it grew and grew; winter and summer it was green, and people who saw it said that it was a beautiful tree.

Christmas came at last, and the tree was the first to be cut down. The axe entered deeply into its stem; the tree fell groaning to the ground; a pain and a faintness overcame it; it was unable to think of the happiness to come, it was sad that it had to leave its home, the spot where it had grown up; it knew well enough that it would never see again the dear old comrades, the little bushes and the flowers, and perhaps not even the birds. Parting was not at all pleasant. The tree did not recover until it was taken from the cart in a court-yard with other trees and heard a man say: "This one is very fine, we only want this one."

Two servants in livery soon came and carried the tree into a large, beautiful room. The walls were all covered with pictures, and by the side of the tile-stove stood big Chinese vases with lions on the lids; there were rocking-chairs, couches covered with silk, on a large table were displayed picture-books and toys of very great value—at least, so the children said. The fir-tree was put into a large vessel filled with sand; but nobody could see that it was a vessel, for it was covered all over with green cloth and placed on a handsome carpet of many colours. How the fir-tree trembled! What was to happen now? The young ladies of the house, aided by the servants, adorned the tree. They hung on its branches little nets cut out of coloured paper and filled with sweets; gilded apples and walnuts were fastened to the tree, as if they grew on it, and more than a hundred small candles, red, blue, and white, were fixed to the branches. Dolls looking exactly like human beings—the tree had never seen anything of the like before—were hanging in the green foliage, and on the very top of the tree they fixed a glittering star of tinsel. It was very beautiful.

"To-night," they all said—"to-night it will shine!"

"Oh, that the evening had come!" thought the tree. "I wish the candles were lighted! And what will happen then? I wonder if the trees will come from the wood to look at me, or if the sparrows will look in at the windows. Am I to grow fast here and remain winter and summer adorned as I am now?"

Indeed, that was not a bad guess! Its longing made its bark ache; barkache for a tree is just as bad as a headache for us.

At last the candles were lighted. What a blaze of light! What a splendour! The tree trembled so much with joy in all its branches that one of the lights set fire to one of its boughs and scorched it.

"Heaven preserve us!" exclaimed the young ladies, and quickly extinguished the flame.

Now the tree was no longer allowed to tremble! That was dreadful. It was so afraid lest it might lose some of its ornaments; it was quite dazzled by all the splendour. Then the folding-doors were thrown open, and the children rushed into the room as if they wished to upset the tree; the elders followed. For a moment the children stood silent with surprise, but only for a moment; then they shouted for joy till the room rang; they danced joyfully round the tree, and present after present was taken down from it.

"What are they doing?" thought the tree. "What is to happen?" The candles burnt gradually down to the boughs on which they were fastened and were put out, and then the children were allowed to plunder the tree. Oh, how they rushed at it; all its branches cracked, and had it not been fastened with the glittering star to the ceiling, they would have upset it. The children were dancing about with their beautiful toys. Nobody took any notice of the tree, except the old nurse, who came and looked at the branches, but only to see if there was not a fig or an apple left on them.

"A story! a story!" cried the children, while they pulled a small stout man towards the tree. He seated himself just underneath the tree, "for there we are in its green shade" he said, "and it will be an advantage to the tree to listen! But I shall only tell one story. Would you like to hear Ivede-Avede or Humpty Dumpty, who fell downstairs, but came to honours after all and married the princess?"

"Ivede-Avede!" cried some, "Humpty Dumpty!" cried others; there was a good deal of crying and shouting. Only the fir-tree was quite silent and thought to itself: "Am I not to take part in this?" but it had already done what it was expected to do.

And the man told the story of Humpty Dumpty who fell downstairs, and after all came to honours and married the princess. And the children clapped their hands and cried: "Go on, tell us another!" They wished also to hear the story of Ivede-Avede, but he only told that of Humpty Dumpty. The fir-tree was standing quite silent and thoughtful; the birds of the wood had never told such stories. "Humpty Dumpty fell downstairs, and yet married the princess. Thus it happens in the world," thought the fir-tree, and believed that it was all true, because such a nice man had told the story. "Well, well! Who knows? Perhaps I shall also fall downstairs and marry a princess!" And it looked forward with joy to being adorned again on the following day with toys, glitter, and fruit.

"To-morrow I shall not tremble!" it thought; "I shall enjoy all my splendour thoroughly. To-morrow I shall hear the story of Humpty Dumpty again, and perhaps also that of Ivede-Avede."

All night the tree was standing silent and thoughtful. In the morning the man-servants and housemaids entered the

room. "Now," thought the tree, "they will adorn me again !"
But they dragged it out of the room, upstairs into the garret,
and placed it there in a dark corner, where no daylight reached
it. "What does this mean?" thought the tree. "What am I to
do here? What can I hear in such a place?" and it leaned against
the wall, and thought and thought. And, indeed, it had time
enough to think; for days and nights passed, but nobody came
upstairs, and when at last somebody did come, it was only to store
away some big chests. Thus the tree was quite hidden; one
might have thought that they had entirely forgotten it.

"Now it is winter," thought the tree. "The ground is so hard ←
and covered with snow that people cannot plant me again !
Therefore, I think, they shelter me here until spring comes. How
thoughtful ! How kind people are to me ! I only wish it was
not quite so dark and so dreadfully lonely here ! Not even
a small hare is to be seen ! How nice it was in the wood, when
the snow covered the ground and the hare was running by; I
should not even mind his jumping right over me, although then I
could not bear the thought of it. It is awfully lonely here, indeed !"

"Squeak, squeak," a little mouse said just then, creeping timidly
forward; another one soon followed. They sniffed at the fir-tree
and slipped into its branches.

"Oh, that it were not so bitter cold," said the mice, "then we
should feel quite comfortable here. Don't you think so, old
fir-tree?"

"I am not old at all !" replied the fir-tree; "there are many
much older than myself."

"Where do you come from?" asked the mice; "what do you
know?" for they were very inquisitive. "Tell us about the most
beautiful place on earth ! Have you been there? Have you
been in the pantry where cheeses lie on the shelves, and hams
hang from the ceiling, where one can dance on tallow candles,
and go in thin and come out fat?"

"I have not been there," said the tree; "but I know the wood
where the sun shines and the birds sing." And then the tree
told the mice all about its youth. The little mice, who had never
heard anything like it before, listened attentively and exclaimed :

"You have seen a great deal, indeed; how happy you must have felt!"

"Do you think so?" said the tree, and reflected on its own story. "After all, those days were not unhappy." Then it told them all about Christmas-eve, when it was so beautifully adorned with cake and lights.

"You must have been very happy, you old fir-tree," replied the mice.

"I am not old at all," repeated the tree, "I only left the wood this winter; I am somewhat forward in my growth."

"How well you can tell stories," said the little mice. Next night they returned with four more little mice, whom they wished to hear what the tree had to relate; the more the tree told them, the more it remembered distinctly all that had happened, and it thought, "Those days were happy indeed, but they may come again. Humpty Dumpty fell downstairs, and married the princess after all; perhaps I may also marry a princess!" And then the fir-tree thought of a pretty little birch in the wood, which appeared to it a beautiful princess.

"Who is Humpty Dumpty?" asked the little mice. And then the tree had to relate the whole tale. It remembered every word of it, and the little mice were so delighted that they nearly jumped to the top of the tree for joy. The next night many more mice came to listen to the tree; and on Sunday two rats came; they, however, said the story was not pretty. The little mice were very sorry, for they began to think less of it.

"Do you know only that one story?" asked the rats.

"Only that one," said the tree, "and that I heard on the happiest night of my life; but then I did not know how happy I was."

"That is a very poor tale," said the rats. "Do you not know one about bacon and tallow candles—a sort of store-room story?"

"No," said the tree.

"We do not care for this one;" thus saying, the rats went off.

In the end also the little mice stayed away, and the tree sighed and said: "How pleasant it was to see all the lively little mice sitting round me when I talked! Now all this is passed. I should be very pleased if they came to fetch me away from here."

But whenever would that happen? One morning people came to tidy the garret; the chests were put aside, the tree was dragged out of its corner and thrown roughly to the ground; a man-servant carried it at once towards the staircase, where the sun was shining.

"Now life is beginning again," thought the tree; it felt the fresh air and the first sunbeams, and soon it was carried into the courtyard. All happened so quickly that the tree forgot to look at itself; there was so much about it to look at. The courtyard bordered on a garden, where all plants were in flower; the roses hung fresh and fragrant over the small fence; the lime-trees were blooming, and the swallows flew about, saying, "Twit, twit, twit, my husband has come!" but they did not mean the fir-tree.

"Now I shall live," exclaimed the fir-tree joyfully, spreading out its branches; but alas! they were all withered and yellow; and it lay between weeds and nettles. The star of gilt paper was still fixed to its top and glittered in the sunshine. Some of the bright children who had been dancing round the tree so merrily on Christmas-eve were playing in the courtyard. One of the smallest came and tore the gilt star off.

"Look, what is still sticking to the ugly fir-tree!" said the child, treading on the branches, which cracked under its boots. And the tree looked at all the fresh and beautiful flowers in the garden; it looked at itself and wished that it had remained in the dark corner of the garret; it remembered its bright youth in the forest, the delightful Christmas-eve, the little mice, which had so quietly listened to the story of Humpty Dumpty.

"All is over," said the old tree. "Oh, that I had enjoyed myself while I could do so! All is passed away."

A man-servant came and chopped the tree into small pieces, until a large bundle was lying on the ground; then he placed them in the fire, under a large copper, where they blazed up brightly; the tree sighed deeply, and each sigh was as loud as a little pistol-shot; the children, who were playing near, came and sat down before the fire, and looking into it cried, "Pop,

pop." But at each little shot, which was a deep sigh, the tree thought of a summer day in the wood, or a winter night there, when the stars sparkled; it remembered the Christmas-eve and Humpty Dumpty, the only fairy tale which it had heard and knew to tell, and then it was all burnt up.

The boys played in the garden, and the smallest had fixed the gilt star which had adorned the tree on its happiest night on his breast. Now all had come to an end, the tree had come to an end, and also the story, for all stories come to an end!

Big Claus and Little Claus

IN a village there once lived two men, who had both the same name. Both were called Claus, but the one had four horses and the other had only a single one. So, to distinguish them from each other, he who had four horses was called "Big Claus," and he who had only one "Little Claus." Now let us hear what happened to both, for it is a true story.

Throughout the whole week Little Claus had to plough for Big Claus and lend him his only horse; then in return big Claus lent him his four, but only once a week, and that was on Sunday. Hurrah! how Little Claus cracked his whip over all the five horses; they were indeed as good as his, on that one day. The sun shone beautifully, all the bells in the church steeple were ringing, and the people, dressed in their best, were going to church, with their hymn-books under their arm, to hear the vicar preach. They saw Little Claus, who was ploughing with five horses, and he was so happy that he kept on cracking his whip and shouting, "Gee-up, all my horses!"

"You must not talk like that," said Big Claus, "only one of them is yours!"

But as soon as some one went by Little Claus forgot that he ought not to say so, and cried: "Gee-up, all my horses!"

"Well, now I must ask you to leave off saying that," said Big Claus; "for if you say it once more, I shall strike your horse on the head, so that it will die on the spot; it will be all over with him then."

"I will really not say so any more," said Little Claus. But as soon as people came near again, and nodded him "good-day," he felt happy, and thought how very fine it looked to have five horses to plough his field; so he cracked his whip once more and cried, "Gee-up, all my horses!"

"I'll gee-up your horses!" said Big Claus, and taking a heavy bar struck Little Claus's only horse on the head, so that it fell down dead on the spot.

"Oh, now I have no longer any horse," said Little Claus, and began to cry. He then took the hide from off his horse and let it dry well in the wind, put it into a sack which he slung across his shoulder, and went to the town to sell it.

He had a very long way to go, through a great, dark wood, and a violent storm came on; he lost his way entirely, and before he came to the right road again it was evening, and much too far to reach the town or to return home before nightfall.

Close to the road lay a large farm; the shutters were up before the windows, but the light could still shine through at the top. "I daresay I shall be able to get permission to stay there for the night," thought Little Claus, and went up and knocked.

The farmer's wife opened the door, but when she heard what he wanted, she told him to be off, saying that her husband was not at home, and that she did not take in strangers.

"Well, then I must lie down outside," said Little Claus, and the farmer's wife shut the door in his face.

Close by stood a large haystack, and between this and the house was a small shed covered with a flat thatched roof.

"I can lie down there," thought little Claus, when he spied the roof; "that will make a splendid bed. I don't suppose the stork will fly down and bite my legs." For a live stork was standing high up on the roof, where it had its nest.

Little Claus now crept up on the shed, where he lay and turned himself over to settle down comfortably. The wooden shutters before the windows did not reach to the top, and so he could see right into the room.

There was a big table laden with wine and roast meat and a splendid fish; at this table were seated the farmer's wife and the sexton, but no one else. She was filling his glass, and he was pegging away with his fork at the fish, for it was his favourite dish.

"How ever could I get some of it, too?" thought Little Claus, and stretched his head out towards the window. Heavens! what a fine cake he saw in there! That was indeed a feast!

Now he heard some one riding from the high road towards the house; that was the woman's husband, who was coming home. He was a very good man, but he had the strange peculiarity that he could never bear to see a sexton; if he caught sight of a sexton he would get quite mad. It was also for this reason that the sexton had gone to see the wife to bid her good-day, because he knew that her husband was not at home, and the good woman therefore placed before him the best fare that she had. But when they heard the husband coming they were startled, and the woman begged the sexton to creep into a great empty chest. He did so, because he knew that the poor man could not bear to see a sexton. The woman hastily hid all the fine things and the wine in her oven, for if her husband had seen them, he would certainly have asked what it meant.

"Ah me!" sighed Little Claus up on his shed when he saw the good things vanishing.

"Is any one up there?" asked the farmer, and cast his eyes up to Little Claus. "What are you lying there for? You had better come with me into the room."

Then Little Claus told how he had lost his way, and begged to be allowed to stay there for the night.

"Most certainly!" said the farmer; "but we must first have something to live on."

The woman received them both in a very friendly manner, laid the cloth on a long table, and gave them a large dish of porridge. The farmer was hungry and ate with a good appetite, but Little Claus could not help thinking of the fine roast meat, fish, and cake which he knew were in the oven. Under the table, at his feet, he had placed the sack containing the horse-hide, which, as we know, he was going to sell in the town. He did not care for the porridge, and therefore trod upon his sack so that the dry hide creaked.

"Hush!" said Little Claus to his sack, treading, at the same time, on it again, when it creaked louder than before.

"What is it that you have in your sack?" asked the farmer.

"Oh, that's a magician!" said Little Claus. "He says we should not eat any porridge, as he has conjured the whole oven full of roast meat, fish and cake."

"Gracious me!" said the farmer, and quickly opened the oven, where he saw all the nice dainty fare which his wife had hidden there, but which he believed the magician in the sack had conjured up for them. The woman dared not say anything, but put the things on the table at once, and so they both ate of the fish, the roast meat and the cake. Little Claus then trod on his sack again, so that the hide creaked.

"What does he say now?" asked the farmer.

"He says that he has also conjured three bottles of wine for us, and that they are standing in the corner near the oven." The woman was now obliged to bring out the wine which she had hidden, and the farmer drank and became very merry. A magician, such as Little Claus had in his sack, he would have very much liked to possess.

"Can he conjure up the devil too?" asked the farmer; "I should like to see him, for I am merry now."

"Yes," said Little Claus, "my magician can do anything that I ask of him. Can't you?" he asked, and trod on the sack to make it creak. "Do you hear? He says, 'Yes,' but the devil is very ugly; we had better not see him."

"Oh, I'm not at all afraid. I wonder what he is like."

"He will take the form of a sexton."

"Ugh!" said the farmer, "that's awful! I must tell you that I cannot bear to see a sexton. But that's nothing; I know that it's the devil, so I can easily put up with it. Now I have courage. But he must not come too near to me."

"Then I will ask my magician," said Little Claus, and treading on the sack held his ear to it.

"What does he say?"

"He says that if you open the chest which is standing in the corner there, you will see the devil crouching inside; but you must hold the lid so that he does not escape."

"Will you help me to hold it?" he said, and went up to the chest

in which the woman had hidden the real sexton, who was sitting inside in a great fright.

The farmer opened the lid a little, and looked in under it. "Ugh!" he cried, and sprang back. "Yes, now I've seen him; he looked exactly like our sexton. Nay, that was terrible."

After that they were obliged to drink, and so they drank till far into the night.

"You must sell me the magician," said the farmer. "Ask what you like for him. I'll give you a whole bushel full of money at once."

"No, I can't do that," said Little Claus. "Just think, how much profit I can get out of this magician."

"I should so much like to have him," said the farmer, and went on begging.

"Well," said Little Claus at last, "as you have been so good as to give me shelter to-night, I'll do it. You shall have the magician for a bushel full of money, but I must have the bushel heaped up."

"That you shall have," said the farmer. "But you must take the chest there with you. I won't keep it in my house an hour; one can never know, perhaps he is still in there."

Little Claus gave the farmer his sack containing the dry hide, and received for it a bushel full of money, heaped up too. The farmer even gave him a truck as well, to carry away the money and the chest.

"Good-bye!" said Little Claus, and went away with his money and the large chest in which the sexton was still concealed.

On the other side of the wood was a large, deep river; the water flowed so rapidly that it was scarcely possible to swim against the stream. A large new bridge had been built across it: Little Claus stopped on the middle of this, and said quite loud so that the sexton in the chest could hear it:

"Whatever am I to do with this stupid chest? It's as heavy as if there were stones in it. I shall only get tired by dragging it farther; I'll throw it into the river. If it swims home to me, well and good, and if it doesn't, it won't matter much."

He then took hold of the chest with one hand and lifted it up a little, as if he wanted to throw it into the water.

"No, don't do that!" cried the sexton in the chest. "Let me out first."

"Ugh!" said Little Claus, and pretended to be frightened. "He's still inside! Then I must throw him into the river quickly, so that he drowns."

"Oh no, no!" shouted the sexton. "I'll give you a whole bushel full of money, if you let me go."

"Oh, well! that's different," said Little Claus, and opened the chest. The sexton crept out quickly, threw the empty chest into the water, and went to his home, where Little Claus received a bushel full of money; he had already received one from the farmer, so he now had his truck full of money.

"See, I was well paid for the horse!" he said to himself, when he shook out all the money into a heap in his room at home. "That will make Big Claus angry, when he hears how rich I have become through my single horse; but I won't tell him all about it."

He then sent a boy to Big Claus to borrow a bushel measure.

"What can he want with that?" thought Big Claus, and smeared some tar on the bottom, so that something of whatever was measured would remain sticking to it. And so it happened, too; for when he got the bushel measure back, three new silver shilling pieces were sticking to it.

"What's that?" said Big Claus, and immediately ran to Little Claus.

"Where did you get so much money from?"

"Oh! that's for my horse-hide; I sold it yesterday evening."

"That's really well paid!" said Big Claus, and running quickly home, took an axe, and struck all his four horses on the head; he then flayed them, and drove to the town with the hides.

"Hides! Hides! Who'll buy hides!" he cried through the streets. All the shoemakers and tanners came running up and asked what he wanted for them.

"A bushel of money for each," said Big Claus.

"Are you mad?" they all cried. "Do you think we have money by the bushel?"

"Hides! Hides! Who'll buy hides!" and to all who asked him what the hides cost, he answered: "A bushel of money."

"He wants to fool us," they all said; so the shoemakers took their straps, and the tanners their leather aprons, and gave Big Claus a sound thrashing.

"Hides! Hides!" they jeeringly called after him; "yes, we'll tan your hide, till the red liquor runs down from you. Out of the town with him!" they cried, and Big Claus had to run as fast as he could, for he had never had such a sound thrashing before.

"Well," he said, when he got home, "Little Claus shall pay me for that; I'll strike him dead for it."

Little Claus's grandmother, who lived with him, had died. She had really been very cross and bad to him, but still he was sorry, and took the dead woman and laid her in his warm bed to see whether she did not come to life again. He would let her lie there the whole night; he himself would go to sleep upon a chair in the corner, as he had often done before.

As he was sitting there in the night, the door opened, and Big Claus came in with his axe. He well knew where Little Claus's bed stood, went straight up to it, and struck the grandmother on the head, thinking that it was Little Claus.

"There," he said, "now you shall not make a fool of me again," and went home.

"That is a very wicked man," thought Little Claus. "He wanted to kill me. It is lucky for grandmother that she was dead already, else he would have taken her life."

He then dressed his grandmother in her Sunday clothes, borrowed a horse of his neighbour and harnessed it to the cart; then he put his grandmother on the back seat, in order that she could not fall out as he drove, and so they rode away through the wood. By sunrise they had arrived at a large inn; here Little Claus stopped and went in to get something to drink. The landlord had a great deal of money: he was a very good man, too, but as passionate as if he were filled with pepper and tobacco.

"Good morning!" he said to Little Claus. "You got into your clothes early to-day."

"Yes," said Little Claus, "I am going to the town with my grandmother; she is sitting outside on the cart, I can't bring her into the room. Will you give her a glass of mead? But you must speak very loud, for she can't hear well."

"Yes, certainly I will," said the landlord, and poured out a large glass of mead, which he took out to the dead grandmother, who was placed upright in the cart.

"Here is a glass of mead from your son," said the landlord. The dead woman, however, did not answer a word, and sat still.

"Don't you hear?" shouted the landlord, as loud as he could; "here is a glass of mead from your grandson."

He shouted it out once more and then still once more, but as she did not move at all from her place he became angry and threw the glass in her face, so that the mead ran down her nose and she fell backwards in the cart; for she had only been placed upright and not tied fast.

"Hallo!" cried Little Claus, rushing out and seizing the landlord by the throat; "you have killed my grandmother. Look here, there is a large hole in her forehead."

"Oh, what a misfortune!" cried the landlord, wringing his hands. "All this comes of my hot temper. My dear Little Claus, I will give you a bushel of money and have your grandmother buried as if she were my own; but keep silent, or they will cut off my head and that would be so unpleasant." So Little Claus got a bushel of money, and the landlord buried his grandmother as if she had been his own.

When Little Claus came home again with all the money, he at once sent his boy over to ask Big Claus to lend him a bushel measure.

"What's that?" said Big Claus. "Have I not killed him? I must go and see for myself." So he himself took the bushel measure over to Little Claus.

"Tell me where you got all that money," he said, and opened his eyes wide when he saw what had been added.

" You didn't kill me, but my grandmother," said Little Claus ; " I have sold her and got a bushel of money for her."

"That's really well paid," said Big Claus; and hurrying home, took an axe and killed his grandmother on the spot.   Placing her in the cart, he drove with her to the town where the apothecary lived, and asked him whether he could buy a dead body.

"Who is it, and where did you get it ? " asked the apothecary.

" It's my grandmother," said Big Claus.   " I killed her to get a bushel of money for her."

"Heaven preserve us ! " said the apothecary.   "You are mad. Don't talk like that, or you will lose your head."   And then he explained to him what a wicked deed he had done, and what a bad man he was, and that he ought to be punished ; this frightened Big Claus so, that he rushed out of the shop into the cart, lashed his horses and drove home.   But the apothecary and all the people thought he was mad, and so let him drive where he liked.

" You shall pay me for that ! " said Big Claus, when he got on the high road outside the town.   "Yes, you shall pay me for it, Little Claus."   As soon as he reached home he took the largest sack that he could find, went over to Little Claus, and said, "You have made a fool of me again.   First I killed my horse, then my grandmother.   That's all your fault, but you shall not fool me again."   With that he took hold of Little Claus round the body and put him in his sack, then took him on his back, and called out to him : "Now I am going to take you away to drown you."

It was a long way that he had to go before he came to the river, and Little Claus was not very light to carry.   The road led close by the church, and the organ was pealing and the people were singing beautifully.   So Big Claus put down his sack with Little Claus in it close to the church door, and thought it might be a very good thing to go in and hear a psalm before going any farther.   Little Claus could not possibly get out of the sack, and all the people were in the church ; so he went in.

"Oh dear! oh dear ! " sighed Little Claus in the sack, turning and twisting about; but it was impossible for him to untie the string. By-and-bye an old cattle-driver with snow-white hair passed by, with a long staff in his hand. He was driving a herd of cows and oxen before him, and these, stumbling against the sack in which Little Claus lay, it was thrown over. "Ah me!"

sighed Little Claus, "I am still so young, and am going already to heaven."

"And I, poor man," said the driver, "who am already so old, cannot get there yet."

"Open the sack," called out Little Claus; "get in instead of me, and you will go to heaven immediately."

"With all my heart," said the driver, and untied the sack, out of which Little Claus crept at once.

"But will you look after my cattle?" asked the old man, as he got into the sack; upon which Little Claus tied it up and went away with all the cows and oxen.

Soon afterwards Big Claus came out of the church and took his sack on his back again, although it seemed to him to have become lighter, for the old cattle-driver was only half as heavy as Little Claus. "How light he is to carry now! That is because

I have heard a psalm." So he went to the river, which was deep and wide, threw the sack, with the old driver in it, into the water, and called out after him, for he believed that it was Little Claus: "Lie there! You will not fool me again." He then went home; but when he came to the place where two roads crossed, he met Little Claus, who was driving his cattle along.

"What's that?" said Big Claus. "Haven't I drowned you?"

"Yes!" said Little Claus. "You threw me into the river scarcely half an hour ago."

"But where did you get these beautiful cattle?" asked Big Claus.

"These are sea-cattle," said Little Claus. "I will tell you the whole story, and thank you for having drowned me, for now I am up in the world and am really rich. How frightened I was while I was in the sack! the wind whistled in my ears as you threw me down from the bridge into the cold water. I immediately sank to the bottom, but did not hurt myself, for down there grows the finest soft grass. I fell on that and the sack was opened at once; a most lovely maiden, with snow-white clothes and a green wreath around her wet hair, took me by the hand and said, "Are you there, Little Claus? Here you have some cattle to begin with. A mile farther on the road there is another large herd, which I will give you." Then I saw that the river formed a great highway for the people of the sea. Down at the bottom they were walking and driving straight from the sea right up into the land, as far as the place where the river ends. It was full of lovely flowers and the freshest grass; the fish, which swam in the water, shot past my ears, just as the birds do here in the air. What lovely people there were there, and what fine cattle grazing in the valleys and on the hills!"

"But why did you come up again to us so quickly?" asked Big Claus. "I shouldn't have done so, if it is so fine down there."

"Well," said Little Claus, "that was good policy on my part. You heard me say that the sea-maiden told me there was a herd of cattle for me a mile farther on the road. Now by the road she meant the river, for she cannot go anywhere else. But I know what windings the river makes, first here and then there, so that it is a long way round; it is much shorter by landing here and cutting across the field back to the river. I save almost half a mile in that way, and get to my cattle more quickly."

"Oh, you are a lucky man," said Big Claus. "Do you think that I should get some cattle too if I went to the bottom of the river?"

"Yes, I think so," said Little Claus. "But I can't carry you in the sack to the river; you are too heavy for me. If you will walk there yourself and creep into the sack, I will throw you in with the greatest pleasure."

"Thank you," said Big Claus; "but if I don't get any sea-cattle when I reach the bottom, I promise you I'll give you a sound thrashing."

"Oh, don't be as bad as that!" So they both went to the river. When the cattle, who were thirsty, saw the water, they ran as fast as they could, to get down to the stream.

"See how they hurry!" said Little Claus. "They are longing to get back to the bottom."

"Yes, but help me first," said Big Claus, "else I'll thrash you;" and he crept into a large sack which had been lying across the back of one of the oxen. "Put a stone into it, or I am afraid I shall not sink to the bottom," he added.

"That's all right!" said Little Claus; but he put a large stone into the sack all the same, tied the string tightly, and then pushed. Plump! there lay Big Claus in the river, and immediately sank to the bottom.

"I don't think he'll find the cattle," said Little Claus, and went home with those that he had.

The Saucy Boy

NCE upon a time there was an old poet, one of those right good old poets.

One evening, as he was sitting at home, there was a terrible storm going on outside; the rain was pouring down, but the old poet sat comfortably in his chimney-corner, where the fire was burning and the apples were roasting.

"There will not be a dry thread left on the poor people who are out in this weather," he said.

"Oh, open the door! I am so cold and wet through," called a little child outside. It was crying and knocking at the door, whilst the rain was pouring down and the wind was rattling all the windows.

"Poor creature!" said the poet, and got up and opened the door. Before him stood a little boy; he was naked, and the water flowed from his long fair locks. He was shivering with cold; if he had not been let in, he would certainly have perished in the storm.

"Poor little thing!" said the poet, and took him by the hand. "Come to me; I will soon warm you. You shall have some wine and an apple, for you are such a pretty boy."

And he was, too. His eyes sparkled like two bright stars, and although the water flowed down from his fair locks, they still curled quite beautifully.

He looked like a little angel, but was pale with cold, and trembling all over. In his hand he held a splendid bow, but it had been entirely spoilt by the rain, and the colours of the pretty arrows had run into one another by getting wet.

The old man sat down by the fire, and taking the little boy on his knee, wrung the water out of his locks and warmed his hands in his own.

He then made him some hot spiced wine, which quickly revived him; so that, with reddening cheeks, he sprang upon the floor and danced around the old man.

"You are a merry boy," said the latter. "What is your name?"

"My name is Cupid," he answered. "Don't you know me? There lies my bow. I shoot with that, you know. Look, the weather is getting fine again—the moon is shining."

"But your bow is spoilt," said the old poet.

"That would be unfortunate," said the little boy, taking it up and looking at it. "Oh, it's quite dry and isn't damaged at all. The string is quite tight; I'll try it." So, drawing it back, he took an arrow, aimed, and shot the good old poet right in the heart. "Do you see now that my bow was not spoilt?" he said, and, loudly laughing, ran away. What a naughty boy to shoot the old poet like that, who had taken him into his warm room, had been so good to him, and had given him the nicest wine and the best apple!

The good old man lay upon the floor crying; he was really shot in the heart. "Oh!" he cried, "what a naughty boy this Cupid is! I shall tell all the good children about this, so that they take care never to play with him, lest he hurt them."

And all good children, both girls and boys, whom he told about this, were on their guard against wicked Cupid; but he deceives them all the same, for he is very deep. When the students come out of class, he walks beside them with a book under his arm, and wearing a black coat. They cannot recognise him. And then, if they take him by the arm, believing him to be a student too, he sticks an arrow into their chest. And when the girls go to church to be confirmed, he is amongst them too. In fact, he is always after people. He sits in the large chandelier in the theatre and blazes away, so that people think it is a lamp; but they soon find out their mistake. He walks about in the castle garden and on the promenades. Yes, once he shot your father and your mother in the heart too. Just ask them, and you will hear what they say. Oh! he is a bad boy, this Cupid, and you must never have anything to do with him, for he is after every one. Just think, he even shot an arrow at old grandmother; but that was a long time ago. The wound has long been healed, but such things are never forgotten.

Now you know what a bad boy this wicked Cupid is.

The Shepherdess and the Sweep

AVE you ever seen a very old wooden cupboard, blackened by age, and decorated with many carved arabesques and foliage? Such a one stood in a sitting-room; it was a legacy from the great-grandmother, and was covered all over with carved roses and tulips. Upon it one could see the most peculiar figures, nd little stagheads with antlers were projecting from them. In the entre of the cupboard stood a carved man; he looked, indeed, ery ridiculous, and he grinned, for one could not possibly call laughing; he had legs like a goat, little horns on his forehead, nd a long beard. The children in the room used to call him Inder-General-Commander-War-Sergeant-in-Chief Billy Goat-gs. That was a name difficult to pronounce, and there are very w who obtain such a title; but to have such a man cut out was rtainly something. There he was! He looked continually wards the table underneath the looking-glass, where a sweet ttle shepherdess of porcelain was standing. Her shoes were lded, her dress was adorned with a red rose; she wore a golden t and crook; in short, she was very beautiful. Close by her ood a little chimney-sweep, as black as coal, and he, too, was of rcelain. He was as clean and nice as any other person; that he as a sweep was only because he was to represent one; the rcelain modeller might just as well have made him a prince, if had liked.

There he was standing with his ladder, and his face was as hite and rosy as a girl's; properly speaking, that was wrong, for it ght to have been a little blackened. He was close by the epherdess, and both were standing on the spots where they had n placed. As they were thus brought together, they had come engaged. They were very suitable for each other; both re young, of the same porcelain and equally fragile.

Close by stood another figure, which was three times as large as this couple; it was an old china-man who could nod. He, too, was made of porcelain, and pretended to be the grandfather of the little shepherdess, but he had no proof of it. He claimed to have power over her, and therefore he had nodded to the Under-General-Commander-War-Sergeant-in-Chief Billy Goatlegs, who paid his addresses to the little shepherdess.

"You will have a husband," said the old china-man, "who, I incline to think, is of mahogany. He can make you Mrs. Under-General-Commander-War-Sergeant-in-Chief Billy Goatlegs; he has a whole cupboard full of silver-plate, which he keeps in secret compartments."

"I do not wish to go into the dark cupboard," said the little shepherdess. "I have heard it said that he has eleven china-women inside the cupboard."

"Then you may well become the twelfth," said the china-man. "To-night, as soon as it rattles in the cupboard, you shall be married, as truly as I am a china-man." Then he nodded again and fell asleep.

But the little shepherdess cried and looked at her beloved one, the porcelain chimney-sweep.

"I entreat you," she said to him, "to take me far, far away, for we cannot stay here."

"I will do anything you please," said the little sweep. "Let us be off at once. I think I shall be able to keep you by my trade!"

"I wish we had already safely got down from the table," she said. "I shall not be happy, until we are far away."

And he comforted her, and showed her how she must put her little feet on the carved corners and the gilded ornaments of the leg of the table; he aided her with his little ladder, and soon they arrived on the floor. When they looked towards the old cupboard, they noticed that there was a great deal of noise in it; all the carved stags put their heads further out, lifted up their antlers, and twisted their necks. The Under-General-Commander-War-Sergeant-in-Chief Billy Goatlegs jumped up with excitement, and called out to the old china-man: "Look, there they are running

way." Then they were terribly frightened, and leapt quickly into
he drawer of the window-seat.

In this drawer were three packs of cards, but none of them was
complete, and a little doll's theatre, which was built up as well as
circumstances permitted.   There a comedy was being performed,
nd all the ladies, diamonds, clubs, hearts, and spades, were sitting
n the front row and fanning themselves with their tulips; all the
naves were standing behind them, showing that they had a head
below as well as above, as all playing-cards have.   The comedy
was about two people who were not to marry each other.   The
shepherdess shed tears over it, for it was exactly her own story.

"I cannot stand this any longer," she said, "I must get out of
he drawer."   But when they got out and looked up towards the
able, the old china-man was awake and shook his whole body,
which was all one piece.

"Now the old china-man is coming," cried the little shepherdess,
nd fell down on her porcelain knees, she was so much afraid.

"I have an idea," said the sweep.   "Shall we creep into the
ig pot-pourri vase yonder in the corner?   There we can repose
n roses and lavender, and throw salt into his eyes when he
comes."

"That will not save us," she said, "for I know that the old
china-man and the pot-pourri vase were one day engaged, and
here always remains a certain friendly feeling between people who
ave once been on such terms.   No, we have no alternative; we
must go out into the wide world."

"Have you really the courage to go with me out into the wide
world?" asked the sweep.   "Have you ever thought how large
he world is, and that we shall never return here?"

"Yes, certainly," was her reply.

Then the sweep looked her straight into the face and said:
"My way leads through the chimney.   Have you really the
courage to go with me through the stove, through the iron case
s well as through the pipes?   Through them we get out into
he chimney, and then I know my way very well.   We shall get
high up, that they can no longer reach us; on the very top is a
ole which leads out into the wide world."

He then led her to the stove-door.

"How black it looks!" she said; but she went with him, not only through the iron case, but also through the pipes, where it was pitch dark.

"Now we are in the chimney," he said. "Look up above you, there is a beautiful star shining."

It was a real star in the sky which was shining straight down upon them, as if it wished to show them the way. They climbed and crept on; it was a dreadful way and very high up. He held her tightly and pointed the best places out to her, where she could put her little porcelain feet safely down; at last they reached the rim of the chimney-pot and sat down, for they were very tired, and that was not wonderful.

The sky, with all its stars, was high above them, the roofs of the town spread out at their feet. They could see very far, far out into the world. The poor shepherdess had not thought that it would be like this; she leant her head on her sweep and began to cry so bitterly that all the gilt came off her girdle.

"That is too much," she said. "I cannot stand it. The world is too large! I wish I were again on the table underneath the looking-glass. I shall not be happy until I have got back there. I have gone out with you into the wide world, now you can take me back again, if you really care so much for me as you say."

The sweep reasoned with her, talked about the old china-man and the Under-General-Commander-War-Sergeant-in-Chief Billy Goatlegs; but she sobbed bitterly, and kissed her little sweep so much, that he could not do otherwise than give in, although it was foolish.

So they returned, with great difficulties, through the chimney, and crept through the pipes and the iron case: that was very unpleasant. When they had arrived in the dark stove they stood and listened behind the door to hear what was going on in the room. But there all was quiet; they peeped in, and there the old china-man was lying on the floor. He had fallen down from the table when he wished to run after them, and was broken into three pieces; the whole back had come off in one piece, and the head had rolled into a corner. The Under-General-Commander-

War-Sergeant-in-Chief Billy Goatlegs stood still in the place where he had always been, and meditated.

"That is terrible," said the little shepherdess. "The old grandfather is broken to pieces, and that is all our fault. I shall never get over this." And then she wrung her hands.

"He can be riveted," said the sweep. "He can be riveted again. Do not be too frightened. If they cement his back and put a good strong rivet into his neck, he will be as good as new, and may still say many disagreeable things to us."

"Do you think so?" she asked. Then they crept up to the table and returned to their former places.

"Here we are again on the same spot," said the sweep. "We might have saved all the trouble."

"Oh, that grandfather were riveted again!" said the shepherdess. "Is that very expensive?"

And he was riveted. The people had his back cemented, and a good strong rivet was put into his neck; he was as good as new again, but he could no longer nod.

"You seem to have become haughty since you broke to pieces," said the Under-General-Commander-War-Sergeant-in-Chief. "I think you have no cause to be so conceited. Am I to have her, or am I not?"

The sweep and the little shepherdess looked quite piteously at the old china-man; they feared lest he might nod again. But he could not do so. It was very unpleasant for him to tell the people that he had a rivet in his neck. Thus the two lovers remained together, blessed the grandfather's rivet, and loved each other till they broke to pieces.

The Goloshes of Fortune

I. A Beginning.

T a house in East Street, Copenhagen, not far from the King's New Market, a very large party had assembled; evidently the host aimed at receiving invitations in return, as he had invited so many people. Half of the guests had already sat down at the card-tables, while the others seemed to be waiting for the answer to their hostess's question, "What shall we do now?" The entertainment had advanced far enough for the people to be getting more and more animated. Among various other subjects, the conversation turned upon the Middle Ages. Some held the opinion that the Middle Ages were more interesting than our own time; and Counsellor Knapp stood up for this opinion so warmly, that the lady of the house sided with him at once, and both eagerly declaimed against Oerstedt's treatise in the Almanac "On Ancient and Modern Times," in which the main preference is given to our own age. The Counsellor held that the times of the Danish King Hans were the best and most prosperous.

While this was the subject of the conversation, which was only interrupted for a moment by the arrival of a newspaper containing nothing worth reading, let us look into the anteroom, where the cloaks, sticks, and goloshes belonging to the guests were lying. Here two women were sitting, the one young, the other more advanced in years. One might have thought they were servants who had come to accompany their mistresses home; but upon looking more closely at them, one was soon convinced that they were not common servants; their appearance was too dignified, their skins too delicate, and their dresses too elegant. They were two fairies.

The youngest was not Fortune herself, it is true, but the hand-

maid of one of her ladies in waiting, who carried the smaller gifts about. The elder one looked somewhat gloomy; she was Care, who always transacts all her business personally, for only then does she know that it is well done.

They were telling each other where they had been during the day. Fortune's messenger had only carried out some unimportant commissions; for instance, she had saved a new hat from a shower of rain, obtained a bow from a titled nonentity for an honest man, &c.; but she had now something of greater consequence to do. "I must also tell you," she said, "that to-day is my birthday, and in honour of it a pair of goloshes have been intrusted to me, which I am to bring to mankind. These goloshes have the property, that whoever puts them on is instantly transported to the place and age where he or she most desires to be; every wish regarding time or place of existence is at once realised, and thus man can for once be happy here below."

"Believe me," said Care, "he will be most unhappy, and bless the moment when he is once more rid of the goloshes."

"Is that your opinion?" replied the other. "Now I shall put them down at the door; some one will take them, and become the happy man."

Such was their conversation.

II. What Happened to the Counsellor.

It was late; Counsellor Knapp, deeply lost in thought over the time of King Hans, wished to go home; but fate so arranged matters that, instead of his own goloshes, he put on those of Fortune, and walked out into East Street.

The magic power of the goloshes instantly carried him back to the times of King Hans, and his feet sank deeply into the mud and mire of the street, which was not paved in those days.

'It is awfully dirty here," said the Counsellor; "why, the good firstones are gone and the lamps are all out."

The moon had not yet risen high enough; the atmosphere was somewhat thick, so that all the surrounding objects were not to be recognised in the darkness. When he came to the next corner, he found a lamp before a picture of the Holy Virgin, but the light it gave was so small that he only noticed it when he was passing underneath it, and his eyes fell upon the painted figures of the Mother and Child.

"That is evidently a curiosity shop," he thought, "and they have forgotten to take in their sign."

Several people in the costume of that age then passed by him.

"How funnily they are dressed up! No doubt they are returning from a masquerade."

Suddenly the sound of drums and fifes struck his ears. He saw the flaring light of torches, and stopped. A very extraordinary procession passed before him. First marched a band of drummers, beating their instruments with great skill; they were followed by attendants with cross-bows and lances. The principal person in the procession was a clergyman. The astonished Counsellor asked what all this meant, and who the clergyman was.

"The Bishop of Zealand," was the answer.

"Good heavens!" sighed the Counsellor, "what does the Bishop intend to do?" Then he shook his head; he could not believe it possible that the man was the bishop.

Still torturing his brains on this point, he passed through East Street and over High Bridge Place. The bridge, which he used to cross in order to reach Castle Square, was nowhere to be found; he at last reached the bank of a shallow river, where he saw two men with a boat.

"Would the gentleman like to cross over to the Holm?" they asked him.

"To the Holm?" said the Counsellor, who was quite unconscious that he lived in a different age. "I wish to go to Christian's Port, in Little Turf Street."

The two men stared at him.

"Only tell me where the bridge is," he said. "It is unpardonable that they have not lighted the lamps here, and it is as muddy as if it were a marsh."

The more he talked to the boatmen, the less intelligible their language became to him.

"I do not understand your Bornholmish," he said at last in an angry tone, and left them. He could not find the bridge, nor was there any rail-fence. "It is a downright shame that things are in such disorder here," he said. He had never thought his age more miserable than he did this evening. "I think it will be best for me to take a droske,"* he thought. But where were the cabs? None were visible. "I shall have to return to King's Newmarket to find a vehicle, otherwise I shall never reach Christian's Port." Then he went back to East Street, and had nearly come to the end of it, when the moon broke through the clouds.

"Good heavens! What strange building have they erected here!" he exclaimed when he saw the East Gate, which in

* A cab is called "droske" in Copenhagen.

those days stood at the end of East Street. He found, however, one of the wickets still open, and passed through it, in the hope of reaching the King's Newmarket; but there were wide meadows before him, with a few bushes growing upon them, and a broad canal or river streaming through them. A few wretched wooden huts, belonging to Dutch sailors, stood on the opposite bank. "Either what I see is a *fata morgana*, or I am intoxicated," lamented the Counsellor. "If I only knew what all this means!" He returned again, firmly believing that he was ill. Walking back through the same streets, he looked more closely at the houses, and noticed that most of them were only built of lath and plaster, and had thatched roofs.

"I do not feel at all well;" he sighed, "and yet I have only taken one glass of punch. But punch does not agree with me, and it is altogether wrong to serve punch with hot salmon. I shall tell the agent's wife so. Would it be wise to go back now, and let them know how I feel? No, no, it would look too ridiculous; and then, after all, the question is, if they are still up." He looked for the house, but was unable to find it.

"This is dreadful; I cannot even recognise East Street again. I do not see a single shop; there are only wretched old houses, as if I were in Roeskilde or Ringstedt. There is no longer any doubt; I am ill, and it is useless to stand on ceremonies. But where in all the world is the agent's house? It is no longer the same; but in yonder house I see some people still up. Alas! I am very ill." He soon arrived at a half-opened door, and saw the light inside. It was an inn of that period, a sort of public-house. The room looked very much like a Dutch bar: a number of people, sailors, citizens of Copenhagen, and a few scholars, sat there in lively conversation, with their mugs before them, and paid little attention to the Counsellor coming in.

"I beg your pardon," said the Counsellor to the landlady, "I have been suddenly taken ill; would you kindly send for a cab to drive me to Christian's Port?"

The woman looked at him and shook her head. Then she addressed him in German. The Counsellor, supposing that she could not speak Danish, repeated his request in German; this, in addition to his dress, made the woman feel sure that he was a foreigner; but she understood that he was unwell, and brought him a jug of water: it tasted very much of sea-water, although it had been fetched from the well outside.

The Counsellor rested his head upon his hand, drew a deep breath and thought over all the strange things around him.

"Is that this evening's number of the *Day**?" he asked mechanically when he saw the woman putting a large piece of paper aside.

She did not know what he meant, but she gave him the paper. It was a woodcut representing a phenomenon which had been seen in the city of Cologne.

"That is very old," said the Counsellor, and became quite cheerful at the sight of this old curiosity. "How did you get this are cut? It is highly interesting, although the whole is but a able. These phenomena are now explained as polar lights; they probably are caused by electricity."

Those who sat next to him, and heard his speech, looked at him with great surprise, and one of them rose, politely raised his hat, and said in a serious tone, "You are certainly a very learned man, monsieur."

"Not at all," replied the Counsellor; "I can only talk about things that everybody is supposed to understand."

"*Modestia* is a fine virtue," said the man. "Moreover, I have to add to your explanation *mihi secus videtur;* yet in the present case I willingly suspend my *judicium.*"

"May I ask with whom I have the honour to speak?" replied the Counsellor.

"I am a Bachelor of Divinity," said the man.

This answer was enough for the Counsellor; title and dress were in accordance with each other. "Surely," he thought, "this man is an old village schoolmaster, such a specimen as one still meets with sometimes in the upper parts of Jutland."

"Although here we are not in a *locus docendi,*" began the man again, "I request you to take the trouble to give us a speech. You are surely well read in the ancients."

* Evening paper at Copenhagen.

"Oh, yes," replied the Counsellor, "I am very fond of reading old and useful books, but I am also interested in new ones—with the exception of every-day stories, of which we have so many in reality."

"Every-day stories?" asked the Bachelor of Divinity.

"Why, yes; I mean the modern novels."

"Oh!" said the man, smiling, "they certainly contain a great deal of wit, and are read at Court. The King especially likes the romance by Iffven and Gaudian which treats of King Arthur and his valiant Knights of the Round Table. He has made jokes about it to his courtiers."

"This one certainly I have not read yet," said the Counsellor. "It must be quite a new one, published by Heidberg."

"No," replied the man, "Heiberg is not the publisher, but Gotfred of Gehmen." *

"Is he the author?" asked the Counsellor; "that is a very old name. Was it not the name of the first Danish printer?"

"Yes, he is our first printer," said the scholar.

So far everything went fairly well; now one of the citizens spoke of the dreadful plague which had raged a few years ago, meaning that of the year 1484. The Counsellor thought he spoke of the cholera, and so they could discuss it, unaware of the fact that each spoke of something else. The war against the freebooters had happened so lately that it was unavoidably mentioned; the English pirates, they said, had seized some ships that were in the harbour. The Counsellor, in the belief that they meant the events of 1801, was strongly against the English. The latter part of the conversation, however, did not go off so smoothly; they could not help contradicting each other every moment; the good Bachelor of Divinity was dreadfully ignorant, so that the simplest remark of the Counsellor seemed to him too daring or too fantastic. They often looked at each other in aston-ishment, and when matters became too difficult, the scholar began to talk Latin, hoping to be better understood, but all was of no avail.

"How do you feel now?" asked the landlady, pulling the

* First printer and publisher in Denmark, under the reign of King Hans.

Counsellor's sleeve. Only then his memory returned; in the course of the conversation he had forgotten all that had happened.

"Good heavens! where am I?" he said, and he felt quite dizzy when he thought of it.

"Let us have claret, mead, or Bremen beer," cried one of the guests. "And you shall drink with us."

Two girls came in; one had on a cap of two colours. They poured the wine out, and made curtseys. The Counsellor felt a cold shiver run down his back. "What does all this mean?" he said. But he had to drink with them, they asked him so politely. He was quite in despair, and when one of them said that he was intoxicated, he did not doubt it for a moment, and only requested them to get him a droske. Now they thought he spoke the Muscovite language. Never in his life had he been in such rude and vulgar company. "One would think that the country had gone back to Paganism," he thought; "this is the most terrible moment in all my life."

Just then the idea struck him that he would stoop under the table and creep towards the door. He carried this out, but when he was near the door, the others discovered his intention; they took hold of his feet, and to his great good fortune, pulled off the goloshes, and at once the whole enchantment was broken.

The Counsellor distinctly saw a street lamp burning, and behind it a large building; it all seemed familiar and grand to him. He was in East Street, as we know it now, and was resting on the pavement with his legs towards the door, and opposite sat the watchman, asleep.

"Goodness gracious! have I really lain here in the street dreaming?" he said. "Yes, this is East Street. How beautifully light and pleasant it looks! That glass of punch must have had a dreadful effect upon me."

Two minutes later, he sat in a cab, and drove to Christian's Port. He thought of all the anguish he had suffered, and praised the present, his own age, with all his heart, as being, in spite of its shortcomings, much better than the age in which he had existed a short while ago.

III. The Watchman's Adventures.

"Well, I never!" said the watchman; "there are a pair of goloshes. They evidently belong to the lieutenant who lives up there, for they are close by his door." The honest man would gladly have rung the bell and returned them to their owner, for there was still a light upstairs, but he did not wish to wake up the other people in the house, so he left them there. "I am sure a pair of such things must keep one's feet very warm," he said. "How nice and soft the leather is!" They fitted his feet exactly. "How strange things are in this world! This man, now, might go into his warm bed, and yet he does not do so, but walks up and down in his room. He is a fortunate man. He has neither wife nor child; he is out every evening. I wish I were in his place, I should certainly be happy."

No sooner had he uttered this wish than the goloshes carried it out; the watchman became the lieutenant in body and mind.

There he was, standing upstairs in the room, holding a sheet of pink note-paper between his fingers, on which was written a poem —a poem from the lieutenant's own pen. Who has not had, once in his life, a poetical moment? Then, if one writes down one's thoughts, they are poetry.

Such poems people only write down when they are in love, but a prudent man never has them printed. To be a lieutenant, poor and in love—this forms a triangle; or one might better describe it as half the broken die of fortune. That is just what the lieutenant thought at this moment, and therefore leant his head against the window frame and sighed. "The poor watchman down in the street is much happier than I. He does not know what I call want. He has a home, a wife and children, who share his joys and sorrows. I should be much happier if I could change places with him, and live with only his hopes and expectations. I am sure he is much happier than I."

Instantly the watchman became a watchman again, for, through the goloshes of Fortune, he had become, body and soul, the lieutenant; but as such he felt less contented than before, and preferred what he had despised a short time ago. He was a watchman again.

"That was a hideous dream," he said, "but very curious; I felt as if I were the lieutenant up there, and that was by no means a pleasure. I missed my wife and children, who are always ready to smother me with their kisses."

He sat down again and nodded; he could not quite get over the dream; the goloshes were still on his feet. A shooting star passed over the sky.

"There it goes" he said, "and yet there are plenty left. I should like to look a little more closely at these things, especially at the moon, for she would not slip so easily out of one's hands. The student my wife does washing for, says that when we are dead we shall fly from one planet to another. That is wrong, although it would not be at all bad. I wish I could take a little leap up there. I should not mind leaving my body here on the steps."

There are some things in this world that must be spoken of with caution, and one ought to be still more careful when one has the goloshes of Fortune upon one's feet. Now, let us see what happened to the watchman.

Everybody knows how quickly one can move from one place to another by steam, having experienced it either on a railway or a steamboat. But this speed is not more than the crawl of the sloth or creeping of a snail in comparison to the swiftness with which light travels. It flies nineteen million times faster than the quickest railway engine. Death is an electric shock to our hearts; the delivered soul vanishes away on the wings of electricity. Sunlight requires about eight minutes and a few seconds to perform a journey of more than ninety-five millions of miles; the soul travels as quickly on the wings of electricity. The distance between the various celestial bodies is not greater to it than we should find the distance between the houses of friends living in the same town quite close together. The electric shock to our hearts costs us our bodies, unless we have by chance the goloshes of Fortune on our feet, like the watchman.

In a few seconds the watchman had traversed the distance of two hundred and sixty thousand miles to the moon, which consists, as everybody knows, of much lighter material than our earth; something like new-fallen snow, as we should say. He had arrived on one of the numerous circular mountains which one sees on Dr. Maedler's large map of the moon. The inside was a basin of about half a mile in depth. Down below was a town; to get an idea of its appearance, the best thing would be to pour the white of an egg into a glass of water; the substance here was just as soft, and formed similar transparent towers, domes, and terraces, floating in the thin air like sails. Our globe hung above his head, like a dark red ball.

He soon noticed a great many beings, surely intended to be what we call "men," but they were very different from us. If they had been arranged in rank and file, and painted, one would certainly say, "What a beautiful arabesque!" They also had a language, but how could the soul of a watchman be expected to understand it? Nevertheless, it did understand the moon-language, for a soul has much greater faculties than we commonly suppose. Have we not frequent proof of its dramatic power in dreams? Then all our friends appear to us in their own character and voice, so exactly like the reality that we should have great difficulty in imitating them in our waking hours. Does not our soul often recall persons of whom we have not thought for years?

Suddenly they appear before our mental eyes in such living reality that we are able to recognise their minutest peculiarities. Truly, our soul's memory is a dreadful thing, for it will be able one day to recall every sin, every evil thought, we ever had; and then we shall have to give an account of every light word which was in our hearts or on our lips.

Thus the watchman's soul understood the language of the inhabitants of the moon very well. They were discussing our earth, and had doubts as to its being inhabited; they asserted the air there must be too thick for any moon-being to live in. They were of opinion that the moon only was inhabited; that it was _the_ celestial body where the ancient inhabitants of the world lived.

They also talked politics; but let us leave them, and return to East Street, and see what happens to the watchman's body. He was still sitting motionless on the steps, his staff having fallen out of his hand, while his eyes looked fixedly towards the moon, where his honest soul was rambling about.

"What's o'clock, watchman?" asked one of the passers-by. But the watchman gave no answer. Then the man gently fillipped his nose, which caused him to lose his equilibrium, and fall, full length, on the ground, like a dead man. His comrades were frightened; he seemed quite lifeless, and remained in the same condition. The incident was reported and discussed, and later on in the morning the body was taken to the hospital.

It might have turned out a capital joke if the soul had come back and looked for its body in East Street, without being able to find it. Probably it would first go to the Police Station, from thence to the Lost Property Office, that inquiries might be made, and in the end repair to the hospital. But we need not trouble our minds on that point, for souls are most clever when they act on their own responsibility; only the bodies make them stupid.

As I have stated, the watchman's body was carried to the hospital; there it was taken to the room where the bodies were washed, and naturally, the first thing they did was to take off the goloshes, whereupon the soul was obliged to return to the body. It at once started straight for the body, and in a few moments the man was alive again. He declared that he had never in all his life passed such a dreadful night, and not for any amount of money would he care to have such sensations again; but he got over it all right.

He was able to leave the hospital the same day, but the goloshes remained there.

IV. A CRITICAL MOMENT—A MOST EXTRAORDINARY JOURNEY.

Every inhabitant of Copenhagen knows the entrance to Frederick's Hospital, but as probably also some people who have not seen Copenhagen will read this story, it will be well to give a short description of it.

Towards the street the hospital is surrounded by an iron railing of considerable height, the thick bars of which stand so far apart that sometimes, as the story goes, some of the most slender young medical assistants have squeezed themselves through and paid little visits to town. Their heads were the most difficult to be brought through, and therefore here, as in other things in this world, those who had the smallest heads were the best off. This information will be sufficient for our narrative.

One of the volunteers, of whom one could only say that he had a great head in the physical sense, was on watch one evening; the rain was pouring down; but in spite of these two obstacles he wished to go out.

Just for a quarter of an hour, he thought; he need not trouble the porter, especially if he could slip through the bars. He noticed the goloshes which the watchman had forgotten; it did not strike him in the least that they were those of Fortune; they would render him good service in the bad weather, he thought, and so put them on. The point was now, if he could squeeze himself through the bars—he had never tried before. They were now in front of him.

"I wish I had my head outside," he said, and instantly, although it was very thick and large, it glided smoothly through the bars; the goloshes seemed to know how to do that very well; now he tried to pass his body through too, but this was impossible.

"I am too stout," he said; "I thought my head was the worst; but it is my body that I can't get through."

Now he tried to withdraw his head again, but he was unable to do so; he could move his neck about comfortably, and this was all. At first he felt very angry, but soon became discouraged. The goloshes of Fortune had placed him in this awkward position, and, unluckily, it never came into his mind to wish himself free again. Instead of wishing, he struggled to get his head out of the bars, but all his attempts were in vain. The rain was pouring down; not a soul was to be seen in the street; he could not reach the bell at the porter's lodge. How could he get out? He felt certain he would have to stop there until the next morning, then they would be obliged to send for a blacksmith to file through the iron bars. But all this would take time; all the charity children

would be going to their school opposite, all the inhabitants of the
adjoining sailor's quarter would flock together to see him in the
stocks; there would be a large crowd, no doubt! "Ugh!" he
cried, "the blood is rushing to my head; I must go mad! Yes, I
am going mad; oh, I wish I were free, then perhaps I might feel
better." He ought to have said this sooner, for the thought was
scarcely expressed when his head was free, and he rushed up to
his room, quite upset by the fright which the goloshes had caused
him.

Now we must not think it was all over for him. No; the
worst was still to come.

The night and the following day passed; nobody claimed the
goloshes. In the evening a recital was to take place on the plat-
form of a private theatre in a far-off street. The house was filled
in every part; the volunteer from the hospital was among the
audience, and seemed to have entirely forgotten what had happened to him the night before. He had put on the goloshes,
as no one had claimed them, and they rendered him good
service, for the streets were very dirty. A new poem, entitled
"Aunty's Spectacles," was being recited, in which the spectacles
were described as enabling the person who wore them in a large
assembly to read the people like cards, and to predict from them
all that would happen in the coming year.

The spectacles pleased him; he would have very much liked to
have such a pair. He thought, one might perhaps be able to look
straight into people's hearts, if one made good use of them, and
that surely would be much more interesting than to see what
would happen in the coming year; the latter, one would be sure
to see, but not the former.

"I think if I could look into the hearts of the ladies and gentle-
men in the first row, they would seem to me to form a sort of
large warehouse; oh, how my eyes would wander about in it!
In the heart of that lady, sitting there, I am sure I should find a
milliner's shop, in the next one the shop is empty, but a cleaning
would do it no harm. Would there also be some shops with
sound articles to be found in them?" "Yes, yes," he sighed, "I
know one in which everything is genuine, but there is already

a clerk in it, and that, in fact, is the only thing I have to find fault with. One might be invited to come into various others and inspect them. I wish I could pass like a little thought through these hearts!"

That was the catch-word for the goloshes; the volunteer shrunk together, and at once began a most extraordinary journey through the hearts of the occupiers of the first row. The first heart through which he passed belonged to a lady; it seemed to him that he was in one of the rooms of an orthopædic museum, where the plaster casts of deformed limbs are arranged on the walls, the only difference being, that while in the museum the casts are formed when the people enter, they were formed and kept in this heart after they had left. There were casts of the bodily and mental deformities of the lady's female friends carefully preserved.

Quickly he glided into another lady's heart. It appeared to him to be like a large holy church; the white dove of innocence fluttered over the high altar. He would have gladly knelt down, but he had no time—he had to go into the next heart; the sound of the organ was still ringing in his ears, and he felt he had become a new and better man, so that he did not feel unworthy to enter the next sanctuary, where he saw a sick mother in a miserable garret-room. But God's bright sun was shining through the window, splendid roses were growing in the little flower-box on the roof, and two sky-blue birds were singing of the joys of childhood, while the sick mother implored God to bless her daughter.

Then he crept on all-fours through an overcrowded butcher's shop; wherever he turned there was nothing but meat. It was the heart of a rich and respectable man, whose name you will certainly find in the directory.

Thence he came into the heart of this gentleman's wife; it was nothing but an old dilapidated pigeon-house. The husband's portrait served as a weathercock, and was connected with the doors, so that they opened and shut whenever he turned his head.

In the next heart he found a cabinet of mirrors, like those one sees in the castle of Rosenburg. But the mirrors magnified in an incredible degree. The insignificant *I* of the proprietor sat in the centre of the floor, like the Dalai-Lama, admiringly contemplating his own greatness.

Next he thought he had entered a narrow case, full of pointed needles, and said, "No doubt, this is the heart of an old maid." But such was not the case; it belonged to a young officer with several orders, whom people considered a man of intellect and heart. The poor volunteer was quite dizzy when he came out of the last heart in the row; he could not collect his thoughts, and fancied his too strong imaginative powers had run away with him.

"Good heavens!" he sighed, "I have a strong tendency to go mad, without doubt, and in here it is intolerably hot; the blood is rushing to my head." Just then he remembered his critical situation the evening before, when he had stuck fast between the bars of the hospital railing.

"Surely that was when I caught it," he thought; "I must do something for it in time. Perhaps a Russian bath would do me good. I wish I were already on the top-shelves."

There he lay on the top-shelf of the vapour-bath, fully dressed, with boots and goloshes still on, and the water dropped down from the ceiling on his face.

"Ugh!" he cried, and jumped down to take a plunge-bath.

The attendant cried out loudly in his surprise at seeing a man with all his clothes on.

The volunteer fortunately had enough presence of mind to whisper in his ear, "It is for a bet."

Upon arriving home, he at once placed a large mustard plaster on his neck and another on his back, to draw out the madness.

The next morning he had a very sore back, and that was all he gained through the goloshes of Fortune.

V. THE CLERK'S TRANSFORMATION.

The watchman, whom surely we have not yet forgotten in the meantime, remembered the goloshes which he had found, and carried with him to the hospital.

He went to fetch them, and when neither the lieutenant nor anybody else in the same street recognised them as their property, he took them to the police-office.

"They look exactly like my own goloshes," said one of the clerks, looking at the goloshes, and placing them by the side of his own. "It requires more than a shoemaker's eye to distinguish the difference —— "

"Mr. Clerk," said an attendant, who entered the room with some papers. The clerk turned round and spoke to the man afterwards, when he looked at the goloshes again, he was uncertain whether the pair on the left or on the right were his. "The wet ones must be mine," he thought; but in this he was wrong—they were the goloshes of Fortune; and after all it is not so wonderful, for a police-clerk can make mistakes like anybody else.

He put the goloshes on, thrust some papers into his pocket, took some others under his arm (the latter he was to read at home, and make abstracts of their contents), and went out. By chance it was Sunday morning, and splendid weather. "A trip to Fredericksburg would do me good," he thought, and thither he bent his steps.

No one could be more quiet and steady than this young clerk. We will not grudge him the little walk; after so much sitting, it will no doubt be beneficial to him. At first he walked on mechanically without thinking of anything at all, and therefore gave the goloshes no opportunity of proving their magic powers. In the Avenue he met an acquaintance, a young Danish poet, who told him that he intended to start the next day for a summer tour.

"Are you really off again?" asked the clerk. "You are indeed a luckier and freer man than one of us. You can go wherever you like, but we always have a chain to our feet."

"But it is fastened to the bread-tree," replied the poet. "You need not have a care for the morrow, and when you grow old you will receive a pension."

"But you are better off, after all," said the clerk. "It must be

pleasure to sit down and write poetry. Everybody has some-
hing pleasant to say to you, and you are your own master.
'ome and try what it is like to be obliged to sit in court and
sten to all sorts of frivolous cases."

The poet shook his head; the clerk did the same, and so they
arted, each retaining his own opinion.

"They are peculiar people, these poets," thought the clerk.
I should very much like to try and enter into such a nature, and
ecome a poet myself, for I am certain I should not write such
imentations as the others. To-day is a splendid spring day for a
oet! The air is exceptionally clear, the clouds look beautiful,
nd the green grass has such a fragrance. For many years I
ave not felt as I do now."

From these remarks we see that he had already turned a poet.
'o express such feelings would in most cases be considered
diculous. It is foolish to think a poet is a different being from
ther men; there may be some among the latter who have far
1ore poetical minds than professional poets. But a poet has
better memory, he can retain ideas and thoughts until
1ey are clearly fixed and expressed in words; and that
thers cannot do. But the transition of an ordinary nature to a
oetical one must needs be noticeable, and so it was with the
lerk.

"What a delicious fragrance!" he said. "How much it reminds
1e of the violets at Aunt Laura's. That was when I was a small
oy. Dear me! I have not thought of that for a long time.
ood old lady! She used to live near the canal. She always kept
green branch or a few green shoots in water, however hard the
inter was. The violets smelt sweet when I was putting hot pennies
:ainst the frozen window-panes to make peep-holes. And I had
fine view through them. There lay the ships out in the canal,
ozen in and deserted by their crews; a lonely crow was the
ily living thing on board. But when spring came, all became
ive; with cries and shouting the ice was burst, the ships were
rred and rigged, and then they started for distant lands. I have
ways remained here, and shall always be obliged to do so, and
: in a police office, while other people take passports for

abroad. That's my fate." And he sighed deeply. Suddenly he stopped. "Good heavens! what can be the matter with me? I have never thought and felt like this. The spring air must be the cause of it. It alarms me, and yet it is not disagreeable!" He felt in his pockets for his papers. "They will soon make me think of something else," he said, and his eyes glided over the first page :

"'Mrs. Sigbirth: Original Tragedy, in Five Acts,'" he read. "What's this? It's my own handwriting. Have I written this tragedy? 'The Intrigue on the Promenade; or, Fast Day: a Vaudeville.' But wherever have I got these things? Somebody must have put them into my pocket. And here is a letter."

It was from a theatrical manager; the plays were refused, and the letter was written in not over-polite language.

"H'm—H'm," said the clerk, and seated himself on a bench. His thoughts were very elevated, and his nerves highly strung. Involuntarily he plucked a flower growing near him; it was a common daisy. What botanists tell us in many a lecture, this flower tells us in a minute. It told the story of its birth, of the power of the sunlight, which, spreading out the fine petals, compels them to breathe forth sweet fragrance. Then he thought of the struggle of life, which in the same way awakens feelings in our breast. Air and light are the flower's lovers, but light is the favoured one. It turns towards the light, and when light vanishes, it folds its petals and sleeps in the arms of the air.

"Light adorns me," said the flower.

"But the air enables thee to breathe," whispered the poet.

A little way off, a boy was splashing with a stick in the water of a marshy ditch, so that the drops of water flew up to the green branches; the clerk thought of the millions of animalculæ which were thrown up in each drop of water, which, considering their size, must produce in them the same feeling as if we were thrown up high into the clouds. When the clerk thought of the great change that had taken place in him, he smiled.

"I am asleep and dreaming! It is strange how naturally one can dream and all the time one knows that he is only dreaming. I hope I may be able to remember this dream to-morrow when

am awake. I feel unusually excited. What a clear perception I
ave of everything, and how free I feel! But I am sure, should I
emember anything of it to-morrow, it will seem stuff and nonsense;
omething of the like has happened to me before. All the clever
nd beautiful things one hears of and speaks about in dreams, are
ke the underground treasure; when one digs it up, it looks rich
nd beautiful, and in the daylight it is but stones and faded
eaves. "Ah!" he sighed sadly, and looked at the singing birds
opping merrily from branch to branch, "they are much better
ff than I! Flying is a fine art. Happy is he who has been born
ith wings. If I could transform myself into a bird, I should
hoose to be a lark."

Immediately his coat-tails and sleeves became wings, his clothes
eathers, and the goloshes, claws; he noticed it and smiled to
imself. "Well, now! I see that I am dreaming, but I never had
uch a foolish dream!"

He flew up into the green branches and sang, but there was no
oetry in his song; the poetical mind was gone. The goloshes, like
nybody else who wishes to do a thing well, could only do one
hing at a time. He wished to be a poet: he became one. Then
e desired to be a little bird, and by becoming one, his former
haracter disappeared.

"This is charming indeed," he said. "In the daytime I sit
t the police office among the most uninteresting official papers;
t night I can dream, and fly about as a lark in the park of
redericksburg. One might really write a popular comedy about
ll this."

Then he flew down into the grass, turned his head from side to
ide, and pecked the flexible blades of grass with his beak, which,
proportion to his present size, appeared to him as large as
alm-leaves in North Africa. The next moment all became as
ark as night around him. Something, as it seemed to him, of
normous size was thrown over him; it was a sailor boy's cap.
hand then came underneath the cap, and seized the clerk by
e back and wings so tightly that he cried out. In his fright
e instinctively shouted out, "You rascal, I am a clerk in the
olice office." But this only sounded to the sailor boy like

"Tweet, tweet." He tapped the bird on its beak and walked off.

In the avenue he met two schoolboys of the upper class—that is, from the social point of view; for as far as their abilities were concerned they belonged to the lowest class in the school; they bought the bird for a small sum, and thus the clerk was brought back to Copenhagen.

"It is a good thing that I am dreaming," said the clerk, "otherwise I should certainly feel very angry! First I was a poet, now I am a lark. Surely the poetical nature has transformed me into this little bird! It is a very poor story, especially if one falls into boy's hands. I should very much like to know how it will end."

The boys took the bird into a very elegantly furnished room; a stout, amiable-looking lady received them. She was not at all pleased to see that they had brought home such a common field bird, as she called the lark. She would only allow them to keep it for the day, and they had to put the bird into an empty cage near the window.

"Perhaps it will please Polly," she added, and nodded to a large green parrot which was proudly rocking itself in its ring in a beautiful brass cage. "To-day is Polly's birthday," she said foolishly, "the little field-bird wants to congratulate it."

Polly did not reply a single word, and continued to rock itself, but a pretty canary, which had been brought away from its warm native country only last summer, began to warble sweetly.

"Squaller!" cried the lady, and threw a white cloth over the cage.

"Tweet, tweet," it sighed; "this is a terrible snowstorm." And then became silent.

The clerk, or, as the lady called him, the field-bird, was put into a small cage close by the canary and not far from the parrot. All that Polly could say (and it sounded sometimes most comical) was, "No, let us be men." What it said besides was no more intelligible than the warbling of the canary; but the clerk, being now a bird himself, understood his comrades very well.

"I flew about beneath green palms and flowering almond-trees," sang the canary. "I used to fly with my brothers and sisters over the beautiful flowers and smooth clear lakes, at the bottom of which one could see the plants waving their leaves. I also saw many fine-looking parrots, which could tell the most amusing tales."

"They were wild birds," replied the parrot, "they were not educated. No, let us be men. Why don't you laugh? When the lady and all the other people laugh you ought to do so also. It is a great shortcoming not to be able to appreciate fun. No, let us be men."

" Do you remember the handsome girls who used to dance in the tents near the flowering trees?" asked the canary. "Have you forgotten the sweet fruit, and the cooling juice of the wild herbs?"

"Oh, yes, I remember it all," replied the parrot; "but I am much more comfortable here. I have good food, and am well treated; I know I am clever, and I do not ask for more. Let us be men. You are a poet, as men call it; I possess sound knowledge and wit; you are a genius, but you lack discretion. You rise up to those high notes of yours, and then they cover you over. They dare not treat me like that. I was more expensive. My beak gains me consideration, and I can be witty. No, let us be men."

"Oh, my warm native country," sang the canary. "I will sing of your dark green trees, your calm bays, where the branches kiss the smooth, clear water. I will sing of all my shining comrades' joy, where the plants grow by the desert springs."

"Leave off those mournful strains," said the parrot. "Sing something that makes one laugh. By laughing you show that you possess the highest mental accomplishments. Have you ever seen a horse or a dog laugh? No, they can cry out; but laugh—only man has the gift of laughing." Then it laughed "Ha, ha, ha!" and added, "Let us be men."

"You poor little grey bird of the North," said the canary, "you are a prisoner here, like us. Although it is cold in your woods, you have freedom there. Fly away; they have forgotten to close the door of your cage, and the top window is open. Fly away!"

The clerk instinctively obeyed, and hopped out of the cage. At the same moment the half-open door leading into the next room creaked, and stealthily, with green shining eyes, the cat came in and chased him. The canary fluttered in the cage, the parrot opened its wings, and cried, "Let us be men." The clerk felt a mortal fright and flew out through the window, over houses and streets, until he was obliged to rest himself a little.

The house opposite his resting-place seemed familiar to him; the windows stood open; he flew in—it was his own room.

He perched himself on the table, and said, "Let us be men," involuntarily imitating the parrot. Instantly he became the clerk again, but he was sitting on the table.

"Oh dear," he said, "I wonder how I came up here, and fell asleep. That was a disagreeable dream. After all, it was nothing but stuff and nonsense."

VI. THE BEST THING THE GOLOSHES DID.

The next day, early in the morning, when the clerk was still in bed, somebody knocked at his door; his neighbour, a young student of theology, who lived in the same storey, walked in.

"Lend me your goloshes," he said; "it is damp in the garden, but the sun shines so brightly that I should like to smoke a pipe out there." He put on the goloshes and was soon in the garden below, in which a plum-tree and a pear-tree were growing. Even such a small garden is considered a wonderful treasure in the centre of big cities.

The student walked about in the garden; it was only six o'clock, and from the street he heard the sound of a post-horn.

"Travelling, travelling," he exclaimed. "That is the most desirable thing in the world, that is the aim of all my wishes. The restlessness which I often feel would be cured by travelling. But I ought to be able to go far away. I should like to see beautiful Switzerland, to travel through Italy, and ——"

It was well that the goloshes acted instantly, otherwise he might have gone too far, not only for himself, but for us too.

He was travelling in the heart of Switzerland, closely packed

with eight others in a diligence. He had a headache, his neck
was stiff with fatigue, the blood had ceased to circulate in his feet,
they were swollen, and the boots pinched. He was half-asleep
and half-awake. In his right-hand pocket he carried his letters of
credit; in his left, the passport; and some gold coins sewn in a
little bag he wore on his chest. Whenever he dozed off he woke
up imagining he had lost one or other of his valuables, and
started up suddenly; then his hand would move in a triangle from
the right over the breast to the left, to feel if they were still in their
places. Umbrellas, sticks and hats were swinging in a net in front
of him, and almost entirely deprived him of the view, which was
very imposing; he looked at it, but his heart sang what, at least,
one poet we know of has sung in Switzerland, although he had
not yet printed it—

> *I dreamt of beauty, and I now behold it*
> *Mont Blanc doth rise before me, steep and grey!*
> *Were my purse full, I should esteem it*
> *The greatest joy in Switzerland to stay."*

Grand, serious, and dark was all nature around him. The pine-
woods looked as small as heather on the high rocks, the summits
of which towered into the misty clouds; it began to snow; an icy
wind was blowing.

"Ugh!" he shivered, "I wish we were on the other side of the
Alps; there it would be summer, and I should have raised money
on my credit notes. I am so anxious about my money that I do
not enjoy Switzerland. Oh! I wish I had already come to the
other side."

And there he was on the other side, in Central Italy, between
Florence and Rome. The lake Thrasymene lay before his eyes,
and looked in the evening light like fiery gold between the dark
blue mountains. Here, where Hannibal defeated Flaminius,
vines were peacefully growing; by the wayside, lovely half-naked
children watched over a herd of swine under the flowering laurel-
trees. If we could describe this picture correctly, all would
exclaim, "Beautiful Italy!"

But neither the student, nor any of his travelling companions in the carriage of the vetturino, said anything of the sort. Venomous flies and gnats flew into the carriage by thousands; they tried to drive them away with myrtle branches, but in vain; the flies stung them nevertheless. There was not one among them whose face was not swollen from their painful stings. The poor horses looked dreadful; the flies covered them in swarms, and it was only a momentary relief when the coachman dismounted and swept the flies off.

Now the sun set, and a sudden icy cold pervaded all nature—much like the cold air in a tomb when we enter it on a hot summer day; the mountains round about appeared wrapped in that peculiar green which we see in some old oil paintings, and which, if we have not witnessed it in the south, we believe to be unnatural. It was a superb spectacle, but the travellers' stomachs were empty and their bodies exhausted with fatigue; all they were longing for was good night quarters, but what could they find? They looked more longingly for this than they did at the magnificent scenery before them.

The road led through an olive grove, much like a road between pollard willow trees at home. Here was at last a lonely inn. A dozen crippled beggars were lying down before it; the liveliest of them looked, to use one of Marryat's phrases, "like the eldest son of Hunger having just come of age"; the others were either blind or had paralysed feet, and crept about on their hands, or they had crippled arms and fingerless hands. That was misery in rags, indeed!

"*Excellenza miserabili,*" they sighed, and stretched forth their crippled limbs. The landlady herself, barefooted and with disorderly hair and a soiled blouse, received the guests.

The doors were fastened with strings; the floors of the rooms consisted of bricks, and were broken in many places; bats flew about under the ceilings, and there was a vile odour within.

"Lay the table down in the stable," said one of the travellers. "There, at least, we know what we breathe."

The windows were opened to allow the fresh air to enter; but the crippled arms and continual lamenting, "*Miserabili excellenza,*"

came in quicker than the air.   Many inscriptions covered the
walls ; half of them were not in favour of the *Bella Italia !*

Supper, when served, consisted of watery soup, with pepper and
rancid oil.   The latter was the chief ingredient in the salad.   Musty
eggs and fried cockscombs were the best dishes ; even the wine
had a peculiar taste ; it was a nauseous mixture.

At night the travellers' boxes were placed against the door,
and one of them had to watch while the others slept.   It was the
student's turn to watch.   Oh, how unbearably close the room
was !   The heat was oppressive ; the gnats buzzed and stung, the
miserabili outside groaned in their dreams.

"Travelling," said the student, "would be a pleasure if one had
no body.   If the body could rest and the mind fly about.   Where-
ever I go I feel a want that oppresses me ; I wish for something
better than the moment can give me ; something better—nay, the
best ; but where and what is it ? "

No sooner had he uttered this wish than he was at home again.
The long white curtains were hanging before the window, and
in the middle of the room stood a black coffin ; in it he slept the
sleep of death.   His wish was fulfilled ; his body rested, his spirit
was free to travel.

"Consider no man happy until he rests in the grave," were the
words of Solon.   In this case their truth was confirmed.   Every
dead body is a sphinx of immortality.   The sphinx in the black
coffin answered the questions which the student two days before
had written down :

> "*O Death, thou stern dark angel, we do find*
> *Nought but the tombs that thou dost leave behind!*
> *Will not the soul on Jacob's ladder upward pass,*
> *Or only rise as sickly churchyard grass ?*
>
> "*The world doth seldom see the greatest woes—*
> *Ye lonely suffering ones! ye now repose!*
> *Your hearts were often more opprest by care,*
> *Than by the earth your coffin-lid doth bear.*"

Two beings were moving about in the room ; we know them
already.   One was the fairy Care, the other was the messenger of
Fortune.   They bent over the dead.

" Now you see," said Care, " what happiness your goloshes have brought to mankind ! "

" They, at least, brought a lasting gift to him who slumbers here," answered Fortune's messenger.

" Oh, no," said Care. " He passed away at his own wish ; he was not summoned. His mental power was not strong enough to discern the treasures Fate had destined him to discover. I will render him a good service now."

And she pulled the goloshes from his feet; the sleep of death was at once ended ; the awakened man raised himself. Care disappeared, and with her the goloshes; probably she considered them her property.

The Flying Trunk

 HERE was once a merchant who was so rich that he could pave the whole street, and almost a little lane too, with silver. But he did not do so ; he knew how to employ his money differently. If he spent a shilling, he got back four ; such a clever merchant was he—till he died.

His son now got all this money. He lived merrily, went masquerading every night, made kites out of dollar-notes, and played at ducks and drakes on the sea-shore with gold pieces instead of stones. In this manner the money could easily come to an end, and it did so. At last he possessed no more than four shillings, and had no other clothes than a pair of slippers and an old dressing-gown. His friends now no longer troubled themselves about him, as they could not of course walk along the streets with him ; but one of them, who was good-natured, sent him an old trunk, with the remark, "Pack up !" That was indeed very nice of him, but he had nothing to pack up, so he sat down in the trunk himself.

It was a wonderful trunk. As soon as you pressed the lock, the trunk could fly. He pressed, and away it flew with him through the chimney, high up above the clouds, farther and farther away. But as often as the bottom creaked a little he was in great terror lest the trunk might go to pieces ; in that case he would have turned a mighty somersault.

Heaven preserve us ! In this manner he arrived in the country of the Turks. He hid the trunk in the wood under the dry leaves, and then went into the town. He could do so very well, for among the Turks everybody went about like that—in a dressing-gown and slippers. Meeting a nurse with a little child, he said, "I say, you Turkish nurse, what grand castle is that close by the town, in which the windows are so wide open ? "

"The Sultan's daughter lives there," she replied. "It was prophesied that she would be very unhappy about a lover, and therefore no one may go to her, unless the Sultan and Sultana are there too."

"Thank you," said the merchant's son ; and going out into the wood, sat down in his trunk, flew up on the roof and crept through the window into the Princess's apartments. She was lying on the sofa asleep, and was so beautiful that the merchant's son could not help kissing her. At this she awoke, and was greatly terrified ; but he said he was a Turkish god, who had come down to her from the sky, and that pleased her.

They sat down next to one another, and he told her little stories about her eyes : that they were the most glorious dark lakes, in which thoughts were swimming about like mermaids. And he told her of her forehead, that it was a mountain of snow with the most splendid halls and images.

They were indeed fine stories ! Then he asked the Princess for her hand, and she said "Yes" at once.

"But you must come here on Saturday," she said. "The Sultan and the Sultana will be here to tea then. They will be very proud at my marrying a Turkish god. But mind you bring a very pretty little tale with you, for my parents like them immensely. Mother likes them moral and high-flown, but father likes merry ones, at which he can laugh."

"Yes, I shall bring no other marriage gift than a story," said he, and so they parted. But the Princess gave him a sword ornamented with gold pieces, and the latter were very useful to him.

So he flew away, bought himself a new dressing-gown, and sitting down in the wood made up a story: it was to be ready by Saturday, and that was no easy task. By the time he had got it ready Saturday had come. The Sultan, the Sultana and the whole Court were at the Princess's to tea. He was received very graciously.

"Will you tell us a tale?" said the Sultana. "One that is deep and instructive."

"But something to laugh at, too," said the Sultan.

"Certainly," he replied, and commenced. And now pay attention:

"Once upon a time there was a box of matches which were very proud of their high descent. Their genealogical tree—that is to say, the great fir-tree, of which each of them was a little splinter—had been a high old tree in the forest. The matches were now lying between a tinder-box and an old iron pot, and they were telling about their youth. 'Yes,' said they, 'when we were upon the green branches, then we were really upon the green branches. Every morning and evening there was diamond tea, that was the dew: we had sunshine the whole day long, and when the sun shone the little birds had to tell stories. We could very well see that we were rich too, for the other trees were only dressed in summer, while our family had means for green dresses both in summer and winter.

"'But one day the woodman came; that was the great revolution; and our family was split up. The head of the family received a post as mainmast on a splendid vessel which could sail round the world, if it wished; the other branches settled in different places, and we now hold the office of kindling a light for the common herd. That is how such grand people as we have come down to the kitchen.'"

"My fate shaped itself in another way," said the iron pot next to which the matches were lying. "From the time I first came into the world, much scrubbing and cooking has gone on inside me. I look after the material wants of life, and occupy the first place in the house. My only pleasure is to be on the shelf after dinner, very nice and clean, and to carry on a sensible conversation with my comrades. But with the exception of the pail, which now and then gets taken down into the yard, we always live within our four walls. The only one who brings us any news is the market basket, but it speaks very unassuringly about the government and the people ; indeed, only the other day an old pot fell down from fright and broke into pieces. It is a Liberal, I tell you ! "

" Now you're talking too much," interrupted the tinder-box, and the steel struck against the flint, so that it gave out sparks. 'Had we not better have a pleasant evening ? "

"Yes, let us talk about who is the grandest," said the matches.

"No, I don't like to talk about myself," objected the pot. 'Let us get up an evening's entertainment. I will begin by telling a story of every-day life—something that any one can take an interest in and derive pleasure from, too.

"On the Baltic by the Danish coast ——"

" That's a pretty beginning ! " said all the plates. " That will be a story which we shall like."

"Yes, I passed my youth there, in a quiet family. The furniture was polished, the floor was scrubbed, and every fortnight clean curtains were hung up."

"How interesting you make your story," said the broom. One can hear at once that the teller is a man who has loved much among women. Something so pure runs through all."

" Yes, that is so," said the pail, and jumped for joy, so that the water splashed all over the floor.

And the pot continued telling its story, the end of which was just as good as the beginning.

All the plates rattled for joy, and the broom got some green parsley out of the dust-hole and made a wreath for the pot, for it knew that this would make the others angry. " If I present him with a wreath to-day," it thought, "he will have to give me one to-morrow."

"Now I will dance," said the tongs, and did so. Heavens! how high she could lift up one leg. The old chair-cushion in the corner burst when he saw it. "Shall I get a wreath too?" asked the tongs; and she got one.

"Still, they're only common people," thought the matches.

Now the tea-urn was asked to sing; but she said she had caught cold and could not sing unless she were boiling. That was mere affectation, however; she would not sing unless she were standing on the table with the family.

By the window was stuck an old goose-quill, with which the maid wrote. There was nothing remarkable about it, except that it had been dipped far too deep into the ink. But it was proud of that. "If the tea-urn will sing," it said, "let her alone. Outside there is a nightingale in a cage which can sing. It is true that it has learnt nothing, but we'll leave that out of the question this evening."

"I don't think it at all right," said the tea-kettle—he was kitchen singer and half-brother to the tea-urn—"that such a foreign bird should be heard. Is that patriotic? Let the market-basket decide."

"I should only be angry," said the market-basket; "there is such a conflict going on within me as no one would believe. Is this a proper way in which to pass an evening? Would it not be more sensible to put the house in order? Every one ought to go to his own place, and I would lead the game. That would be quite another thing."

"Yes, let us make a noise," they all said. Then the door opened, and the servant came in, at which they all stood still; not one stirred. But there was not a single pot who did not know what he could do and how grand he was. "Yes, if I had liked," each one thought, "we might have had a right merry evening."

The maid took the matches and lit the fire with them. Heavens! what sparks they threw out, and how they burst into flame!

"Now, everybody can see that we are first," they thought.
"How we shine, and with what light!" And they were
burnt up.

"That was a fine story," said the Sultana. "I feel quite
transplanted to the kitchen among the matches. Yes, now you
shall have our daughter."

"Indeed you shall," said the Sultan; "you shall marry our
daughter on Monday." And they made him feel quite one of
the family.

The wedding was settled, and on the evening before it the whole
city was illuminated. Biscuits and cakes were thrown among
the people; the street boys stood upon their toes, shouting
"Hurrah" and whistling on their fingers. It was uncommonly
grand.

"Well, I suppose I shall have to treat them to something too,"
thought the merchant's son. So he bought some rockets and
crackers, and every kind of fireworks that you can think of, put
them in his trunk and flew up to the sky with them.

Bang, bang! How they went off and cracked!

All the Turks jumped so high that their slippers flew over
their ears; such a display they had never yet seen. Now they
could understand that it was the god of the Turks himself who
was to marry the Princess.

As soon as the merchant's son had come down again into the
wood with his trunk, he thought, "I'll just go into the town to
hear what impression it made." And it was natural that he
should wish to know that.

What stories the people did tell! Every one whom he asked
about it had seen it in his own way; but all thought it beautiful.

"I saw the god of the Turks himself," said one. "His eyes
were like shining stars, and his beard like foaming water."

"He flew in a mantle of fire," said another. "The sweetest
little cherubs peeped out of its folds."

Indeed they were fine things that he heard, and on the following day he was to be married.

So he went back to the wood to get into his trunk; but what

had become of it? The trunk was burnt. A spark from the fireworks had fallen into it and had set it alight, and now the trunk lay in ashes. He could not fly any more, nor get to his bride.

She stood on the roof the whole day and waited, and is probably waiting still. But he wanders through the world telling tales, which are, however, no longer such merry ones as the one he told about the matches.

The Little Match Girl

I was terribly cold; it snowed and was almost dark on this, the last evening of the year. In the cold and darkness, a poor little girl, with bare head and naked feet, went along the streets. When she left home, it is true, she had had slippers on, but what was the use of that? They were very large slippers; her mother had worn them till then, so big were they. So the little girl lost them as she sped across the street, to get out of the way of two carts driving furiously along. One slipper was not to be found again, and a boy had caught up the other and run away with it. So the little girl had to walk with naked feet, which were red and blue with cold. She carried a lot of matches in a red apron, and a box of them in her hand. No one had bought anything of her the live-long day; no one had given her a penny.

Shivering with cold and hunger, she crept along, poor little thing, a picture of misery.

The snow-flakes covered her beautiful fair hair, which fell in long tresses about her neck: but she did not think of that now. Lights were shining in all the windows, and there was a tempting smell of roast goose, for it was New Year's Eve. Yes, she was thinking of that.

In a corner formed by two houses, one of which projected beyond the other, she crouched down in a little heap. Although she had drawn her feet up under her, she became colder and colder ; she dared not go home, for she had not sold any matches nor earned a single penny.

She would certainly be beaten by her father, and it was cold at home, too; they had only the roof above them, through which

the wind whistled, although the largest cracks had been stopped up with straw and rags.

Her hands were almost numb with cold. One little match might do her good, if she dared take only one out of the box, strike it on the wall and warm her fingers. She took one out and lit it. How it sputtered and burned !

It was a warm, bright flame, like a little candle, when she held her hands over it; it was a wonderful little light, and it really seemed to the child as though she was sitting in front of a great iron stove with polished brass feet and brass ornaments. How the fire burned up, and how nicely it warmed one ! The little girl was already stretching out her feet to warm these too, when—out went the little flame, the stove vanished, and she had only the remains of the burnt match in her hand.

She struck a second one on the wall; it threw a light, and where this fell upon the wall, the latter became transparent, like a veil; she could see right into the room. A white table-cloth was spread upon the table, which was decked with shining china dishes, and there was a glorious smell of roast goose stuffed with apples and dried plums. And what pleased the poor little girl more than all was that the goose hopped down from the dish, and with a knife and fork sticking in its breast, came waddling across the floor straight up to her. Just at that moment out went the match, and only the thick, damp, cold wall remained. So she lighted another match, and at once she sat under the beautiful Christmas tree; it was much larger and better dressed than the one she had seen through the glass doors at the rich merchant's. The green boughs were lit up with thousands of candles, and gaily-painted figures, like those in the shop-windows, looked down upon her. The little girl stretched her hands out towards them and—out went the match. The Christmas candles rose higher and higher till they were only the stars in the sky; one of them fell, leaving a long fiery trail behind it.

"Now, some one is dying," thought the little girl, for she had been told by her old grandmother, the only person she had ever loved, and who was now dead, that when a star falls a soul goes up to heaven.

She struck another match on the wall; it was alight once more, and before her stood her old grandmother, all dazzling and bright, and looking very kind and loving.

"Grandmother!" cried the little girl. "Oh! take me with you. I know that you will go away when the match is burnt out; you will vanish like the warm stove, like the beautiful roast goose, and the large and splendid Christmas-tree." And she quickly lighted the whole box of matches, for she did not wish to let her grandmother go. The matches burned with such a blaze that it was lighter than day, and the old grandmother had never appeared so beautiful nor so tall before. Taking the little girl in her arms, she flew up with her, high, endlessly high, above the earth; and there they knew neither cold, nor hunger, nor sorrow—for they were with God.

But in the cold dawn, the poor little girl was still sitting—with red cheeks and a smile upon her lips—in the corner, leaning against the wall : frozen to death on the last evening of the Old Year. The New Year's sun shone on the little body. The child sat up stiffly, holding her matches, of which a box had been burnt. "She must have tried to warm herself," some one said. No one knew what beautiful things she had seen, nor into what glory she had entered with her grandmother on the joyous New Year.

Ole Luk-Oie

HERE is no one in the world who knows so many stories as Ole Luk-Oie. He can tell them beautifully !

Towards evening time when children are still sitting nicely at table or on their stools, Ole Luk-Oie comes. He creeps up the stairs very quietly, for he always walks in his socks ; he opens the doors gently, and whish ! he squirts sweet milk into the children's eyes in tiny drops, but still quite enough to prevent them from keeping their eyes open and therefore from seeing him. He steals behind them, and blows softly on their necks, and this makes their heads heavy. Of course it does not hurt them, for Ole Luk-Oie is the children's friend; he only wants them to be quiet, and that they are not until they have been put to bed.

He wants them to be quiet only to tell them stories.

When the children are at last asleep, Ole Luk-Oie sits down upon their bed. He has fine clothes on; his coat is of silk, but it is impossible to say of what colour, for it shines green, red and blue, according as he turns. Under each arm he carries an umbrella; the one with pictures on it he opens over good children, and then they dream the most beautiful stories all night; but the other, on

which there is nothing at all, he opens over naughty children, and
then they sleep as though they were deaf, so that when they awake
in the morning they have not dreamt of the least thing.

Now we shall hear how during one week Ole Luk-Oie came to a
little boy named Hjalmar every evening, and what he told him
There are seven stories : for there are seven days in the week.

MONDAY.

"Look here," said Ole Luk-Oie in the evening, when he had
put Hjalmar to bed; " I'll just make things look nice."

And all the flowers in the flower-pots grew into large trees
stretching out their long branches across the ceiling and along the
walls, so that the room looked like a beautiful arbour ; and all the
branches were full of flowers, every flower being finer than a rose
and smelling sweetly. If one wanted to eat them, they were

sweeter than jam. The fruits shone like gold, and there were cakes simply bursting with currants. Nothing like it had ever been seen before. But at the same time terrible cries were heard coming from the table-drawer in which Hjalmar's school-books lay.

"Whatever is the matter?" said Ole Luk-Oie, going to the table and opening the drawer. It was the slate, upon which a terrible riot was going on amongst the figures, because a wrong one had got into the sum, so that it was nearly falling to pieces; the pencil hopped and skipped at the end of its string, as if it were a little dog who would have liked to help the sum, but it could not. And from Hjalmar's copy-book there also came the sounds of woe, terrible to hear. On every page there stood at the beginning of each line a capital letter, with a small one next to it; that was for a copy. Now next to these stood some other letters which Hjalmar had written, and these thought they looked just like the two first. But they lay there as if they had fallen over the pencil-lines upon which they ought to have stood.

"Look, this is the way you ought to hold yourselves up," said the copy. "Look, slanting like this, with a powerful up-stroke."

"Oh, we should like to," said Hjalmar's letters; "but we can't, we are too weak."

"Then you must take some medicine," said Ole Luk-Oie.

"Oh, no," they cried, and stood up so gracefully that it was a pleasure to see them.

"Well, we cannot tell any stories now!" said Ole Luk-Oie; I must drill them. One, two! one, two!" And in this way he drilled the letters. They stood up quite gracefully, and looked as nice as only a copy can do. But when Ole Luk-Oie had gone and Hjalmar looked at them in the morning, they were just as weak and miserable as before.

TUESDAY.

As soon as Hjalmar had gone to bed, Ole Luk-Oie touched all the furniture in the room with his little magic squirt, whereupon it immediately began to talk.

Every piece spoke about itself, with the exception of the spittoon, which stood quietly there and got very angry at their being so vain as to talk only about themselves, to think only about themselves, and to take no notice whatever of it, which stood modestly in the corner and allowed itself to be spat upon.

Over the wardrobe hung a large picture in a gilt frame; it was a landscape. There might be seen large old trees, flowers in the grass, and a wide river flowing round the wood, past many castles, and far out into the stormy sea.

Ole Luk-Oie touched the picture with his magic squirt, and the birds immediately began to sing, the branches of the trees to move, and the clouds to sail past; their shadows could be seen gliding along over the landscape.

Then Ole Luk-Oie lifted Hjalmar up to the frame and put his little feet into the picture, right among the high grass; there he stood. The sun shone down upon him through the branches of the trees. He ran to the water and got into a small boat which was lying there; it was painted red and white, the sails glittering like silver; and six swans, wearing golden crowns round their necks and brilliant blue stars on their heads, drew the boat along, past the green wood where the trees tell of robbers and witches, and where the flowers speak of the dainty little elves and of what the butterflies have told them.

Most lovely fishes, with scales like silver and gold, swam after the boat; now and then they took a jump, making the water splash. Birds, blue and red, small and large, also followed, flying in two long rows.

The gnats danced and the cockchafers said: "Boom, boom!" They all wanted to follow Hjalmar, and each had a story to tell.

What a pleasant voyage it was! At times the woods were thick and dark, at times full of sunlight and flowers like the most beautiful garden. There were great castles built of glass and of marble, and on the balconies stood princesses, who were all little girls whom Hjalmar knew very well, and with whom he had formerly played. Every one of them stretched out her hands,

offering him the prettiest sugar-heart that you could find in a
sweetstuff shop. Hjalmar caught hold of one side of the sugar-
heart as he sailed by, and the princess also holding on tightly, each
got a piece of it ; she the smallest, Hjalmar the biggest. At every
castle little princes were keeping guard, shouldering their golden
swords and showering down raisins and tin-soldiers ; it was easy to
see that they were real princes.

Sometimes Hjalmar sailed through forests, sometimes through
great halls or through the middle of a town ; he also came to the
town in which lived the nurse who had carried him when he was
still a little boy and who had always been so good to him. She
nodded and beckoned to him, and sang the pretty little verse
which she had herself composed and sent to Hjalmar :

> *"I think of thee full many a time,*
> *My own dear darling boy ;*
> *To kiss thy mouth, thine eyes, thy brow,*
> *Was once my only joy.*

> *"I heard thee lisp thy first sweet words,*
> *Yet from thee I was torn ;*
> *May Heaven be e'er that angel's shield*
> *Whom in my arms I've borne."*

And all the birds sang too, the flowers danced on their stalks,
and the old trees nodded as if Ole Luk-Oie were also telling them
stories.

WEDNESDAY.

How the rain was pouring down outside ! Hjalmar could hear
it in his sleep, and when Ole Luk-Oie opened one of the windows
the water came up to the window-sill. It formed quite a lake,
and a most splendid ship lay close to the house.

"If you would like to sail with us, little Hjalmar," said Ole
Luk-Oie, "you can reach foreign countries to-night, and get back
here by the morning."

Then Hjalmar suddenly found himself dressed in his Sunday
clothes in the middle of the beautiful ship ; the weather at once
became fine, and they sailed through the streets, cruised round

the church, and were soon sailing on a great stormy sea. They sailed until they lost sight of land, and could see only a flight of storks which were coming from Hjalmar's home and going to warm climates. They were flying in a line one after another, and had already come very far. One of them was so tired that his wings could scarcely carry him any longer; he was the last in the line, and was soon left a long way behind, finally sinking lower and lower with outspread wings. He flapped them once or twice more, but it was of no use; first he touched the rigging of the vessel with his feet, then he slid down from the sail, and at last he stood on the deck.

The cabin-boy took him and put him into the fowl-coop with the hens, ducks, and turkeys; there stood the poor stork, a prisoner among them.

"Look at the fellow," said all the fowls, and the turkey-cock puffed himself out as much as he could, and asked him who he was; the ducks waddled backwards and jostled each other, quacking: "What a fool! What a fool!" And the stork told them about the heat of Africa, about the pyramids, and about the ostrich who runs across the desert like a wild horse; but the ducks did not understand him, and nudged each other, saying: "I suppose we all agree that he is very stupid."

"Of course he is very stupid," said the turkey; and then he gobbled. So the stork was silent and thought of his Africa.

"What beautifully thin legs you have," said the turkey-cock. "What do they cost a yard?"

"Quack, quack, quack!" grinned all the ducks; but the stork pretended not to have heard it.

"You might laugh anyhow," said the turkey-cock to him; "for it was very wittily said. But perhaps it was too deep for you. Ha, ha! he is not very clever. We will keep to our interesting selves." And then he gobbled, and the ducks quacked. It was irritating to hear how they amused themselves.

But Hjalmar went to the fowl-coop, opened the door and called the stork, who hopped out to him on the deck. He had now had a good rest, and he seemed to nod at Hjalmar, as if to thank him. He then spread his wings and flew to the warm countries;

but the hens cackled, the ducks quacked, and the turkey-cock turned red as fire in his face.

"To-morrow we shall make soup of you," said Hjalmar; and with that he awoke and found himself between his linen sheets. But it was a strange journey upon which Ole Luk-Oie had taken him that night.

THURSDAY.

"Do you know what?" said Ole Luk-Oie; "only don't be frightened, and you will see a little mouse here." And he held out his hand with the pretty little animal in it. "She is come to invite you to a wedding. There are two little mice, who are going to enter the state of matrimony to-night. They live under the floor of your mother's pantry, which must be a fine place to dwell in."

"But how can I get through the little mouse-hole in the floor?" asked Hjalmar.

"Let me look after that," said Ole Luk-Oie. "I will soon make you small." And then he touched Hjalmar with his little magic squirt, making him immediately smaller and smaller, until at last he was only as big as a finger. "Now you can borrow the clothes of the tin soldier; I think they will fit you, and it looks well to wear a uniform when you are in company."

"So it does," said Hjalmar, and in a moment he was dressed like the prettiest little tin soldier.

"Will you be good enough to sit in your mother's thimble?" said the little mouse; "then I shall have the honour of drawing you along."

"Dear me! will you take so much trouble yourself?" said Hjalmar; and in that fashion they drove to the mouse's wedding.

At first they came to a long passage under the floor, just high enough to enable them to drive along with the thimble, and the whole passage was illuminated with lighted tinder.

"Doesn't it smell delightful here?" asked the mouse, who was drawing him along. "The passage is smeared with bacon-rind. There can be nothing nicer!"

They now came into the hall where the wedding was to take place. On the right-hand side stood all the little lady-mice whispering and squeaking as though they were having rare fun; on the left stood all the gentlemen-mice stroking their whiskers with their paws. In the middle of the hall could be seen the bride and bridegroom standing in the hollowed-out rind of a cheese; they were kissing each other in a shameless manner before the eyes of all, for they were already betrothed and on the point of being married.

More strangers were continually arriving; the mice were almost treading each other to death, and the bridal pair had placed themselves right in the doorway, so that it was impossible to go in and out. The whole room, like the passage, had been besmeared with bacon-rind, and that was all the refreshments; for dessert, however, a pea was shown, in which a mouse of the family had bitten the name of the bridal pair—that is to say, of course only the initials. But what a novel idea it was!

All the mice agreed that it had been a splendid wedding, and that the conversation had been most agreeable.

Then Hjalmar drove home again. He had certainly been in distinguished society, but he had also had to huddle himself up a good deal, to make himself small, and to wear the uniform of a tin soldier.

FRIDAY.

"You would hardly believe how many grown-up people there are who would only be too pleased to have me," said Ole Luk-Oie. "Particularly those who have done something bad. 'Dear little Ole,' they say to me, 'we cannot close our eyes, and so we lie awake the whole night and see all our wicked deeds sitting like ugly little goblins on the bedstead, and squirting hot water over us; we wish you would come and drive them away, so that we could get a good sleep.' Then they sigh deeply. 'Indeed we would willingly pay for it; good-night, Ole, the money is on the window-sill.'

"But I don't do it for money," said Ole Luk-Oie.

"What are we going to do to-night?" asked Hjalmar.

"Well, I don't know whether you would like to go to another wedding to-night; it is of quite a different kind to last night's. Your sister's big doll—the one that looks like a man and is called Hermann—is going to marry the doll Bertha. Besides this it is the bride's birthday, and therefore they will receive a great many presents."

"Yes, I know that," said Hjalmar. "Whenever the dolls want new clothes, my sister says it is a birthday or a wedding; that has happened quite a hundred times already."

"Yes, but to-night is the hundred and first wedding, and when that number is reached, everything is over. That is why this one will be quite unlike any other. Only just look!"

And Hjalmar looked upon the table. There stood the little doll's house with lights in the windows, and all the tin soldiers presenting arms in front of it. The bride and bridegroom were sitting on the floor and leaning against the leg of the table; they seemed very thoughtful, and for this they had perhaps good cause. Ole Luk-Oie, dressed in grandmother's black gown, married them. When the ceremony was over, all the furniture in the room began to sing the following beautiful song, written by the lead-pencil to the air of the soldiers' tattoo:

> " We'll troll the song out like the wind,
>   Long live the bridal pair !
>   They're both so dumb, so stiff and blind,
>   Of leather made, they'll wear.
>   Hurrah, hurrah, though deaf and blind
>   We'll sing it out in rain and wind."

And now came the presents; they had, however, declined to accept any eatables, love being enough for them to live on.

"Shall we take a country-house, or would you rather travel?" asked the bridegroom. To settle this, the swallow, who had travelled a great deal, and the old hen, who had hatched five broods of chicks, were asked for their advice.

The swallow spoke of the beautiful warm countries, where the grapes grow large and full, where the air is so mild and the mountains have such colours as are never seen on them in our country.

" But still they have not our broccoli," said the hen. " I was once in the country for a whole summer with all my chicks; there was a sand-pit, into which we might go, and scrape up, and then we were admitted to a garden full of broccoli. Oh, it was grand! I cannot imagine anything nicer."

"But one head of cabbage is just like another," said the swallow; "and then we very often have bad weather here."

" Well, one gets used to that," said the hen.

" But it is cold here, and it freezes."

" That is good for cabbages," said the hen. " Besides, it can be warm here too. Didn't we have a summer, four years ago, that lasted five weeks? It was almost too warm to breathe. And then we have not poisonous animals, as they have there; and we are free from robbers. He must be a wicked man who does not think that our country is most beautiful. He really does not deserve to be here."

And then the hen wept and added: " I have travelled too. I rode for more than twelve miles in a coop. Travelling is by no means a pleasure."

"The hen is a sensible woman," said the doll Bertha. " I don't in the least care for mountain travelling myself, for you only go up and down again. No, we will go into the gravel-pit outside the gate and take a walk in the cabbage-garden."

And so they did.

SATURDAY.

"Shall I hear any stories to-night?" asked little Hjalmar, as soon as Ole Luk-Oie had sent him to sleep.

"We have no time for any this evening," said Ole Luk-Oie, opening his beautiful umbrella over him. "Just look at these Chinamen!"

The umbrella looked like a large Chinese bowl with blue trees and pointed bridges, and with little Chinamen nodding their heads.

"We must have the whole world cleaned up by to-morrow morning," said Ole Luk-Oie, "for it is a holiday, it is Sunday. I will go to the church-steeple and see whether the little church goblins are polishing the bells, so that they may sound sweetly; I will go out into the fields and see whether the wind is blowing the dust off the grass and the leaves ; and what is the most necessary work of all, I must fetch down the stars to polish them. I take them in my apron; but first each one must be numbered, and the holes in which they are fixed must also be numbered, so that they may be put back in their right places. They would otherwise not hold fast and we should have too many falling stars, one tumbling down after another.

"Look here; do you know, Mr. Ole Luk-Oie," said an old portrait which hung on the wall in Hjalmar's bedroom, "I am Hjalmar's great-grandfather? I thank you for telling the boy tales; but you must not put wrong ideas into his head. The stars cannot be taken down. The stars are worlds, just like our earth, and that is the beauty of them."

"Thank you, old great-grandfather," said Ole Luk-Oie; "thank you. You are the head of the family; you are its founder; but I am still older than you. I am an old heathen; the Greeks and Romans called me the God of Dreams. I have visited the grandest houses, and still go there. I know how to deal both with the humble and the great. Now, you may tell your stories." And Ole Luk-Oie went away and took his umbrella with him.

"Well! One must not even give one's opinion any more," grumbled the old portrait.

And Hjalmar awoke.

SUNDAY.

"Good evening," said Ole Luke-Oie. Hjalmar nodded and sprang up to turn his great-grandfather's portrait against the wall, so that it could not interrupt, as it had done yesterday.

"You must tell me some stories about the five green peas who lived in one pod; about the leg of the cock which went courting the leg of the hen; and about the darning-needle who was so grand that she fancied she was a sewing-needle."

"You can have too much of a good thing," said Ole Luk-Oie. 'You know very well that I prefer showing you something. I will show you my brother. He is also called Ole Luk-Oie, but he never comes to any one more than once, but when he does come to them, he takes them with him on his horse and tells them stories. He only knows two ; one is so extremely beautiful that no one in the world can imagine anything like it ; the other is most awful and horrible—it cannot be described."

Then Ole Luk-Oie lifted little Hjalmar up to the window, saying : "Now you will see my brother, the other Ole Luk-Oie. They call him Death.   Do you see, he does not look so bad as in the picture books, where they make him out to be a skeleton.   That splendid hussar uniform that he is wearing is embroidered with silver ; a black velvet mantle floats behind him over the horse. See at what a gallop he rides."

And Hjalmar saw how this Ole Luk-Oie rode away, taking both young and old upon his horse.   Some he placed before him and others behind, but he always asked first:

"How is your report for good behaviour ?"

"Good," they all replied.

"Yes, but let me see it myself," said he ; and then each one had to show him his book of reports.   All those who had 'Very good' and 'Excellent' were placed in front upon the horse and heard the delightful story ; but those who had 'Pretty good' and 'Middling' had to get up behind and listen to the horrible tale ; they trembled and wept, and wanted to jump down from the horse, but could not do so, because they had immediately grown fast to it.

"But Death is a most beautiful Ole Luk-Oie," said Hjalmar. "I am not afraid of him."

"Neither should you be," said Ole Luk-Oie ; "only take care that you get good reports."

"Well, that's instructive," muttered the great-grandfather's portrait.   "It is of some use to give one's opinion occasionally."

Now he felt satisfied.

And that is the story of Ole Luk-Oie ; perhaps he will tell you some more to-night himself.

The Ugly Duckling

HE country was looking beautiful. It was summer; the wheat was yellow, the oats were green, the hay stood in stacks on the green meadows, and the stork strutted about on his long red legs chattering Egyptian, for he had learnt that language from his mother. All around the fields and meadows were large forests, and in the middle of these forests deep lakes. Yes, it was really glorious out in the country. In the sunshine one could see an old country seat surrounded by deep canals, and from the wall, right down to the water, there grew large burdock leaves, which were so high that little children could stand upright under the tallest. It was as wild there as in the thickest wood. A duck, who was hatching her young, sat on her nest here, but she got very tired of waiting for the young ones to come. She rarely had visitors, for the other ducks preferred swimming about in the canals to waddling up and sitting down under a burdock leaf to gossip with her.

At last one egg cracked after another. "Chick, chick;" all the yolks were alive, and the little heads peeped out.

"Quack, quack!" said the duck; so they all hurried up as fast as they could, and looked about on all sides under the green leaves. Their mother let them look as much as they liked, because green is good for the eyes.

"How large the world is," said all the little ones; for, of course, they had much more room now than in the egg.

"Do you think this is the whole world?" said the mother; "why, that stretches far beyond the other side of the garden, right into the parson's field, but I have never been there yet. I suppose you are all here?" she continued, getting up. "No, you are not; the largest egg is still lying here. How long will this last? I'm getting tired of it!" And so saying she sat down again.

"Well, how are you getting on?" said an old duck, who had come to pay her a visit.

"This egg takes such a long time," answered the sitting duck; "it will not break. But just look at the others; are they not the daintiest ducklings that were ever seen? They all look like their father, the rascal—he doesn't come to pay me a visit."

"Let me see the egg that will not break," said the old duck. "Depend upon it, it is a turkey's egg. I was once deceived in the same way myself, and had a lot of trouble and bother with the young ones, for they are afraid of the water. I couldn't get them into it; I quacked at them and I hacked at them, but it was of no use. Let me see the egg. Yes, that is a turkey's egg. Let it alone and rather teach the other little ones to swim."

"I'll just sit on it a little while longer," said the duck; "having sat so long now, I may as well sit a few days more."

"As you like," said the old duck, and went away.

At last the big egg broke. "Tweet, tweet," said the young one, creeping out. It was very big and ugly. The duck looked at it. "That's a mighty big duckling," said she; "none of the others look like that; could he be a young turkey-cock? Well, we shall soon get to know that; he will have to go into the water, if I have to push him in myself."

The next day the weather was gloriously fine; the sun shone down on all the green leaves, and the mother duck went down to the canal with her whole family. She sprang with a splash into the water, and as she went "Quack, quack!" one duckling after another jumped in. The water closed over their heads, but they soon came up again, and swam beautifully; their legs moved by themselves, and all were in the water. Even the ugly little grey one was swimming too.

"No, he is not a turkey," said the duck; "look how beautifully he moves its legs, and how upright he holds itself; he is my own child. And if you only look at him properly, he is really very pretty. Quack, quack! Come with me; I will take you into society, and introduce you to the duck-yard; but mind you always keep near me, so that no one treads on you; and beware of the cat."

So they came into the duck-yard. There was a terrible noise

inside, for there were two families who were fighting about the head of an eel; and after all the cat got it.

"You see, such is the way of the world," said the mother-duck, sharpening her beak, for she, too, wanted the eel's head. "Now, use your legs," said she; "try to hurry along, and bend your necks before the old duck there; she is the most distinguished of

all here. She is of Spanish blood, that is why she is so fat; and you see she has a red rag round her leg. That is something extremely grand, and the greatest distinction a duck can attain; it is as much as to say that they don't want her to get lost, and that she may be recognised by man and beast. Hurry up! Don't turn your feet inwards; a well-educated duckling turns his feet outwards as much as possible, just like his father and mother. Look, like that! Now bend your neck and say 'Quack!'"

And they did as she told them; but the other ducks all around looked at them and said, quite loud: "Look there! Now we are to have that lot too; as if we were not enough already. And, fie! how ugly that one duckling is; we will not stand that." And one of the ducks immediately flew at him, and bit him in the neck.

"Leave him alone," said the mother; "he is doing no one any harm."

"Yes, but he is too big and strange-looking," said the duck who had bitten him; "and therefore he must be whacked."

"They are pretty children which the mother has," said the old duck with the rag round her leg; "they are all fine, except one, which has turned out badly. I wish she could hatch him over again."

"That cannot be, your highness," said the duckling's mother; "he is not handsome, but he has a very good heart, and swims as beautifully as any other; indeed, I may say, somewhat better. I think he will grow prettier and get to look a little smaller in time. He has lain too long in the egg, and therefore not received the right shape." And with this she scratched the little one's neck and smoothed his feathers. "Besides," she said, "he is a drake, and therefore it does not matter so much. I think he will become very strong and fight his way through the world."

"The other ducklings are very pretty," said the old duck; "pray make yourselves at home, and if you find an eel's head, you may bring it to me."

So now they felt at home. But the poor duckling who had been the last to leave his shell, and who was so ugly, was bitten, pushed, and made a fool of, and that by the hens as well as by the ducks. "He is too big," they all said, and the turkey-cock, who had come into the world with spurs, and therefore thought himself an emperor, puffed himself up like a ship in full sail, and bore down upon him, gobbling and getting quite red in the face. The poor duckling did not know where to stand or where to go; he was distressed at being so ugly and the jest of the whole duck-yard.

So passed the first day, and afterwards things grew worse and worse. The poor duckling was chased about by all; even his sisters were unkind to him, and kept on saying: "If only the cat would catch you, you hideous creature!" And his mother said, "Would that you were far away!" The ducks bit him, the hens beat him, and the girl who had to feed the poultry kicked him away with her foot.

So he ran and flew over the hedge, frightening away the little birds in the bushes. "That is because I am so ugly," thought the duckling, closing his eyes, but running on just the same. So he came to a great moor, where some wild ducks lived; here he lay the whole night, being tired and sorrowful.

Towards morning the wild ducks flew up and gazed at their new comrade.

"Pray, who are you?" they asked, and the duckling turned in all directions, and greeted them as well as he could.

"You are exceptionally ugly!" said the wild ducks; "but that does not matter to us as long as you do not marry into our family."

Poor thing! he was really not thinking of marrying, but only wanted permission to lie among the reeds and drink a little moor water. So he lay two whole days; then two wild geese, or rather ganders, came by; they had not long crept out of their shell, and that is why they were so bold.

"Listen, comrade," they said; "you are rather ugly but we like you very well; will you come with us and be a bird of passage? On another moor near this place there are some nice sweet wild geese, all females too, every one of whom can say 'Quack!' You would be in a fair way to make your fortune there, ugly as you are."

"Bang! bang!" went a gun, and the two wild ganders fell down dead among the reeds, and the water became red with their blood. "Bang! bang!" came again, and whole flocks of wild geese flew up out of the reeds. Once more came a shot. There was a great hunting party going on, and the huntsmen were lying all round the moor; some were even sitting up in the branches of the trees, which stretched far out over the reeds. The blue smoke dispersed itself into the thick trees and far out over the water, like clouds; the hounds came splashing across the moor, the reeds and the rushes bending in all directions. What a fright the poor duckling was in! He turned his head to put it under his wing, but at the same moment a terribly large dog stood quite close to him, his tongue hanging far out of his mouth, his eyes gleaming angrily, hideously. Craning forward straight at the duckling, he showed his sharp teeth, and——splash! splash! he was gone again, without touching him.

"Oh, how thankful I am!" sighed the duckling; "I am so ugly that even the dog will not bite me."

And so he lay still whilst the shots whistled through the reeds, one report following another.

It was late in the day before all was quiet, but the poor little one did not dare to stir even then; he waited several hours more before he looked round, and then hurried away from the moor as fast as he could. He ran over fields and meadows, though there was such a storm raging that it was difficult for him to get along at all.

In the evening he reached a wretched little peasant's hut; it was in such bad repair that it did not know itself on which side to fall, and therefore remained standing. The wind whistled so round the duckling that he was obliged to sit down in order to withstand it, and it grew worse and worse. He then noticed that the door had fallen from one of its hinges, and hung so to one side that he could creep into the room through the gap, which he did.

Here lived a woman with her tom-cat and her hen. The tom-cat, whom she called her little son, could put his back up and purr; he could even give out sparks, but that was only when he was stroked the wrong way. The hen had very small short legs and was therefore called "Chickling Short-legs"; she laid good eggs, and the woman loved her like her own child. The next morning they immediately noticed the strange duckling, and the tom-cat began to purr and the hen to cluck.

"What's the matter?" said the woman, looking round; but she could not see well, and took the duckling to be a fat duck who had lost her way. "That's indeed a rare catch," said she. "Now I can have duck's eggs. I hope it's not a drake. That we must find out."

And so the duckling was taken on trial for three weeks, but no eggs came.

The tom-cat was master in the house, and the hen was mistress, and they used always to say "We and the world," for they believed themselves to be the half, and by far the better half too. The duckling thought that it was possible to be of another opinion, but that the hen would not allow.

"Can you lay eggs?" she asked.

"No."

"Well, then you will have the goodness to be quiet."

And the tom-cat said, "Can you set your back up, purr and give out sparks?"

"No."

"Then you may have no opinion when reasonable people are speaking."

So the duckling sat in the corner and was in a bad humour; here the fresh air and the sunshine came in to him, and excited in him such a strong desire to swim on the water that he could not help telling the hen of it.

"What are you thinking of?" asked the latter. "You have nothing to do, and that is why you get these fancies. Either lay eggs or purr, and then they will pass away."

"But it is so nice to swim on the water," said the duckling; "so delightful to let it close over your head and to dive to the bottom."

"Well, that seems a fine pleasure," said the hen. "I think you must be mad. Ask the tom-cat—he is the wisest creature I know —whether he likes to swim on the water or to dive under. I won't speak of myself. Ask even our mistress, the old woman; there is no one in the world wiser than she. Do you think she has a longing to swim and to let the water close over her head?"

"You don't understand me," said the duckling.

"We don't understand you? Who then would be able to understand you? I don't suppose you pretend to be wiser than the tom-cat and the old woman—I won't speak of myself at all. Don't get silly things into your head, child, and be thankful 'for all the kindness that has been shown you. Have you not come into a warm room, and are you not in the society of those from whom you can learn something? But you are a fool, and it is disagreeable to have anything to do with you. Believe me, I wish you well. I tell you unpleasant things, and it is in this way that one's real friends may be known. Only learn to lay eggs or to purr and send out sparks."

"I think I shall go out into the wide world," said the duckling.

" Well, do so," said the hen.

So the duckling went; he swam upon the water, he dived down, but none of the animals took any notice of him, on account of his ugliness.

The autumn now came; the leaves in the wood turned yellow and brown; the wind caught them and made them dance about; and up in the air it was very cold. The clouds were heavy with hail and snow-flakes, and the raven sat on the hedge and croaked with cold; indeed, it made one shiver only to think of it. The poor duckling had by no means a good time. One evening—there was a glorious sunset—a flock of beautiful large birds came out of a thicket. The duckling had never seen such handsome ones; they were of dazzling whiteness, with long slender necks. They were swans; and uttering a peculiar cry they spread their long, splendid wings and flew away out of the cold region to warmer countries and open seas.

They rose so high, that a strange feeling came over the ugly young duckling. He turned round and round in the water like a wheel, stretched his neck high up in the air after them, and uttered such a loud and peculiar cry that he was quite frightened by it himself! Oh! he could not forget the beautiful happy birds, and when he could see them no longer he dived down to the bottom; on coming up again he was almost beside himself. He did not know what the birds were called, nor whither they were flying; yet he loved them as he had never loved any one before. He did not envy them at all. How could it occur to him to wish himself such loveliness as that? He would have been quite happy if only the ducks had suffered him to be among them—the poor, ugly creature.

The winter became cold, very cold. The duckling was obliged to swim about in the water to prevent it from freezing over entirely, but every night the opening in which he swam became smaller and smaller. It froze so hard that the ice cracked; the duckling was obliged to use his legs continually, so that the hole should not close up. At last he got tired, lay quite still, and froze fast in the ice.

Early next morning a peasant came by, and seeing what had

happened, went up, broke the ice in pieces with his wooden shoe, and carried the duckling home to his wife. There he revived.

The children wanted to play with him ; but the duckling thought they wished to do him some harm, and in his terror jumped right into the milk-pail, so that the milk flew about the room. The farmer's wife clapped her hands at him, upon which he flew into the butter-vat, then down into the meal tub, and out again. What a sight he looked ! The woman screamed and struck at him with the tongs, and the children, all laughing and screaming, knocked each other down in trying to catch him. It was a good thing for him that the door was open, and that he could slip out among the bushes into the freshly fallen snow. There he lay, quite worn out.

But it would be too sad to relate all the trouble and misery that the duckling had to endure during the severe winter. He was lying on the moor among the reeds when the sun began to shine warmly again. The larks were singing; it was beautiful spring.

Then once more the duckling was able to use his wings; they were much stronger, and carried him along more swiftly than before, and ere he was aware of it, he found himself in a large garden, where an elder-tree scented the air, and bent its long green branches down to the winding canal. Oh, what beauty, what vernal freshness was here ! And out of the thicket came three splendid white swans ; they ruffled their feathers and swam lightly on the water. The duckling knew the splendid creatures, and was seized with a strange sadness.

" I will fly to them, to those royal birds ! And they will kill me, because I, who am so ugly, dare to come near them. Better to be killed by them than to be bitten by the ducks, beaten by the hens, kicked by the girl who minds the poultry-yard, and to suffer so much in winter." So he flew into the water and swam towards the beautiful swans. They perceived him, and shot down upon him with all their feathers up. " Only kill me," said the poor creature, bowing his head to the level of the water and awaiting his death. But what did he see in the clear water ? He saw beneath him his own image, no longer an awkward dark grey bird, ugly and deformed, but a swan himself.

It matters little whether one has been born in a duck-yard so long as one has been hatched from a swan's egg.

He felt quite happy at having suffered so much trouble and care. Now only could he rightly value the good fortune that greeted him. And the large swans swam round him and stroked him with their beaks.

Some little children came into the garden and threw bread and corn into the water. The youngest one cried, "There is a new one;" and the other children also shouted with glee, "Yes, a new one has come," dancing about and clapping their hands. They ran to their father and mother, and bread and cake was thrown into the water, while every one said, "The new one is the finest; so young and so beautiful!" And the old swans bowed down before him.

Then he felt quite ashamed, and put his head under his wing; he really did not know what to do. He was all too happy, but not at all proud. He remembered how he had been persecuted and despised, and now he heard every one saying that he was the most beautiful of all beautiful birds. Even the elder-tree bowed down before him till its branches touched the water, and the sun shone warm and bright. Then he shook his feathers, stretched his slender neck, and from the bottom of his heart joyfully exclaimed, "I never even dreamed of such happiness when I was still the ugly duckling."

Twelve by the Mail

T was intensely cold, the sky was studded with stars, there was no breath of air stirring.

"Boom!" An old earthen pot was flung against the neighbour's door. "Bang, bang!" A gun was fired off. They were greeting the New Year. It was New Year's Eve! The church-clock was striking Midnight.

"Ta-ta-ra, ta-ta-ra!" The heavy mail-coach came lumbering up and stopped before the gate of the town. There were twelve passengers in it, for all seats were occupied.

"Hip, hip, hurrah!" cried the people in the houses of the town, where they were keeping New Year's Night, and rose when the clock struck twelve with their glasses in their hands, drinking the health of the New Year.

"A Happy New Year to you!" was the cry. "A pretty wife! plenty of money! no trouble and sorrow!"

Such were the good wishes expressed amid clinking of glasses. There was singing and ringing! Before the gate of the town stopped the mail-coach with twelve guests, the passengers.

And who were these strangers? Each of them had his passport and luggage with him; they even brought presents for you, for me, and for all the inhabitants of the little town. But who were they, what did they intend to do, and what did they bring with them?

"Good morning!" they called out to the sentry at the town-gate

"Good morning!" answered the sentry, for the clock had already struck twelve o'clock.

"Your names? your business?" the sentry asked the first who left the coach.

"Look for yourself in my passport," replied the man. "I am *I!*" And he was indeed a man, clad in a large bearskin and wearing fur boots. "I am the man on whom many people set their hopes. Come and see me to-morrow and I shall give you a New Year's gift. I throw coppers and silver among the people, and give balls—to wit, thirty-one; but more nights I cannot sacrifice. My ships are frozen in, but in my office it is warm and pleasant. My name is January; I am a merchant, and carry all my accounts with me."

Then the second alighted from the coach. He was a jovial fellow; he was theatrical manager, arranger of masquerades and all sorts of amusements that one could think of. His luggage consisted of a big cask.

"We shall drive the cat out of this cask at carnival time," he said. "I shall give you and myself pleasure. We shall be merry

every day. I have not too long to live—in fact, of all the family
my life is the shortest, for I shall only become twenty-eight days
old. Sometimes they allow me one day more, but I don't trouble
myself about that. Hurrah!"

"You must not shout so!" said the sentry.

"Why shouldn't I?" replied the man. "I am Prince Carnival
travelling under the name of Februarius."

Then the third left the coach. He looked the very picture of
fasting; he carried his nose very high, for he was related to the
"forty knights," and he was a weather-prophet. But this is not
a remunerative trade, and therefore he was in favour of fasting.
He had a bunch of violets in his button-hole, but it was very small.

"March, March!" cried the fourth after him, slapping his
shoulders, "do you not smell something? Come quick into the
guardroom; they are drinking punch there, which is your favourite
beverage; I can smell it outside. March, Mr. Martius!" But it
was not true, he only wished to tease him by making him an
April fool; for with such merriment the fourth generally made
his entrance into the town. He looked very smart, worked but
very little, and kept more holidays than others. "I wish there was
a little more steadiness in the world," he said, "but sometimes
one is in good, sometimes in bad, humour, always according to circumstances; one has continually to change one's dress, for sometimes it rains and sometimes the sun shines. I am a sort of house
agent and undertaker; I can laugh and weep according to circumstances. I have my summer-clothes here in my portmanteau,
but it would be foolish to put them on. Here I am! On Sundays
I take a walk in shoes and white silk stockings, and with a muff."

After him a lady alighted from the coach. Her name was Miss
May. She wore a summer dress and goloshes, her frock was of a
light green, and anemones adorned her hair; she smelt so
strongly of thyme that the sentry could not help sneezing.
"Health and prosperity to you," she said, greeting him. How
pretty she was! She was a singer, but not a theatrical vocalist
nor a ballad-singer; she was a songstress of the grove; she
roamed about in the green forests and sang for her own pleasure
and amusement.

"Now comes the young married woman," they cried from inside the coach, and a young, beautiful and distinguished-looking woman stepped out. One could see that Mrs. June was not accustomed to do much for herself, but rather to be waited upon. On the longest day in the year she gave a great dinner-party, that her guests might have time to eat the numerous courses which were served. Although she had her own carriage, she travelled like the others by the mail, in order to show people that she was not haughty. But she was not unaccompanied, for her younger brother Julius was with her. He looked very well fed, wore summer clothes and a straw hat. He had but little luggage, as it was burdensome to carry in the great heat; he had only a pair of bathing-drawers with him.

Then the mother alighted, Mrs. August, a wholesale fruiterer, the proprietress of many fish-ponds and a farmer, wearing a large crinoline; she was stout and hot, worked hard, and carried the beer out to her labourers in the field herself. "In the sweat of thy brow thou shalt eat thy bread," she used to say; "that is written in the Bible. When the work is done follow the excursions into the country, dance and play under the green trees, and the harvest festivals." She was an excellent house-keeper.

After her a man came out of the coach who was a painter; he was the famous colourist, September; he would repair to the woods and change the colour of the leaves according to his ideas; and soon it gleamed with crimson, russet, and gold. The master could whistle like a starling; he was a quick worker, and decorated his beer-jug with a twining branch of hops, so that it looked beautiful; he had a strong sense of beauty. There he stood with his colour-box, which made up his whole luggage.

He was followed by a landowner, who only thought of ploughing and preparing the field in the seed-month, and who was fond of field sports. Mr. October had his dog and gun with him, and carried nuts in his game-bag. "Crack, crack!" He had a great deal of luggage, including even an English plough; he talked about agriculture, but on account of the coughing and groaning of his neighbour one could not hear much of it.

It was November who coughed so much when he got out. He suffered a great deal from colds, and blew his nose continually; and yet he declared that he must accompany the servant-girls to their new places and initiate them into their winter service; his cold, he thought, would soon be better when he began wood-cutting, for he was a master woodcutter, and the president of the guild. He passed his evenings cutting wood for skates, for he knew well, he said, that in a few weeks these articles would be in great demand for the people's amusement.

Finally, the last passenger made her appearance—the old mother December, carrying a foot-warmer with her. The old woman was shivering with cold, but her eyes were as bright as two stars. She held a flower-pot in her arm, in which a little fir-tree was growing. "This tree," she said, "I will take care of and cherish, that it may thrive and grow very tall, till Christmas-eve; it must reach from the floor to the ceiling, and will be covered with glittering lights, gilded apples, and cut-out figures. The foot-warmer warms me like a stove; I shall take a story-book out of my pocket and read it aloud, until all the children in the room are quiet, and all the little figures on the tree become alive; and the little wax angel on the top of the tree opens his wings of tinsel, flies down from his green resting-place, and kisses all the children and grown-up people in the room. Nay, he also kisses the poor children who stand outside in the street and sing the Christmas song of the "Star of Bethlehem."

"Well, the coach may drive off," said the sentry, "now we have all the twelve. And the luggage cart may come up."

"First let the twelve come in to me," said the captain of the guard, "one after the other. I shall keep their passports here; they are all available for one month; when it is gone I shall give them a character on the passports. Now, Mr. January, please walk in."

And Mr. January accepted the invitation.

When a year is gone, I shall tell you what the twelve passengers have brought you, myself, and all of us. At present I do not know it, and perhaps they do not know it themselves; for it is a strange time we live in.

The Little Mermaid

AR out in the ocean the water is as blue as the petals of the finest corn-flower, and as transparent as the purest glass. But it is very deep, much deeper indeed than any anchorchain can fathom; many steeples would have to be piled one on the top of the other in order to reach from the bottom to the surface of the water. Down there live the sea-folks.

You must not think that there is nothing but the bare white sand at the bottom of the ocean; no, on the contrary, there grow the most peculiar trees and plants, having such pliable trunks, stalks, and leaves that they stir at the slightest movement of the water, as if they were alive. All the big and small fishes glide through their branches as birds fly through the trees. Where the ocean is deepest stands the sea-king's castle; its walls are built of coral, and the high arched windows are cut out of the clearest amber; the roof is covered all over with shells, which open and close according as the current of the water sets. It looks most beautiful, for each of them is filled with pearls of priceless value; a single one of them would be a fit ornament for a queen's diadem.

The sea-king had been a widower for many years, and his aged mother was keeping house for him. She was a clever woman, but she was very proud of her noble birth; therefore she wore twelve oysters on her tail, while other distinguished sea-folks were only allowed to wear six. In every other respect she deserved unmingled praise, especially for her tender care of the sea-princesses, her grand-daughters. They were six in number, and the youngest was the most beautiful of all. Her skin was as clear and delicate as the petals of a rose, her eyes as blue as the sea in its greatest depth; but she also, like the others, had no legs—her body ended in a fish-tail. All day long the princesses used to play about in the spacious halls of the castle, where flowers blossom from the walls.   When the large amber windows were thrown open the fishes came swimming to the princesses, as the swallows sometimes fly in when we open the windows; the fishes were so tame that they ate out of their hands, and suffered the princesses to stroke them.

In front of the castle was a large garden in which bright red and dark blue flowers were growing; the fruit glittered like gold, and the flowers looked like flames of fire; their stalks and leaves were continually moving.   The ground was covered with the finest sand, as blue as the flame of sulphur.   A peculiar blue light was shed over everything; one would rather have imagined one's self to be high up in the air, having above and below the blue sky, than at the bottom of the sea.   When the sea was calm one could see the sun; it looked like an immense purple flower, from which the light streamed forth in all directions.

Each of the little princesses had her own place in the garden, where she was allowed to dig and to plant at her pleasure.   One gave her flower-bed the shape of a whale, another preferred to form it like a little mermaid; but the youngest made hers as round as the sun, and her flowers were also of the purple hue of the sun.   She was a peculiar child, always quiet and sensitive; while her sisters thought a great deal of all sorts of curious objects which they received from wrecked ships, she only loved her purple flowers, and a beautiful figure, representing a boy, carved out of clear white marble, which had come from some wreck to the bottom of the sea.   She had planted a red weeping-willow close by the marble figure, which throve well and was hanging over it with its fresh branches reaching down to the blue sand and casting a violet-coloured shadow.   Like the branches, this shadow was continually moving, and it gave one the impression as if the top and the roots of the tree were playing together and trying to kiss each other.

The little mermaid liked most of all to hear stories about mankind above, and the grandmother had to tell her all she knew about ships, towns, and animals; she was very much surprised to hear that on earth the flowers were fragrant (the sea-flowers had no smell) and that the woods were green, that the fishes which one saw there on the trees could sing beautifully and delight everybody. The grandmother called the little birds fishes; otherwise her grand-daughters would not have understood her, as they had never seen a bird.

"When you are fifteen years old," said the grandmother, "you will be allowed to rise up to the surface of the sea and sit on the cliffs in the moonlight, where the big ships will be sailing by. Then you will also see the woods and towns."

In the following year the eldest princess would complete her fifteenth year; the other sisters were each one year younger than the other; the youngest therefore had to wait fully five years before she could go up from the bottom of the sea and look at the earth above. But each promised to tell her sisters what she liked best on her first visit; for their grandmother, they thought, did not tell them enough—there were so many things on which they wished to be informed. None of them, however, longed so much to go up as the youngest, who had to wait the longest time, and was always so quiet and pensive. Many a night she stood at the open window and looked up through the dark blue water, watching the fishes as they splashed in the water with their fins and tails. She could see the moon and the stars—they looked quite pale, but appeared through the water much larger than we see them. When something like a dark cloud passed over her and concealed them for a while, she knew it was either a whale, or a ship with many human beings, who had no idea that a lovely little mermaid was standing below stretching out her white hands towards the keel of their ship.

The eldest princess now completed her fifteenth year, and was allowed to rise up. When she came back she had to tell about hundreds of things: the greatest pleasure, she said, was to lie in the moonlight on a sandbank, when the sea was calm, and to look at the near coast and the large town where the lights sparkled like many hundreds of stars; to hear the music and noise caused by the clamour of carriages and human voices, to see the many church-steeples and to listen to the ringing of the bells. The youngest sister listened attentively to all this, and when she again, at night, stood at the open window and looked up through the dark-blue water, she thought of the great town, with all its bustle and noise, and imagined she heard the ringing of the bells in the depth of the sea.

In the following year the second sister's turn came to rise up to the surface of the sea and to swim whither she pleased. She came up just as the sun was setting, and this aspect she considered the most beautiful of all she saw. The whole sky looked like gold, and she could not find words to describe the beautiful clouds. Purple and violet, they were sailing by over her head; but even quicker than the clouds she saw a flight of wild swans flying towards the sun; she followed them, but the sun sank down and the rosy hue on the surface of the water and in the clouds vanished.

The year after, the third sister rose up. She was the boldest of all, and swam up the mouth of a broad river. She saw beautiful green hills covered with vines. Strongholds and castles peeped out of the splendid woods; she heard the birds sing, and the sun was shining so warmly that she had often to dive down and cool her burning face. In a little creek she found a troop of human children playing; they were quite naked, and splashed in the water; she wished to play with them, but they ran away, terrified. Then a little black animal, a dog, came—she had never seen one before—and barked so dreadfully at her that she was frightened, and hurried back as fast as she could to the open sea. But she could never forget the stately woods, the green hills, and the nice children who could swim, although they had no fish-tails.

The fourth sister was not so daring; she remained out in the open sea, and declared that there it was most pleasant to stay. There, she said, one could look around many miles, and the sky appeared to one like an immense glass globe. She had also seen ships, but only from a great distance; they looked to her like seagulls. The playful dolphins, she said, threw somersaults, while the big whales spouted up the sea-water through their nostrils, as if many hundred fountains were playing all around her.

Now the fifth sister's turn came, and as her birthday was in winter she saw something different from her sisters on her first visit. The sea looked quite green; enormous icebergs were floating around her—every one of them was like pearl, she said, although they were much higher than the church-steeples built by men. They had the most peculiar shapes and glittered like diamonds. She had seated herself on one of the highest, and while the wind was playing with her hair she noticed how the ships were tossed about; towards the evening the sky became covered with black clouds, it lightened and thundered, and the big ice-blocks reflected the flashes of lightning while they were tossed up by the roaring sea. The sailors reefed all their sails, for they were terrified and anxious; but she was sitting quietly on the floating iceberg, and watching how the flashes of lightning descended zigzag into the foaming sea.

The first time one of the sisters came to the surface, all the new and beautiful things charmed her; but now, being as grown-up girls allowed to rise whenever they pleased, all this became indifferent to them, and after a month they declared that it was best down below in their own home. On many a night the five sisters would rise to the surface of the water arm-in-arm, in a row, and sing, for they had beautiful voices, much finer than any human being ever has; and when a storm was approaching, and they thought that some ships might be wrecked, they swam in front of them, singing of the beautiful things at the bottom of the sea, and bidding the people not to be afraid, but come down. The people, however, did not understand them, and mistook their singing for the noise of the wind; they never saw the treasures below, for when the ship went down they were drowned, and only arrived dead at the sea-king's castle. When her sisters thus went up arm-in-arm, the youngest princess used to stand alone and follow them with her eyes; then she often felt as if she must cry; but mermaids have no tears, therefore they suffer much more than we do.

"Oh! that I were already fifteen years old," she said; "I know I shall love the world above, and the people that dwell in it, very much."

At last she was fifteen. "You are now grown up," said her
grandmother, the old dowager-queen, to her; "now let me adorn
you like your sisters." She placed a wreath of white lilies on
her head, the petals of the flowers being half-pearls; and in
order to show her high rank the old lady caused eight oysters
to be fixed to her grand-daughter's tail.

"They hurt me, Granny," said the little mermaid. "Never
mind, my child, pride must suffer pain," replied the old lady. The
little princess would have gladly taken off all her ornaments and the
heavy wreath; her purple flowers would have suited her much
better, but she could not offend her grandmother. "Farewell!"
she said, and rose up as lightly as a bubble. The sun had just
set when she lifted her head out of the water, but the clouds were
still coloured like purple and gold; the evening-star sparkled
beautifully through the rose-tinted atmosphere; the air was mild
and fresh, and the sea perfectly calm. There was a big ship with
three masts lying before her; only one sail was set, as not a breath
of air was stirring; the sailors were sitting about on deck and in
the rigging. There were music and dancing on board, and when it
became dark many hundreds of coloured lamps were lighted, and

it looked as if the flags of all nations were floating in the air. The little mermaid swam up close to the cabin windows, and when the waves lifted her up she could see many well-dressed people through the clear panes. The most beautiful of them was a young prince with large black eyes—he certainly seemed not older than sixteen; it was his birthday, and that was the cause of all this rejoicing. The sailors were dancing on deck, and when the young prince stepped out of the cabin-door hundreds of rockets were thrown up into the air, and became for some moments as bright as day. The little mermaid was frightened, and dived under the water; but soon she lifted up her head again, and then it seemed to her as if all the stars were falling down from the sky. She had never seen such a display of fireworks. Large Catherine-wheels turned rapidly round, splendid fiery fishes flew through the air, and all was reflected by the bright calm sea. On the ship it was so light that one could distinctly see everything, even the smallest rope. And the young prince was so beautiful! He shook hands with the people and smiled graciously, while the music sounded dreamily through the starry night.

It became very late, but the little mermaid could not turn her eyes away from the ship and the beautiful prince. The coloured lamps were extinguished; no more rockets were sent up nor cannons fired off. But in the sea, deep below, was a strange murmuring and humming, while the little mermaid was rocking on the waves and looking into the cabin. Soon the wind began to blow; one sail after another was furled; the waves rose up high; flashes of lightning were seen in the distance; a terrible storm was approaching. Then all the sails were reefed. The large ship in its rapid course was tossed about like a nutshell by the waves, which rose up as high as mountains, as if they would roll over the top of the masts. The ship dived like a swan down between the waves, and was then carried up again by them to a great height. The little mermaid thought it was a pleasant journey; not so the sailors. The ship creaked and groaned; her strong planks were bending under the weight of the heavy waves which entered into her; the mainmast was broken like a reed; the ship lay over on her side, and the water rushed over her. The little mermaid then perceived that the crew was in danger; she herself had to be careful, lest the posts and planks floating about on the water might hurt her. For moments it was so dark that one could distinguish nothing, but when it lightened everything was visible. The little mermaid was looking out for the prince; she saw him sink down into the depths when the ship broke up. She was very pleased, for now she thought he would come down to her. But soon she remembered that men cannot live in the water, and that he would arrive dead at her father's castle. No, he must not die! Heedless of the beams and planks floating on the waters, she dived down to the bottom, and came up again in search of the prince. At last she found him; his strength was failing him; he was no longer able to swim in the storm-tost sea; his arms and legs became powerless; his beautiful eyes closed; he would surely have died had not the little mermaid come to his assistance. She held up his head, and let the waves drift them where they would.

Next morning the storm had abated, but not a plank was visible of the ship anywhere; the sun rose purple and radiant out of the water, and seemed to impart new life to the prince's cheeks; his eyes, however, remained closed. The mermaid kissed his beautiful forehead, stroked back his wet hair; he looked to her very much like the white marble figure in her little garden at home. She kissed him again and again, and wished that he were alive.

Now she had before her eyes the dry land, where high mountains towered into the clouds, while the snow was glittering on their summits, and looking like swans resting there. Down on the coast were magnificent green woods, and quite in the foreground stood a church or a convent—she did not know which; but at any rate it was a building. Lemon and orange trees were growing in the garden, and high palms stood before the gate. The sea formed a little bay here and was quite calm, although very deep; she swam straight to the cliff, where the fine white sand had been washed ashore, and put him down, taking special care that his head was raised up to the warm sunshine. Then all

the bells began to ring in the large white building, and many
young girls passed through the garden. The little mermaid swam
farther out, hid herself behind some rocks, covered her hair and
breast with sea-foam, lest anybody might see her little face, and
watched to see who would come to the poor prince. After a
while a young girl came to the spot where the prince was lying;
at first she seemed very much frightened, but she soon recovered
herself, and called some people. The little mermaid saw that the
prince came back to life, and smiled at all who stood around him,
but at her he did not smile; he little knew that she had saved

him. She was very sad; and when they had taken him into the
large building, she dived down and so returned to her father's
castle.

She had always been silent and pensive; now she was still more
so. Her sisters asked her what she had seen when she went up
for the first time, but she told them nothing. Many a morning
and many an evening she returned to the spot where she had
left the prince; she saw how the fruit in the garden became ripe
and was gathered, how the snow melted on the high mountains;
but she never caught sight of the prince, and each time she
returned home she was more mournful than before.

Her only consolation was to sit in her little garden, and to put
her arms round the marble figure which resembled the prince,
but she no longer looked after her flowers. Her garden became

a wilderness; the plants straggled over the paths, and twined their long stalks and leaves round the trunks and branches of the trees, so that it became quite dark and gloomy.

At last she could bear it no longer, and confided her troubles to one of her sisters, who of course told the others. These, and a few other mermaids who mentioned it confidentially to their intimate friends, were the only people who were in the secret. One of them knew the prince, and could tell them where his kingdom was. She also had witnessed the festival on board the ship.

"Come, dear sister," said the other princesses; and arm-in-arm, in a long row, they rose up to the spot where the prince's castle stood. It was built of bright yellow stone, and had broad marble staircases, one of which reached right down to the sea. Magnificent gilt cupolas surmounted the roof, and in the colonnades, running all round the building, stood lifelike marble statues. Through the clear panes in the high window could be seen splendid halls, where costly silk curtains and beautiful tapestry hung, and the wall was covered with paintings so exquisite that it was a pleasure to look at them. In the centre of the largest hall a fountain played; its jets rose as high as the glass cupola in the ceiling, through which the sun shone upon the water and the beautiful plants growing in the great basin.

Now she knew where he dwelt, and near there she passed many an evening and many a night on the water. She swam much closer to the shore than any of the others would have ventured; nay, she even went up the narrow canal under the magnificent marble balcony which threw a large shadow on the water. Here she sat and gazed at the young prince, who thought that he was quite alone in the moonlight. Often she saw him sailing in a stately boat, decorated with flags, and with music on board. She listened from behind the green rushes; and when the wind caught her long silver-white veil, and people noticed it, they imagined it was a swan opening its wings. Many a time at night, when the fishermen were upon the sea with torches, she heard them say many good things about the prince, and she was glad that she had saved his life when he was drifting half-dead upon the waves; she remembered how his head had rested on her bosom, and how fervently she had kissed him, but he knew nothing about it, and did not even dream of her. Her love for mankind grew from day to day, and she longed more and more to be able to live among them, for their world seemed to her so much larger than hers. They could cross the sea in large ships, and ascend mountains towering into the clouds. The lands which they possessed, both woods and fields, stretched farther than her eyes could reach. There were still so many things on which she wished to have information, and her sisters could not answer all her questions; therefore she asked her grandmother, who knew the upper world very well, and appropriately styled it "the countries above the sea."

"If human beings are not drowned," asked the little mermaid, "can they live for ever? Do they not die as we do down here in the sea?"

"Yes" replied the old lady. "They also die, and their life is even shorter than ours. We sometimes live to be three hundred years old; but when we cease to exist here we are turned into foam on the surface of the water, and have not even a grave in the depth of the sea among those we love. We never live again; our souls are not immortal; we are like the green seaweed, which, when once severed from its root, can never grow again. Men, on the other hand, have a soul which lives for ever after the body has become dust; it rises through the sky, up to the shining stars. As we rise out of the sea, and behold all the countries of the earth, so they rise to unknown glorious regions which we shall never see."

"Why have we not also an immortal soul?" asked the little mermaid, sorrowfully. "I would gladly give all the years I have yet to live, if I could be a human being only for one day, and to have the hope of seeing that marvellous country beyond the sky."

"You must not dream of that," replied the old lady. "We are much happier and better off than mankind above."

"Then I shall die, and drift on the sea as foam, never hearing the music of the waves, or seeing the beautiful flowers and the red sun. Is there not anything I can do in order to obtain an immortal soul?"

"No!" said the grandmother. "Only if a man would love you so much that you would be dearer to him than father or mother, if he would cling with all his heart and all his love to you, and let the priest place his right hand into yours, with the promise to be faithful to you here and to eternity, then his soul would flow over into your body, and you would receive a share of the happiness of mankind. He would give you a soul and yet keep his own. But that can never happen! What is beautiful here below, your fish tail, they consider ugly on earth—they do not know any better; up there one must have two clumsy limbs, which they call legs, in order to be beautiful."

The little mermaid sighed, and looked at her fish-tail mournfully. "Let us be merry," said the old lady. "Let us dance and make the best of the three hundred years of our life. That is truly quite enough; afterwards repose will be more pleasant. To-night we will have a court ball."

Such a splendid sight is never seen on earth. The walls and the ceiling of the large ballroom were of thick transparent glass. Several hundred enormous shells, purple and bright green, stood at each side in long rows, filled with blue fire, which lit up the whole room and shone through the walls so that the sea outside was quite illuminated; one could see countless fishes, of all sizes, swimming against the glass walls; the scales of some gleamed with purple, others glittered like silver and gold. A broad stream ran through the middle of the ballroom, upon which the sea-folks, both men and women, danced to the music of their own sweet songs. Human beings have not such beautiful voices. The little mermaid sang best of all, and the whole court applauded with fins and tails. For a moment she felt a joy in her heart at the thought that she possessed the most beautiful voice of all living on earth or in the sea. But soon her mind returned to the world above; she could not forget the beautiful prince, nor cease grieving that she did not possess an immortal soul like his. Therefore she stole out of her father's castle; and while within the others enjoyed songs and merriment, she sat sorrowfully in her little garden.

Then she heard a bugle sound through the water, and thought, "Surely now he is sailing above, he who fills my mind, and into whose hands I should like to entrust my fate. I will dare all in order to obtain him and an immortal soul! While my sisters are dancing in my father's castle I will go to the sea-witch, whom I have always feared so much ; perhaps she can advise and help me."

Then the little mermaid left her garden and went out to the roaring whirlpools where the witch dwelt. She had never gone that way before; no flowers, no seaweed even, was growing there —only bare grey sandy soil surrounded the whirlpools, where the water rushed round like mill-wheels and drew everything it got hold of down into the depths. She had to pass right through these dreadful whirlpools in order to reach the witch's territory. For a good part of the way the road led over warm bubbling mud ; this the witch called her peat-moor. Behind this her house stood, in a strange wood, for all the trees and bushes were polypes—half-animals and half-plants. They looked like snakes, with many hundred heads, growing out of the ground. All the branches were slimy arms with fingers like supple worms, every limb was moving from the root to the highest branch, all they could seize out of the sea they clutched and held fast, never letting it go again. The little mermaid stopped timidly in front of them ; her heart was beating with fear, she nearly turned back again; but then she thought of the prince and the immortal soul, and regained her courage. She twisted her long flowing hair round her head, lest the polypes might seize it ; she crossed her hands upon her breast, and shot through the water like a fish, right past the dreadful polypes, which stretched out their supple arms and fingers after her. She saw that each of them had seized something and held it tightly with hundreds of little arms. The polypes held in their arms white skeletons of people who had perished at sea and had sunk into the depth, the oars of ships, and chests, skeletons of land animals, and a little mermaid whom they had caught and strangled : this latter was the most dreadful sight to the little princess.

Then she came to a big marshy place in the wood, where large fat water-snakes were rolling about, and showing their ugly light yellow bodies.

In the middle of this place stood a house, built with the white bones of shipwrecked people; there the sea-witch sat, letting a toad eat out of her mouth, as we should feed a little canary with sugar. The ugly fat water-snakes she called her little chickens, and allowed them to crawl all over her.

"I know very well what you want," said the sea-witch. "It is silly of you, but you shall have your way; you will become wretchedly unhappy, my beautiful princess. You wish to get rid of your fish-tail and have two limbs instead, which men use for walking, that the young prince may fall in love with you and that you may gain him, and an immortal soul." Thus saying the old witch laughed loud and hideously, so that the toads and the snakes fell to the ground, where they wriggled about. "You are just in good time," said the witch; "if you had come to-morrow after sunrise, I should not have been able to help you for a whole year. I will prepare you a drink, and you must swim ashore before the sun rises, and sit down and drink it; then your tail will disappear and shrink together into what mankind call legs; but it will hurt you, as if a sharp sword pierced you. Every man who sees you will say that you are the most beautiful girl he has ever seen. You will keep your gracefulness, and no dancer will be able to move as lightly as you; but at each step that you take you will feel as though you trod on a sharp knife, and as if your blood must flow. If you are ready to suffer all this, I will help you."

"Yes!" said the little mermaid, with a trembling voice; and she thought of the prince and the immortal soul.

"But remember," said the witch, "if you have once received a human form you can never become a mermaid again; you will never be able to return again to your sisters and to your father's castle; and if you fail to gain the prince's love, so that he forgets, for your sake, father and mother, clings to you with body and soul, and makes the priest join your hands, that you become man and wife, you will not obtain an immortal soul. On the first morning after he has wedded another, your heart will break, and you will become foam on the water."

"I will have it," said the little mermaid, and turned as pale as death.

"But you must pay me," said the witch, "and it is not a little that I ask. You have the most beautiful voice of all who live at the bottom of the sea; you may think you can bewitch him with it; but this voice you must give me. I will have the best thing you possess in exchange for my costly drink, for I must give you my own blood, that the drink may be strong enough, and as cutting as a two-edged sword."

"If you take my voice," said the little mermaid, "what is left to me?"

"Your fine figure," said the witch, "your gracefulness and your speaking eyes—with these you may easily capture a human heart. Now, have you lost your courage? Put out your little tongue, that I may cut it off in payment, and I will give you the wonderful drink."

"Do it," said the little mermaid; and the witch placed her pot on the fire to prepare the draught.

"Cleanliness is a good thing" she said, and scoured the kettle with snakes which she had tied into a bundle; then she pricked herself in the breast and let her black blood drop into it. The steam rose up in the strangest shapes; any one who could have seen it, would have been frightened to death. Every moment the witch threw new things into the pot, and when it boiled the sound was like the weeping of a crocodile. At last the drink was ready, and looked like the clearest water.

"There it is," said the witch, and cut the little mermaid's tongue off; so now she was dumb, and could neither sing nor speak. "If the polypes should seize you when you go back through my wood," said the witch, "you have only to throw one drop of this fluid over them, and their arms and fingers will break into a thousand pieces." But the little mermaid had no need of it; the polypes shrunk back in fear at the sight of the sparkling drink, which shone in her hand like a glittering star.

Thus she passed quickly through the wood and the marsh and the roaring whirlpools. She could see her father's castle; the torches in the ballroom were all extinguished; they were all asleep; she dared not go to them; now she was dumb and on the point of leaving them for ever, she felt as though her little heart would break. She stole into the garden, took a blossom from each of her sisters' flower-beds, kissed her hands a thousand times towards the castle, and rose up through the dark blue sea. The sun had not yet risen when she reached the prince's castle and went up the magnificent marble steps. The moon was shining more brightly than usual. The little mermaid took the burning draught, and felt as though a two-edged sword pierced her tender body; she fainted, and lay there as if dead. When the sun rose out of the sea she awoke and felt a sharp pain but just before her stood the beautiful young prince. He fixed his black eyes upon her, so that she cast hers down, and noticed that her fish tail had disappeared, and that she had, instead, two of the prettiest feet any girl could wish for. As she had no clothes she wrapped herself in her long hair. The Prince asked her who she was, and where she came from; she looked at him sweetly and yet mournfully with her dark blue eyes, for she was unable to speak. Then he took her by the hand and led her into the castle. At every step she took she felt, as the witch had told her in advance, as if she trod upon needles and knives; but she suffered it willingly, and stepped as lightly as a soap-bubble at the prince's side, who, with all the others, admired her graceful movements.

They gave her splendid dresses of silk and muslin to put on, and she was the most beautiful of all women in the castle; but she was mute, and could neither sing nor speak. Lovely slaves, dressed in silk and gold, came to sing before the prince and his royal parents. One sang better than all the rest, and the prince clapped his hands and smiled at her. Then the little mermaid became sorrowful; she knew that she had been able to sing much more sweetly, and thought, " Oh ! if he only knew that in order to be with him I have sacrificed my voice for ever !"

Then the slaves danced graceful dances to the loveliest music; and the little mermaid lifted her beautiful white arms, balanced herself on tiptoe, and glided, dancing, over the floor; none of them could equal her. At every movement her beauty became still more apparent, and her eyes spoke more deeply to the heart than the songs of the slaves. All were charmed, especially the prince, who called her his little foundling. She danced again, and

again, although she felt, whenever her feet touched the ground as
though she trod upon sharp knives. The prince wished her
always to remain with him, and gave her permission to sleep on a
velvet cushion before his door.

He had her dressed like a page, that she might accompany him
on horseback. They rode through the fragrant woods, where the
green boughs touched their shoulders and the birds sang in the
fresh foliage. She climbed with the prince to the summits of the
high mountains, and although her tender feet bled so much that
even others could see it, she smiled and followed him until they
saw the clouds sailing beneath their feet, like a flight of birds
travelling to foreign countries. At home, in the prince's castle,
when the others slept at night, she went out on the broad marble
staircase ; it was cooling for her burning feet to stand in the cold
sea-water, and then she thought of those below in the deep. One
night her sisters came up arm in arm ; they sang mournfully as
they floated on the water; she beckoned to them, and they
recognised her and told her how much she had grieved them.
After this she saw them every night, and once she also saw her
old grandmother, who had not come up to the surface for many,
many years, and the Sea King with his crown on his head. They
stretched out their hands towards her, but they did not venture so
close to the land as her sisters.

The prince cared more for her from day to day ; he loved her as
one would love a dear good child, but he never had the least
thought of marrying her; and yet she had to become his wife
before she could obtain an immortal soul, otherwise she would
turn to foam on the sea the morning after his wedding. "Don't
you love me most of all ?" the mermaid's eyes seemed to say
when the prince took her in his arms and kissed her beautiful
forehead.

"Yes, I care most for you," he said, "for you have the best
heart of them all. You are most devoted to me, and resemble a
young girl whom I once saw, but whom I shall certainly not find
again. I was on board a ship which was wrecked; the waves
washed me ashore near a sacred temple, where several young girls
officiated. The youngest of them found me on the beach, and

saved my life. I only saw her twice; she would be the only girl in the world I could love; but you are like her, and you almost efface her likeness from my heart. She belongs to the sacred temple, and therefore my good fortune has sent you to me. Let us never separate."

"Alas! he does not know that I have saved his life," thought the little mermaid. "I carried him across the sea towards the wood where the temple stands; I was sitting behind the foam, looking to see if any one would come to him. I saw the beautiful girl whom he loves better than me." She sighed deeply, for she could not weep. "The girl belongs to the sacred temple, he has said. She will never come out into the world; they will never meet again; but I am near him, and see him every day. I will care for him, love him, and sacrifice my life for him."

But soon the rumour spread that the prince was to marry the beautiful daughter of a neighbouring king, and that was why they were, equipping a magnificent ship. They say the prince is travelling to see the neighbouring king's country, but in reality he goes to see his daughter. A large suite is to accompany him. The little mermaid shook her head and smiled; she knew the prince's thoughts much better than the others. "I must travel," he had said to her; "I must go and see the beautiful princess, for my parents wish it; but they will not compel me to marry her. I cannot love her; she is not like the beautiful girl in the temple, whom you resemble. Should I one day select a bride, I should prefer you, my dumb foundling with the eloquent eyes." And he kissed her ruby lips, and played with her long tresses, and placed his head on her bosom, so that she began to dream of human happiness and an immortal soul.

"You are not afraid of the sea, my dumb child?" he said to her when they were standing on the stately ship that was to take him to the neighbouring king's country. He told her of the storm and of the calm, of the strange fishes in the deep, and of the marvellous things divers had seen there. She smiled at his words, for who knew more about the things at the bottom of the sea than she did? In the moonlight night, when all were asleep except the man at the wheel, she sat on board, gazing down into the

clear water. Then she imagined she saw her father's castle; and
her grandmother with her silver crown on her head, looking up
through the violent currents at the ship's keel. Her sisters came
up to the surface, looked mournfully at her, and wrung their white
hands. She beckoned them, smiled, and wished to tell them she
was comfortable and happy, but a sailor boy approached her, and
her sisters dived under, so that he thought the white objects he
had seen were foam on the surface of the water.

The next morning the ship arrived in the harbour of the neighbouring king's splendid city. All the church bells were merrily
pealing, trumpets were sounding from the high towers, while the
soldiers paraded, with colours flying and bayonets glittering.
Every day another festivity took place; balls and entertainments
followed one another; but the princess had not yet come. They
said she was being educated in a sacred temple far away, where
she was learning every royal virtue. At last she arrived. The little
mermaid was anxious to see her beauty, and did not fail to
acknowledge it when she saw her. She had never seen a lovelier
being; her complexion was clear and delicate, and behind dark
lashes smiled a pair of dark blue, faithful-looking eyes.

"You are she who saved me when I was lying like a dead
body on the beach," said the prince, and he pressed his blushing
bride to his heart. "I am too happy," he said to the little
mermaid. "My greatest hopes have been realised. You will be
glad to hear of my happiness, for you have always been so kind to
me." The little mermaid kissed his hand, and felt as if her heart
was going to break. She knew that she was to die on his wedding
morning, and turn to foam on the sea.

The church bells pealed, heralds rode through the streets and
announced the engagement. On all the altars sweet-smelling
oil burnt in costly silver lamps. The priests swung their censers;
bride and bridegroom joined hands, and received the bishop's
blessing. The little mermaid was dressed in silk and gold, and
carried the bride's train; but her ears did not hear the festive
music, her eyes did not see the sacred ceremony; she thought of
the night of her death, and all that she had lost in this world.

The very same evening bride and bridegroom went on board

the ship; the cannons roared; the flags streamed in the wind; in the middle of the ship a beautiful tent of purple and gold was erected for the royal couple.

The sails swelled in the wind, and the ship glided gently and lightly through the smooth sea. When it became dark, coloured lamps were lit, and the sailors danced merrily on deck. The little mermaid could not help thinking of the first time she rose to the surface, when she had witnessed the same splendour and joy; she danced madly, hovering like a swallow when it is pursued. All applauded her, for she had never danced so well. It was like sharp knives cutting her tender feet, but she did not feel it; her heart suffered much greater pain. She knew that it was the last evening that she was to be with him—him for whom she had deserted her relatives and her home, sacrificed her sweet voice, and daily suffered endless pain, while he had not the slightest idea of it. It was the last night that she could breathe the same air with him, and see the deep sea and the starry sky; eternal night, without thought or dream, was waiting for her who had not been able to gain a soul. On board the ship joy and merriment lasted till long past midnight; she laughed and danced while her heart was full of thoughts of death. The prince kissed his beautiful bride, and she fondly touched his dark curls, and arm in arm they retired to rest in the magnificent tent.

Then all became still on board; only the man at the wheel remained at his post. The little mermaid rested her white arms on the railing of the ship, and looked towards thé east for the morning dawn; the first sunbeam she knew would kill her. She saw her sisters rising out of the waves; they were as pale as herself; their beautiful long hair was no longer fluttering in the wind—it was cut off. "We have given it to the witch, that we might help you, and save you from death to-night. She has given us a knife; here it is! Look how sharp it is! Before the sun rises you must thrust it into the prince's heart, and when the warm blood spurts upon your feet, they will grow together again into a fish-tail, and you will be a mermaid once more; then you can come back to us, and live your three hundred years before you become dead salt sea-foam. Hasten! You or he must die

before the sun rises. Our grandmother is so grieved, her white
hair has also been cut off by the witch's scissors. Kill the prince
and return to us! Hasten! Do you see that red streak in
the sky? In a few minutes the sun will rise, and then you must
die!"

Then they heaved a mournful sigh, and disappeared in the
waves.

The little mermaid drew back the purple curtain at the door of
the tent, and saw the beautiful bride lying with her head on the
prince's breast. She bent down and kissed his forehead, and
looked up to the sky, where daybreak was approaching; then she
looked at the sharp knife, and again at the prince, who murmured
his bride's name in his dreams. Only she was in his thoughts,
and the knife trembled in the little mermaid's hand. Suddenly
she threw it far out into the sea, and where it fell the waves
looked red, and it seemed as if drops of blood were spurting
up out of the water. As she was passing away she looked
once more at the prince, then threw herself down from the ship
into the sea, and felt her body dissolving into foam.

The sun rose out of the sea, and his rays fell with gentleness
and warmth upon the cold sea-foam; the little mermaid felt
no pain of death. She saw the bright sun, and above her were
hovering hundreds of transparent beings; their language was
melodious, but so ethereal that no human ear could hear them,
and no earthly eye could see them; they were lighter than
air, and floated about in it without wings. The little mermaid
noticed that she had a body like theirs, which rose higher and
higher out of the foam.

"Where am I coming to?" she asked, and her voice sounded
like that of the other beings—so ethereal that no earthly music
could equal it. "To the daughters of the air," replied the others.
"The mermaids have no immortal souls, and can never obtain
one unless they gain the love of human beings; their eternal
existence depends on another's power. The daughters of the air
have no immortal soul either, but they can obtain one for themselves by good actions. We fly to the hot countries where the
poisonous vapours kill mankind, and bring them cool breezes.

We spread the fragrance of the flowers through the air, and refresh and heal them. When we have striven for three hundred years to achieve all the good that is in our power, we obtain an immortal soul, and share the eternal happiness of mankind. You poor little mermaid, you have striven with all your heart for

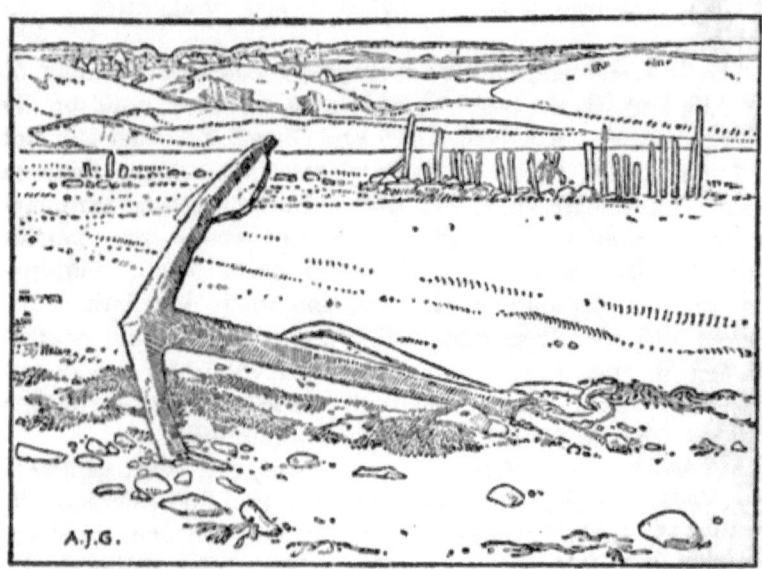

the same object; you have endured and suffered; now you have risen to the aërial world; and now, after three hundred years of good works, you will gain an immortal soul for yourself."

And the little mermaid raised her eyes up to the sun and felt tears in them for the first time.

On the ship there was life and noise once more; she saw how the prince and his beautiful bride were looking for her; mournfully they gazed at the glittering foam, as if they knew that she had thrown herself into the waves. Invisibly she kissed the bride's forehead and caressed the prince; then she rose with the other children of the air up to the rosy cloud which sailed through the ether.

"After three hundred years we float thus into the eternal Kingdom of God!"

"But we may get there sooner," whispered one of the daughters of the air. "Invisibly we penetrate into the houses of human beings, where they have children, and for every day on which we find a good child that causes its parents joy and deserves their love, God shortens our period of probation. The child does not know when we fly through the room, and if we smile for joy, one of the three hundred years is taken off; but if we see a naughty or wicked child, we must shed tears of sorrow, and every tear augments our period of probation by one day.

The Lovers

 TOP and a little ball lay together among other toys in a drawer. The top said to the little ball one day, "Shall we be sweethearts, as we are lying together here in the same drawer?" But the little ball, which was covered with red morocco, and thought as much of itself as any young lady, would not even reply to such a proposal.

On the next day the little boy to whom the toys belonged took the top, painted it red and yellow, and drove a nail with a brass head into it, so that the top looked very beautiful when it was spinning round.

"Look at me," it said to the little ball. "What do you say to this? Shall we be sweethearts now? We are so well suited to each other; you jump and I dance. No two people could be happier than we two."

"Really, do you think so?" replied the little ball. "You evidently do not know that my father and mother were morocco slippers, and that I have a Spanish cork in my body."

"Very well, but I am made of mahogany," said the top. "The mayor himself has turned me, for he has a lathe of his own which causes him a great deal of pleasure."

"Can I depend upon this being true?" asked the little ball.

"May I never be whipped again, if I do not speak the truth," replied the top.

"You know very well how to plead your cause," said the little

ball. "But I cannot comply with your wishes, for I am as good as engaged to a swallow. Whenever I fly up into the air it puts its head out of the nest and asks me : 'Will you?' And in myself I have already said Yes, and that is as much as half an engagement; but I will promise never to forget you."

"What is the good of that to me?" said the top ; and they spoke no more to each other.

Soon after this conversation the boy took out the little ball. The top saw it flying high up into the air, like a bird, till it was no longer visible : it always came back, and every time it touched the ground it made a high leap; this was either because it was desirous to fly up again, or because it had a Spanish cork in its body.

When the boy threw it up for the ninth time, the little ball did not come back; he looked everywhere for it, but could not find it—it was gone.

The next day the ball was taken out by the boy.

"I know very well where it has gone to," sighed the top, "it is in the swallow's nest, and has married the swallow." The more the top thought of this, the more it loved the little ball; and its love increased for the very reason that its wish could not be

fulfilled, for the little ball had married another; and the top
twirled round and hummed, and was continually thinking of the
little ball, which, to its imagination, became more and more
beautiful. Thus the years passed by, and its love grew quite
old.

The top itself was no longer young; but one day it was gilded
all over, and looked more beautiful than it had ever done before.
Now it was a golden top, and leapt and twirled till it hummed.
But suddenly it jumped too high and was gone.

They sought it everywhere, even in the cellar, but it was not to
be found.

Where was it?

It had jumped into the dust-bin, where all sorts of rubbish were
lying: old cabbage stalks, dust and dirt, that had fallen down
through the gutter.

"Here, I am well placed indeed! Here my gilding will soon
disappear. Oh, what company I have come into!" And then it
looked at a long naked cabbage stalk and at a peculiar round
thing that was much like an old apple; but it was no apple—it
was an old ball which had lain for many years in the gutter and
was soaked through with water.

"Heaven be thanked! here is an equal at last; somebody to
whom one can talk," said the little ball, and looked at the gilded
top. "I was originally covered with morocco, and sewn by the
hands of a young lady, and have a Spanish cork in my body; but
nobody will think so now. I was on the point of marrying a
swallow, but then I dropped into the gutter, and there I remained
more than five years, and was thoroughly soaked through. You
can believe me, it was a very long time for a little ball."

But the top said nothing; it thought of its old love, and the
more the little ball talked, the more it became certain that this
was its old sweetheart. Just then the servant came to throw
some rubbish into the dust-bin. "Ah, there is the gilt top,"
she said.

Thus the top came again to respectability and honour, but the
little ball was never heard of again. The top did not mention its
old love any more, for love vanishes when one's sweetheart has

lain five years in the gutter and become soaked through ; one does not recognise it again, if one meets it in the dust-bin.

Thumbelina

NCE upon a time there was a woman who wished very much to have a very small child, but she did not know where to get one. So she went to an old witch and said to her : " I would so very much like to have a small child ; can you tell me where I can get one ? "

"Oh, we shall soon be able to manage that," said the witch. "Here is a barleycorn ; it is not of the same kind that grows in the farmer's field, or that the chickens get to eat. Put it into a flower-pot, and you will see something."

"Thank you," said the woman, and gave the witch twelve shillings, for that was the price of it. Then she went home and planted the barleycorn ; immediately there grew up a large hand-some flower, looking like a tulip ; the leaves, however, were tightly closed, as though it were still a bud. "It is a beautiful flower," said the woman, kissing its red and yellow leaves ; but as she kissed it the flower opened with a bang. It was a real tulip, as could now be seen ; but in the middle of the flower, on the green velvety pistils, sat a tiny maiden, delicately and gracefully formed. She was scarcely half a thumb's length high, and there-fore she was called Thumbelina.

A neat polished walnut-shell served Thumbelina for a cradle, blue violet leaves were her mattresses, and a rose-leaf her blanket. There she slept at night, but in the daytime she played about on the table, where the woman had put a plate with a wreath of flowers round it, the stalks of which stood in water. On this water floated a large tulip leaf, and on this she could sit and row from one side of the plate to the other, having two white horse-hairs for oars. It looked wonderfully pretty. She could sing, too, and indeed, so tenderly and prettily as had never been heard before.

One night, as she was lying in her pretty bed, an old toad came creeping in through the window, in which there was a broken pane. The toad was a very ugly one, large and wet; it hopped down upon the table, where Thumbelina lay sleeping under the red rose-leaf.

"She would be a pretty wife for my son," said the toad, taking the walnut-shell in which Thumbelina was sleeping, and hopping with it through the window, down into the garden.

There flowed a great wide brook, the margin of which was swampy and marshy, and here lived the toad with her son. Ugh! he was so ugly and nasty, and looked just like his mother "Croak, croak! Crek-kek-kex!" was all that he could say when he spied the graceful little girl in the walnut-shell.

"Don't speak so loud, else you'll wake her," said the old toad. "She might run away from us, for she is as light as swan's-down, so we will put her on one of the broad leaves of the water-lily in the brook; that will be just like an island for her, she is so light and small. She will not be able to run away from there while we are getting ready the state-room under the marsh, where you are to live and keep house."

AJ.G.

Out in the brook there grew a great many water-lilies with broad green leaves, which looked as though they were floating on the water; the leaf which lay farthest off was the largest, to this the old toad swam out, and laid the walnut-shell with Thumbelina upon it.

Tiny Thumbelina woke early in the morning, and when she saw where she was she began to cry very bitterly; for there was water on every side of the great green leaf, and she could not get to land.

The old toad was sitting in the marsh decking out her room

with reeds and yellow flowers—it was to be made very pretty for the new daughter-in-law; then she swam out with her ugly son to the leaf where Thumbelina was. They wanted to fetch her pretty bed, which was to be placed in the bridal chamber before she herself entered it. The old toad bowed low in the water before her and said: "Here you have my son; he will be your husband, and you will live in great splendour down in the marsh."

"Croak, croak! Crek-kek-kex!" was all that the son could say. Then they took the pretty little bed and swam away with it, leaving Thumbelina sitting alone on the green leaf, crying, for she did not want to live with the nasty old toad, or have her ugly son for a husband. The little fishes swimming down in the water had both seen the toad and also heard what she had said; so they put out their heads, for they wanted to see the little girl too. As soon as they saw her they thought her so pretty that they felt very sorry that she was to go down to the ugly toad. No, that should never be! They assembled together down in the water, round the green stalk that held the leaf on which the tiny maiden stood, and with their teeth they gnawed away the stalk; the leaf floated away down the stream with Thumbelina—far away, where the toad could not reach her.

Thumbelina sailed by many towns, and the little birds sitting in the bushes saw her and sang, "What a lovely little girl!" The leaf went floating away with her farther and farther, and so Thumbelina travelled right out of the country.

A pretty little white butterfly kept fluttering around her, and at last sat down upon the leaf. Thumbelina pleased him, and she was very glad of it, for now the toad could not reach her, and it was so beautiful where she was; the sun was shining on the water, making it sparkle like the brightest silver. She took her girdle, and tied one end of it round the butterfly, fastening the other end of the ribbon to the leaf; it glided along much quicker now, and she too, for of course she was standing on it.

A great cockchafer came flying along, who spied her, and immediately clasped his claws round her slender waist and flew up with her into a tree. The green leaf floated down the stream, and the butterfly with it; for he was bound fast to the leaf and could not get away.

Heavens! how frightened poor Thumbelina was when the cockchafer flew up into the tree with her. But she was mostly grieved for the sake of the beautiful white butterfly which she had bound fast; in case he could not free himself, he would be obliged to starve. But the cockchafer did not care about that. He sat down with her on the largest green leaf of the tree, gave her the honey from the flowers to eat, and told her that she was very pretty, although she was not at all like a cockchafer.

Later on all the other cockchafers who lived in the tree came to pay a visit; they looked at Thumbelina and said, "She has not even more than two legs; that looks miserable!" "She hasn't any feelers," said another. "She has such a narrow waist, and looks quite human. Ugh, how ugly she is!" said all the lady cockchafers; and yet Thumbelina was very pretty—even the cockchafer who had carried her off admitted that. But when all the others said she was ugly, he at last believed it too, and would no longer have her; she might go where she liked. So they flew from off the tree with her and put her upon a daisy; she wept because she was so ugly that the cockchafers would not have her, and yet she was the loveliest little girl that one could imagine—as delicate and as tender as the most beautiful rose-leaf.

The whole summer through poor Thumbelina lived alone in the great forest. She wove herself a bed out of blades of grass, and hung it under a shamrock, in order to be protected from the rain; she gathered the honey out of the flowers for food, and drank of the dew that was on the leaves every morning. In this way summer and autumn passed, but now came winter—the long, cold winter. All the birds who had sung so beautifully about her flew away; the trees became bare and the flowers faded. The large shamrock under which she had lived dried up, and there remained nothing of it but a withered stalk; she was dreadfully cold, for her clothes were in tatters, and she herself was so small and delicate. Poor little Thumbelina, she would be frozen to death. It began to snow, and every snow-flake that fell upon her was like a whole shovelful thrown upon us; for we are so tall, and she was only an inch long. So she wrapped herself in a dry leaf, but that tore in half and would not warm her; she was shivering with cold.

Close to the wood to which she had now come lay a large corn-field; but the corn was gone long since, and only the dry naked stubbles stood up out of the frozen ground. These were like a forest for her to wander through, and oh! how she was trembling with cold. In this state she reached the door of a field-mouse who occupied a hole under the corn stubbles. There the mouse lived comfortably, had a whole room full of corn, a splendid kitchen and larder. Poor Thumbelina stood before the door like a little beggar girl, and asked for a piece of a barleycorn, for she had not had a bit to eat for two days.

"You poor little creature!" said the field-mouse—for she was really a good old mouse—"come into my warm room and dine with me."

Now, being pleased with Thumbelina, she said: "If you like, you can stay with me the whole winter, but you must keep my

room clean and neat, and tell me tales, for I am very fond of them."
And Thumbelina did what the good old field-mouse wished, and
in return was treated uncommonly well.

"Now we shall soon have a visit," said the field-mouse; "my
neighbour is in the habit of visiting me once a week. He is even
better off than I am; has large rooms, and wears a beautiful black
velvety fur. If you could only get him for a husband you would
be well provided for. But he cannot see. You must tell him the
prettiest stories that you know."

But Thumbelina did not trouble herself about it; she did not
think much of the neighbour, for he was only a mole.

He came and paid a visit in his black velvety fur. He was so
rich and so learned, said the field-mouse, and his dwelling was
twenty times larger than hers; he possessed great learning, but
he could not bear the sun and the beautiful flowers. Of the
latter he seldom spoke, for he had never seen them.

Thumbelina had to sing, and she sang: "Cockchafer,
cockchafer, fly away," and "When the parson goes afield."
So the mole fell in love with her because of her beautiful voice:
but he said nothing, for he was a prudent man.

A short time before, he had dug a passage through the earth
from his house to theirs, and the field-mouse and Thumbelina
received permission to take a walk in this passage as often as they
liked. But he begged them not to be afraid of the dead bird
which lay there. It was an entire bird, with feathers and beak,
who had probably died only a short time before, and was buried
just where the mole had made his passage.

The mole took a piece of decayed wood in his mouth, for that
glimmers like a light in the dark, and then went on in front, and
lighted them through the long dark passage. When they came
to the spot where the dead bird lay, the mole thrust his broad
nose against the ceiling and pushed the earth up, so that a large
hole was made, through which the light could shine down. In
the middle of the floor lay a dead swallow, with its beautiful
wings pressed close to its sides and its feet and head drawn under
its feathers; the poor bird had certainly died of cold. This
grieved Thumbelina very much; she was very fond of all the

little birds who had sung and twittered so beautifully to her all the summer. But the mole kicked him with his crooked legs, and said, "He doesn't pipe any more now. How miserable it must be to be born a little bird! Thank Heaven, that can happen to none of my children; such a bird has nothing but his tweet, and is obliged to starve in winter."

"Yes, you may well say that as a sensible man," said the field-mouse. "What does the bird get for all his twittering when winter comes? He must starve and freeze. But I suppose that is considered very grand."

Thumbelina said nothing; but when the two others had turned their backs upon the bird, she bent down, and putting the feathers aside which covered its head, she kissed him upon his closed eyes.

"Perhaps it was he who sang so beautifully to me in the summer," she thought. How much pleasure he has given me, the dear, beautiful bird!"

The mole now stopped up the hole through which the daylight shone in, and then accompanied the ladies home. But at night Thumbelina could get no sleep; so she got up from her bed and wove a fine large carpet of hay, which she carried along, and spread out over the dead bird. She also laid the tender stamina of flowers, which were as soft as cotton, and which she had found in the field-mouse's room, around the bird, so that he might lie warm.

"Good-bye, you beautiful little bird," she said. "Good-bye and many thanks for your beautiful singing in summer, when all the trees were green and the sun shone down warm upon us." Then she laid her head upon the bird's heart. But the bird was not dead; he was only lying there benumbed, and having now been warmed again was coming back to life.

In autumn all the swallows fly away to warm countries; but if there is one who is belated, it gets so frozen that it drops down as if dead, and remains lying where it falls, and soon the cold snow covers it.

Thumbelina trembled, so frightened was she, for the bird was big, very big, compared with her, who was only an inch long.

But she took courage, and laying the cotton more closely round the poor swallow, she fetched a leaf of mint which she herself had used as a blanket, and laid it over the bird's head.

The next night she again stole up to him; he was alive, but very weak, and could open his eyes only for a short moment to look at Thumbelina, who stood before him with a piece of decaying wood in her hand, for she had no other lantern.

"Thank you, my pretty little child," said the sick swallow to her. "I have been so beautifully warm. Soon I shall get my strength back and will then be able to fly about in the warm sunshine outside."

"Oh!" said she, "it is cold outside; it is snowing and freezing. Stay in your warm bed; I will take care of you."

Then she brought the swallow some water in a leaf of a flower. This the swallow drank, and told her how he had torn one of his wings on a thorn-bush, and had therefore been unable to fly so quickly as the other swallows who had flown far away to warm countries. So he had at last fallen to the ground, but could not remember anything more, and did not at all know how he had come there.

So he remained down there the whole winter, and Thumbelina nursed and tended him with all her heart; neither the mole nor the field-mouse knew anything about it, for they did not like the poor swallow at all.

As soon as spring came, and the sun warmed the earth, the swallow said good-bye to Thumbelina, who opened the hole which the mole had made up above. The sun shone in beautifully upon them, and the swallow asked her whether she would go with him; she could sit upon his back, he said, and they would fly far into the green forest. But Thumbelina knew that it would grieve the old field-mouse if she left her like that. "No, I cannot," she said.

"Good-bye, good-bye, you good pretty little girl!" said the swallow, and flew out into the sunshine. Thumbelina looked after him, and the tears came into her eyes, for she was very fond of the poor swallow.

"Tweet, tweet," sang the bird and flew into the green forest.

Thumbelina was very sad.　She got no permission to go out into the warm sunshine.　The corn which had been sown on the field over the house of the field mouse grew up high into the air; it was a thick wood for the poor little girl who was only an inch high.

"Now you are a bride, Thumbelina," said the field-mouse. "Our neighbour has asked for your hand.　What a great piece of luck for a poor child!　Now you will have to make your outfit, both woollen and linen clothes; for you must lack nothing when you are the mole's wife."

Thumbelina had to turn the spindle, and the field-mouse hired four spiders to weave for her day and night.　Every evening the mole used to visit them, and was always saying that at the end of the summer the sun would not shine so warm by a long way, that it was burning the earth as hard as a stone.　Yes, when the summer was over he would celebrate his marriage with Thumbelina. But the latter was not at all pleased, for she could not bear the tiresome mole.　Every morning when the sun rose, and every evening when it set she stole out to the door, and when the wind parted the ears of corn, so that she could see the blue sky, she would think how bright and beautiful it was out there, and would have a great longing to see the dear swallow again.　But he never came back; he had probably flown far away into the beautiful green wood.

When autumn came, Thumbelina had her whole outfit ready.

"You are to be married in four weeks," said the field-mouse to her.　But Thumbelina wept, and said she would not have the tiresome mole.

"Fiddlesticks!" said the field-mouse; "don't be obstinate, or I will bite you with my white teeth.　He is a fine man whom you are going to marry.　The Queen herself has not such black velvety fur.　He has a full kitchen and cellar.　Be thankful for it!"

Now the wedding was to take place.　The mole had already come to fetch Thumbelina; she was to live with him deep down under the earth, and never come out to the warm sunshine, for that he did not like.　The poor little girl was very sad; she was now to say good-bye to the beautiful sun, which, while she lived with the field-mouse, she had always had permission to look at from the door. "Good-bye, bright sun!" she said, and stretched her arms out high, and walked a little way off from the house of the field-mouse, for now the corn was cut and there remained only the dry stubbles. "Good-bye, good-bye!" she said, and wound her arms round a little red flower which was still blooming there. "Greet the little swallow for me, if you see him." "Tweet, tweet," suddenly sounded above her head; she looked up, and saw the little swallow, who was just flying by. When he spied Thumbelina, he was very pleased; she told him how unwilling she was to marry the ugly mole, and that she would have to live deep down under the earth, where the sun never shone. She could not held crying in telling it.

"The cold winter is coming now," said the little swallow; "I am flying away to warm countries; will you come with me? You can sit on my back; then we shall fly away from the ugly mole and his dark room, far away over the mountains, to warm countries, where the sun shines more beautifully than here, where it is always summer and there are glorious flowers. Do fly with me, dear little Thumbelina—you who saved my life when I lay frozen in the dark underground cellar."

"Yes, I will go with you," said Thumbelina; and she seated herself on the bird's back, with her feet on his outspread wing, binding her girdle fast to one of his strongest feathers. Then the swallow flew up into the air, over forest and sea, high up over the great mountains, where snow always lies. And Thumbelina began to freeze in the cold air, but then she crept under the bird's warm feathers, and only put out her little head to admire all the beauty beneath her.

At last they came to the warm countries. There the sun shone far brighter than here, the sky seemed twice as high, and in the ditches and on the hedges grew the finest green and blue grapes. In the woods hung citron and oranges; the air was heavy with the scent of myrtle and mint, and on the high roads the prettiest little children ran and played with large coloured butterflies. But the swallow flew still farther, and it became more and more beautiful. Under the most majestic green trees by the blue lake stood a marble castle of dazzling whiteness, all of the olden time. Vines wound themselves round the tall pillars, and up above there were a number of swallows' nests, and in one of these lived the swallow who was carrying Thumbelina.

"This is my house," said the swallow. "But it would not be proper for you to live with me here, and my arrangements are not such as you would be satisfied with. Pick out for yourself one of the most beautiful flowers that are growing down there; then I will put you into it, and you shall have everything as nice as you can wish.'

"That is glorious!" she said, clapping her little hands.

There lay a large white marble pillar which had fallen to the ground and broken into three pieces; between these grew the finest large white flowers. The swallow flew down with Thumbelina, and set her upon one of the broad petals. But what was her surprise! There in the middle of the flower sat a little man, as white and transparent as if he were made of glass; he wore the prettiest golden crown on his head, and had splendid little wings on his shoulders; he himself was no bigger than Thumbelina. He was the angel of the flower. In every flower lived such a little man or woman; but this one was the king of all.

"Heavens! how beautiful he is!" whispered Thumbelina to the swallow. The little prince was very frightened at the sight of the swallow, for it was a giant bird compared to him, who was so small and delicate. But when he spied Thumbelina he was greatly pleased; she was the prettiest little girl he had ever seen. He therefore took his golden crown from off his head, and put it upon hers, asking her what her name was, and whether she would be his wife; then she should be queen of all the flowers. He was indeed quite a different man to the son of the toad, and the mole with the black velvety fur. She said "Yes" to the grand prince. And out of every flower came a lady and a gentleman, so dainty that they were a pleasure to behold. Each one brought Thumbelina a present; but the best of all was a pair of beautiful wings from a large white fly; these were fastened on to Thumbelina's back, and now she too could fly from flower to flower.

There was much rejoicing, and the little swallow sat up in his nest, and was to sing the bridal song; this he did as well as he could, although in his heart he was sad, for he was so fond of Thumbelina, and would have liked never to separate himself from her.

"You shall not be called Thumbelina," said the Flower Angel to her. "That is an ugly name, and you are too pretty for it. We will call you Maia." "Good-bye, good-bye!" said the little swallow with a heavy heart, and flew away from the warm countries back to Denmark. There he had a little nest over the window where the man lives who can tell tales. To him he sang "Tweet, tweet." That is how we know the whole story.

The Flax

HE flax was standing in full bloom; it had pretty blue flowers, as delicate as the wings of a moth, if not more so. The sun was warming it with his rays, the rain-clouds watered it; and that was as beneficial to the flax as it is to little children to be washed and afterwards kissed by their mothers. It makes them look much brighter. So it did the flax.

"People say I am standing very well," said the flax; "that I have a good length to make a piece of strong linen. Oh, I am so very happy! I am certainly the happiest of all plants! How well I am cared for! And I shall be useful! How much I enjoy the warm sun, how much the rain refreshes me. I am exceedingly happy—nay, I am the happiest of all plants."

"That is all very well," said a fence-post; "you do not know the world as well as I, for I have plenty of knots in me." And then it groaned quite piteously:

> "*Snip, snap, snurre—*
> *Bassellurre:*
> *Ended is the song.*"

"No, it is not ended," said the flax, "the sun will shine to-morrow, or the rain will refresh us. I feel how I am growing. I see that I am in full flower, I am the happiest of all plants."

One day people came, seized the flax and pulled it out by the roots; that was very painful! They placed it in water as if they intended to drown it, and afterwards hung it over a fire, as if they wished to fry it. It was dreadful!

"One cannot always be happy," said the flax; "one must also suffer in order to become experienced."

And things much worse happened to it. The flax was steeped, roasted, broken, and hackled. How could it possibly know the names of the various operations they performed upon it? Afterwards the flax was put on the spinning-wheel. "Whirr, whirr," the wheel turned so rapidly round that the flax was not able to gather its thoughts.

"How very happy I was," it thought, whilst it suffered agonies of pain; "one must be contented with the good one has enjoyed in the past. Contented, contented!" Thus the flax still said, when it was put on the loom. A large piece of beautiful linen was woven from it, and all the flax, to the very last stalk, was used up for this one piece.

"But this is marvellous; I should never have thought it! Fortune favours me very much indeed. The fence-post knew something after all when it sang:

> *Snip, snap, snurre—*
> *Bassellurre.*'

The song is by no means ended. No, on the contrary, now it only begins. That is very extraordinary. I have suffered a great deal, no doubt, but now I have turned out something useful. I am the happiest of all plants! How strong and fine, how white and long I am. It is something very different from being only a plant, although it bears flowers; as a plant, one is not so much looked after, and gets water only when it rains. Now I am well cared for; the maid turns me over every morning, and at night she gives me a shower-bath with the watering-pot; the pastor's wife has even made a speech in praise of me; she said that I was the best piece of linen in the whole parish. I cannot possibly be happier than I am now!"

The linen was taken into the house and operated upon with scissors. How they cut and tore it, and pricked it with sewing-needles; it was by no means a pleasure! They made twelve garments of it of a kind which people do not like to mention, although nobody can get on without them; they made a whole dozen out of one piece of linen.

"Look at me now," said the flax, "only now I have become something really useful, and clearly understand what I am destined for in this world. What a blessing! Now I am useful, and so everybody ought to be, for that is the only true happiness in the world. Although they have cut twelve pieces of me, all the twelve are one and the same; we just make up the dozen. What an exceptional luck!"

Years and years passed: the garments were so much worn that they began to fall to pieces.

"There must be an end one day," said every piece. "I should have very much liked to last a little longer, but one must not expect more than is possible."

Then they were torn into rags and tatters. "It is all over now," they thought, when they were ground in a mill, soaked, and boiled, and went through various processes they were unable to remember. But they became beautiful white paper.

"That is a surprise indeed, and what a pleasant one," said the paper. "Now I am finer than before, and now they will write upon me. That is an extraordinary good fortune.

And really the most interesting stories and beautiful stanzas were written upon the paper, and there was only one ink-blot; of course this was quite an exceptional chance. And the people heard what was written upon it; it was good and clever, and made them better and enlightened them. Thus the words written on this paper produced a great blessing.

"That is more than I ever dreamt of, when I was a little blue flower in the field. How could it come into my mind that I should be destined to give mankind pleasure and knowledge? I can hardly believe it, and yet it is true. God knows that I have myself done nothing more with my feeble strength than what was necessary for my existence and growth, and yet He heaps honour after honour upon me. Whenever I think, 'Now the song is ended,' I pass into something better and higher. Now I shall probably travel about in the world, that all people may read what is written upon me. It can't be otherwise; it is most likely. I have so many great thoughts written upon me as I had formerly blue flowers. I am indeed the happiest of all plants."

The paper, however, was not sent on travels—nay, it was taken to the printer's, and there the whole manuscript was set up in type, and a book, or rather many hundreds of books were made of it, so that many more might have pleasure and profit from the writing than was possible if the paper on which it was written had been sent about in the world; no doubt it would have fallen to pieces before it had performed half its journey.

"Certainly, this is the wisest thing that could be done," thought the written paper, "although it never struck me. I remain at home, and am honoured like an old grandfather, for that I am indeed to all new books. Thus some good can be done. I should not have been able to wander so much about. Only he who wrote the book has looked at me, for every one of his words run out of his pen straight upon me. I am the happiest of all!"

Then the paper was tied up in a bundle with other papers, and thrown into a cask which stood in the wash-house.

"When the work is done, it is pleasant to rest," said the paper. "It is wise to collect one's thoughts and to reflect on all that lives in one. It is only now that I thoroughly understand all that is written upon me. I wonder what will happen now? Surely there will be progress again; one always advances—that I know by my own experience."

One day all the paper was taken out of the cask and placed on the hearth; it was to be burnt, for people said it must not be sold to tradesmen to wrap butter or sugar in it. All the children of the house were standing round the fireplace, for they wished to see the paper burning; it flamed up so beautifully, and afterwards one could see so many red sparks flying about in the ashes: one after another of the sparks disappeared as quickly as the wind. They called it "seeing the children coming out of school": the last spark was the schoolmaster. They thought they knew all about it, but that was a mistake. We, however, shall soon know.

All the old paper, the whole bundle of it, was put on the fire and was soon ablaze. "Ugh," it said, and flamed up high. "Ugh, that is not at all pleasant;" but when all was alight the bright flames reached much higher than the flax would ever have been able to stretch its little blue flowers, and the flames shone more brightly than the linen could ever have done. All the written letters turned red for a moment, and all the words and thoughts they expressed vanished in the flames. "Now I am flying straight up to the sun," said a voice in the flame; and it seemed as if a thousand voices repeated it, and the flames came out of the chimney-pot.

And finer than the flames, invisible to human eyes, there were rising up as many little beings as the flax had had flowers. They were still lighter than the flame that had borne them, and when it was extinguished and nothing left of the paper but black ashes, they danced once more over the ashes, and wherever they touched it red sparks leapt up. "The children came out of school, and the last was the schoolmaster." That was a pleasure! And the children sang:

> "*Snip, snap, snurre—*
> *Bassellurre:*
> *Ended is the song.*"

But all the little invisible beings said: "The song is never ended —that is the best of all; and therefore I am the happiest of all in the world."

Of course the children could neither hear nor understand it, and that was quite right, for children must not know everything.

The Princess and the Pea

ONCE upon a time there was a prince who wanted to marry a princess; but she would have to be a real princess. He travelled all over the world to find one, but nowhere could he get what he wanted. There were princesses enough, but it was difficult to find out whether they were real ones. There was always something about them that was not as it should be. So he came home again and was sad, for he would have liked very much to have a real princess.

One evening a terrible storm came on; there was thunder and lightning, and the rain poured down in torrents. Suddenly a knocking was heard at the city gate, and the old king went to open it.

It was a princess standing out there in front of the gate. But, good gracious! what a sight the rain and the wind had made her look. The water ran down from her hair and clothes; it ran down into the toes of her shoes and out again at the heels. And yet she said that she was a real princess.

"Well, we'll soon find that out," thought the old queen. But she said nothing, went into the bed-room, took all the bedding off the bedstead, and laid a pea on the bottom; then she took twenty mattresses and laid them on the pea, and then twenty eider-down beds on top of the mattresses.

On this the princess had to lie all night. In the morning she was asked how she had slept.

"Oh, very badly!" said she. "I have scarcely closed my

eyes all night. Heaven only knows what was in the bed, but I was lying on something hard, so that I am black and blue all over my body. It's horrible!"

Now they knew that she was a real princess because she had felt the pea right through the twenty mattresses and the twenty eider-down beds.

Nobody but a real princess could be as sensitive as that.

So the prince took her for his wife, for now he knew that he had a real princess; and the pea was put in the museum, where it may still be seen, if no one has stolen it.

There, that is a true story.

The Garden of Paradise

NCE upon a time there was a king's son. No one had so many fine books as he; he could read in them about everything that had happened in this world, and see pictures of it all in beautiful engravings. He could get information upon every nation and every country; but there was not a word to say where the Garden of Paradise was to be found, and that happened to be just what he thought most about.

His grandmother had told him when he was still little, and was about to go to school for the first time, that every flower in this Garden of Paradise was made of the nicest cake, and that the pistils contained the finest wines; that history was written on some of them, and geography or tables on others, so that one had only to eat cake to know one's lesson. The more one ate, the more history, geography, and tables one would learn.

At that time he believed it. But soon, when he was a bigger boy, and had learned more and become wiser, he understood well enough that there must be quite a different kind of delight in the Garden of Paradise.

"Oh, why did Eve pluck from the tree of knowledge? Why did Adam eat of the forbidden fruit? If I had been he, it would

not have happened. Sin would never have come into the world."
He said this then, and he still said so when he was seventeen
years old. The Garden of Paradise occupied all his thoughts.

One day he was walking in the wood alone, for that was his
greatest pleasure. The sun went down, and the sky became

clouded over. The rain came down as though the whole of
heaven were a single sluice-gate, out of which the water poured;
and it was as dark as it is only at night in the deepest well. He
often slipped on the wet grass, and often fell over the smooth
stones which protruded from the wet rocky ground. Everything
was dripping with water; there was not a dry thread on the poor
prince. He was obliged to clamber over great boulders, where
the water welled up out of the high moss. He was almost fainting, when he heard a strange rushing sound and saw before him a
large illuminated cave. There was such a large fire burning in the
middle that a stag could have been roasted before it. And indeed
this was being done. A splendid stag with long horns had been

placed upon a spit and was being slowly turned between two
felled pine-trunks. An elderly woman, tall and strong, looking
like a man in woman's clothes, was sitting by the fire and throwing
on one piece of wood after another.

"Come nearer," she said; "sit down by the fire, so that your
clothes may dry."

"There's a terrible draught here," said the prince, sitting down
on the floor.

"It will be worse when my sons come home," answered the
woman. "You are here in the Cave of the Winds; my sons are
the four winds of the world. Can you understand that?"

"Where are your sons?" asked the prince.

"Well, it is difficult to answer when people ask stupid
questions," said the woman. "My sons do just as they like:
now they are playing at shuttlecock with the clouds up there in
the king's hall." And with these words she pointed upwards.

"Indeed!" said the prince. "But I must say you speak rather gruffly, and are not so gentle as the women I usually have about me."

"Well, I suppose they have nothing else to do. I must be hard, if I wish to keep my boys in order; but that I can do, although they are obstinate fellows. Do you see these four sacks hanging on the wall? They are as frightened of those as you used to be of the rod behind the mirror. I can bend those boys together, I tell you, and then I pop them into the sack; we make no ceremony about it. Then they sit there and dare not stir out before I think fit. But here we have one of them."

It was the North-wind, who brought in icy coldness; large hail-stones skipped upon the floor, and snowflakes fluttered around. He wore bearskin trousers and jacket, and a sealskin cap came down over his ears; long icicles hung down from his beard, and one hailstone after another slid down from the collar of his jacket.

"Don't go near the fire at once," said the prince. "You might get your hands and face frostbitten."

"Frostbitten?" said the North-wind, and laughed out loud. "Cold is my greatest pleasure. And pray what tailor's son may you be? How did you come into the Cave of the Winds?"

"He is my guest," said the old woman; "and if you are not satisfied with this explanation, you will find your way into the sack. Do you understand me now?"

That settled the matter; and the North-wind told whence he came, and where he had been almost a whole month.

"I come from the Polar Sea," said he. "I have been on Bear Island with the Russian walrus-hunters. I sat at the helm and slept when they set sail from the North Cape, and when I awoke now and then the stormy petrel was flying about my legs. What a strange bird that is! It makes a quick stroke with its wings, holds them stretched out and unmoved, and is then in full flight."

"Come, don't make your tale too long," said the mother of the winds. "So you came to Bear Island?"

"It is a beautiful place. The ground would do for dancing on, smooth as china. The half-thawed snow mixed with a little moss, sharp stones and the skeletons of walruses and ice-bears lay all around, as well as giant arms and legs covered with mouldy green. One would have believed that the sun had never shone upon it at all. I blew the fog off a little in order to see the hut. It was built of wreckage, covered over with walrus hides, the flesh side of which had been turned outwards; a live polar bear was sitting on the roof growling. I went to the shore, and looking into the birds' nests, saw the naked young ones, who were crying with their beaks wide open. I blew down into their thousand throats, and they learned to keep their beaks shut. A little farther off, the walruses were rolling about like live entrails, or giant worms with swine-heads and teeth a yard long."

"You tell your story beautifully, my son," said the mother. "My mouth waters when I listen to you."

"Then the hunting began. The harpoon was thrust into the breast of the walrus, so that the steaming blood rushed over the ice like a fountain. Then I remembered my sport too. I blew and made my ships, the towering icebergs, shut in the boats. Hey! how the men whistled and shouted; but I whistled still louder. They were obliged to throw the bodies of the dead walruses, the boxes and the cordage out upon the ice. I shook snow-flakes over them, and let them float southwards, in their hemmed-in vessels, with what they had caught, to taste the sea-waters. They will never come to Bear Island again."

"Then you have been doing mischief," said the mother of the winds.

"The good that I have done others may tell about," said he. "But here we have my brother from the West. I like him best of all : he smells of the sea, and brings a fine coldness with him."

"Is that the little Zephyr?" asked the prince.

"It is indeed Zephyr," said the old woman. "But he is by no means little. Years ago he was a pretty boy, but that time is now past."

He looked like a savage, and wore a padded hat, so that he should not hurt himself in falling. In his hand he held a mahogany club, hewn in the mahogany forests of America. It was no plaything!

"Where do you come from?" asked his mother.

"From the forest-wastes," said he, "where the water-snake lies in the wet grass and people seem to be unnecessary."

"What did you do there?"

"I looked into the deepest river and saw how it hurled itself from the rocks, became dust and flew up to the clouds to carry the rainbow. I saw the wild buffalo swimming in the stream, and how the current carried him away. He floated along with a flock of wild ducks, who flew into the air when they came to the waterfall. But the buffalo had to go down; that pleased me, and I raised a storm that shivered the oldest trees into splinters."

"And is that all you have done?" asked the old woman.

"I have turned somersaults in the savannahs; I have stroked the wild horses, and shaken down the coker-nuts. Dear me! what stories I could tell. But one must not say everything that one knows. You know that very well, old lady." And he kissed his mother so boisterously that she almost fell backwards. He was a terribly wild boy.

The South-wind now came in, wearing a turban and the flowing mantle of a Bedouin.

"It is very cold out here," said he, throwing some more wood upon the fire. "It is easy to see that the North-wind came in first."

"It is hot enough here to roast an ice-bear," said the North-wind.

"You are an ice-bear yourself," answered the South-wind.

"Do you want to be put into the sack?" asked the old woman. "Sit down on that stone there, and tell me where you have been."

"In Africa, mother," he answered. "I went lion-hunting with the Hottentots in the country of the Kaffirs. Grass grows on the plains there as green as an olive. The ostrich ran a race with me, but I am still quicker than he. I came to the desert and to the yellow sand, where it looks just like the bottom of the sea. I met a caravan : they were killing their last camel to get some drinking water, but they got only a little, after all. The sun burned from overhead and the sand from underfoot. The far-stretching desert was boundless. I danced about in the fine loose sand, and whirled it up into great pillars. What a dance that was! You should have seen how despondently the dromedary stood there, and how the trader drew his caftan over his head. He threw himself down before me as before Allah, his god. Now they are buried; a pyramid of sand is heaped up over them all. When I blow that away, the sun will bleach their white bones;

then travellers will see that human beings have been there before. Otherwise that would not be believed in the desert."

"Then you have only done evil," said his mother. "Into the sack with you!" And before he knew where he was she had caught the South-wind round the body, and popped him into the sack. He rolled himself over and over on the ground, but she sat down on him, and he had to lie still.

"These boys of yours are lively," said the prince.

"They are," she answered, "but I know how to keep them in order. Here comes the fourth!"

This was the East-wind, dressed like a Chinaman.

"Oh, so you come from that quarter?" said his mother. "I thought that you had been in the Garden of Paradise."

"I am not going there until to-morrow," said the East-wind. "That will be a hundred years since I have been there. I come from China now, where I danced round the porcelain tower and made all the bells jingle. The officials were being beaten in the street; bamboo canes were split across their shoulders, and they were all people from the first to the ninth grade. They shouted: 'Many thanks, my paternal benefactor.' But the cry did not come from their hearts, and I jingled the bells and sang: 'Tsing, tsang, tsu!'"

"You are mischievous," said the old woman. It is a good thing that you are going to the Garden of Paradise to-morrow; you always learn better manners there. Take a good draught at the fountain of wisdom, and bring a bottleful home for me."

"I will!" said the East-wind. "But why have you put my brother of the south into the sack? Out with him! He must tell me about the phœnix bird; the princess in the Garden of Paradise always likes to hear about it, when I pay her a visit every hundred years. Open the sack, and then you will be my sweetest mother, and I will give you two bags full of tea, as green and as fresh as I picked it on the spot where it grew."

"Well, for the sake of the tea, and because you are my pet boy, I will open the sack." She did so, and the South-wind crept out; but he looked quite dejected, because the stranger prince had seen his disgrace.

"Here is a palm-leaf for the princess," said he. "This leaf was given me by the phœnix, the only bird of that kind in the world. It has traced upon it with its beak the whole story of its life during the hundred years that it has lived. Now she can read for herself how the phœnix bird set fire to its nest and sat in it while it was consumed by the flames, like a Hindoo widow. How the dry twigs crackled! What a smoke and a vapour there were! At length all had been destroyed by the flames; the old phœnix bird had become ashes. But its egg lay red and glowing in the fire; suddenly it burst with a great clap, and the young one flew out, and that one now reigns over all birds, and is the only phœnix bird in the world. It has bitten a hole in the palm-leaf I gave you; that is its greeting to the princess."

"Let us eat something," said the mother of the Winds. So they all sat down together and ate of the roast stag. The young prince sat by the side of the East-wind, and therefore they soon became good friends. "I say," said the prince, "just tell me what princess that is of whom you were talking so much just now, and where is the Garden of Paradise situated?"

"Ho, ho!" said the East-wind; "would you like to go there? Well, then, fly with me to-morrow. But I must tell you this: no human being has been there since the time of Adam and Eve. I suppose you know them from your Bible history?"

"Of course," said the prince.

"At that time, when they were driven out, the Garden of Paradise sank into the earth; but it retained its warm sunshine, its balmy air, and all its beauty. The fairy queen lives there now; there lies also the Island of Happiness, where Death never comes and where all is beautiful. If you get upon my back to-morrow, I will take you with me; I think we shall be able to manage it. But leave off talking now, because I want to go to sleep."

And then they all went to sleep.

Early in the morning the prince awoke, and was not a little surprised to find himself already high above the clouds. He was sitting on the back of the East-wind, who held him fast; they were so high up in the air that forests and meadows, rivers and seas looked as though painted on a map.

"Good morning," said the East-wind. "You might just as well sleep a little longer, because there is not much to be seen on the flat country beneath us, unless you have a mind to count the churches. They stand like little lumps of chalk on the green board." What he called a green board were the fields and meadows.

"It was very rude of me not to say good-bye to your mother and your brothers," said the prince.

"Such things are excusable if one is asleep," said the East-wind. And thereupon they flew along still faster. It could be heard by the tree-tops, for when they flew over them all the branches and the leaves rustled; it could be heard by the sea and the lakes, for wherever they flew the waves rose higher, and the great ships dipped low into the water, like swans swimming.

Towards evening, when it was getting dark, the large towns were an extremely pretty sight, with all the lights being kindled, first here and then there. It was just like watching all the little sparks as they vanish one after another from a burnt piece of paper. At this the prince clapped his hands; but the East-wind begged him not to do so, and rather to hold on tight, as otherwise he might easily fall, and remain hanging from the top of a church steeple.

The eagle in the dark forests flew very lightly, but the East-wind flew more lightly still. The Cossack on his little steed sped very swiftly across the plain, but the prince rode more swiftly still. "Now you can see the Himalayas," said the East-wind. "They are the highest mountains in Asia, and we shall soon reach the Garden of Paradise." Then they turned more towards the south, and soon the air was balmy with spices and flowers. Figs and pomegranates were growing wild; red and white grapes hung from the wild vines. Here they both descended and stretched themselves on the soft grass, where the flowers nodded to the wind, as if they wanted to say, "Welcome!"

"Are we now in the Garden of Paradise?" asked the prince.

"Dear me! no," answered the East-wind. "But we shall soon get there. Do you see yonder cliff and the wide cave in front of which the vines hang like a long green curtain? We must go through there to get in. Wrap yourself up in your cloak; the sun burns here; but one step farther, and it will be as cold as ice.

The bird which flies past the cave has one wing in the warmth of summer, and the other in the cold of winter."

"Indeed! So that is the way to the Garden of Paradise," said the prince. They now entered the cave. Oh, how icy cold it was! But it did not last long; the East-wind spread out his wings, and they shone like the brightest fire. What a cave it was! The great boulders, from which the water trickled down, hung above them in the strangest forms. In one place it was so narrow that they had to creep along on hands and feet, and in another as high and wide as in the open air. It looked like subterranean chapels with mute organ-pipes and petrified organs.

"I suppose we are going to the Garden of Paradise by the road of Death?" asked the prince. But the East-wind answered not a syllable, only pointing forwards, where the most beautiful blue light was streaming towards them. The boulders above became more and more hazy, till at last they looked like a white cloud in the moonlight. Now they breathed a beautiful balmy air, as fresh as on the mountains, as fragrant as among the roses of the valley. A river flowed there, as clear as the air itself, and the fish were like silver and gold. Purple eels, which gave forth blue sparks with every movement, were playing beneath the surface, and the broad leaves of the water-lily had all the colours of the rainbow. The flower itself was a glowing orange-coloured flame, which was fed by the water, just as oil keeps a lamp continually burning. A strong marble bridge, so delicately and artistically carved as though it were of lace and seed-pearls, led over the water to the Island of Happiness, where the Garden of Paradise was.

The East-wind took the prince in his arms, and carried him across. The flowers and leaves sang the most beautiful songs of his childhood, but with such sweet modulations as no human voice can command. Were they palm-trees or gigantic water-plants that grew here? The prince had never before seen trees so large and full of sap, and hanging there in long garlands were the most wonderful creepers, such as are only found, painted in colours and gold, on the margins of old missals or wound about initial letters. They were the strangest compounds of birds, flowers, and stalks. Close by, on the grass, stood a group of

peacocks with their bright tails spread out. It was really so ! But
when the prince touched them he found that they were not birds,
but plants ; they were large plantain-leaves, that shone here like
the majestic tail of the peacock. Lions and tigers sprang like
agile cats in and out of the green hedges, which were as fragrant
as the flowers of the olive-tree ; but they were tame. The wild
wood-pigeon shone like the finest pearl, and beat her wings against
the lion's mane ; the antelope, so shy elsewhere, stood by and
nodded its head, as if it wished to join them in their play.

There now appeared the Fairy of Paradise. Her raiment was
resplendent as the sun, and her face wore a smile like that of a
glad mother when she is happy on account of her child. She was
young and fair, and the loveliest maidens, each wearing a bright
star in her hair, followed her. The East-wind gave her the leaf
on which the phœnix bird had written, and it made her eyes
sparkle with joy. She took the prince by the hand, and led him
into her castle, where the walls had colours like those of the
brightest tulip petals when they are held in the sunlight. The
ceiling itself was a large shining flower, and the more one looked
up at it the deeper seemed to be its cup. The prince went to the
window and looked through one of the panes : there was the Tree
of Knowledge, and Adam and Eve standing close by. " Were they
not driven out ? " he asked. And the Fairy smiled and explained
to him that Time had stamped its picture on every pane ; but
not as pictures are generally seen. Here there was life in them.
The leaves of the trees moved ; the people came and went just as
anything is seen in a mirror. And he looked through another pane
and saw Jacob's dream, with the ladder reaching up to heaven, and
angels with great wings were floating up and down. Indeed, everything that had happened in this world lived and moved in the glass
panes ; such artistic pictures could only be engraved by Time.

The fairy smiled and led him to a large lofty hall, the walls of
which appeared to be transparent. Here were many portraits,
one more beautiful than the other. Millions of happy faces were
seen, all smiling and singing in beautiful harmony. The top ones
were so small that they looked smaller than the smallest rose-buds
when they are drawn, no larger than a pin's head on paper. In the

middle of the hall stood a large tree with luxuriant branches hanging down; golden apples peeped out like oranges from between the green leaves. It was the Tree of Knowledge, of whose fruit Adam and Eve had eaten. From each leaf there trickled a bright red dew-drop; it looked as if the tree were weeping tears of blood.

"Let us get into the boat now," said the fairy, "and we will have some refreshments on the billowy water. Our bark will not move from the spot, but all the countries of the earth will glide past before our eyes."

And it was wonderful to behold how the whole coast moved. First came the high, snow-clad Alps, with clouds and dark fir-trees; the horn sent forth its melancholy note, and the shepherd sang lustily in the valley. Then the banana-trees trailed their long hanging branches over the boat; black swans swam upon the water, and the strangest animals and flowers appeared on the river-bank: it was New Holland, the fifth quarter of the globe, which with a view of its blue mountains now swept by. One could hear the chant of the priests and see the savages dancing to the sound of the drums and the bone trumpets. The pyramids of Egypt, their tops reaching the clouds, ruined pillars and sphinxes, half buried in the sand, sailed past in like manner. The Northern Lights shone out over the extinct volcanoes of the Arctic regions: a firework display which no one could imitate. The prince was very happy, for he saw a hundred times as much as we can tell of here.

"And can I always stay here?" he asked.

"That depends upon yourself," answered the fairy. "If you do not wish to do, as Adam did, what is forbidden, you can always stay here."

"I will never touch the apples on the Tree of Knowledge," said the prince.

"There are thousands of kinds of fruit here, just as fine as they are. Try yourself, and if you are not strong enough, go back with the East-wind, who brought you here. He is now about to fly back, and will not let himself be seen here for a hundred years; that time will pass for you in this place as if it were a hundred hours, but it is a long time to resist temptation. Every evening when I leave you, I must call to you: "Come with me!" I must beckon you to me with my hand. But stay where you are. Do not go with me, or else your desire would grow stronger at every step. You would then reach the hall where the Tree of Knowledge grows; I sleep under its fragrant, hanging branches. You will bend over me, and I must smile, but if you press a kiss upon my mouth, Paradise will sink deep into the earth, and be lost to you. The piercing wind of the desert will whistle round you, and the cold rain will trickle upon your head. Sorrow and trouble will be your lot."

" I will stay here," said the prince. And the East-wind kissed him on the forehead and said: " Be strong; then we shall meet each other here again after a hundred years. Farewell, farewell ! " And the East-wind spread out his great wings; they shone like lightning in harvest-time, or like the North-light in winter.

" Farewell, farewell ! " re-echoed all the flowers and trees. Rows of storks and pelicans flew like waving ribbons, and accompanied him to the boundaries of the garden.

" Now let us begin our dances," said the fairy. " Towards the end, when I am dancing with you, and the sun is sinking, you will see me beckon you, and hear me call to you to come with me. But do not do so. For a hundred years I must repeat it every evening; on every occasion, as soon as the time is past, you will have gained more strength, and at last you will no longer even think of it. To-night is the first time; now I have warned you."

The fairy then led him into a large hall of white transparent lilies; the yellow stamina in each flower formed a little golden harp, from the strings of which came notes like those of a flute. The most beautiful maidens, graceful and slender, clad in wavy gauze, so that their charming limbs could be seen, glided through the dance, and sang how beautiful it was to live, that they would never die, and that the Garden of Paradise would flourish for ever.

The sun was setting; the whole sky became the colour of gold, and gave the lilies the appearance of the most lovely roses. The prince drank the sparkling wine which the maidens handed him, and felt a happiness that he had never experienced before. He saw the background of the hall open itself, and the Tree of Knowledge standing in a splendour which blinded his eyes; the singing there was soft and sweet, like his mother's voice, and it seemed as though she were singing : " My child, my beloved child !"

Then the fairy beckoned to him, and called so sweetly, "Come with me! Come with me !" that he rushed towards her, forgetting his promise, forgetting it already on the first evening, while she beckoned and smiled. The fragrance, the spicy fragrance, all around became stronger; the harps sounded much sweeter, and it seemed as if the millions of smiling heads in the hall, where the tree grew, nodded and sang: "One should know everything. Man is lord of the earth." And they were no longer tears of blood that fell from the leaves of the Tree of Knowledge; they were brilliant red stars, which the prince thought he saw. "Come with me! Come with me !" sang the quivering tones, and with every step the prince's cheeks burned more hotly, his blood rushed more quickly through his veins. "I must," said he. "It is no sin—can be none. Why may I not follow beauty and joy? I will see her sleep; there is no harm done if I refrain from kissing her. And I shall not kiss her. I am strong; I have a firm will."

And the fairy, throwing aside her dazzling raiment, bent back the boughs, and a moment after she was concealed behind them.

"I have not yet sinned," said the prince; "neither will I do so."

And then he drew the boughs aside; she was already asleep, as beautiful as only the fairy in the Garden of Paradise can be. She smiled in her dream, but he bending down over her, saw tears trembling between her eyelids.

"Do you weep on my account?" he whispered. "Do not weep, you lovely creature. Now only do I understand the bliss of Paradise. It is rushing through my blood, through my thoughts; I feel the strength of the cherub and of eternal life in my earthly body. May eternal night come over me! One minute such as this is riches enough !" And he kissed the tears from her eyes; his mouth touched hers.

There came a crash of thunder more deep and terrible than had ever been heard. Everything rushed together; the beautiful fairy, the blooming Garden of Paradise sank, sank lower and lower. The prince saw it sink into the black night; it shone in the distance like a twinkling little star. Icy coldness ran through his limbs; he closed his eyes and lay for a long time as one dead.

The cold rain beat into his face, the sharp wind flew about his head, and his senses returned. "What have I done!" he sighed. "I have sinned, like Adam—sinned, so that Paradise has sunk far away." He opened his eyes and still beheld the star in the distance, the star that shone like the lost Paradise—it was the morning-star in the heavens. He rose and found himself in the great forest near the Cave of the Winds; the mother of the winds was sitting beside it; she looked angry and raised her hand in the air.

"Already, on the first evening," she said. "I thought as much! Well, if you were my son you would go into the sack."

"He shall go in," said Death. He was a strong old man, with a scythe in his hand and with large black wings. "He shall be laid in the coffin, but not yet. I will only mark him, and let him wander about a little while longer in the world to repent of his sins and to become good and better. But I shall come one day when he least expects it, put him into the black coffin, place it on my head and fly up to the star. There too blooms the Garden of Paradise, and if he is good and pious, he shall enter; but if his thoughts are wicked and his heart is still full of sin, he will sink deeper with his coffin than Paradise sank, and I shall fetch him up only every thousand years, so that he either sinks still deeper or reaches the star—that star which shines yonder."

The Snowman

"IT is so bitterly cold that my whole body creaks," said the snowman. "The wind is wonderfully invigorating. How that glowing thing up there is staring at me!" He meant the sun, who was just setting. "He shall not make me wink; I will hold the pieces tightly." For you must know that he had two large triangular pieces of red tile in the place of eyes in his head; an old rake represented his mouth and therefore he had also teeth.

He was born amidst the cheering of the boys, and greeted by the tinkling of sledge-bells and the cracking of whips.

The sun set, the full moon rose large, round and clear on the blue sky. "There he is again on the other side!" said the snow-man. Of course he fancied the sun was showing himself again. "I thought I had cured him of staring. Now let him hang there, and give me a light, that I may see myself. I wish I knew how to move, I should so much like to walk about. If I could, I should like to go down and slide on yonder ice, as I have seen the boys do ; but I don't know how—I can't even walk."

"Away, away!" barked the old dog in the yard; he was some-what hoarse, and could no longer well pronounce the proper "Wow, wow." He had become hoarse when he used to live indoors and lie all day long under the warm stove. "The sun will soon teach you how to run; I have seen him teach your predecessor last year, and his predecessors before him. Away, away, they are all gone."

"I do not understand you, friend," said the snowman. "Do you mean to say that she up there is to teach me walking?" He meant the moon. "I have certainly seen her walk a little while ago when I looked her straight in the face, but now she comes creeping from the other side."

"You are dreadfully ignorant," replied the dog, "but that is no wonder, for you have only just been put up. She whom you see up there is the moon; he whom you have seen going off a little while ago was the sun; he is returning to-morrow, and is sure to teach you how to run down into the ditch. We shall soon have a change in the weather, I feel it by the pain I have in my left hind leg; the weather is going to change."

"I do not understand him," said the snowman, "but it strikes me that he speaks of something disagreeable. He who was so staring at me and afterwards went off—the sun, as he calls him—is not my friend; so much I know for certain."

"Away, away," barked the dog; turned three times round him-self, and crept back into his kennel to sleep.

The weather really changed. On the next morning the whole country was enveloped in a dense fog; later on an icy wind began to blow, it was bitter cold; but when the sun rose, what a splendour! Trees and bushes were covered with a hoar-frost, they looked like a wood of white coral; all the branches seemed to be strewed over with shiny white blossoms. The many delicate boughs and twigs, which are in the summer completely hidden by the rich foliage, were all visible now. It looked very much like a snowy white cobweb; every twig seemed to send forth rays of white light. The birch-tree moved its branches in the wind, as the trees do in the summer; it was marvellously beautiful to look at.

And when the sun rose the whole glittered and sparkled as if small diamonds had been strewed over them, while on the snowy carpet below large diamonds or innumerable lights seemed to shine even more white than the snow.

"How charming!" said a young girl who stepped out into the garden with a young man. Both stopped near the snowman, and then looked admiringly at the glittering trees. "There is no more beautiful scene in the summer," she said, and her eyes were beaming. "And we can't possibly have such a fellow there in the summer," replied the young man, pointing at the snowman.

The girl laughed, nodded at the snowman, and then both walked over the snow, so that it creaked under their feet like starch.

"Who were these two?" asked the snowman of the dog. "You are longer in the yard than I; do you know them?"

"Certainly I do," replied the dog. "She has stroked me, and he has given me a meat-bone. I shall never bite those two."

"But what are they?" asked the snowman again.

"Lovers," was the dog's answer. "They are going to live together in one kennel, and gnaw on the same bone. Away, away!"

"Are they beings like ourselves?" asked the snowman.

"They are members of the master's family," replied the dog. "Of course one knows very little if one has only been born yesterday. I can see that from you! I have the age and the knowledge too. I know all in the house. I also knew a time when I was not obliged to be chained up here in the cold. Away, away!"

"The cold is splendid," said the snowman. "Go on, tell me more; but you must not rattle so with the chain, for you make me shudder if you do ."

"Away, away!" barked the dog. "They say I was once a dear little boy. Then I used to lie on a chair covered with velvet, up in the mansion, or sit on the mistress's lap; they kissed me upon the mouth and wiped my paws with an embroidered handkerchief. They called me Ami, dear sweet Ami. But later on I became too big for them, and they gave me to the housekeeper; thus I came down into the basement. You can look in at the window from the place where you are standing. You can look down into the room where I was one day master, for master I was at the housekeeper's. The rooms were not so grand as above in the mansion, but they were more homely; I was not continually touched and pulled about by the children, and the food was just as good, if not better, than at the mansion. I had my own cushion, and there was a stove in the room, which is at this time of the year the best thing in the world. I used to creep under the stove; there was enough room for me. I am still dreaming of this stove. Away, away!"

"Does a stove look nice?" asked the snowman. "Does it resemble me?"

"The very contrary of you! It is as black as a raven and has a long neck with a broad brass band round it. It eats so much fuel that the fire comes out of its mouth. One must keep at its side, close by or underneath it; there one is very comfortable. Perhaps you can see it from your place."

The snowman looked and noticed something, brightly polished with a broad brass band round it; in its lower parts the fire was visible. A strange feeling overcame the snowman; he had no idea what it was, nor could he explain the cause of it; but all beings, even those who are not snowmen, know it.

"Why did you leave her?" asked the snowman, for he had a notion that the stove was a woman. "How could you leave such a place?"

"I was compelled to," replied the dog; "they threw me out of the house and fastened me up here with the chain. I had bitten the youngest son of the squire in the leg, because he pushed away the bone which I was gnawing with his foot. Bone for bone, I think. But this they took very ill of me, and from this time forward I was chained up. And I have lost my voice, too—do you not hear how hoarse I am? Away, away! I can no longer bark like other dogs. Away, away! That was how it ended."

The snowman was no longer listening to him; he looked unswervingly at the basement into the housekeeper's room, where the stove was standing on its four iron legs, as high as the snowman.

"What a strange noise I hear within me," he said. "Shall I never get in there? It is such an innocent wish of mine, and they say innocent wishes are sure to be fulfilled. I must go in there, and lean against her, even if I must break the window."

"You will never get in there," said the dog, "and if you come close to the stove you are gone. Away, away!"

"I am already now as good as gone," replied the snowman, "I believe I am fainting."

The snowman was all day long looking in at the window. In the dawn the room appeared still more inviting; a gentle light shone out of the stove, not like that of the moon or the sun, but such light as only a stove can produce after being filled with fuel. When the door of the room was opened, the flame burst out at the mouth of the stove—that was its custom. And the flame was reflected on the white face and breast of the snowman, and made him appear quite ruddy.

"I can no longer stand it," he said; "how well it suits her to put out her tongue!"

The night was long, but it did not appear so to the snowman, for he was standing there deeply lost in his pleasant thoughts, which were so freezing that it creaked.

In the morning the window-panes of the basement were covered with ice; the most beautiful ice-flowers that one could wish for were upon them; but they concealed the stove.

The ice on the window-panes would not thaw; the snowman could not see the stove which he imagined to be such a lovely woman. It groaned and creaked within him; it was the very weather to please a snowman ; but he did not rejoice—how could he have been happy with this great longing for the stove ?

"That is a dreadful disease for a snowman," said the dog ; "I suffered myself from it one day, but I have got over it." "Away, away !" he barked. "We shall soon have a change in the weather," he added.

The weather changed ; it was beginning to thaw. The warmer it became, the more the snowman vanished away. He said nothing, he did not complain ; that is the surest sign.

One morning he broke down ; and lo! in the place where he had stood, something like a broomstick was sticking in the ground, round which the boys had built him up.

"Well, now I understand why he had such a great longing," said the dog ; "I see there is an iron hook attached to the stick, which people use to clean stoves with ; the snowman had a stove-scraper in his body, that has moved him so. Now all is over. Away, away !"

And soon the winter was gone. "Away, away," barked the hoarse dog, but the girls in the house were singing :

> "*Thyme, green thyme, come out, we sing,*
> *Soon will come the gentle spring ;*
> *Ye willow trees, your catkins don :*
> *The sun shines bright and days roll on.*
> *Cuckoo and lark sing merrily too,*
> *We also will sing Cuckoo ! cuckoo !*"

And nobody thought of the snowman.

Holger Danske

N Denmark, close by the Oeresund, stands the old castle of Kronborg ; hundreds of ships, English, Russian, and Prussian, pass through the sound every day and fire salutes to the old castle—"Boom, boom !"—and the old castle returns their salutes with cannons, for in the language of cannons "Boom" means "Good-day" and "Thank you." In the winter-

THE SLEEP OF HOLGER DANSKE.

time no ships can sail by there, for then the water is frozen right across to the Swedish coast, and has quite the appearance of a high-road. There the Danish and Swedish flags are streaming in the wind, and Danes and Swedes bid each other " Good-day " and " Thank you," not with cannons, but with cordial shaking of hands ; each comes to buy the bread and cake of the other, for you know other people's bread and butter tastes better than one's own. But the old castle of Kronborg is by far the most beautiful sight of all ; there Holger Danske is sitting in a deep, dark cellar, into which nobody can go. He is clad in an armour of iron and steel, and rests his head on his strong arms; his long beard hangs down over the marble table, and has grown through it. He sleeps and dreams, but in his dream he sees all that is going on in Denmark. Every Christmas-eve an angel of God comes to him and tells him that all he has dreamt is true, and that he might go on sleeping, as Denmark is in no real danger; but should it ever get into trouble, the old Holger Danske will rise and burst the table in withdrawing his beard. Then he will strike with his sword, so that the dint of his strokes will be heard through all the countries of the world.

An old grandfather was telling all this about Holger Danske to his little grandson, and the little boy knew that all his grandfather said was true. While the old man spoke he busily carved a large wooden figure, intended to represent Holger Danske and to be fixed to the prow of a ship, for he was a carver in wood—that is to say, a man who carves the figures of persons in wood, which are to be fixed to the fronts of ships according to the names they receive. Now he had carved Holger Danske, who was standing there so proudly with his long beard, holding his broad sword in one hand while the other rested on the Danish arms.

The old man said so much about distinguished Danish men and women that it seemed to his little grandson in the end as if he knew quite as much as Holger Danske, who after all was only dreaming. And when the child was put to bed he thought so much about all he had heard, that he pressed his chin against the counterpane, believing he had a long beard which had grown through it.

The grandfather went on working : he was carving the last part of the figure, the arms of Denmark. When he had finished and looked at the whole and thought of all he had read and heard of, and what he had told his little grandson, he nodded, wiped his spectacles and put them on again, saying: "Well, well, Holger Danske will not come in my lifetime, but the little boy there in bed may have a chance of seeing him one day, when there is really need." The old man nodded again; the more he looked at his figure of Holger Danske, the more he was satisfied with his work; it seemed to him to become coloured, and the armour to gleam like iron and steel; the hearts in the Danish arms turned more and more red, and the lions with the golden crowns on their heads were leaping.*

"Indeed, there is no more beautiful coat of arms in the world," said the old man. "The lions represent strength, the hearts kindness and love!" He looked at the uppermost of the lions and thought of King Canute, who subjected the great England to the Danish throne; the second lion reminded him of Waldemar, who united Denmark and conquered the Wendish territories; when he looked at the third lion he thought of Margaret, who united Denmark with Sweden and Norway. When he looked at the red hearts they seemed to glow more than before; they became flames which moved, and in his mind he followed each of them.

The first flame led him into a narrow dark prison; there sat a prisoner, a beautiful woman, Eleanor Ulfeld,† the daughter of Christian the Fourth, and the flame took the shape of a rose on her bosom, and became one with the heart of this noblest and best of all Danish women.

"That is a heart indeed in Denmark's arms," said the old grandfather. And his mind followed the second flame far out into the sea, where the cannons roared and smoke enveloped the ships; it fixed itself in the shape of the ribbon of an order to the breast

---

* The Danish arms consist of three lions between nine hearts.

† Eleanor was the wife of Corfitz Ulfeld, who was accused of high treason. The only crime of this high-minded woman was her faithful love to her unhappy husband. She passed twenty-two years in a dreadful prison, and was only delivered after the death of her prosecutor, Queen Sophia Amelia.

of Hvitfeld* when he blew himself up with his ship in order to
save the fleet.

The third flame led him to the miserable huts in Greenland,
where the missionary Hans Egede † ruled in word and deed with
love ; the flame became a star on his breast—that was another
heart of the Danish coat of arms.

The old man's mind hastened on in front of the fourth flame ;
he knew where it would go. In the wretched room of a peasant
woman stood Frederick the Sixth, and wrote his name with chalk
on a beam ; the flame was burning on his breast and in his heart,
and there in the peasant's room his heart became a heart of the
Danish arms.

The old man wiped his eyes, for he had known King Frederick
with his silvery locks and honest blue eyes, and loved him ; he
folded his hands and was silent for a moment. Just then the old
man's daughter-in-law entered the room, and said : "It is late ; you
must go to rest ; supper is ready."

"The figure you have carved is very beautiful, Holger Danske,
and our whole old coat of arms," she continued. "I feel as if I
have seen this face before."

"No, that is impossible," said the grandfather; "but I have
seen it, and I have endeavoured to carve it in wood as I have kept
it in my memory. It was when the English were in the port, on
the memorable second of April when we gave proof that we were
all old Danes. On board the *Denmark*, where I fought in the
squadron of Steen Bille, there was a man by my side whom the
balls seemed to fear. He merrily sang old songs and fought as if
he were more than a man. I remember him still very well, but
whence he came and whither he went nobody knows. I have
often thought that he was perhaps Holger Danske himself, who
had swam down from Kronborg in order to help us in the hour
of danger ; that was my idea, and that is his likeness."

* When Hvitfeld's ship, the *Danebrog*, in the battle on the Kjöge Bay,
710, caught fire, this gallant man blew himself up in order to save the
own and the Danish fleet, against which the ship was drifting.

† Hans Egede went in 1721 to Greenland, and worked there as a mission-
ry for fifteen years under very hard conditions.

And the figure cast a great shadow all over the wall and part of the ceiling; it seemed as if the real Holger Danske was casting it, for it moved; but this might also have been caused by the flame, which did not burn steadily.   And the daughter-in-law kissed the old man and led him to the big easy chair near the table; and there she and the old man's son, who was the father of the little boy in bed, had their supper.   The grandfather spoke of the Danish lions and the Danish hearts, of their strength and kindness; he declared that there existed yet another strength besides that of the sword; he pointed to the shelves filled with old books, where Holberg's comedies stood which were so much read and so amusing, it seemed almost as if all the persons of bygone days could be recognised in them.   "He, too, knew how to strike a blow," said the grandfather, "for he ridiculed as much as he could the follies and prejudices of the people."   Then the grandfather nodded towards the looking-glass where the almanac with the picture of the Round Tower * was hanging, and said: "Tycho Brahe was also a man who made use of the sword, not to cut flesh and bone, but to make the path on the sky through the stars more distinct.   And *he*, whose father belonged to my trade, the old wood-carver's son, *he* whom we have often seen with his white curls and broad shoulders, he who is known all over the world—he could shape the stone; but I can only carve wood.   Well, well, Holger Danske can appear in many shapes, so that all the world hears of Denmark's strength.   Let us drink Bertel's † health !"

The little boy in bed saw distinctly the old castle of Kronborg and the Oeresund, the real Holger Danske who was sitting deep below with his beard grown to the marble table and dreaming of all that happens here above.   Holger Danske was also dreaming of the humble little room where the wood-carver sat; he heard all that was said, and nodded in his dream, saying: "Yes, remember me, ye Danish people—keep me in your memory.   I shall return to you in the hour of danger !"

And outside before the Kronborg the bright day shone; the wind carried the sounds of the bugle over from the neighbouring

* Observatory at Copenhagen.
† Bertel Thorwaldsen, the famous sculptor.

country; the ships sailed by and saluted "Boom, boom!" and from the Kronborg it echoed "Boom, boom!" But Holger Danske did not awake, however strong the cannons roared, for it was only "Good day" and "Thank you." They must fire more strongly if they wish to wake him up; but one day he will wake up, for there is still life in Holger Danske.

The Red Shoes

 NCE upon a time there was a little girl, pretty and dainty. But in summer-time she was obliged to go barefooted because she was poor, and in winter she had to wear large wooden shoes, so that her little instep grew quite red.

In the middle of the village lived an old shoemaker's wife; she sat down and made, as well as she could, a pair of little shoes out of some old pieces of red cloth. They were clumsy, but she meant well, for they were intended for the little girl, whose name was Karen.

Karen received the shoes and wore them for the first time on the day of her mother's funeral. They were certainly not suitable for mourning; but she had no others, and so she put her bare feet into them and walked behind the humble coffin.

Just then a large old carriage came by, and in it sat an old lady; she looked at the little girl, and taking pity on her, said to the clergyman, "Look here, if you will give me the little girl, I will take care of her."

Karen believed that this was all on account of the red shoes, but the old lady thought them hideous, and so they were burnt. Karen herself was dressed very neatly and cleanly; she was taught to read and to sew, and people said that she was pretty. But the mirror told her, "You are more than pretty—you are beautiful."

One day the Queen was travelling through that part of the country, and had her little daughter, who was a princess, with her.

All the people, amongst them Karen too, streamed towards the castle, where the little princess, in fine white clothes, stood before the window and allowed herself to be stared at. She wore neither a train nor a golden crown, but beautiful red morocco shoes; they were indeed much finer than those which the shoemaker's wife had sewn for little Karen. There is really nothing in the world that can be compared to red shoes!

Karen was now old enough to be confirmed; she received some new clothes, and she was also to have some new shoes. The rich shoemaker in the town took the measure of her little foot in his own room, in which there stood great glass cases full of pretty shoes and white slippers. It all looked very lovely, but the old lady could not see very well, and therefore did not get much pleasure out of it. Amongst the shoes stood a pair of red ones, like those which the princess had worn. How beautiful they were! and the shoemaker said that they had been made for a count's daughter, but that they had not fitted her.

"I suppose they are of shiny leather?" asked the old lady. "They shine so."

"Yes, they do shine," said Karen. They fitted her, and were bought. But the old lady knew nothing of their being red, for she would never have allowed Karen to be confirmed in red shoes, as she was now to be.

Everybody looked at her feet, and the whole of the way from the church door to the choir it seemed to her as if even the ancient figures on the monuments, in their stiff collars and long black robes, had their eyes fixed on her red shoes. It was only of these that she thought when the clergyman laid his hand upon her head and spoke of the holy baptism, of the covenant with God, and told her that she was now to be a grown-up Christian. The organ pealed forth solemnly, and the sweet children's voices mingled with that of their old leader; but Karen thought only of her red shoes. In the afternoon the old lady heard from everybody that Karen had worn red shoes. She said that it was a shocking thing to do, that it was very improper, and that Karen was always to go to church in future in black shoes, even if they were old.

On the following Sunday there was Communion. Karen looked first at the black shoes, then at the red ones—looked at the red ones again, and put them on.

The sun was shining gloriously, so Karen and the old lady went along the footpath through the corn, where it was rather dusty.

At the church door stood an old crippled soldier leaning on a crutch; he had a wonderfully long beard, more red than white, and he bowed down to the ground and asked the old lady whether he might wipe her shoes. Then Karen put out her little foot too. "Dear me, what pretty dancing-shoes!" said the soldier. "Sit fast, when you dance," said he, addressing the shoes, and slapping the soles with his hand.

The old lady gave the soldier some money and then went with Karen into the church.

And all the people inside looked at Karen's red shoes, and all the figures gazed at them; when Karen knelt before the altar and put the golden goblet to her mouth, she thought only of the red shoes. It seemed to her as though they were swimming about in the goblet, and she forgot to sing the psalm, forgot to say the "Lord's Prayer."

Now every one came out of church, and the old lady stepped into her carriage. But just as Karen was lifting up her foot to get in too, the old soldier said: "Dear me, what pretty dancing shoes!" and Karen could not help it, she was obliged to dance a few steps; and when she had once begun, her legs continued to dance. It seemed as if the shoes had got power over them. She danced round the church corner, for she could not stop; the coachman had to run after her and seize her. He lifted her into the carriage, but her feet continued to dance, so that she kicked the good old lady violently. At last they took off her shoes, and her legs were at rest.

At home the shoes were put into the cupboard, but Karen could not help looking at them.

Now the old lady fell ill, and it was said that she would not rise from her bed again. She had to be nursed and waited upon, and this was no one's duty more than Karen's. But there was a

grand ball in the town, and Karen was invited. She looked at
the red shoes, saying to herself that there was no sin in doing
that; she put the red shoes on, thinking there was no harm
in that either; and then she went to the ball, and commenced to
dance.

But when she wanted to go to the right, the shoes danced to
the left, and when she wanted to dance up the room, the shoes

danced down the room, down the stairs through the street, and
out through the gates of the town. She danced, and was obliged
to dance, far out into the dark wood. Suddenly something shone
up among the trees, and she believed it was the moon, for it was
a face. But it was the old soldier with the red beard; he sat
there nodding his head and said: "Dear me, what pretty dancing
shoes!"

She was frightened, and wanted to throw the red shoes away;
but they stuck fast. She tore off her stockings, but the shoes had
grown fast to her feet. She danced and was obliged to go on
dancing over field and meadow, in rain and sunshine, by night
and by day—but by night it was most horrible.

She danced out into the open churchyard; but the dead there

did not dance. They had something better to do than that. She wanted to sit down on the pauper's grave where the bitter fern grows; but for her there was neither peace nor rest. And as she danced past the open church door she saw an angel there in long white robes, with wings reaching from his shoulders down to the earth; his face was stern and grave, and in his hand he held a broad shining sword.

"Dance you shall," said he, "dance in your red shoes till you are pale and cold, till your skin shrivels up and you are a skeleton! Dance you shall, from door to door, and where proud and wicked children live you shall knock, so that they may hear you and fear you! Dance you shall, dance—— !"

"Mercy!" cried Karen. But she did not hear what the angel answered, for the shoes carried her through the gate into the fields, along highways and byways, and unceasingly she had to dance.

One morning she danced past a door that she knew well; they were singing a psalm inside, and a coffin was being carried out covered with flowers. Then she knew that she was forsaken by every one and damned by the angel of God.

She danced, and was obliged to go on dancing through the dark night. The shoes bore her away over thorns and stumps till she was all torn and bleeding; she danced away over the heath to a lonely little house. Here, she knew, lived the executioner; and she tapped with her finger at the window and said:

"Come out, come out! I cannot come in, for I must dance."

And the executioner said: "I don't suppose you know who I am. I strike off the heads of the wicked, and I notice that my axe is tingling to do so."

"Don't cut off my head!" said Karen, "for then I could not repent of my sin. But cut off my feet with the red shoes."

And then she confessed all her sin, and the executioner struck off her feet with the red shoes; but the shoes danced away with the little feet across the field into the deep forest.

And he carved her a pair of wooden feet and some crutches, and taught her a psalm which is always sung by sinners; she kissed the hand that had guided the axe, and went away over the heath.

"Now, I have suffered enough for the red shoes," she said; "I will go to church, so that people can see me." And she went quickly up to the church-door; but when she came there, the red shoes were dancing before her, and she was frightened, and turned back.

During the whole week she was sad and wept many bitter tears, but when Sunday came again she said: "Now I have suffered and striven enough. I believe I am quite as good as many of those who sit in church and give themselves airs." And so she went boldly on; but she had not got farther than the churchyard gate when she saw the red shoes dancing along before her. Then she became terrified, and turned back and repented right heartily of her sin.

She went to the parsonage, and begged that she might be taken into service there. She would be industrious, she said, and do everything that she could; she did not mind about the wages as long as she had a roof over her, and was with good people. The pastor's wife had pity on her, and took her into her service. And she was industrious and thoughtful. She sat quiet and listened when the pastor read aloud from the Bible in the evening. All the children liked her very much, but when they spoke about dress and grandeur and beauty she would shake her head.

On the following Sunday they all went to church, and she was asked whether she wished to go too; but, with tears in her eyes, she looked sadly at her crutches. And then the others went to hear God's Word, but she went alone into her little room; this was only large enough to hold the bed and a chair. Here she sat down with her hymn-book, and as she was reading it with a pious mind, the wind carried the notes of the organ over to her from the church, and in tears she lifted up her face and said: "O God! help me!"

Then the sun shone so brightly, and right before her stood an angel of God in white robes; it was the same one whom she had seen that night at the church-door. He no longer carried the sharp

sword, but a beautiful green branch, full of roses ; with this he
touched the ceiling, which rose up very high, and where he had
touched it there shone a golden star.   He touched the walls, which
opened wide apart, and she saw the organ which was pealing
forth ; she saw the pictures of the old pastors and their wives,
and the congregation sitting in the polished chairs and singing

from their hymn-books.   The church itself had come to the poor
girl in her narrow room, or the room had gone to the church.   She
sat in the pew with the rest of the pastor's household, and when
they had finished the hymn and looked up, they nodded and said,
"It was right of you to come, Karen."
    "It was mercy," said she.
    The organ played and the children's voices in the choir
sounded soft and lovely.   The bright warm sunshine streamed
through the window into the pew where Karen sat, and her heart
became so filled with it, so filled with peace and joy, that it broke.
Her soul flew on the sunbeams to Heaven, and no one was there
who asked after the *Red Shoes*.

The Little Elder-tree Mother

HERE was once a little boy who had caught cold; he had gone out and got wet feet. Nobody had the least idea how it had happened; the weather was quite dry. His mother undressed him, put him to bed, and ordered the teapot to be brought in, that she might make him a good cup of tea from the elder-tree blossoms, which is so warming. At the same time, the kind-hearted old man who lived by himself in the upper storey of the house came in; he led a lonely life, for he had no wife and children; but he loved the children of others very much, and he could tell so many fairy tales and stories, that it was a pleasure to hear him.

"Now, drink your tea," said the mother; "perhaps you will hear a story."

"Yes, if I only knew a fresh one," said the old man, and nodded smilingly. "But how did the little fellow get his wet feet?" he then asked.

"That," replied the mother, "nobody can understand."

"Will you tell me a story?" asked the boy.

"Yes, if you can tell me as nearly as possible how deep is the gutter in the little street where you go to school."

"Just half as high as my top-boots," replied the boy; "but then I must stand in the deepest holes."

"There, now we know where you got your wet feet," said the old man. "I ought to tell you a story, but the worst of it is, I do not know any more."

"You can make one up," said the little boy. "Mother says you can tell a fairy tale about anything you look at or touch."

"That is all very well, but such tales or stories are worth nothing! No, the right ones come by themselves and knock at my forehead saying: 'Here I am.'"

"Will not one knock soon?" asked the boy; and the mother

smiled while she put elder-tree blossoms into the teapot and poured
boiling water over them. "Pray, tell me a story."

"Yes, if stories came by themselves; they are so proud, they
only come when they please.—But wait," he said suddenly,
"there is one. Look at the teapot; there is a story in it now."

And the little boy looked at the teapot; the lid rose up
gradually, the elder-tree blossoms sprang forth one by one, fresh
and white; long boughs came forth; even out of the spout they
grew up in all directions, and formed a bush—nay, a large elder
tree, which stretched its branches up to the bed and pushed the
curtains aside; and there were so many blossoms and such a
sweet fragrance! In the midst of the tree sat a kindly-looking
old woman with a strange dress; it was as green as the leaves,
and trimmed with large white blossoms, so that it was difficult to
say whether it was real cloth, or the leaves and blossoms of the
elder-tree.

"What is this woman's name?" asked the little boy.

"Well, the Romans and Greeks used to call her a Dryad," said
the old man; "but we do not understand that. Out in the sailors'
quarter they give her a better name; there she is called elder-tree

mother. Now, you must attentively listen to her and look at the beautiful elder tree."

" Just such a large tree, covered with flowers, stands out there ; it grew in the corner of an humble little yard ; under this tree sat two old people one afternoon in the beautiful sunshine. He was an old, old sailor, and she his old wife; they had already great-grandchildren, and were soon to celebrate their golden wedding, but they could not remember the date, and the elder-tree mother was sitting in the tree and looked as pleased as this one here. ' I know very well when the golden wedding is to take place,' she said ; but they did not hear it—they were talking of bygone days.

" ' Well, do you remember ? ' said the old sailor, ' when we were quite small and used to run about and play—it was in the very same yard where we now are—we used to put little branches into the ground and make a garden.'

" ' Yes,' said the old woman, ' I remember it very well; we used to water the branches, and one of them, an elder-tree branch, took root, and grew and became the large tree under which we are now sitting as old people.'

" ' Certainly, you are right,' he said; ' and in yonder corner stood a large water-tub ; there I used to sail my boat, which I had cut out myself—it sailed so well ; but soon I had to sail somewhere else.'

" ' But first we went to school to learn something,' she said, ' and then we were confirmed; we wept both on that day, but in the afternoon we went out hand in hand, and ascended the high round tower and looked out into the wide world right over Copenhagen and the sea ; then we walked to Fredericksburg, where the king and the queen were sailing about in their magnificent boat on the canals.'

" ' But soon I had to sail about somewhere else, and for many years I was travelling about far away from home.'

" ' And I often cried about you, for I was afraid lest you were drowned and lying at the bottom of the sea. Many a time I got up in the night and looked if the weathercock had turned; it turned often, but you did not return. I remember one day distinctly : the rain was pouring down in torrents; the dustman had come to the house where I was in service; I went down with the dust-bin and stood for a moment in the doorway, and looked at the dreadful weather. Then the postman gave me a letter; it was from you. Heavens! how that letter had travelled about. I tore it open and read it; I cried and laughed at the same time, and was so happy! Therein was written that you were staying in the hot countries, where the coffee grows. These must be marvellous countries. You said a great deal about them, and I read all while the rain was pouring down and I was standing there with the dust-bin. Then suddenly some one put his arm round my waist——'

"'Yes, and you gave him a hearty smack on the cheek,' said the old man.

"'I did not know that it was you—you had come as quickly as your letter; and you looked so handsome, and so you do still. You had a large yellow silk handkerchief in your pocket and a shining hat on. You looked so well, and the weather in the street was horrible!'

"'Then we married,' he said. 'Do you remember how we got our first boy, and then Mary, Niels, Peter, John, and Christian?'

"'Oh yes; and now they have all grown up, and have become useful members of society, whom everybody cares for.'

"'And their children have had children again,' said the old sailor. 'Yes, these are children's children, and they are strong and healthy. If I am not mistaken, our wedding took place at this season of the year.'

"'Yes, to-day is your golden wedding-day,' said the little elder-tree mother, stretching her head down between the two old people, who thought that she was their neighbour who was nodding to them; they looked at each other and clasped hands. Soon afterwards the children and grandchildren came, for they knew very well that it was the golden wedding-day; they had already wished them joy and happiness in the morning, but the old people had forgotten it, although they remembered things so well that had passed many, many years ago. The elder tree smelt strongly, and the setting sun illuminated the faces of the two old people, so that they looked quite rosy; the youngest of the grand-children danced round them, and cried merrily that there would be a feast in the evening, for they were to have hot potatoes ; and the elder mother nodded in the tree and cried 'Hooray' with the others."

"But that was no fairy tale," said the little boy who had listened to it.

"You will presently understand it," said the old man who told the story.   "Let us ask little elder-tree mother about it."

"That was no fairy tale," said the little elder-tree mother ; "but now it comes!   Real life furnishes us with subjects for the most wonderful fairy tales; for otherwise my beautiful elder-bush could not have grown forth out of the teapot."

And then she took the little boy out of bed and placed him on her bosom ; the elder branches, full of blossoms, closed over them ; it was as if they sat in a thick leafy bower which flew with them through the air; it was beautiful beyond all description. The little elder-tree mother had suddenly become a charming young girl, but her dress was still of the same green material, covered with white blossoms, as the elder-tree mother had worn ; she had a real elder blossom on her bosom, and a wreath of the same flowers was wound round her curly golden hair; her eyes were so large and so blue that it was wonderful to look at them.   She and the boy kissed each other, and then they were of the same age and felt the same joys.   They walked hand in hand out of the bower, and now stood at home in a beautiful flower garden.   Near the green lawn the father's walking-stick was tied to a post.   There was life in this stick for the little ones, for as soon as they seated themselves upon it the polished knob turned into a neighing horse's head, a long black mane was fluttering in the wind, and four strong slender legs grew out.   The animal was fiery and spirited ; they galloped round the lawn.   "Hoorray! now we shall ride far away, many miles!" said the boy; "we shall ride to the nobleman's estate where we were last year."   And they rode round the lawn again, and the little girl, who, as we know, was no other than the little elder-tree mother, continually cried, "Now we are in the country!   Do you see the farmhouse there, with the large baking stove, which projects like a gigantic egg out of the wall into the road?   The elder tree spreads its branches over it, and the cock struts about and scratches for the hens.   Look how proud he is! Now we are near the church; it stands on a high hill, under the spreading oak trees; one of them is half dead! Now we are at the smithy, where the fire roars and the half-naked men beat with their hammers so that the sparks fly far and wide. Let's be off to the beautiful farm!" And they passed by every-thing the little girl, who was sitting behind on the stick, described, and the boy saw it, and yet they only went round the lawn. Then they played in a side-walk, and marked out a little garden on the ground; she took elder-blossoms out of her hair and planted them, and they grew exactly like those the old people planted when they were children, as we have heard before. They walked about hand in hand, just as the old couple had done when they were little, but they did not go to the round tower nor to the Fredericksburg garden. No; the little girl seized the boy round the waist, and then they flew far into the country. It was spring and it became summer, it was autumn and it became winter, and thousands of pictures reflected themselves in the boy's eyes and heart, and the little girl always sang again, "You will never forget that!" And during their whole flight the elder-tree smelt so sweetly; he noticed the roses and the fresh beeches, but the elder-tree smelt much stronger, for the flowers were fixed on the little girl's bosom, against which the boy often rested his head during the flight.

"It is beautiful here in spring," said the little girl, and they were again in the green beechwood, where the thyme breathed forth sweet fragrance at their feet, and the pink anemones looked lovely in the green moss. "Oh! that it were always spring in the fragrant beechwood!"

"Here it is splendid in summer!" she said, and they passed by old castles of the age of chivalry. The high walls and indented battlements were reflected in the water of the ditches, on which swans were swimming and peering into the old shady avenues. The corn waved in the fields like a yellow sea. Red and yellow flowers grew in the ditches, wild hops and convolvuli in full bloom in the hedges. In the evening the moon rose, large and round, and the hayricks in the meadows smelt sweetly. "One can never forget it!"

"Here it is beautiful in autumn!" said the little girl, and the atmosphere seemed twice as high and blue, while the wood shone with crimson, green, and gold. The hounds were running off, flocks of wild fowl flew screaming over the barrows, while the bramble bushes twined round the old stones. The dark-blue sea was covered with white-sailed ships, and in the barns sat old women, girls, and children picking hops into a large tub; the young ones sang songs, and the old people told fairy tales about goblins and sorcerers. It could no be more pleasant anywhere.

"Here it's agreeable in winter!" said the little girl, and all the trees were covered with hoar-frost, so that they looked like white coral. The snow creaked under one's feet, as if one had new boots on. One shooting star after another traversed the sky. In the room the Christmas tree was lit, and there were song and merriment. In the peasant's cottage the violin sounded, and games were played for apple quarters; even the poorest child said, "It is beautiful in winter!"

And indeed it was beautiful! And the little girl showed everything to the boy, and the elder-tree continued to breathe forth sweet perfume, while the red flag with the white cross was streaming in the wind; it was the flag under which the old sailor had served. The boy became a youth; he was to go out into the wide world, far away to the countries where the coffee grows. But at parting the little girl took an elder-blossom from her breast and gave it to him as a keepsake. He placed it in his prayer-book, and when he opened it in distant lands it was always at the place where the flower of remembrance was lying; and the more he looked at it the fresher it became, so that he could almost smell the fragrance of the woods at home. He distinctly saw the little girl, with her bright blue eyes, peeping out from behind the petals, and heard her whispering, "Here it is beautiful in spring, in summer, in autumn, and in winter," and hundreds of pictures passed through his mind.

Thus many years rolled by. He had now become an old man, and was sitting, with his old wife, under an elder-tree in full bloom. They held each other by the hand exactly as the great-grandfather and the great-grandmother had done outside, and, like them, they talked about bygone days and of their golden wedding. The little girl with the blue eyes and elder-blossoms in her hair was sitting high up in the tree, and nodded to them, saying, "To-day is the golden wedding!" And then she took two flowers out of her wreath and kissed them. They glittered at first like silver, then like gold, and when she placed them on the heads of the old people each flower became a golden crown. There they both sat like a king and queen under the sweet-smelling tree, which looked exactly like an elder-tree, and he told his wife the story of the elder-tree mother as it had been told him when he was a little boy. They were both of opinion that the story contained many points like their own, and these similarities they liked best.

"Yes, so it is," said the little girl in the tree. "Some call me Little Elder-tree Mother; others a Dryad; but my real name is 'Remembrance.' It is I who sit in the tree which grows and grows. I can remember things and tell stories! But let's see if you have still got your flower."

And the old man opened his prayer-book; the elder-blossom was still in it, and as fresh as if it had only just been put in. Remembrance nodded, and the two old people, with the golden crowns on their heads, sat in the glowing evening sun. They closed their eyes and—and——

Well, now the story is ended! The little boy in bed did not know whether he had dreamt it or heard it told; the teapot stood on the table, but no elder-tree was growing out of it, and the old man who had told the story was on the point of leaving the room, and he did go out.

"How beautiful it was!" said the little boy. "Mother, I have been to warm countries!"

"I believe you," said the mother; "if one takes two cups of hot elder-tea it is quite natural that one gets into warm countries!" And she covered him up well, so that he might not take cold. "You have slept soundly while I was arguing with the old man whether it was a story or a fairy tale!"

"And what has become of the little elder-tree mother?" asked the boy.

"She is in the teapot," said the mother; "and there she may remain."

The Darning Needle

HERE was once upon a time a darning needle, which thought itself so fine that it imagined that it ought to be a sewing needle. "Take care that you hold me tightly," said the darning needle to the fingers which took it up. "Do not drop me, for if I fall on the ground one will certainly not find me again, I am so fine!"

"That's what you say," said the fingers, and seized her round the body.

"Look out! I am coming with a suite!" said the darning needle, and dragged a long thread after it; but there was no knot in the thread. The fingers directed the needle straight towards the cook's slipper. The upper leather was torn and had to be mended.

"That's degrading work," said the darning needle; "I shall never get through it; I shall break, I shall break!" And really it broke. "Did I not tell you so?" said the darning needle, "I am too fine."

"Now it's good for nothing," said the fingers; but yet they had to hold it. The cook fixed a knob of sealing-wax to the needle, and fastened her neckerchief with it. "So! now I am a scarf-pin," said the needle. "I knew very well that I should come to honour; when one is worthy one gets on in the world!" And then it laughed to itself; but one never sees when a darning needle laughs. It sat there as proudly as if it was in a state carriage, and looked in all directions.

"May I ask if you are made of gold?" it inquired of a pin, its neighbour. "You have a bright exterior, and a head of your own, although it is but small! You must endeavour to grow, for it is not every one who receives a knob of sealing-wax!" Thus saying, the darning needle raised itself so proudly that it fell out of the neckerchief, straight into the sink which the cook was rinsing down. "Now I am going on my travels," said the darning needle, "I hope I shall not be lost!" But it was lost indeed. "I am too fine for this world," it said, when it was lying in the gutter, "but I know who I am, and that is always a little pleasure." And the darning needle kept its proud bearing, and did not lose its cheerful temper. All sorts of things passed over it; chips, straws, and bits of old newspaper. "Look how they sail," said the darning needle, "they do not know what is underneath them! I am sticking fast here. See, there goes a chip, thinking of nothing in the world but itself—a chip! There is a straw drifting by; how it turns round and round! Don't think only of yourself; you might easily run against a stone. There floats a piece of newspaper; and although what is printed upon it was forgotten long ago, it gives itself airs. I am sitting here patiently and quietly; I know who I am, and that I shall continue to be!"

One day something lay by the side of it which glittered so splendidly that the darning needle thought it was a diamond; but it was only a piece of a broken glass bottle, and because it was so bright the darning needle spoke to it, and introduced itself as a scarf-pin. "I suppose you are a diamond?"—"Yes, something of that kind." And then they both thought each other something very precious; they spoke of the pride of the world.

"I have been in a girl's box," said the darning needle, "and this girl was a cook; she had five fingers on each hand, but I have never seen anything so conceited as these fingers! And yet they were only there to take me out of the box, and put me back again."

"Were they very distinguished?" asked the piece of glass.

"Distinguished!" said the darning needle; "no, but haughty. They were five brothers, all born fingers. They held proudly together, although they were of different lengths. The first, the thumb, was short and thick; it stood out of the rank, and had only one joint in its back and could only make one bow; but it said, if it was cut off a man's hand he could not be a soldier. Sweet-tooth, the second finger, was put into sweet and sour dishes, pointed to the sun and the moon, and made the downstrokes when the fingers wrote. Longman, the third, looked over the heads of all the others. Gold rim, the fourth, wore a golden girdle round the waist; and little Playman did nothing at all, and was proud of it. They did nothing but brag, and therefore I left them."

"And now we sit here and glitter," said the piece of glass. At the same moment more water rushed into the gutter; it overflowed, and carried the piece of glass away. "So, now it is promoted," said the darning needle, "but I remain here; I am too fine; but that is my pride, and I have good reason for it!" And it sat there proudly and had many great thoughts. "I am almost inclined to think I am the child of a sunbeam, I am so fine! It seems to me as if sunbeams were always looking for me here under the water also! I am so fine that my mother cannot find me. If I had my old eye, the one that broke off, I believe I should cry, but I shall not do it—it is not considered good breeding to cry."

One day, a few urchins lay grubbing in the gutter, where they found old nails, farthings, and suchlike treasures. It was dirty work, but it caused them great pleasure. "Oh!" cried one, who had pricked himself with the darning needle, "look, what a fellow."

"I am not a fellow, I am a miss," said the darning needle, but nobody listened to it. The sealing wax had come off and the needle had turned black; but black makes one look thinner, and therefore it thought itself finer than ever.

"Here comes an egg-shell drifting along," said the boys, and they stuck the darning needle firmly into it. "White walls, and I am black myself," said the darning needle; "that is very becoming; now one can see me at least. I wish I may not become seasick and break." But it did not become seasick, nor did it break.

"It is a good thing against seasickness if one has a steel stomach, and does not forget that one is something better than a man. Now my seasickness is past; the finer one is, the more one can bear!"

"Crack," cried the eggshell, as a heavy cart went over it.

"Good heavens!" said the darning needle, "how it presses! Now I shall become seasick after all. I am breaking!"

But it did not break, although the heavy cart passed over it; it lay there full length, and there it may stay.

The Last Dream of the Old Oak

(A CHRISTMAS STORY)

N a wood, high up on the steep shore, near the open sea, stood a very old oak tree. It was three hundred and sixty-five years old, but all this long time had not appeared any longer to the tree than the same number of days to us human beings. We are awake in the daytime, we sleep at night, and then we have our dreams. It is different with a tree; it is awake during three seasons, and only begins to sleep towards the winter. Winter is its resting-time, its night after a long day, consisting of spring, summer, and autumn.

On many a warm summer day the ephemera—the fly that lives but one day—danced round its crown, lived and felt happy in the sunshine, and then the little creature rested a moment in quiet contentment on one of the large fresh oak leaves, and the oak tree would say: "Poor little one! your whole life is but one day! How very short! It is sad indeed!"

"Sad? What do you mean by that?" the ephemera used to ask. "All around me it is so wonderfully light, warm, and beautiful, and that makes me glad."

"But only one day, and then it is all over!"

"Over," repeated the ephemera; "What does *over* mean? Is it not over with you too?"

"No; I live perhaps thousands of your days, and my days consist of entire seasons! That is so long that you are unable to reckon it up!"

"No. I don't understand you! You have thousands of my days, but I have thousands of moments in which I can be merry and happy. Does all the splendour of this world cease to exist when you die?"

"No," said the tree; "that will probably last much longer—indefinitely longer than I am able to imagine."

"But then we have both the same time to live, (
differently." And the ephemera danced and fle\
air, rejoicing in the possession of its wonderful win{
velvet; it enjoyed the warm air, which was satu
spicy fragrance of the clover fields, the dog rose:
honeysuckle, the garden hedges, thyme, the prin
mint. The fragrance was so strong that the ephen
intoxicated with it. The day was long and beaut
and sweet pleasures, and when the sun set the littl(
agreeably tired of all the delight. Its wings wc
support it, and gently and slowly it glided down
blades of grass, nodded as an ephemera can
asleep, peacefully and joyfully. It was dead.
ephemera," said the oak, "that was really too short

The same dance, the same questions and ans'
falling asleep, occurred again on every summer da\
itself through whole generations of ephemeras,
equally merry and happy.

The oak stood awake in the spring, its morning;
midday; and the autumn, its evening; soon its rest
was approaching. The winter was at hand. Alrea
sang "Good night! good night!" Here dropp(
dropped a leaf. "We will stir you and shake you
go to sleep! We shall sing you to sleep, we shall
sleep, and surely it will do your old twigs good; th
with delight and joy. Sleep sweetly! sleep sweet!
three hundred and sixty-fifth night; properly sp(
only a stripling! Sleep sweetly! The clouds w
down and make you a covering to keep your feet
sweetly—and pleasant dreams!"

The oak stood there, deprived of its foliage, to g(
whole long winter and to dream many a dream; al
thing that had happened to it, as in the drea
beings. The large tree was once small—nay, an a
its cradle. According to human calculation, it was
fourth century; it was the largest and best tree in
over-towered by far all the other trees with its crowi

from a great distance out at sea, and served as a landmark to the sailors. Of course, it had no idea that so many eyes looked for it. High up in its green crown the wood-pigeon built her nest, and the cuckoo made its voice heard; and in autumn, when its leaves looked like hammered copper, the birds of passage rested themselves there before they flew across the sea. Now, however, it was winter; the tree stood there without leaves, and one could see how crooked and knotty the branches were that grew out of the stem. Crows and jackdaws came and sat alternately on it while they talked about the hard times which were now beginning, and how difficult it was to find food in the winter.

Towards the holy Christmas time the tree dreamt a most beautiful dream. It had a distinct notion of the festive time, and it seemed to the tree as if all the church bells round about were merrily pealing, and as if all this took place on a bright, mild, and warm summer day. Fresh and green its mighty crown spread forth, the sunbeams were playing between the leaves and branches, the air was filled with the fragrance of herbs and blossoms; coloured butterflies chased each other, the ephemeras danced about as if all was only there for them to enjoy. All the tree had seen happening round it during many years passed before it in a festive procession. It saw the knights and noble ladies of bygone days on horseback, with waving plumes on their heads, the falcons on their wrists, riding through the wood; the bugle sounded, the hounds barked; it saw hostile warriors in coloured garments, with glittering arms, spears, and halberds, pitching tents and striking them again; the watch-fires were burning while they sang and slept under the branches of the oak tree; it saw lovers in quiet happiness meet at its trunk in the moonlight and cut their names, their initials, into the dark-green bark. Guitars and Æolian harps were once—many, many years ago—hung in the branches of the oak by merry travellers; now they were hanging there again, and their wonderful sounds rang forth. The wood-pigeons cooed as if they wished to tell what the tree was feeling, and the cuckoo called out to it how many days it had yet to live. Then the tree felt new life streaming into it, down to the smallest root and high up into the topmost branches and leaves.. It felt how it spread and extended—nay, it felt, by means of its roots, that there was also warmth and life deep below in the earth; its force was increasing, it grew higher and higher, the trunk shot up, there was no resting; more and more it grew, the crown became fuller, spread out, and raised itself, and in measure as the tree grew, its happiness and its longing to reach higher and higher increased, right up to the bright warm sun. It had already grown up into the clouds, which sailed under it like flights of birds of passage, or large white swans. Every leaf of the tree had the gift of sight, as if they had eyes to see. The stars became visible to it in broad daylight; they were large and sparkling, each of them glittered as mildly and clearly as a pair of eyes; they recalled to its memory well-known kind eyes—children's eyes, lovers' eyes— who had met under the tree. It was a marvellous moment, so full of joy and delight! And yet amidst all this joy the tree felt a desire, a longing wish, that all the other trees down in the wood— all the bushes, all the herbs and flowers—might be able to rise with it, see all this splendour, and feel this joy. The great majestic oak, with all its grandeur, was not quite happy without having them all, great and small, around it, and these feelings of longing passed through all the leaves and branches as vigorously as they would pass through a human breast. The crown of the tree was rocking to and fro as if it were seeking something in its deep longing; it was looking back. Then it smelt the fragrance of the thyme, and soon the still stronger scent of the honeysuckle and violet; it seemed as if the cuckoo was answering it.

Yes, through the clouds the green tops of the wood became visible, and below the oak recognised the other trees—how they grew and rose. Bushes and herbs shot high up, several tearing themselves up by the roots and flying up the quicker. The birch tree was the quickest of all; like a white flash of lightning its slender stem shot up in a zigzag line, the branches surrounding it like green gauze and flags. The whole wood, even the brown feathery reed, grew up; the birds followed and sang, and on a long blade of grass which fluttered in the air like a green silk ribbon sat a grasshopper, cleaning his wings with his legs; the cockchafers and the bees were humming; every bird was singing as well as it could; sounds and songs of joy and gladness rose up to heaven.

"But where is the little blue flower that grows near the water," cried the oak, "and the harebell and the little daisy?" Indeed, the old oak wished to have them all around it.

"Here we are! Here we are!" echoed from all sides.

"But where is the beautiful thyme of last summer?—and wasn't there a bed of snowdrops here last year?—and the crab-apple that bloomed so beautifully, and the splendour of the woods during the whole year! Oh! that it were only born now, that it were only here now; then it could be with us!"

"We are here! We are here!" sounded voices still higher, as if they had flown up in advance.

"No! that is too beautiful to be believed!" exclaimed the old oak. "I have them all, both great and small; not one is forgotten! How is all this happiness imaginable? How is it possible?"

"In God's eternal kingdom it is possible and imaginable," sounded through the air.

The old tree, which was incessantly growing, felt its roots tearing themselves away from the earth. "That is right so, that is the best of all," said the old tree. "No fetters are holding me any longer; I can rise to the highest light and splendour, and all my beloved ones are with me, both great and small. All! All!"

That was the dream of the old oak, and while it thus dreamed a terrible storm was raging over land and sea—on holy Christmas Eve. The sea was rolling heavy waves against the shore; the tree, which crackled and groaned, was torn out of the ground by the roots at the very moment when it was dreaming that its roots tore themselves out of the earth. It fell to the ground. Its three hundred and sixty-five years had now passed away like the one day of the ephemera.

On Christmas morn, when the sun rose, the storm had abated. All the church bells were merrily pealing; out of every chimney top, even from the smallest and humblest cottage, the smoke rose up in blue clouds, like the smoke which rose from the altars of the Druids when they offered thankofferings. The sea became gradually calm; and on board a large ship which had been struggling all night with the storm, and happily got through it, all the flags were hoisted as a sign of Christmas joy.

"The tree is gone! The old oak, our landmark on the coast," said the sailors, "it has fallen during last night's storm. Who can replace it? No one!"

Such a funeral oration, short and sincere, was pronounced on the tree, which lay stretched out on the snow near the shore; and over it passed the sound of the psalms from the ship—songs of Christmas joy, and of the redemption of the human soul through Christ, and of eternal life:

> *"Christians, awake! salute the happy morn,*
> *Whereon the Saviour of the world was born;*
> *Rise to adore the mystery of love*
> *Which hosts of angels chanted from above.*
> *Hallelujah, Hallelujah."*

Thus sounded the old hymn, and every one on board the ship felt himself edified by song and prayer, as the old tree had done in its last most beautiful dream, on Christmas morn.

The Wild Swans

AR from here, where the swallows fly when it is winter with us, there lived a king who had eleven sons, and one daughter, called Elise.) The eleven brothers were princes, and went to school with stars on their breasts and swords at their sides. They wrote with diamond pencils on gold slates, and learning by heart came as easy to them as reading; one could see at once that they were princes. Their sister Elise sat upon a little plate-glass stool, and had a picture-book that had been bought for half a kingdom.

Oh, the children were extremely well cared for, but it was not to be always so.   Their father, who was king of the whole country, married a wicked queen, who did not love the poor children at all.   That they found out the very first day.   There were grand doings at the castle, and the children were playing at "visiting"; but instead of having as many cakes and roasted apples as they used to have, the queen gave them only some sand in a teacup and told them they could pretend it was something.

The following week she took little Elise to live with some peasants in the country, and it was not long before she told the king so much that was untrue about the poor princes that he would have nothing more to do with them.

"Go out into the world and gain your own living," said the wicked queen. "Fly, like the great dumb birds!"   But she could not make matters as bad as she wished, for they became eleven beautiful wild swans.

With a strange cry they flew out of the castle windows, far away over the park and into the wood.

It was still early in the morning when they passed the place where their sister Elise lay sleeping in the peasant's hut.   Here they hovered about the roof, stretched their long necks and flapped their wings; but no one heard or saw them.   They were obliged to go farther, high up in the clouds, out into the wide world; so they flew on to a great dark forest which extended as far as the seashore.

Poor little Elise stood in the peasant's hut playing with a green leaf, for she had no other plaything.   She pricked a hole in the leaf, and looking up at the sun through it, she seemed to see her brothers' bright eyes, and whenever the warm sunbeams fell upon her cheeks she thought of all their kisses.

One day passed just like the other.   When the wind blew through the great edge of rose bushes before the house it would whisper to the roses : "Who can be more beautiful than you?" But the roses would shake their heads and say "Elise!"   And when the old woman sat before the door on Sundays reading her hymn-book, the wind would turn over the leaves and say to the book: "Who can be more pious than you?"   And the hymn-book would answer, "Elise." It was the pure truth too, what the roses and the hymn-book said.

When she was fifteen years old she was to go home; and when the queen saw how beautiful she was she disliked her more than ever. She would gladly have changed her into a wild swan like her brothers; but she did not dare to do so at once, because the king wished to see his daughter.

Early in the morning the queen went into the bath, which was built of marble and furnished with soft cushions and the most splendid coverings. She took three toads, and, kissing them, said to one: "Get on Elise's head when she enters the bath, so that she may become dumb like you." "Get on her forehead," she said to the other, "and let her become ugly like you, so that her father may not know her!" "Rest on her heart!" she whispered to the third; "let her become wicked, so that she may be tormented." Putting the toads into the clear water, which immediately turned green, she called Elise, undressed her, and made her get in too. As Elise dived under, one of the toads got into her hair, another upon her forehead, and the third upon her breast. She, however, appeared not to notice them, and as soon as she stood up, three red poppies were floating on the water. Had the creatures not been poisonous and kissed by a witch, they would have been changed into red roses. But having rested on her head, her forehead, and her heart, they were bound to become flowers of some kind. She was too pious and innocent for sorcery to have any power over her.

When the wicked queen saw that, she rubbed Elise all over with walnut juice, so that she became dark brown, smeared an evil-smelling salve over her pretty face and entangled her glorious hair. It was impossible to recognise the beautiful Elise.

When her father saw her he was quite startled, and said she was not his daughter. No one knew her except the watch-dog and the swallows; but they were merely poor animals who had nothing to say.

Then poor Elise wept and thought of her eleven brothers who were all away. She stole out of the castle sorrowfully, and walked the whole day over fields and moors till she reached the great forest. She did not know where to go, but she felt extremely miserable and longed for her brothers: she supposed that they, like her, had been driven out into the world, and she determined to seek and find them.

She had been in the forest only a short time when night came on ; then she entirely lost her way. So she lay down on the soft moss, said her evening prayer, and leaned her head against the stump of a tree. A deep silence reigned, the air was mild, and all around in the grass and in the moss there gleamed, like green fire, hundreds of glow-worms ; when she touched a branch gently with her hand, the glimmering insects fell down upon her like falling stars.

All night long she dreamed of her brothers ; they were playing again as when they were children, writing with the diamond pencils on the golden slates and looking at the beautiful picture-book that had cost half a kingdom. But on the slate they did not make, as formerly, noughts and strokes ; they wrote, instead, of the daring deeds they had done and of all they had seen and gone through. And in the picture-book everything was alive ; the birds sang, and the people came out of the book and spoke to Elise and her brothers. But when she turned over a leaf, they immediately jumped back, so that there should be no confusion.

When she awoke, the sun was already high in the heavens. It is true she could not see it, for the branches of the tall trees were so closely entwined overhead. But the sunbeams played among them like a wavy golden veil, while the foliage gave forth a sweet fragrance and the birds almost sat upon her shoulders. She heard the splashing of water, for there were a number of large springs which all flowed into a lake having the softest sand for its bed. Although thick bushes grew all around it, the deer had made an opening in one place, and through this Elise went down to the water.

It was so clear that if the wind had not moved the branches and bushes one would have believed that they were painted on the surface ; so distinctly was every leaf reflected in it, both those upon which the sun shone and those which were in the shade.

As soon as Elise perceived her own face, she was quite startled, so brown and ugly did it look; but when she wetted her little hand and rubbed her eyes and forehead, her skin appeared as white as before. Then she undressed and got into the fresh water. A more beautiful king's daughter than she could not be found in the wide world.

When she had dressed herself again and plaited her long hair, she went to the bubbling spring, drank out of the hollow of her hand, and wandered far into the forest, without knowing whither. She thought of her brothers, and of the good God who would certainly not forsake her. He had made the wild crab-apples grow to feed the hungry, and now led her to a tree the branches of which bent under the weight of their fruit. Here she made her mid-day meal, put some props under the branches, and then penetrated into the darkest part of the forest. It was so still that she could hear her own footsteps, as well as the rustling of every dry leaf that bent under her feet. Not one bird was to be seen, not a single ray of the sun could penetrate the thick dark foliage. The tall stems stood so close together, that when she looked straight before her, it seemed as if she was enclosed by palisades on all sides. Here was a solitude such as she had never known before.

The night became very dark; not a single little glow-worm glimmered in the moss. Sorrowfully she laid herself down to sleep. Then it seemed to her as though the boughs above her were parted, and the good God looked down upon her with kindness, and little angels peeped out from above and behind Him.

When she awoke in the morning she did not know whether she had dreamed it or whether it had really happened.

After walking a few steps she met an old woman with some berries in her basket; the old woman gave her some of them, and Elise asked whether she had not seen eleven princes riding through the forest.

"No," replied the old woman; "but yesterday I saw eleven swans with golden crowns on their heads swimming in the river close by."

And she led Elise a short distance farther to a slope, at the foot of which a streamlet wound its way. The trees on its banks stretched their long leafy branches out towards each other, and where by their natural growth they could not reach across, the roots had been torn out of the earth, and hung, entwined with the branches, over the water.

Elise bade the old woman farewell, and went along the stream to the place where it flowed out to the great open shore.

The whole glorious sea lay before the young girl, but not one sail appeared upon it: not a single boat was to be seen. How was she to get any farther? She gazed on the innumerable little pebbles on the shore; the water had worn them all smooth and round. Glass, iron stones, everything that was lying washed together there, had received its shape from the water, which was, however, softer than her dainty hand.

"It rolls on unweariedly, and thus it makes hard things smooth. I will be just as indefatigable. Thanks for your lesson, you clear rolling waves; my heart tells me that some day you will carry me to my brothers."

Upon the seaweed that had been washed ashore lay eleven white swans' feathers, which Elise collected into a little bunch. Some drops of water lay upon them: whether they were dewdrops or tears no one could tell. It was very lonely on the sea-shore, but she did not feel it, for the sea afforded constant variety; indeed, more in a few hours than the lovely inland lakes presented in a whole year. When a great black cloud came it seemed as if the sea wished to say: "I can look black too"; and then the wind would blow and the waves turn their white linings outside. But when the clouds shone red, and the winds slept, then the sea was as smooth as a rose-leaf; sometimes green, sometimes white. But however peaceful it might be, there was always a slight movement on the shore; the water would heave gently, like the bosom of a sleeping child.

Just as the sun was about to set, Elise saw eleven wild swans, with golden crowns on their heads, flying towards the land; they flew one behind the other, and looked like a long white ribbon. Then Elise ascended the slope and hid behind a bush; the swans descended close to her and flapped their great white wings.

As the sun sank beneath the water, the swans' feathers suddenly disappeared, and there stood eleven beautiful princes—Elise's brothers.

She uttered a loud cry, for although they had altered very much, she knew that they were, and felt that they must be, her brothers. She sprang into their arms and called them by their names; and

the princes felt very happy when they saw their little sister, and recognised her too, who was now so tall and beautiful. They laughed and wept, and soon they had told each other how wickedly their stepmother had behaved towards them all.

"We brothers," said the eldest, "fly about as wild swans when the sun is in the heavens; as soon as it has set, we again return to our human shape. We therefore have to be very careful to find a safe resting-place by sunset, for if at that time we should be flying up towards the clouds, we should be hurled down into the depths in our human form. We do not live here; there is a country just as beautiful as this across the sea, but it is a long way off. We have to cross the great ocean, and there is no island on our way where we can rest for the night; only one little rock rises up from the waters midway, and that is only just large enough to

VOL. I.

BUT one of them, the youngest remained
behind, and the swan laid his head in her
lap and she stroked his wings; and the
whole day they remained together. 25

accommodate us if we stand very close together. When the sea is very rough, the water dashes up right over us, but still we thank Heaven for this resting-place. There we pass the night in our human form; if it were not for this rock we could never visit our dear native land, for we require two of the longest days in the year for our flight. Only once a year are we permitted to visit our home; we may stay here for eleven days and fly over the great forest from whence we can see the castle in which we were born, and where our father lives, and catch a glimpse of the high church-tower where our mother lies buried. Here it seems as if even the trees and bushes were related to us; here the wild horses career across the steppes as we saw them do in our childhood; here the charcoal-burner sings the old songs to which we danced when children; here is our native land, hither we feel drawn, and here we have found you, dear little sister. We can stay here two days longer; then we must away across the sea to a glorious country, which, however, is not our native land. How can we get you away? We have neither ship nor boat."

"In what manner can I release you?" asked their sister. And they sat talking nearly the whole night, taking only a few hours' slumber. Elise was awakened by the beating of the swans' wings as they rustled above her. Her brothers were again transformed, and flew in great circles, and at last went far away; but one of them, the youngest, remained behind, and the swan laid his head in her lap and she stroked his wings; the whole day they were together. Towards evening the others came back, and when the sun had set they stood there in their natural forms.

"To-morrow we fly away from here, and cannot come back before a whole year has gone by. But we cannot leave you like that. Have you courage to go with us? My arms are strong enough to carry you through the wood; ought not, then, all our wings be strong enough to fly with you across the sea?"

"Yes, take me with you," said Elise.

They were occupied the whole night in making a great strong net out of the pliable willow bark and tough reeds. On this Elise laid herself, and when the sun rose, and her brothers were changed into wild swans, they seized the net with their bills and flew with

their dear sister, who was still asleep, high up towards the clouds.
The sunbeams fell right upon her face, so one of the swans flew
over her head so that his broad wings might overshadow her.

They were far away from land when Elise awoke; she thought
she was still dreaming, so strange did it seem to her to be carried
across the sea, high up in the air. At her side lay a branch with
beautiful ripe berries and a bunch of sweet carrots; the youngest
of her brothers had picked them and laid them there for her. She
smiled at him gratefully, for she recognised him; he it was who
flew over her and shaded her with his wings.

They were so high that the largest ship they saw beneath them
looked like a white sea-gull lying on the water. A large cloud
stood behind them looking just like a mountain, and upon it
Elise saw her own shadow and that of the eleven swans in
gigantic proportions. It was a picture more splendid than she
had ever seen before. But as the sun rose higher and the cloud
remained farther behind, the floating shadow picture vanished.

The whole day they flew on like an arrow rushing through the
air; but they went slower than usual, for now they had their sister
to carry. Bad weather came on and evening drew near; Elise
looked anxiously at the setting sun, and still the lonely rock in the
ocean was not to be seen. It seemed to her as if the swans were
making stronger efforts with their wings. Alas! it was through her
that they did not get along fast enough. When the sun had set
they must become human and fall into the sea and drown. Then
she sent up a prayer to Heaven from the bottom of her heart, bu

still she perceived no rock. The black clouds came nearer, forming themselves into one great threatening wave, which shot forward as if it were of lead, while continuous flashes of lightning lit
up the sky.

The sun was now just at the water's edge. Elise's heart beat
fast; suddenly the swans shot down, and so quickly that she
thought she should fall, but still they sailed on for a little. The
sun was already half below the water when she perceived the little
rock beneath her. It looked no larger than if it were a seal
putting its head above the water. The sun sank very fast; it
looked only like a star as her foot touched the firm ground, and
then it vanished like the last spark in a piece of burnt paper. She
saw her brothers standing arm-in-arm around her, but there was
only just room enough for them and her, not more.

The sea dashed against the rock and covered them with its
spray; the heavens were ablaze with continuous flashes of
lightning, and the thunder rolled in peal upon peal; but sister and
brothers held each other by the hand and sang psalms, from which
they gathered comfort and courage.

In the early dawn the sky was serene and calm; as soon as the
sun rose, the swans flew away with Elise from the island. The
sea still ran high; it seemed to them, high up in the air, as if the
white foam on the dark green sea were millions of swans swimming upon the water.

When the sun rose higher Elise saw before her, half floating in
the air, a mountainous land with shining masses of ice on its
heights; in the middle of it rose a castle quite a mile long, with
row upon row of stately pillars, while beneath waved forests of
palms and gorgeous flowers. She asked whether that was the land
for which they were making; but the swans shook their heads, for
what she beheld was the beautiful but ever-changing castle in the
air of the Fata Morgana; into this they might bring no human
being. As Elise gazed upon it, mountains, woods, and castle fell
into an indistinct heap, and twenty proud churches, all alike, with
tall spires and pointed windows, stood in their place. She thought
she heard the organ pealing, but it was only the sea that she
heard. When she came quite close to the churches they changed

to a whole fleet sailing away beneath her, but when she looked down it was only a sea-mist floating on the water. Thus she had a constant change before her, till, at last, she saw the real land for which they were making; there arose the most beautiful blue mountains with cedar forests, cities, and castles. Long before the sun went down she was sitting on a rock in front of a great cave which was overgrown with delicate green creepers looking like embroidered carpets.

"Now we shall see what you dream of here to-night," said the youngest brother showing her her bedroom.

"Heaven grant that I may dream how I can release you," said she. This thought filled her mind completely, and she fervently prayed to Heaven for help; indeed, even in her sleep she continued to pray. Then it seemed to her as if she were flying high up into the air, to the castle among the clouds of the Fata Morgana; and the fairy came towards her, beautiful and radiant, but still bearing a close resemblance to the old woman who had given her berries in the forest and had told her of the swans with the golden crowns.

"Your brothers can be released," she said, "but have you courage and perseverance? Water is indeed softer than your dainty hands, and yet it changes the shape of stones; but it does not feel the pain which your fingers will feel; it has no heart, and therefore does not suffer the anxiety and torment which you must endure. Do you see the stinging-nettle that I hold in my hand? Many of the same kind grow around the cave in which you sleep; now remember that only that kind, and those which grow upon the graves in the churchyard, are of any use. Those you must pluck, although they will make your hands full of blisters. If you tread these nettles underfoot, you will get flax: of this you must plait and weave eleven shirts of mail with long sleeves; throw these over the eleven swans, and the charm will be broken. But remember that from the moment when you begin this task until it is finished, even if it should take years to do, you may not speak; the first word that you utter will go like a deadly dagger straight to your brothers' hearts. Upon your tongue depends their life. Remember all that I tell you!"

And at the same time she touched her hand with the nettle ; it was like a burning fire, and awoke Elise. It was broad daylight, and close to where she had slept lay a nettle like the one she had seen in her dream. Then she fell upon her knees to offer up her thanks to Heaven, and went out of the cave to begin her task.

With her delicate hands she caught hold of the hateful nettles; they stung like fire and raised great blisters on her hands and arms ; but she would bear it gladly if she could but release her dear brothers. She trod on every nettle with her bare feet and plaited the green flax.

When the sun had gone down her brothers returned and were frightened at finding her so dumb ; they believed it was a new charm of their wicked stepmother. But when they saw her hands they understood what she was doing for their sake. The youngest brother wept, and wherever his tears fell she felt no pain and the burning blisters vanished.

She passed the night at her work, for she could not rest until she had released her dear brothers. The following day, whilst the swans were away, she sat in her solitude ; but never before had the time flown so quickly as now. One shirt of mail was already finished, and now she was beginning the second.

Suddenly a hunting-horn was heard among the hills, and she was seized with fear. The sound came nearer and nearer, and she heard the baying of hounds ; she fled in terror into the cave, and binding the nettles which she had collected and prepared into a bundle, sat down upon it.

Immediately a great dog came leaping up out of the ravine, and soon afterwards another and yet another ; they kept running to and fro, baying loudly. In a few minutes all the huntsmen were before the cave, and the most handsome among them was the king of that country. He went up to Elise, for he had never seen a more beautiful maiden.

" How did you come hither, you lovely child ? " he asked.

Elise shook her head ; she dared not speak, for her brothers' deliverance and life were at stake. She also hid her hands under her apron, so that the king should not see what she had to suffer.

" Come with me ! " he said ; " you shall not stop here. If you are as good as you are beautiful I will clothe you in silk and velvet, place a golden crown upon your head, and you shall live in my grandest castle and reign!" Then he lifted her upon his horse. She wept and wrung her hands, but the king said: "I only wish for your happiness. Some day you will thank me for it." With these words he galloped away across the mountains, holding her before him on his horse, and the hunters galloped behind.

When the sun went down, the beautiful royal city with its churches and cupolas lay before them. The king led her into the castle, where great fountains were splashing in the marble halls, and where walls and ceilings were adorned with paintings. But she had no eyes for all this, she only wept and mourned. She passively allowed the women to dress her in royal robes, to plait pearls in her hair, and to draw on dainty gloves over her blistered fingers.

When she stood there in her splendour she was dazzlingly beautiful, so that the courtiers bowed low before her. The king chose her for his bride, although the archbishop shook his head, and whispered that the beautiful forest maiden was certainly a witch who dazzled the eyes and fooled the heart of the king.

The king, however, did not listen to this, but ordered the music to play, the costliest dishes to be served, and the loveliest maidens to dance before them. And she was led through fragrant gardens into splendid halls, but never a smile came upon her lips or from her eyes: she stood there a picture of grief. Then the king opened a little chamber close by, where she was to sleep; it was hung with costly green tapestry and resembled the cave in which she had been. On the floor lay the bundle of flax which she had made from the nettles, and under the tapestry hung the shirt of mail which she had already completed. All these things one of the huntsmen had taken with him as curiosities.

"Here you can dream yourself back in your former home!" said the king. "Here is the work that occupied you there; now, in the midst of all your splendour it will be pleasant for you to recall that time."

When Elise saw the work she was so anxious about, a smile

played round her mouth and the blood came back to her cheeks. She thought of her brothers' deliverance, and kissed the king's hand, while he pressed her to his heart and had the marriage feast proclaimed by all the church bells. The beautiful dumb maiden out of the wood became queen of the land.

Then the archbishop whispered evil words into the king's ear, but they did not reach his heart. The marriage was to take place; the archbishop himself had to place the crown upon her head, and he maliciously pressed the narrow circlet down tightly upon her brow so that it pained her. But a heavier band encompassed her heart—sorrow for her brothers. She did not feel bodily pain. Her lips were dumb, for a single word would have caused her brothers to die, but her eyes spoke of tender love for the good handsome king who did everything to please her. He became dearer to her from day to day, and oh! how she wished that she could confide in him and tell him of her sorrows. But she was forced to be dumb, and to remain so until she had finished her task. Therefore at night she crept away from his side, went into the little chamber which had been decorated like the cave, and wove one shirt of mail after the other. But when she began the seventh, she had no more flax.

She knew that in the churchyard there grew nettles that she could use; but she must pluck them herself, and how was she to get there?

"Oh, what is the pain in my fingers compared to the torture that my heart endures?" thought she. "I must venture it. Heaven will not withdraw its protection from me."

In fear and trembling, as though what she intended doing were a wicked deed, she crept down into the garden in the moonlight night and went through the lanes and the lonely streets to the churchyard. There she saw a circle of vampires sitting on one of the broadest tombstones. These hideous witches took off their rags, as if they were going to bathe, and then digging up the newly-made graves with their long skinny fingers, they snatched out the corpses with fiendish greed and ate the flesh. Elise had to pass close by them, and they fastened their evil glances upon her; but she prayed quietly, collected the stinging nettles, and carried them home to the castle.

Only one person had seen her; it was the archbishop, for he was awake when other people slept. Now he knew that he was right in his opinion, that all was not with the queen as it should be: she was a witch, and therefore she had cast a spell over the king and the people.

He secretly told the king what he had seen and what he feared. And when the hard words fell from his lips the images of the saints in the church shook their heads as though they wished to say, " It is not so; Elise is innocent! " But the archbishop interpreted it in a different way; in his opinion they bore witness against her and shook their heads at her sins. Then two big tears rolled down the king's cheeks; he went home with doubt in his heart and pretended to be asleep in the night. But no peaceful slumber came to his eyelids, and he noticed that Elise got up. Every night she did the same, and every time he followed her softly and saw her vanish into her room.

From day to day his looks grew darker; Elise saw it, but did not understand the reason; but it made her anxious, and what did she not suffer in her heart for her brothers! Her hot tears fell upon the royal velvet and purple; they lay there like glittering diamonds. And all who saw the rich splendour wished to be queen. In the meantime she had almost finished her work; only one shirt of mail was still wanting, but she had no more flax and not a single nettle. Therefore she was obliged to go once more, for the last time, to the churchyard to pluck a few handfuls. She thought with terror of this lonely walk and of the horrible vampires; but her will was firm as well as her faith in Providence.

Elise went; but the king and the archbishop were following her. They saw her disappear by the gate leading into the churchyard, and when they approached it, they saw the vampires sitting on the tombstone as Elise had seen them; and the king turned aside, for among them he believed her to be whose head had rested on his breast only that evening.

" The people must condemn her," he said: and the people condemned her to be burnt.

Out of the splendid regal halls she was led into a dark damp hole, where the wind whistled in through the grated window; instead of velvet and silk, they gave her the bundle of nettles that she had collected. She could lay her head upon them and the hard stinging coats of mail which she had woven were to be her coverlet. But they could have given her nothing more dear to her; she took up her work again and prayed to Heaven. Outside

the street-boys sang mocking songs about her; not a soul comforted her with a kind word.

Towards evening there was a rustling of swans' wings close to the grating; it was the youngest of her brothers. He had found his sister, and she sobbed aloud for joy, though she knew that the next night would probably be the last she had to live. But now the work was almost ended, and her brothers were here.

The archbishop now came, to be with her in her last hours: that he had promised to the king. But she shook her head and begged him with looks and gestures to go. That night she had to finish her work, otherwise all would have been in vain; the pain, the tears, and the sleepless nights. The archbishop went away with nothing but evil words for her; but poor Elise knew that she was innocent and went on with her work.

The little mice ran about upon the floor and dragged the nettles up to her feet in order to help in some way too, and the thrush sat upon the window grating and sang all night as merrily as it could, so that Elise should not lose courage.

In the morning twilight, about an hour before sunrise, the eleven brothers stood at the castle gate and requested to be taken before the king. They were told that that could not be ; that it was not daylight yet : that the king was asleep and could not be disturbed. They begged and threatened so, that the sentinels came up, and even the king himself came out and asked what the matter was. Just then the sun rose and no brothers were now to be seen, but eleven wild swans flew away over the castle.

The whole people streamed out of the city gates ; they were going to see the witch burnt. A broken-down old horse drew the cart along on which she sat ; they had dressed her in a gown of coarse sackcloth, and her glorious hair hung loose about her beautiful head. Her cheeks were deadly pale ; her lips moved slightly, whilst her fingers were busied with the green flax. Even on the way to her death she did not interrupt the work she had begun ; ten shirts of mail lay at her feet, and she was now working at the eleventh. The mob jeered at her.

" Look at the red witch, how she mutters ! She has no hymn-book in her hand ; no, there she sits with her hideous sorcery—tear it from her into a thousand pieces."

And they all crowded upon her and wanted to tear up the shirts of mail ; then eleven wild swans came flying up and sat round her on the cart, beating their great wings. Now the mob fell back terrified. " It is a sign from heaven ! She cannot be guilty," many whispered. But they did not dare to say so aloud.

As the executioner seized her by the hand she quickly threw the eleven shirts of mail over the swans. Immediately eleven beautiful princes stood there. But the youngest had a swan's wing instead of an arm, for one sleeve was wanting in his shirt of mail—that one she had not quite finished.

" Now I may speak," said she. " I am innocent."

And the people who saw what had happened bowed down before her as before a saint ; she, however, sank lifeless into her brothers' arms, the suspense, anguish, and pain having told upon her.

"Yes, she is innocent," said the eldest brother, and then he related all that had taken place. Whilst he spoke a fragrance as of millions of roses spread itself in the air, for every piece of wood piled around the stake had taken root and was sending out shoots. There stood a fragrant hedge, tall and thick, full of red

roses ; on the top was a flower of dazzling whiteness, gleaming like a star. This the king plucked and placed upon Elise's bosom, whereupon she awoke with peace and happiness in her heart.

All the church bells rang of their own accord and the birds came in great flocks. There was a wedding procession back to the castle such as no king had ever seen.

The Shadow

IN hot countries the sun is very strong; people turn mahogany brown, and in the hottest countries they are even burnt to niggers. This time it was, however, only as far as the hot countries that a learned man from the cold regions had come. He believed that he would be able to walk about there in the same way as he did at home, but he soon found out his mistake. He had to stay at home like other sensible people; the window-shutters and the doors were closed the whole day, and it looked just as if everybody in the house were asleep or had gone out. The narrow street of high houses where he lived was so situated that the sun fell upon it from morning till night, making it really unbearable. The learned man from the cold regions was, although a young man, a wise one; he felt as though he were sitting in a burning oven, and this injured his health, and he became thin. Even his shadow shrivelled up and became smaller than it used to be at home; the sun went so far as to take it away altogether, and it only re-appeared in the evening after that luminary had set. It was a pleasure to see it return. As soon as the light was brought into the room the shadow stretched itself up the wall, and even made itself so tall that it reached the ceiling; it was obliged to stretch itself in order to get its strength back. The learned man used to go out upon the balcony to stretch himself, and as soon as the stars appeared in the beautiful clear sky he seemed to come back to life. People now appeared on all the balconies in the street, and in warm countries there is a balcony before every window, for one must have fresh air even if one is accustomed to getting mahogany brown. Then there was life above and below. Below, all the cobblers and tailors—among whom is included everybody else—came out into the street; they brought out tables and chairs and lights. Thousands of lights were lit. One talked, another sang, and some walked about; carriages passed and mules trotted by, the bells which they wear on their harness tinkling merrily. On one side was heard the chant of a funeral procession, on the other the tolling of the church bells. Yes, there was indeed life in the street at such an hour. Only in one house—the one opposite to which the learned man from the north lived—it was very quiet. And yet somebody lived there, for on the balcony there were flowers which bloomed beautifully even in the heat of the sun; this they could not have done if they had not been watered, and there must have been somebody to do that. Besides, the doors were half opened towards evening; but then it was dark, at least in the front room, while music was heard proceeding from the inner one. The learned stranger thought this music particularly fine, but that might have been only a fancy of his, for he thought everything in these warm countries excellent, with the exception of the sun. The stranger's landlord told him that he did not know who had taken the house opposite; no one had ever been seen, and as to the music, it seemed to him terribly tedious. "It is just as if some one were sitting there practising a piece that he can't play: always the same piece. 'I shall play it after all,' he thinks, but he won't play it, however long he may practise."

One night the stranger awoke. He always slept with the balcony door open; the wind blew aside the curtain hanging before it, and it seemed to him as though there were a strange light coming from the balcony of the house opposite. All the flowers shone like flames of the most beautiful colours, and in the midst of the flowers stood a lovely graceful maiden. She seemed to be all aglow, and it quite dazzled his eyes, but he had opened them too wide, having just woke up out of his sleep. With one jump he was out of bed. Softly he crept behind the curtain; but the maiden was gone, the splendour was gone, and the flowers no longer shone, although they stood there as beautiful as ever. The door was ajar, and from inside came such sweet and lovely music that one could really go into raptures about it. It was like sorcery; but who lived there? Where was the actual entrance? For towards both the street and the side-street the whole of the

ground floor was taken up by shops, and surely people could not
go through these to get upstairs.

One evening the stranger was sitting on his balcony: a light
was burning in the room close behind him, and it was therefore
natural for his shadow to fall upon the wall of the house opposite.
Yes, there it sat, among the flowers on the balcony, and when the
stranger moved the shadow moved too.

"I believe my shadow is the only living thing to be seen over
there," said the learned man. "See how nicely it sits there among
the flowers. The door is only half closed: now my shadow ought
to have the sense to go in, have a look round, and then come
back and tell me what it has seen. "Yes, you would make
yourself useful by doing that," he said in a joke. "Be good
enough to go in. Well, why don't you go?" He then nodded to
the shadow, and the shadow nodded back. "Well, go! but don't
stay away altogether." The stranger got up, and the shadow on
the balcony opposite got up too; the stranger turned round, and
if any one had paid particular attention to it he would have seen
how the shadow went straight through the half-opened balcony
door of the opposite house at the same moment that the stranger
entered his room and let fall the long curtains.

The next morning the learned man went out to get a cup of
coffee and to read the papers. "How's this?" he said when he
came into the sunshine. "I've lost my shadow. Then it really
went away last night and did not come back; this is most
annoying!"

He was vexed; not so much because his shadow was gone, but
because he knew that there was already a story of a man without
a shadow. Everybody in his own country knew that story, and
when he returned home and told his own tale they would say that
it was only an imitation, and he did not care about having that
said of him. He therefore resolved to say nothing about it, which
was very sensible of him.

In the evening he again went out upon his balcony; he had
placed the light just behind him, for he knew that a shadow
always likes to have its master for a screen, but he could not
entice it to come out. He made himself first small and then tall,

but there was no shadow, and there came no shadow. He said
" Hem, hem !" but that was of no use either.

It was very, very vexing ; but in warm countries everything grows
very quickly, and after the lapse of a week he perceived, to his
great joy, that a new shadow was growing out of his legs when he
walked in the sunshine : the roots must therefore have remained.
After three weeks' time he had a tolerable shadow, which
continued to grow during his journey back to the north till it was
at last so tall and so broad that he could well have spared
half of it.

When the learned man came home he wrote books about all
that was true, and good, and beautiful in the world ; and days and
years—many years—passed.

One evening as he was sitting in his room there was a gentle
tap at the door. "Come in," he said ; but as nobody appeared
he got up and opened the door. There stood a man before him
so excessively thin that it made him feel quite queer, but as the
man was also very well dressed he took him to be an important
personage.

" With whom have I the honour of speaking ? " he asked.

" Ah ! " said the fine gentleman, " I hardly expected that you
would recognise me. I have grown so much body that I have
both flesh and clothes. I suppose you never thought of seeing
me in this condition ? Don't you know your old shadow ? You
doubtless never believed that I would ever come back. Things
have gone exceedingly well with me since I saw you last, and I
have amassed fortune in every way. I could easily buy myself
free from servitude if I wished to do so." He rattled a bunch of
valuable seals which hung from his watch, and passed his hand
over the massive gold chain which he wore round his neck. And
how the diamond rings on his fingers glittered ! Everything was
real too !

" I am utterly bewildered ! " said the learned man. " What
does all this mean ? "

" Well, certainly nothing usual," answered the shadow. " But
you are not like ordinary men yourself, and, as you well know, I
have trodden in your footsteps since childhood. As soon as you

thought that I was old enough to go out into the world alone I went my own way, and I am now in brilliant circumstances. But a kind of longing came over me to see you once more before you die, and I wanted to see these places again, for one always loves one's native country. I know that you have grown another shadow; have I anything to pay to it or to you? If so, kindly say so."

"But is it really you?" said the learned man. "It is indeed astonishing. I should never have believed that one could ever see one's old shadow again turned into a human being."

"Do tell me what I have to pay," said the shadow, "for I would not like to be in any one's debt."

"How can you talk like that?" said the learned man. "What debt can there be? You are as free as any one else. I am exceedingly glad of your good fortune. Sit down, my old friend, and just tell me how all this came about, and what you have seen in the warm countries and in that house opposite to which we used to live."

"Well, I will tell you," said the shadow, sitting down; "but you must promise me never to tell any one in the town here, wherever you may meet me, that I was once your shadow. I intend to become engaged; I can support more than one family."

"Have no fear," said the learned man; "I will tell no one who you really are. Here is my hand; I promise it upon my honour as a man!"

"Upon my honour as a shadow!" said the other. He was, of course, obliged to speak like that.

It was, however, most wonderful how much of a human being he had become. He was dressed in the finest black cloth, and wore patent leather boots and an opera hat—that is, a hat which can be closed up till it looks all brim and crown. We will say nothing more of the seals, the gold chain, and the diamond rings, with which we are already acquainted. Yes, the shadow was exceedingly well dressed, and it was, in fact, this that made him look quite like a man.

"Now I will tell you all about it," said the shadow; and then he put down his feet with the patent leather boots as hard as he could on the arm of the learned man's new shadow, which was lying like a dog at his feet. This he did either out of pride or because he thought the new shadow might stick to him. But the shadow lying down remained very still, in order that he might hear all about it : he was also desirous to know how he might free himself and become his own master.

"Do you know who lived in the house opposite us?" said the shadow. "That was the most charming of all! It was Poetry. I was there for three weeks, and that is exactly the same as living three thousand years and reading everything that is composed and written. For this I tell you and it is true : I have seen everything, and I know everything."

"Poetry!" cried the learned man. "It is true she only lives as a hermitess in large cities. Poetry! Yes, I saw her for one short moment, but sleep was still in my eyes ; she was standing on the balcony radiant as the northern lights, in the midst of flowers with living flames. Tell me, tell me! You were on the balcony. You went in at the door and then——"

"Then I found myself in the front room," said the shadow. "You were sitting on the other side and continually looking across into the room. It was not lit up, but there was a kind of twilight ; one door after another stood open in a long row of rooms and halls, and at the end it was so bright that the mass of light would have killed me if I had reached the maiden. But I was prudent ; I took my time, and that one is obliged to do."

"And what did you see then?" asked the learned man.

"I saw everything! And I will tell you all about it ; but—you must really not put it down to pride on my part—as a free man, and considering the knowledge that I possess, to say nothing of my position and circumstances, I wish you would speak to me a little more respectfully."

"I beg your pardon," said the learned man, "but my way of speaking is an old habit, and it is therefore difficult to drop. You are perfectly right, I will think of it in future. But now do tell me all that you saw."

"All," said the shadow, "for I saw all and I know all."

"How did it look in the inner rooms?" asked the learned man.

" Were they like the cool grove? Were they like a holy temple? Were the halls like the starry heavens seen from the mountain-tops?"

" Everything was there," said the shadow. "I certainly did not go right inside, for I remained in the twilight of the outer room, but that was an excellent position. I saw everything and know everything. I have been in the antechamber of the Court of Poetry."

" But what did you see? Did the gods of antiquity pass along the lofty halls? Did you see the combats of the ancient heroes? Did sweet children play there and tell their dreams?"

" I tell you that I was there, and from that you must understand that I saw everything that was to be seen. If you had gone there, you would not have remained a human being, but I became one, and at the same time I obtained a knowledge of my inmost nature, of what is born in me, and the relationship in which I stood to Poetry. When I was still with you I never thought of such things; but you know that whenever the sun rose or set I was often wonderfully tall, and in the moonlight I was almost more notice-able than yourself. At that time I did not understand my inner self; it was made plain to me in the antechamber when I became a human being. I came out fully mature, but you were no longer in the warm countries. I was ashamed of myself to go about as a human being in the condition in which I then was. I wanted boots and clothes and the whole of that human outfit that distin-guishes a man. I made my way—yes, I think I can trust you with this, for you will not put it into a book—I made my way under the cook's cloak; I hid myself under it, and the woman did not know how much she was hiding. It was only in the evening that I went out, and walked about the streets in the moonlight. I stretched myself up along the wall, which tickles one very pleasantly in the back; I ran up and down, looked through the highest windows into grand halls, as well as through the attic windows which nobody could reach, and I saw what no one saw, what no one was supposed to see. It is really a wicked world after all; I would not care to be a man if it were not the generally accepted idea that it is an honour to be one. I saw the most incredible things among men and women, among parents, and 'sweet incomparable children.' I saw what no one knows, but which all would so much like to know : their neighbour's evil deeds. Had I published a newspaper, it would have been read, but I wrote straight to the evil-doers themselves, and in every town I came I created terror. They were so afraid of me that they loved me to excess. Professors made me a professor ; tailors gave me new clothes (I am well provided) ; coiners made money for me ; women said that I was beautiful—and so I became the man I now am. I must now bid you adieu. Here is my card, I live on the sunny side, and am always at home when it rains." And the shadow went.

"That was very remarkable," said the learned man.

Days and years passed away, and the shadow came again.

"How do you do ? " he asked.

"Ah ! " sighed the learned man ; "I am writing about the true, the good, and the beautiful ; but no one cares to hear about such things. I am in despair, for I take it to heart."

"That I never do," said the shadow ; "I grow strong and fat as every one should try to be. You don't understand the world, and that makes you ill—you must travel. I am going to make a tour this summer ; will you go with me ? I should like to have a travelling companion ; will you come as my shadow ? It would be a great pleasure to me, and I will pay your expenses."

"I suppose you are going very far ? " asked the learned man.

"Some might call it so," said the shadow. "A journey will do you a deal of good. Will you be my shadow ? You shall have everything paid for you."

"The idea is too mad," said the learned man.

"But so is the world," said the shadow, "and it will remain so."

With that he went away.

Everything went wrong with the learned man ; sorrow and trouble followed him, and what he wrote about the true, the good, and the beautiful, was like casting pearls before swine. At length he fell ill.

"You really look like a shadow," people said to him, and at

these words a shudder ran through the learned man, for he had his own thoughts on the matter.

"You must go and drink the waters," said the shadow, who one day paid him a visit. "There is no other help for you. I will take you with me for old acquaintance' sake. I will pay your expenses, and you shall write a description of the journey to entertain me on the way. I want to go to a watering-place; my beard does not grow quite as it ought, which is as bad as being ill, for one must have a beard. Now be reasonable, and accept my offer; we will travel as comrades."

And they travelled. The shadow was now master, and the master, shadow. They drove, they rode, and they walked together, sometimes next to each other, sometimes before or behind each other, according to the position of the sun. The shadow always took care to secure the place of honour; the learned man hardly noticed it, for he had a very kind heart and exceedingly mild and friendly manners. One day the master said to the shadow, "As we have become travelling comrades in this way and have also grown up together from childhood, shall we not call each other 'thou'? It sounds so much more familiar."

"What you say," said the shadow, who was now really the master, "is very kind and straightforward; I will now be just as kind and straightforward. You, who are a learned man, know very well how strange nature is. There are some people who cannot bear the smell of brown paper—it makes them ill, while it makes others' flesh creep to hear a pane of glass scratched with a nail; I myself have a similar feeling when I hear you address me as 'thou.' I feel as though I were thrust back into my old position with you—pressed to the earth. You see it is only a matter of feeling, not pride. I cannot let you say 'thou' to me, but I will willingly call you 'thou,' and so your wish will be half fulfilled."

And now the shadow called its former master "thou." "That's rather cool," thought the latter, "that I have to say 'you' to him, while he says 'thou' to me"; but he was obliged to put up with it.

They came to a watering-place where there were a great many

strangers, and among them a very pretty princess whose malady consisted in being too sharp-sighted, which was very alarming.

She at once perceived that the new arrival was quite a different kind of person from all the others. "It is said that he is here to make his beard grow, but I recognise the real cause—he cannot cast a shadow."

Her curiosity now being aroused, she immediately entered into conversation with the stranger on the promenade. Being a king's daughter, it was not necessary for her to make any ceremonies, so she told him straight out: "Your illness consists in your being unable to cast a shadow."

"Your royal highness must be well on the road to recovery," said the shadow. "I know that your illness consists in seeing too sharply, but that is past, and you are cured. I have a very uncommon shadow. Don't you see the person who always walks next to me? Other people have common shadows, but I don't like what is common. People often give their servants better cloth for their liveries than they wear themselves, and so I have allowed my shadow to dress himself up like a man; as you see, I have even given him a shadow. It costs a great deal, but I like to have something uncommon."

"What!" said the princess, "can I be really cured? These baths are the best that exist; the waters have quite marvellous powers nowadays. But I sha'n't go from here yet, for it is only just beginning to be amusing; the strange prince—for he must be a prince—pleases me immensely. I only hope his beard won't grow, for if it does he will be off again."

In the evening the king's daughter danced with the shadow in the great ballroom. She was light, but he was still lighter; she had never seen such a dancer before. She told him from what country she came, and he knew the country; he had been there, but she was away at the time. He had looked through the windows of the castle, both the upper and the lower ones; there he had learnt one thing and another, and could therefore give the princess answers and make allusions that greatly astonished her. She thought he must be the cleverest man in the world, and she conceived a great respect for all that he knew. And when she danced with him again she fell in love with him; and that the shadow perceived very well, for she almost looked him through and through with her eyes. They danced together once more, and she was nearly telling him of her love, but she was judicious, and thought of her country and her kingdom and of the many people over whom she was to reign.

"He is a clever man," she said to herself; "that is good. And he dances excellently; that is good too. But I wonder whether he has good sound knowledge. That is just as important; he must be examined." And she immediately put a difficult question to him which she herself could not have answered; and the shadow pulled a long face.

"You can't answer me that," said the princess.

"I knew that already when I was a child," said the shadow. "I believe even my shadow, standing by the door there, could answer that."

"Your shadow," said the princess; "that would be very strange."

"I don't say for certain that he can," said the shadow, "but I should almost think so. He has followed me now for so many years, and he has heard so much from me, that I should think so. But your royal highness will permit me to draw your attention to the fact that he is so proud of passing for a man that if he is to be put into a good humour—and that he must be to answer correctly—he should be treated just like a human being.

"I like that!" said the princess.

And now she went up to the learned man at the door and spoke with him about the sun and the moon, about the green forests and nations both near and far, and the learned man answered very wisely and well.

"What a man that must be, who has such a clever shadow!" she thought. "It would be a real blessing for my people and my kingdom if I chose him. I will do so!"

And the matter was soon agreed to between the princess and the shadow, but no one was to know anything of it till she had returned to her country.

"No one; not even my shadow," said the shadow, and for that he had special reasons.

They came to the country where the princess ruled when she was at home. "Listen, my friend," said the shadow to the learned man; "now I am as happy and powerful as any one can become, and now I will do something special for you. You shall live with me in the castle, you shall drive with me in the royal carriage, and you shall have a hundred thousand dollars a year; but you must allow yourself to be called a shadow by each and every one, and may never say that you have ever been a man. And then once every year, when I sit in the sun on the balcony to show myself, you must lie at my feet as befits a shadow; for I will tell you that I am going to marry the princess, and the wedding will take place this evening."

"No, that is too mad!" said the learned man. "I won't do it, and I sha'n't do it; why, it means cheating the whole country and the princess too! I'll tell everything: that I am a man, and that you are a shadow merely dressed up in men's clothes."

"No one would believe you," said the shadow. "Be reasonable, or I'll call out the guard."

"I am going straight to the princess!" said the learned man.

"But I shall go first," said the shadow, "and you'll go to prison." And it was so too, for the sentries obeyed the one whom they knew the princess was going to marry.

"You are trembling," said the princess when the shadow came into her room. "Has anything happened? You must not be ill to-day, just as we are going to get married."

"I have experienced the most terrible thing that can happen to one," said the shadow. "Just fancy—such a poor shadow brain cannot stand much—just fancy, my shadow has gone mad; he imagines that he has become a man, and that—only just fancy!— that I am his shadow."

"How terrible!" said the princess. "He is locked up, I suppose?"

"Of course; I fear he will never recover."

"Poor shadow!" cried the princess. "He is very unfortunate; it would be a real kindness to rid him of his life. And if I consider the matter rightly—how in our time the people are only too ready to take the part of the lower against the higher—it appears to me necessary to have him quietly put away."

"That's really hard, for he was a faithful servant," said the shadow, and he pretended to sigh.

"You are a noble character!" said the princess, and bowed before him.

In the evening the whole city was illuminated, and cannon were fired "Boom!"—and the soldiers presented arms. What a wedding it was! The princess and the shadow came out upon the balcony to show themselves and receive another "Hurrah!" The learned man heard nothing of all these festivities, for he was already executed.

The Old Street Lamp

AVE you ever heard the story of the old street lamp? It is not particularly amusing, it is true, but still it is worth hearing for once.

It was a very honest old lamp, that had done its duty for many, many years, but was now to retire from active service. It felt like an old ballet-dancer who dances for the last time, and who on the morrow will sit in her garret forgotten. The lamp was very anxious indeed about the next day, for it knew that it was to appear for the first time in the Town Hall and be examined by the burgomaster and the council to see whether it was fit for further service or not.

It was to be decided whether it was in future to show its light for the inhabitants of one of the suburbs, or in some factory in the country; its way might even lead straight to an iron foundry to be melted down. In the latter case anything might indeed be made of it, but the thought whether it would then retain the recollection of having formerly been a street lamp troubled it terribly. Whatever might happen to it, this much was certain:

that it would be separated from the watchman and his wife, who looked upon it as belonging to their family. When the lamp was hung up for the first time, the watchman was a sturdy young man; it happened at the very same hour when he first entered on his duties. Yes, it was certainly a long time ago, that it became a lamp and he a watchman. The wife was at that time rather proud. Only when she went by in the evening would she deign to notice the lamp; in the daytime, never. But now, of late years, when they all three, the watchman, his wife, and the lamp, had grown old, the wife had also tended it, cleaned it, and provided it with oil. The old couple were thoroughly honest; never had they cheated the lamp of one drop of its proper measure of oil.

It was its last evening in the street, and on the morrow it was to go to the Town Hall; these were two gloomy thoughts. No wonder that it did not burn brightly. But many other thoughts passed through it too. To how much had it lent its light! How much it had seen! Perhaps quite as much as the burgomaster and the council. But it did not give utterance to these thoughts, for it was a good, honest old lamp, which would never have hurt any one, least of all the authorities. It thought of many things, and from time to time its flame flickered up. At such moments it had a feeling that it, too, would be remembered. "There was that handsome young man—it is certainly a long time ago—who had a letter on pink paper with gilt edges. It was so daintily written, as if by a lady's hand. Twice he read it and kissed it and looked up at me with eyes which plainly said, 'I am the happiest of men!' Only he and I knew what was written in this first letter from his love. Yes, there is still another pair of eyes that I remember. It is something wonderful how thoughts jump about. There was a funeral procession in the street; the young beautiful lady lay on a grand hearse in a coffin covered with flowers and wreaths, and the number of torches darkened my light. The people stood in crowds along the houses, and all followed the funeral as it passed. But when the torches were out of my sight and I looked round, a single person still stood leaning against my post, weeping. Never shall I forget those mournful eyes that looked up to me!" These and similar thoughts occupied the old street lamp, which was burning to-day for the last time.

The sentry who is relieved from his post at least knows his successor and may whisper a few words to him. The lamp did not know who was to succeed it, and yet it might have given a few useful hints regarding rain and fog, and some information as to how far the rays of the moon fell upon the pavement, and from what side the wind generally blew, and many other things.

On the bridge of the gutter stood three persons who wished to introduce themselves to the lamp, believing that the latter itself had the bestowal of the office it filled. The first person was a herring's head, which could shine in the dark too. He thought it would be a great saving of oil if he were stuck up on the post. Number two was a piece of rotten wood, which also shines in the dark. It believed itself to be descended from an old stock, once the pride of the forest. The third person was a glow-worm; whence it had come the lamp could not understand, but there it was, and it could give light too. But the rotten wood and the herring's head swore by all that they held sacred that it only gave light at certain times, and could therefore not be taken into account.

The old lamp declared that none of them gave sufficient light to fill the post of a street lamp; but none of them believed that. They were therefore very glad to hear that the office could not be given away by the lamp itself, declaring that it was much too decrepit to choose aright.

At the same moment the wind from the street corner came rushing along and passed through the air-holes of the old lamp. "What do I hear?" he said; "you are going away to-morrow? Do I meet you to-day for the last time? Then I must give you something at parting; I am now going to blow into your brain-box in such a way that in future you will not only be able to remember all that you have seen and heard, but it will be so bright within you that you will be able to see all that is read about, or spoken of, in your presence."

"Oh, that is really much, very much," said the old lamp.

"I thank you heartily. I only hope I shall not be melted down."

"That won't happen just yet," said the wind. "Now I am blowing memory into you ; if you get many presents like that, you will be able to pass your old days very pleasantly."

"I only hope I shall not be melted down," said the lamp. "Or should I, in that case, also retain my memory ? "

"Old lamp, be sensible," said the wind, and blew.

At that moment the moon came out from behind some clouds.

"What do you give the lamp ? " asked the wind.

"I give nothing," answered the moon. "I am on the wane, and the lamps have never given me light; on the contrary, I have often given the lamps light." With these words it again hid itself behind the clouds to escape from further demands.

A drop now fell down upon the lamp as if from the roof; the drop declared that it came from the grey clouds, and that it was also a present, and perhaps the best of all. "I will penetrate you so thoroughly that you will have the power to turn into rust and to crumble away in a single night, if you wish it."

This seemed to be a very bad present to the lamp, and the wind thought the same. "Does no one give any more? Does no one give any more? " he blew as loud as he could.

There fell a bright shooting star, forming one long band of light.

"What was that? " cried the herring's head. "Didn't a star fall down? I verily believe it went into the lamp. Really, if such high-placed personages compete for this post, we may say good night and betake ourselves home."

And they all three did so. The old lamp shed a wonderfully strong light. "That was a splendid present !" it said. "The bright stars, which have always been my greatest joy, and which shine as I have never been able to shine, although I have tried with all my might, have yet noticed me, the poor old lamp, and have sent me a present, consisting in the power of letting those I love see all that I remember, and which I myself see as plainly as if it stood before me. And herein lies true pleasure; for joy that cannot be shared with others is only half joy."

"Such sentiments do you honour," said the wind. "But for that, wax lights will be necessary. If these are not lit up in you, your rare powers will be of no use to others. Do you see?—the stars have not thought of that; they take you and every other light to be wax candles. But I must go down." And the wind went down.

"Good heavens! Wax lights!" said the lamp. "I never had such things till now, and don't suppose I shall get them in the future. I only hope I shall not be melted down."

The next day—well, the next day we shall do better to pass over. The next evening the lamp was reclining in an armchair. Guess where. At the old watchman's. He had begged of the burgomaster and council, in consideration of his long and faithful services, the favour of being allowed to keep the old lamp, which he himself had set up and lit for the first time on his first day of office, four-and-twenty years ago.

He looked upon it as his child, for he had no other; and the lamp was given to him.

Now it lay in the armchair, near the warm stove. It seeemed as if it had got bigger, for it occupied the chair all alone.

The old people sat at supper and cast kindly glances at the old lamp, which they would gladly have given a place at the table.

They certainly only occupied a cellar, six feet below the ground, and one had to go along a stone passage to get to the room. But inside it was very comfortable and warm, strips of cloth having been nailed along the door. Everything was clean and neat; there were curtains round the little bedsteads and before the little windows. On the window-sill stood two curious flower-pots which Christian the sailor had brought from the East and West Indies. They were only of clay, and represented two elephants whose backs were wanting; in their place there sprang up from the earth with which one figure was filled the most beautiful chives: that was the kitchen garden. Out of the other grew a large geranium: that was the flower garden. On the wall hung a large coloured picture: the Congress of Vienna. There they had all the kings and emperors at once. A kitchen clock with heavy weights went "tick, tick," and always went fast too; but the old people thought that this was much better than going slow. They ate their supper, and the street lamp lay, as we have said, in the armchair close to the stove. It seemed to the lamp as if the whole world had been turned round and round. But when the old watchman looked at it and spoke of what they two had gone through together—in

rain and fog, in the short bright summer nights, as well as in the long nights of winter, when the snow came down and one longed to be back in the cellar—then the old lamp felt all right again. It saw everything as plainly as if it were now taking place; yes, the wind had provided it with a capital light.

The old people were very active and industrious; not an hour was spent in idleness. On Sunday afternoons some book or other was brought out—preferably a book of travels. And the old man read aloud of Africa, of the great forests, of the elephants which run about wild; and the old woman listened intently, with stolen glances at the clay elephants which served as flower-pots.

"I can almost picture it to myself," said she. And the lamp heartily wished that a wax candle had been there, and could have been lit up within it; then the old woman could have seen everything to the smallest detail, just as the lamp saw it: the high trees, the branches all closely interwoven, the naked black people on horseback, and bands of elephants trampling down the reeds and bushes with their broad clumsy feet.

"What is now the use of all my powers if I get no wax light?" sighed the lamp. "They have only oil and tallow candles, and that won't do."

One day a great heap of wax candle-ends came down into the cellar; the largest pieces served as lights, the small ones the old woman used for waxing her thread. So there were wax candles enough, but it occurred to no one to put a little piece into the lamp.

"Here stand I with my rare powers," thought the lamp. "I carry everything within me, and cannot let them take part in it; they do not know that I am able to transform bare walls into the most gorgeous tapestries, into the most beautiful woods, into everything they can wish for." The lamp was, however, kept clean, and stood shining in a corner where it caught everybody's eye. Strangers considered it a great piece of rubbish; but the old people did not mind that: they loved the lamp.

One day—it was the old watchman's birthday—the old woman approached the lamp, smiling to herself, and said: "I'll have some illuminations to-day in honour of my old man." And the lamp rattled its metal frame and thought: "Well, at last they have a bright idea." But the idea only went as far as oil, and no wax candle came forth. The lamp burned the whole evening, but now saw only too well that the gift of the star would remain a lost treasure for all its life. Then it had a dream—with such faculties there was, of course, nothing wonderful in that. It seemed to it that the old people were dead, and that it had itself come to the iron foundry to be melted down. It felt quite as terrified as the time when it had to go to the Town Hall to be inspected by the burgomaster and the council. But although the power had been given it to fall into rust and dust at will, still it did not do so. It was put into the furnace and turned into an iron candlestick to hold wax candles—as beautiful a candlestick as any one could wish for. It had received the shape of an angel holding a large bouquet, and in the middle of the bouquet the wax candle was to be placed. The candlestick had a place given to it on a green writing-table. The room was very comfortable: many books stood round it, and the walls were hung with beautiful pictures; it belonged to a poet. Everything that he thought or wrote showed itself round about him. Nature changed itself into thick dark forests, into smiling meadows where the storks strutted about, into a ship on the billowy sea, into the clear sky with all its stars.

"What powers lie in me!" said the old lamp, awakening. "I could almost wish to be melted down. But no! that must not be as long as the old people are alive. They love me for my own sake; they have cleaned me and provided me with oil. I am indeed quite as well off as the whole Congress, in the contemplation of which they also take pleasure."

And since that time it enjoyed more inner peace, and that the honest old street lamp had well deserved.

The Neighbouring Families

NE would have thought that something important was going on in the duck-pond, but it was nothing after all. All the ducks lying quietly on the water or standing on their heads in it—for they could do that—at once swam to the sides; the traces of their feet were seen in the wet earth, and their cackling was heard far and wide. The water, which a few moments before had been as clear and smooth as a mirror, became very troubled. Before, every tree, every neighbouring bush, the old farmhouse with the holes in the roof and the swallows' nest, and especially the great rose-bush full of flowers, had been reflected in it. The rose-bush covered the wall and hung out over the water, in which everything was seen as if in a picture, except that it all stood on its head; but when the water was troubled everything got mixed up, and the picture was gone. Two feathers which the fluttering ducks had lost floated up and down; suddenly they took a rush as if the wind were coming, but

as it did not come they had to lie still, and the water once more became quiet and smooth. The roses were again reflected; they were very beautiful, but they did not know it, for no one had told them. The sun shone among the delicate leaves; everything breathed forth the loveliest fragrance, and all felt as we do when we are filled with joy at the thought of our happiness.

"How beautiful existence is!" said each rose. "The only thing that I wish for is to be able to kiss the sun, because it is so warm and bright. I should also like to kiss those roses down in the water, which are so much like us, and the pretty little birds down in the nest. There are some up above too; they put out their heads and pipe softly; they have no feathers like their father and mother. We have good neighbours, both below and above. How beautiful existence is!"

The young ones above and below—those below were really only shadows in the water—were sparrows; their parents were sparrows too, and had taken possession of the empty swallows' nest of last year, and now lived in it as if it were their own property.

"Are those the ducks' children swimming there?" asked the young sparrows, when they saw the feathers on the water.

"If you must ask questions, ask sensible ones," said their mother. "Don't you see that they are feathers, such as I wear and you will wear too? But ours are finer. Still, I should like to have them up in the nest, for they keep one warm. I am very curious to know what the ducks were so startled about; not about us, certainly, although I did say 'peep' to you pretty loudly. The thick-headed roses ought to know why, but they know nothing at all; they only look at themselves and smell. I am heartily tired of such neighbours."

"Listen to the dear little birds up there," said the roses; "they begin to want to sing too, but are not able to manage it yet. But it will soon come. What a pleasure that must be! It is fine to have such cheerful neighbours."

Suddenly two horses came galloping up to be watered. A peasant boy rode on one, and he had taken off all his clothes except his large broad black hat. The boy whistled like a bird, and rode into the pond where it was deepest, and as he passed the

rose-bush he plucked a rose and stuck it in his hat. Now he
looked dressed, and rode on. The other roses looked after their
sister, and asked each other, "Where can she be going to?"
But none of them knew.

"I should like to go out into the world for once," said one;
"but here at home among our green leaves it is beautiful too.

The whole day long the sun shines bright and warm, and in the
night the sky shines more beautifully still; we can see that
through all the little holes in it."

They meant the stars, but they knew no better.

"We make it lively about the house," said the sparrow-mother;
"and people say that a swallows' nest brings luck; so they are
glad of us. But such neighbours as ours! A rose-bush on the
wall like that causes damp. I daresay it will be taken away;
then we shall, perhaps, have some corn growing here. The roses
are good for nothing but to be looked at and to be smelt, or at
most to be stuck in a hat. Every year, as I have been told by my
mother, they fall off. The farmer's wife preserves them and
strews salt among them; then they get a French name which I
neither can pronounce nor care to, and are put into the fire to

make a nice smell. You see, that's their life; they exist only for the eye and the nose. Now you know."

In the evening, when the gnats were playing about in the warm air and in the red clouds, the nightingale came and sang to the roses that the beautiful was like sunshine to the world, and that the beautiful lived for ever. The roses thought that the nightingale was singing about itself, and that one might easily have believed; they had no idea that the song was about them. But they were very pleased with it, and wondered whether all the little sparrows could become nightingales.

"I understand the song of that bird very well," said the young sparrows. "There was only one word that was not clear to me. What does 'the beautiful' mean?"

"Nothing at all," answered their mother; "that's only something external. Up at the Hall, where the pigeons have their own house, and corn and peas are strewn before them every day—I have dined with them myself, and that you shall do in time, too; for tell me what company you keep and I'll tell you who you are—up at the Hall they have two birds with green necks and a crest upon their heads; they can spread out their tails like a great wheel, and these are so bright with various colours that it makes one's eyes ache. These birds are called peacocks, and that is 'the beautiful.' If they were only plucked a little they would look no better than the rest of us. I would have plucked them already if they had not been so big."

"I'll pluck them," piped the young sparrow, who had no feathers yet.

In the farmhouse lived a young married couple; they loved each other dearly, were industrious and active, and everything in their home looked very nice. On Sundays the young wife came down early, plucked a handful of the most beautiful roses, and put them into a glass of water, which she placed upon the cupboard.

"Now I see that it is Sunday," said the husband, kissing his little wife. They sat down, read their hymn-book, and held each other by the hand, while the sun shone down upon the fresh roses and upon them.

"This sight is really too tedious," said the sparrow-mother, who could see into the room from her nest; and she flew away.

The same thing happened on the following Sunday, for every Sunday fresh roses were put into the glass; but the rose-bush bloomed as beautifully as ever. The young sparrows now had feathers, and wanted very much to fly with their mother; but she would not allow it, and so they had to stay at home. In one of her flights, however it may have happened, she was caught, before she was aware of it, in a horse-hair net which some boys had attached to a tree. The horse-hair was drawn tightly round her leg—as tightly as if the latter were to be cut off; she was in great pain and terror. The boys came running up and seized her, and in no gentle way either.

"It s only a sparrow," they said; they did not, however, let her go, but took her home with them, and every time she cried they hit her on the beak.

In the farmhouse was an old man who understood making soap into cakes and balls, both for shaving and washing. He was a merry old man, always wandering about. On seeing the sparrow which the boys had brought, and which they said they did not want, he asked, "Shall we make it look very pretty?"

At these words an icy shudder ran through the sparrow-mother.

Out of his box, in which were the most beautiful colours, the old man took a quantity of shining leaf-gold, while the boys had to go and fetch some white of egg, with which the sparrow was to be smeared all over; the gold was stuck on to this, and the sparrow-mother was now gilded all over. But she, trembling in every limb, did not think of the adornment. Then the soap-man tore off a small piece from the red lining of his old jacket, and cutting it so as to make it look like a cock's comb, he stuck it to the bird's head.

"Now you will see the gold-jacket fly," said the old man, letting the sparrow go, which flew away in deadly fear, with the sun shining upon her. How she glittered! All the sparrows, and even a crow—and an old boy he was too—were startled at the sight; but still they flew after her to learn what kind of a strange bird she was.

Driven by fear and horror, she flew homeward; she was almost sinking fainting to the earth, while the flock of pursuing birds increased, some even attempting to peck at her.

"Look at her! Look at her!" they all cried.

"Look at her! Look at her!" cried her little ones, as she approached the nest. "That is certainly a young peacock, for it glitters in all colours; it makes one's eyes ache, as mother told us. Peep! that's 'the beautiful'." And then they pecked at the bird with their little beaks so that it was impossible for her to get into the nest; she was so exhausted that she could not even say "Peep!" much less "I am your own mother!" The other birds, too, now fell upon the sparrow and plucked off feather after feather until she fell bleeding into the rose-bush.

"Poor creature!" said all the roses; "only be still, and we will hide you. Lean your little head against us."

The sparrow spread out her wings once more, then drew them closely to her, and lay dead near the neighbouring family, the beautiful fresh roses.

"Peep!" sounded from the nest. "Where can mother be so long? It's more than I can understand. It cannot be a trick of hers, and mean that we are now to take care of ourselves. She has left us the house as an inheritance; but to which of us is it to belong when we have families of our own?"

"Yes, it won't do for you to stay with me when I increase my household with a wife and children," said the smallest.

"I daresay I shall have more wives and children than you," said the second.

"But I am the eldest!" exclaimed the third. Then they all got excited; they hit out with their wings, pecked with their beaks, and flop! one after another was thrown out of the nest. There they lay with their anger, holding their heads on one side and blinking the eye that was turned upwards. That was their way of looking foolish.

They could fly a little; by practice they learned to improve, and at last they agreed upon a sign by which to recognise each other if they should meet in the world later on. It was to be one "Peep!" and three scratches on the ground with the left foot.

The young one who had remained behind in the nest made nimself as broad as he could, for he was the proprietor. But this greatness did not last long. In the night the red flames burst through the window and seized the roof; the dry straw blazed up high, and the whole house, together with the young sparrow, was burned. The two others, who wanted to marry, thus saved their lives by a stroke of luck.

When the sun rose again and everything looked as refreshed as if it had had a quiet sleep, there only remained of the farmhouse a few black charred beams leaning against the chimney, which was now its own master. Thick smoke still rose from the ruins, but the rose-bush stood yonder, fresh, blooming, and untouched, every flower and every twig being reflected in the clear water.

"How beautifully the roses bloom before the ruined house," exclaimed a passer-by. "A pleasanter picture cannot be imagined. I must have that." And the man took out of his portfolio a little book with white leaves: he was a painter, and with his pencil he drew the smoking house, the charred beams and the overhanging chimney, which bent more and more; in the foreground he put the large, blooming rose-bush, which presented a charming view. For its sake alone the whole picture had been drawn.

Later in the day the two sparrows who had been born there came by. "Where is the house?" they asked. "Where is the nest? Peep! All is burned and our strong brother too. That's what he has now for keeping the nest. The roses got off very well; there they still stand with their red cheeks. They certainly do not mourn at their neighbours' misfortunes. I don't want to talk to them, and it looks miserable here—that's my opinion." And away they went.

On a beautiful sunny autumn day—one could almost have believed it was still the middle of summer—there hopped about in the dry clean-swept courtyard before the principal entrance of the Hall a number of black, white, and gaily-coloured pigeons, all shining in the sunlight. The pigeon-mothers said to their young ones: "Stand in groups, stand in groups! for that looks much better."

"What kind of creatures are those little grey ones that run

about behind us?" asked an old pigeon, with red and green in her eyes. "Little grey ones! Little grey ones!" she cried.

"They are sparrows, and good creatures. We have always had the reputation of being pious, so we will allow them to pick up the corn with us; they don't interrupt our talk, and they scrape so prettily when they bow."

Indeed they were continually making three foot-scrapings with the left foot and also said "Peep!" By this means they recognised each other, for they were the sparrows from the nest on the burned house.

"Here is excellent fare!" said the sparrow. The pigeons strutted round one another, puffed out their chests mightily, and had their own private views and opinions.

"Do you see that pouter pigeon?" said one to the other. "Do you see how she swallows the peas? She eats too many, and the best ones too. Curoo! Curoo! How she lifts her crest, the ugly, spiteful creature! Curoo! Curoo!" And the eyes of all sparkled with malice. "Stand in groups! Stand in groups! Little grey ones, little grey ones! Curoo, curoo, curoo!"

So their chatter ran on, and so it will run on for thousands of years. The sparrows ate lustily; they listened attentively, and even stood in the ranks with the others, but it did not suit them at all. They were full, and so they left the pigeons, exchanging opinions about them, slipped in under the garden palings, and when they found the door leading into the house open, one of them, who was more than full, and therefore felt brave, hopped on to the threshold. "Peep!" said he; "I may venture that."

"Peep!" said the other; "so may I, and something more too!" And he hopped into the room. No one was there; the third sparrow, seeing this, flew still farther into the room, exclaiming, "All or nothing! It is a curious man's nest all the same; and what have they put up here? What is it?"

Close to the sparrows the roses were blooming; they were reflected in the water, and the charred beams leaned against the overhanging chimney. "Do tell me what this is. How comes this in a room at the Hall?" And all three sparrows wanted to fly over the roses and the chimney, but flew against a flat wall. It was all a picture, a great splendid picture, which the artist had painted from a sketch.

"Peep!" said the sparrows, "it's nothing. It only looks like something. Peep! that is 'the beautiful.' Do you understand it? I don't."

And they flew away, for some people came into the room.

Days and years went by. The pigeons had often cooed, not to say growled—the spiteful creatures; the sparrows had been frozen in winter and had lived merrily in summer: they were all betrothed, or married, or whatever you like to call it. They had little ones, and of course each one thought his own the handsomest and cleverest; one flew this way, another that, and when they met they recognised each other by their "Peep!" and the three scrapes with the left foot. The eldest had remained an old maid and had no nest nor young ones. It was her pet idea to see a great city, so she flew to Copenhagen.

There was a large house painted in many gay colours standing close to the castle and the canal, upon which latter were to be seen many ships laden with apples and pottery. The windows of the house were broader at the bottom than at the top, and when the sparrows looked through them, every room appeared to them like a tulip with the brightest colours and shades. But in the middle of the tulip stood white men, made of marble; a few were of plaster: still, looked at with sparrows' eyes, that comes to the same thing. Up on the roof stood a metal chariot drawn by metal horses and the goddess of Victory, also of metal, was driving. It was *Thorwaldsen's Museum.*

"How it shines! how it shines!" said the maiden sparrow. "I suppose that is 'the beautiful.' Peep! But here it is larger than a peacock." She still remembered what in her childhood's days her mother had looked upon as the greatest among the beautiful. She flew down into the courtyard: there everything was extremely fine. Palms and branches were painted on the walls, and in the middle of the court stood a great blooming rose-tree spreading out its fresh boughs, covered with roses, over a grave. Thither flew the maiden sparrow, for she saw several of her own kind there. A "peep" and three foot-scrapings—in this way she had often greeted throughout the year, and no one here had responded, for those who are once parted do not meet every day; and so this greeting had become a habit with her. But to-day two old sparrows and a young one answered with a "peep" and the thrice-repeated scrape with the left foot.

"Ah! Good-day! good-day!" They were two old ones from the nest and a little one of the family. "Do we meet here? It's a grand place, but there's not much to eat. This is 'the beautiful.' Peep!"

Many people came out of the side rooms where the beautiful marble statues stood and approached the grave where lay the great master who had created these works of art. All stood with enraptured faces round Thorwaldsen's grave, and a few picked up the fallen rose-leaves and preserved them. They had come from afar: one from mighty England, others from Germany and France. The fairest of the ladies plucked one of the roses and hid it in her bosom. Then the sparrows thought that the roses reigned here, and that the house had been built for their sake. That appeared to them to be really too much, but since all the people showed their love for the roses, they did not wish to be behindhand. "Peep!" they said, sweeping the ground with their tails, and blinking with one eye at the roses, they had not looked at them long before they were convinced that they were their old neighbours. And so they really were. The painter who had drawn the rose-bush near the ruined house, had afterwards obtained permission to dig it up, and had given it to the architect, for finer roses had never been seen. The architect had planted it upon Thorwaldsen's grave, where it bloomed as an emblem of 'the beautiful' and yielded fragrant red rose-leaves to be carried as mememtoes to distant lands.

"Have you obtained an appointment here in the city?" asked the sparrows. The roses nodded; they recognised their grey neighbours and were pleased to see them again. "How glorious it is to live and to bloom, to see old friends again, and happy faces every day. It is as if every day were a festival." "Peep!" said the sparrows. "Yes, they are really our old neighbours; we remember their origin near the pond. Peep! how they have got

on. Yes, some succeed while they are asleep. Ah! there's a
faded leaf; I can see that quite plainly." And they pecked at it
till it fell off. But the tree stood there fresher and greener than
ever; the roses bloomed in the sunshine on Thorwaldsen's grave
and became associated with his immortal name.

The Wicked Prince

THERE lived once upon a time a wicked prince
whose heart and mind were set upon conquer-
ing all the countries of the world, and on
frightening the people; he devastated their
countries with fire and sword, and his soldiers
trod down the crops in the fields and destroyed
the peasants' huts by fire, so that the flames
licked the green leaves off the branches, and the fruit hung dried
up on the singed black trees. Many a poor mother fled, her naked
baby in her arms, behind the still smoking walls of her cottage;
but also there the soldiers followed her, and when they found her,
she served as new nourishment to their diabolical enjoyments;
demons could not possibly have done worse things than these
soldiers! The prince was of opinion that all this was right, and
that it was only the natural course which things ought to take.
His power increased day by day, his name was feared by all, and
fortune favoured his deeds.

He brought enormous wealth home from the conquered towns,
and gradually accumulated in his residence riches which could
nowhere be equalled. He erected magnificent palaces, churches,
and halls, and all who saw these splendid buildings and great
treasures exclaimed admiringly: "What a mighty prince!" But
they did not know what endless misery he had brought upon other
countries, nor did they hear the sighs and lamentations which rose
up from the *débris* of the destroyed cities.

The prince often looked with delight upon his gold and his magnificent edifices, and thought, like the crowd: "What a mighty

prince! But I must have more—much more. No power on earth must equal mine, far less exceed it."

He made war with all his neighbours, and defeated them. The conquered kings were chained up with golden fetters to his chariot when he drove through the streets of his city. These kings had to kneel at his and his courtiers' feet when they sat at table, and live on the morsels which they left. At last the prince had his own statue erected on the public places and fixed on the royal palaces; nay, he even wished it to be placed in the churches, on the altars, but in this the priests opposed him, saying: "Prince, you are mighty indeed, but God's power is much greater than yours; we dare not obey your orders."

"Well," said the prince, "then I will conquer God too." And in his haughtiness and foolish presumption he ordered a magnificent ship to be constructed, with which he could sail through the air; it was gorgeously fitted out and of many colours; like the tail of a peacock, it was covered with thousands of eyes, but each eye was the barrel of a gun. The prince sat in the centre of the ship, and had only to touch a spring in order to make thousands of bullets fly out in all directions, while the guns were at once loaded again. Hundreds of eagles were attached to this ship, and it rose with the swiftness of an arrow up towards the sun. The earth was soon left far below, and looked, with its mountains and woods, like a cornfield where the plough had made furrows which separated green meadows; soon it looked only like a map with indistinct lines upon it; and at last it entirely disappeared in mist and clouds. Higher and higher rose the eagles up into the air; then God sent one of his numberless angels against the ship. The wicked prince showered thousands of bullets upon him, but they rebounded from his shining wings and fell down like ordinary hailstones. One drop of blood, one single drop, came out of the white feathers of the angel's wings and fell upon the ship in which the prince sat, burnt into it, and weighed upon it like thousands of hundredweights, dragging it rapidly down to the earth again; the strong wings of the eagles gave way, the wind roared round the prince's head, and the clouds around— were they formed by the smoke rising up from the burnt cities?—

took strange shapes, like crabs many, many miles long, which stretched their claws out after him, and rose up like enormous rocks, from which rolling masses dashed down, and became fire-spitting dragons.

The prince was lying half-dead in his ship, when it sank at last with a terrible shock into the branches of a large tree in the wood.

"I will conquer God!" said the prince. "I have sworn it: my will must be done!"

And he spent seven years in the construction of wonderful ships to sail through the air, and had darts cast from the hardest steel to break the walls of heaven with. He gathered warriors from all countries, so many that when they were placed side by side they covered the space of several miles. They entered the ships and the prince was approaching his own, when God sent a swarm of gnats—one swarm of little gnats. They buzzed round the prince and stung his face and hands; angrily he drew his sword and brandished it, but he only touched the air and did not hit the gnats. Then he ordered his servants to bring costly coverings and wrap him in them, that the gnats might no longer be able to reach him. The servants carried out his orders, but one single gnat had placed itself inside one of the coverings, crept into the prince's ear and stung him. The place burnt like fire, and the poison entered into his blood. Mad with pain, he tore off the coverings and his clothes too, flinging them far away, and danced about before the eyes of his ferocious soldiers, who now mocked at him, the mad prince, who wished to make war with God, and was overcome by a single little gnat.

The Old House

DOWN yonder in the stree
stood an old, old house
It was almost three hur
dred years old according t
the inscription on one of th
beams, which bore the dat
of its erection surrounded b
tulips and trailing hops. Ther
one could read whole verse
in old-fashioned letters, an
over each window a fac
making all kinds of grimace:
had been carved in the bear

One storey projected a lon
way beyond the other, an
close under the roof was
leaden gutter with a dragon
head.　The rain-water was t
run out of the jaws, but it ra
out of the animal's stomacl
for there was a hole in th
gutter.

All the other houses in th
street were still new and nea
with large window-panes an
smooth walls.　It was plainl
to be seen that they wishe
to have nothing to do with th
old house.　Perhaps they wer
thinking : "How long is th
tumble-down old thing to re
main a scandal to the whol
street?　The parapet project

so far that no one can see from our windows what is going on on the other side. The steps are as broad as those of a castle, and as high as if they led to a church steeple. The iron railings look like the gate of a family vault, and they have brass knobs too. It is really too silly ! "

Opposite, there were some more new neat houses, and they thought just as the others ; but at the window sat a little boy with fresh rosy cheeks and clear sparkling eyes, and he was particularly fond of the old house, both by sunshine and by moonlight. And when he gazed across at the wall where the plaster had fallen off, he could make out the strangest pictures of how the street had formerly looked, with its open staircases, parapets, and pointed gables ; he could see soldiers with halberds, and gutters in the form of dragons and griffins. It was a house worth looking at, and in it lived an old man who went about in leather knee-breeches, and wore a coat with great brass buttons, and a wig which it was easy to see was a real one. Every morning another old man came to clean the place for him and to run on errands. With this exception, the old man in the knee-breeches lived quite alone in the old house. Occasionally he came to the window and looked out, and the little boy would nod to him, and the old man would nod back, and so they became acquainted and became friends, although they had never spoken to each other. But indeed that was not at all necessary.

The little boy once heard his parents say: "The old man opposite is very well off; but he is alone ! "

On the following Sunday the little boy wrapped something up in a piece of paper, went into the street with it, and addressing the old man, who ran errands, said: " Here! will you take this to the old man who lives opposite, from me? I have two tin soldiers ; this is one of them, and he shall have it, because I know he is quite alone."

And the old attendant looked pleased, nodded, and took the tin soldier into the old house. Afterwards word was sent over whether the little boy would not like to come himself and pay a visit. His parents gave him leave to do so, and he went over to the old house.

The brass knobs on the staircase railings shone brighter than ever; one would have thought that they had been polished on account of the visit. And it looked just as if the carved trumpeters—for on the door trumpeters had been carved all in tulips—were blowing with all their might; their cheeks were more blown out than before. Yes, they blew, "Ta-ta-ra-ta! The little boy is coming! Ta-ta-ra-ta!" And then the door opened. The whole hall was hung with old portraits of knights in armour, and ladies in silk dresses; and the armour clattered and the silk dresses rustled. And then came a staircase which went up a long way and then down a little bit, and then one found oneself upon a balcony, which was certainly very rickety, with large holes and long cracks; out of all these grew grass, for the whole balcony, the courtyard, and the wall was so overgrown with green that it looked like a garden; but it was only a balcony. Here stood old flower-pots which had faces and asses' ears; but the flowers grew just as it pleased them. In one pot pinks were growing over on all sides—that is to say, the green part of them—sprout upon sprout. And they said quite plainly: "The air has caressed me, the sun has kissed me and promised me a little flower on Sunday, —a little flower on Sunday."

And then one came to a room where the walls were covered with pigskin, and on the pigskin golden flowers had been stamped.

> "*Gilding fades fast,*
> *But pigskin will last!*"

said the walls.

And there stood chairs with high backs, all carved and with arms on each side. "Sit down," they said. "Oh, how it cracks inside me! I am certainly getting gouty, like the old cupboard. Gout in the back—ugh!"

And then the little boy came to the room where the old man was sitting.

"Thank you for the tin soldier, my little friend," said he, "and thank you for coming over to me."

"Thanks, thanks!" or rather, "Crick, crack!" said all the furniture. There was so much of it that the pieces almost stood in each other's way to see the little boy.

And in the middle of the wall hung a picture of a beautiful lady, of young and cheerful appearance, but dressed in the old-fashioned way, with powdered hair and clothes that stood out stiff. She said neither "Thanks" nor "Crack," but looked down with kind eyes upon the little boy, who immediately asked the old man, "Where did you get her from?"

"From the second-hand dealer over the way," said the old man. "There are always a lot of portraits hanging there; no one knows who they were or troubles about them, for they are all buried. But I knew this lady many years ago, and now she has been dead and gone these fifty years."

And under the portrait hung, in a frame, a bouquet of faded flowers; they were certainly half a century old too—at least they looked so.

And the pendulum of the great clock swung to and fro, and the hands moved, and everything in the room grew older still; but no one noticed it.

"They say at home," said the little boy, "that you are always alone."

"Oh!" replied the old man, "the old thoughts, with all that they bring with them, come and visit me; and now you come too. I am very comfortable, I'm sure!"

And then he took from a shelf a book with pictures; there were long processions and the most wonderful coaches, such as are never seen now-a-days; soldiers like the knave of clubs, and citizens with waving banners. The tailors had a banner with a pair of shears on it, held by two lions, and the shoemakers a banner without any shoes, but with an eagle that had two heads, for shoemakers must have everything in such a way that they can say, "That's a pair!" What a picture-book it was!

The old man went into the next room to get some preserves, apples, and nuts. It was really glorious in the old house.

"I can't stand it any longer!" said the tin soldier, who was standing on the chest of drawers. "It is quite too lonely and dull here. No; when once one knows what family life is, there is no getting accustomed to this kind of thing. I cannot stand it! The day seems already long enough; but the evening is longer still. Here it is not at all like it is at your house, where your father and mother always talked pleasantly, and where you and the other sweet children made a capital noise. Dear me! how lonely it is here at the old man's! Do you think he gets any kisses? Do you think he gets friendly looks or a Christmas tree? He'll get nothing but a grave! I can't stand it!"

"You mustn't look at it from the dark side," said the little boy. "All this seems to me extremely beautiful, and all the old thoughts, with all that they bring with them, come and visit here."

"Yes, but I don't see them and I don't know them," said the tin soldier. "I can't stand it!"

"You must!" said the little boy.

The old man came with a most pleased look on his face, and with the finest preserved fruits and apples and nuts; then the little boy thought no more of the tin soldier.

The little boy came home happy and pleased. Days and weeks passed by, during which there was a great deal of nodding both to and from the old house; then the little boy went across again.

The carved trumpeters blew "Ta-ta-ra-ta! There's the little boy! Ta-ta-ra-ta!" The swords and armour on the old knights' portraits clattered, and the silk dresses rustled; the pigskin told tales, and the old chairs had gout in their backs: "Oh!" It was just like the first time, for over there one day or one hour was just like another.

"I can't stand it!" said the tin soldier. "I have wept tin. It is too dull here. Let me rather go to war and lose my arms and legs. That would be at least a change. I can't stand it! Now I know what it means to be visited by one's old thoughts, with all that they bring with them. I have had visits from mine, and you may believe me, that's no pleasure in the long run. I was at last nearly jumping down from the chest of drawers. I saw you all in the house over there as plainly as if you were really here. It was again Sunday morning, and you children were all standing round the table singing the hymn that you sing every morning. You were standing devoutly with folded hands, and father and mother were also feeling very solemn; then the door opened and your little sister Mary, who is not yet two years old, and who always dances when she hears music and singing, of whatever kind it may be, was brought in. She ought not to have done so, but she began to dance, though she could not get into the right time, for the notes were too long drawn; so she stood first on one leg and held her head forward, but she could not keep it up long enough. You all looked very earnest, though it was rather difficult to do so; but I laughed inwardly, and therefore fell down from the table and got a bump, which I have still. It was certainly not right of me to laugh. All this, and everything else that I have gone through, now passes through me again, and these are, no doubt, the old thoughts with all that they bring with them. Tell me, do you still sing on Sundays? And tell me something about little Mary. And how is my comrade, the other tin soldier? He is certainly a very happy fellow. I can't stand it!"

"You have been given away," said the little boy; "you must stay. Can't you see that?"

Then the old man came with a chest in which there were many things to be seen: little rouge-boxes and scent-boxes and old cards, so large and so thickly gilt as one never sees now-a-days. Many little boxes were opened; the piano too, and on the inside of the lid of this were painted landscapes. But it sounded quite hoarse when the old man played upon it; then he nodded to the portrait that he had bought at the second-hand dealer's, and his eyes sparkled quite brightly.

"I'll go to war! I'll go to war!" cried the tin soldier as loud as he could, and threw himself down upon the floor.

Yes, but where had he gone? The old man looked for him and the little boy looked too, but away he was, and away he stopped. "I'll find him some day," said the old man, but he never did; the flooring was too open and full of holes. The tin soldier had fallen through a crack, and there he now lay as in an open grave.

The day passed, and the little boy came home. Several weeks passed by; the windows were quite frozen up, and the little boy had to breathe upon the panes to make a peep-hole to look at the old house. The snow had blown into all the carvings and inscriptions, and covered the whole staircase, as if there were no one in the house. And there was no one in the house, either : the old man had died ! In the evening a carriage stopped at the door, and upon that he was placed in his coffin ; he was to rest in his family vault in the country. So he was carried away ; but no one followed him, for all his friends were dead. The little boy threw kisses after the coffin as it was driven by.

A few days afterwards an auction was held in the old house, and the little boy saw from his window how the old knights and the old ladies, the flower-pots with the long ears, the chairs and the old cupboards, were carried away. One went this way, another that way ; her portrait, that had been bought from the second-hand dealer went back to his shop, and there it remained hanging, for no one cared about the old picture.

In the spring the old house itself was pulled down ; it was an old piece of lumber, people said. You could see from the street straight into the room with the pigskin wall-covering, which was torn down all in tatters, and the green of the balcony hung in confusion around the beams, which threatened a total downfall. And now the place was cleared up.

"That's a good thing !" said the neighbouring houses.

A noble house was built, with large windows and smooth white walls ; but in front of the place where the old house had stood a little garden was laid out and wild vines crept up the neighbours' wall. Before the garden were placed great iron railings with an iron gate, looking very stately. People remained standing before it and looked through. And the sparrows sat in dozens upon the vine branches, all chattering at once as loud as they could, but not about the old house, for that they could not remember, many years having passed—so many, that the little boy had grown into a man, a sturdy man who was a great joy to his parents. He was just married, and had moved with his wife into the house which had the garden in front of it ; and here he stood beside her while she planted a field flower which she thought very pretty ; she planted it with her little hand, pressing the earth close round it with her fingers. "Oh ! what was that ?" She had pricked herself. Out of the soft ground something pointed was sticking up. It was—just fancy !—the tin soldier, the same that had been lost up at the old man's, that had been roaming about for a long time amongst old wood and rubbish, and that had now lain already many years in the earth.

The young wife first dried the soldier with a green leaf, and then with her dainty handkerchief, which smelt delightfully.

The tin soldier felt just as if he were waking up out of a swoon.

"Let me see him!" said the young man. He smiled and then shook his head. "No, it can hardly be the same one; but it reminds me of the story of a tin soldier which I had when I was a little boy." And then he told his wife about the old house and the old man, and the tin soldier which he had sent across to him because he was so lonely; and the tears came into the young wife's eyes when she heard of the old house and the old man.

"But it is quite possible that this is the very tin soldier!" said she. "I will take care of him and remember what you have told me; but you must show me the old man's grave."

"I don't know where that is," he replied, "and no one knows. All his friends were dead; no one tended it, and I was only a little boy."

"Oh! how lonely he must have been!" said she.

"Yes, very lonely!" said the tin soldier; "but it is glorious not to be forgotten."

"Glorious!" exclaimed a voice close by; but no one except the tin soldier saw that it came from a rag of the pigskin hangings, which had now lost all its gilding. It looked like wet earth; but still it had an opinion which it expressed as follows:

> *"Gilding fades fast,*
> *But pigskin will last!"*

But the tin soldier did not believe it.

The Story of a Mother

MOTHER was sitting by her little child; she was very sad, for she was afraid that it was going to die. Its little face was pale, and the little eyes were closed. The child breathed with difficulty, and at times as deeply as if it were sighing, and the mother looked more and more sadly at the little being. There was a knock at the door, and a poor old man came in wrapped up in a large horse-cloth to keep him warm; he had need of it, too, for it was in the depth of winter. Outside every thing was covered with ice and snow, and the wind blew so keenly that it cut one's face.

As the old man was shivering with cold and the child was asleep for a moment, the woman got up and warmed some beer in the oven in a little pot. The old man sat down and rocked the cradle, while the mother also sat down on an old chair next to him, looking at her sick child, who was breathing so heavily, and holding his little hand.

"You don't think I am going to lose it, do you?" she asked. "Heaven will not take it from me."

The old man—it was Death—nodded his head in such a strange way that it might just as well have meant "Yes" as "No." The mother looked down and tears rolled over her cheeks. Her head began to feel heavy; for three days and three nights she had not closed her eyes, and now she slept, but only for a minute; then she jumped up shivering with cold. "What is it?" she asked, looking all around her; but the old man was gone and her little child too. He had taken it with him. The wheels of the old clock in the corner went whirring round; the heavy leaden weight ran right down to the ground, and then the clock stood still.

The poor mother rushed out of the house, calling for her child.

Outside, in the midst of the snow, sat a woman in long black clothes, who said: "Death has been in your room; I saw him hurry away with your little child. He strides along more quickly than the wind, and never brings back what he has taken."

"Only tell me which way he went," said the mother. "Tell me the way, and I will find him."

A]G.

"I know the way," said the woman in black; "but before I tell it you, you must sing me all the songs you sung to your child. I like those songs; I have heard them before, for I am Night, and saw your tears when you were singing them."

"I will sing them all—all!" said the mother. "But do not detain me now; let me overtake him, so that I may get my child back."

But Night sat dumb and motionless. The mother wrung her hands, singing and weeping. There were many songs, but still more tears. Then Night said: "Go to the right into the dark pine forest; thither I saw Death wend his way with the little child."

In the depths of the forest the road divided, and she did not know in which direction to go. There stood a blackthorn bush, without any leaves, or flowers; for it was winter time, and icicles hung from its boughs.

"Have you seen Death pass by with my little child?"

"Yes," replied the blackthorn bush; "but I shall not tell you which road he took unless you first warm me at your bosom. I am freezing to death here—I am turning into pure ice!"

So she pressed the blackthorn bush close to her bosom in order to thaw it completely. The thorns pierced her flesh and her blood flowed in large drops. But the blackthorn bush put forth fresh green leaves and blossomed in the cold winter's night; so warm is the heart of a sorrowing mother. Then the bush told her which road she was to take.

She came to a great lake upon which there was neither ship nor boat. The lake was not frozen hard enough to bear her, nor was it shallow and even enough for her to wade through it, and yet she must cross it if she wished to find her child. Then she lay down to drink the lake dry, but that was impossible for one person to do. The sorrowing mother, however, thought that perhaps a miracle might be wrought.

"No, that will never do," said the lake. "Let us rather see whether we can come to some agreement. I love to collect pearls, and your eyes are two of the brightest I have ever seen; if you will weep them out into me, I will carry you over to the great hot-house where Death lives and where he grows flowers and trees, each one of which is a human life."

"Oh, what would I not give to get back my child!" said the sobbing mother. She wept still more, and her eyes fell down to the bottom of the lake and became two costly pearls. Then the lake took her up as though she were sitting in a swing, and in one sweep wafted her to the opposite shore, where stood a wonderful house, miles in length. It was difficult to say whether it was a mountain with forests and caves, or whether it had been built. But the poor mother could not see it; she had cried out her eyes.

"Where shall I find Death, who took my little child away?" she asked.

"He has not arrived here yet," said an old grey-haired woman, who was walking to and fro and guarding Death's hothouse. "But how did you find your way here, and who helped you?"

"Heaven has helped me," she answered. "It is merciful, and that you will be too. Where shall I find my little child?"

"I don't know it," said the old woman, "and you can't see. Many flowers and trees have faded during the night, and Death will soon come to transplant them. You know very well that every human being has his tree of life or his flower of life, according to how it has been arranged for each. They look just like other plants, but their hearts beat. Children's hearts can beat too. If you try, perhaps you may be able to recognise the heart-beat of your child. But what will you give me if I tell you what else you must do?"

"I have nothing to give," said the unhappy mother. "But I will go to the end of the world for you."

"I have nothing there for you to do," said the old woman; "but you can give me your long black hair: I daresay you know yourself that it is beautiful; it pleases me. You can have my white locks for it; they are better than nothing."

"Is that all you want?" she said. "I will give you that with pleasure." And she gave her her beautiful hair, receiving for it the snow-white locks of the old woman.

Then they went into Death's great hothouse, where flowers and trees grew strangely intermingled. Here stood some delicate hyacinths under glass bells, and great strong pæonies. There grew water-plants, some quite fresh, others somewhat sickly; water-snakes lay upon them, and black crabs clung fast to the stalks. In another place were splendid palm-trees, oaks, and plantains, parsley and blooming thyme. All the trees and flowers bore names; each one was a human life, and the people they represented were still living, some in China, others in Greenland, and all over the world. There were great trees planted in small pots, so that they were cramped and almost bursting the pots; and there was also many a weakly little flower set in rich mould, with moss all round it, and well taken care of and tended. The anxious mother bent down over all the little plants to hear the human heart beating in each, and from among millions she recognised that of her child.

"There it is!" she cried, and stretched out her hand towards a little crocus, which was feebly hanging over on one side.

"Don't touch the flower!" said the old woman, "but stand here, and when Death comes—I expect him every moment—don't let him tear up the plant, but threaten him that you will do the same with the other flowers: that will frighten him! He is responsible for them to Heaven; not one may be pulled up before permission has been given."

Suddenly an icy blast swept through the hall, and the blind mother felt that it was Death who was approaching.

"How could you find the way here?" he asked. "How were you able to come here more quickly than I?"

"I am a mother!" she replied.

Death stretched out his long hand towards the small delicate flower; but she held her hands firmly round it, held them clasped —oh! so closely, and yet full of anxious care lest she should touch one of the petals. Then Death breathed upon her hands, and she felt that this was colder than the cold wind; and her hands sank down powerless.

"You have no power to resist me!" said Death.

"But Heaven has!" said she.

"I only do its will," said Death. "I am its gardener. I take up all its flowers and trees and transplant them into the great Garden of Paradise, into the Unknown Land. How they thrive there and what that life is like I may not tell you."

"Give me back my child!" said the mother, weeping and imploring.

Suddenly she grasped two pretty flowers firmly in her hands and called out to Death: "I will tear up all your flowers, for I am in despair."

"Do not touch them!" said Death. "You say that you are so

unhappy, and would you now make another mother as unhappy as yourself?"

"Another mother!" exclaimed the poor mother, and immediately let both flowers go.

"Here are your eyes," said Death. "I fished them up out of the lake; they were sparkling brightly at the bottom; I did not know that they were yours. Take them back—they are now even brighter than before—and then look down into this deep well. I will utter the names of the two flowers you were about to tear up, and you will see what you were on the point of destroying."

She looked down into the well; it was a glorious thing to see how one of the lives became a blessing to the world, to see how much happiness and joy diffused itself around it. She also saw the life of the other, which consisted in sorrow and want, trouble and misery.

"Both are the will of God!" said Death.

"Which of them is the flower of unhappiness, and which the blessed one?" she asked.

"That I will not tell you," answered Death; "but this you shall learn from me, that one of the flowers is that of your own child. It was the fate of your child that you saw—the future of your own child."

Then the mother shrieked with terror. "Which of them is that of my child? Tell me that! Liberate the innocent child! Release my child from all this misery! Rather take it away! Take it to the Kingdom of God! Forget my tears, forget my entreaties and all that I have done!"

"I don't understand you," said Death. "Will you have your child back, or shall I take it to that place that you do not know?"

Then the mother wrung her hands, and falling on her knees, prayed to the good God: "Hear me not when I pray contrary to Thy will, for Thy will is ever best! Hear me not! Hear me not!"

Her head sank down upon her breast, and Death went with her child to the Unknown Land.

The Bell

IN the narrow streets of a large town people often heard in the evening, when the sun was setting, and his last rays gave a golden tint to the chimney-pots, a strange noise which resembled the sound of a church bell; it only lasted an instant, for it was lost in the continual roar of traffic and hum of voices which rose from the town. "The evening bell is ringing," people used to say; "the sun is setting!" Those who walked outside the town, where the houses were less crowded and interspersed by gardens and little fields, saw the evening sky much better, and heard the sound of the bell much more clearly. It seemed as though the sound came from a church, deep in the calm, fragrant wood, and thither people looked with devout feelings.

A considerable time elapsed: one said to the other, "I really wonder if there is a church out in the wood. The bell has indeed a strange sweet sound! Shall we go there and see what the cause of it is?" The rich drove, the poor walked, but the way seemed to them extraordinarily long, and when they arrived at a number of willow trees on the border of the wood they sat down, looked up into the great branches and thought they were now really in the wood. A confectioner from the town also came out and put up a stall there; then came another confectioner who hung a bell over his stall, which was covered with pitch to protect it from the rain, but the clapper was wanting.

When people came home they used to say that it had been very romantic, and that really means something else than merely taking tea. Three persons declared that they had gone as far as the end of the wood; they had always heard the strange sound, but there it seemed to them as if it came from the town. One of them wrote verses about the bell, and said that it was like the voice of a mother speaking to an intelligent and beloved child; no tune, he said, was sweeter than the sound of the bell.

The emperor of the country heard of it, and declared that he who would really find out where the sound came from should receive the title of " Bellringer to the World," even if there was no bell at all.

Now many went out into the wood for the sake of this splendid berth ; but only one of them came back with some sort of explanation. None of them had gone far enough, nor had he, and yet he said that the sound of the bell came from a large owl in a hollow tree. It was a wisdom owl, which continually knocked its head against the tree, but he was unable to say with certainty whether its head or the hollow trunk of the tree was the cause of the noise.

He was appointed " Bellringer to the World," and wrote every year a short dissertation on the owl, but by this means people did not become any wiser than they had been before.

It was just confirmation-day. The clergyman had delivered a beautiful and touching sermon, the candidates were deeply moved by it; it was indeed a very important day for them : they were all at once transformed from mere children to grown-up people ; the childish soul was to fly over, as it were, into a more reasonable being.

The sun shone most brightly; and the sound of the great unknown bell was heard more distinctly than ever. They had a mind to go thither, all except three. One of them wished to go home and try on her ball dress, for this very dress and the ball were the cause of her being confirmed this time, otherwise she would not have been allowed to go. The second, a poor boy, had borrowed a coat and a pair of boots from the son of his landlord to be confirmed in, and he had to return them at a certain time. The third said that he never went into strange places if his parents were not with him ; he had always been a good child, and wished to remain so, even after being confirmed, and they ought not to tease him for this; they, however, did it all the same. These three, therefore, did not go; the others went on. The sun was shining, the birds were singing, and the confirmed children sang too, holding each other by the hand, for they had no position yet, and they were all equal in the eyes of God. Two of the smallest soon became tired and returned to the town ; two little girls sat down and made garlands of flowers, they, therefore, did not go on. When the others arrived at the willow trees, where the confectioner had put up his stall, they said : " Now we are out here ; the bell does not in reality exist—it is only something that people imagine ! "

Then suddenly the sound of the bell was heard so beautifully and solemnly from the wood that four or five made up their minds to go still further on. The wood was very thickly grown. It was difficult to advance : wood lilies and anemones grew almost too high ; flowering convolvuli and brambles were hanging like garlands from tree to tree ; while the nightingales were singing and the sunbeams played. That was very beautiful ! But the way was unfit for the girls ; they would have torn their dresses. Large rocks, covered with moss of various hues, were lying about ; the fresh spring water rippled forth with a peculiar sound. " I don't think that can be the bell," said one of the confirmed children, and then he lay down and listened. " We must try to find out if it is ! " And there he remained, and let the others walk on.

They came to a hut built of the bark of trees and branches ; a large crab-apple tree spread its branches over it, as if it intended to pour all its fruit on the roof, upon which roses were blooming ; the long boughs covered the gable, where a little bell was hanging. Was this the one they had heard ? All agreed that it must be so, except one who said that the bell was too small and too thin to be heard at such a distance, and that it had quite a different sound to that which had so touched men's hearts.

He who spoke was a king's son, and therefore the others said that such a one always wishes to be cleverer than other people.

Therefore they let him go alone ; and as he walked on, the solitude of the wood produced a feeling of reverence in his breast ; but still he heard the little bell about which the others rejoiced, and sometimes, when the wind blew in that direction, he could hear the sounds from the confectioner's stall, where the others were singing at tea. But the deep sounds of the bell were much stronger; soon it seemed to him as if an organ played an accompaniment—the sound came from the left, from the side where the heart is. Now something rustled among the bushes, and a little boy stood before the king's son, in wooden shoes and such a short jacket that the sleeves did not reach to his wrists. They knew each other: the boy was the one who had not been able to go with them because he had to take the coat and boots back to his landlord's son. That he had done, and had started again in his wooden shoes and old clothes, for the sound of the bell was too enticing—he felt he must go on.

"We might go together," said the king's son. But the poor boy with the wooden shoes was quite ashamed; he pulled at the short sleeves of his jacket, and said that he was afraid he could not walk so fast; besides, he was of opinion that the bell ought to be sought at the right, for there was all that was grand and magnificent.

"Then we shall not meet," said the king's son, nodding to the poor boy, who went into the deepest part of the wood, where the thorns tore his shabby clothes and scratched his hands, face, and feet until they bled. The king's son also received several good scratches, but the sun was shining on his way, and it is he whom we will now follow, for he was a quick fellow. "I will and must find the bell," he said, "if I have to go to the end of the world."

Ugly monkeys sat high in the branches and clenched their teeth. "Shall we beat him?" they said. "Shall we thrash him? He is a king's son!"

But he walked on undaunted, deeper and deeper into the wood, where the most wonderful flowers were growing; there were standing white star lilies with blood-red stamens, sky-blue tulips shining when the wind moved them; apple-trees covered with apples like large glittering soap bubbles: only think how resplendent these trees were in the sunshine! All around were beautiful green meadows, where hart and hind played in the grass. There grew magnificent oaks and beech-trees; and if the bark was split of any of them, long blades of grass grew out of the clefts; there were also large smooth lakes in the wood, on which the swans were swimming about and flapping their wings. The king's son often stood still and listened; sometimes he thought that the sound of the bell rose up to him out of one of these deep lakes, but soon he found that this was a mistake, and that the bell was ringing still farther in the wood. Then the sun set, the clouds were as red as fire; it became quiet in the wood; he sank down on his knees, sang an evening hymn and said: "I shall never find what I am looking for! Now the sun is setting, and the night, the dark night, is approaching. Yet I may perhaps see the round sun once more before he disappears beneath the horizon. I will climb up these rocks, they are as high as the highest trees!" And then, taking hold of the creepers and roots, he climbed up on the wet stones, where water-snakes were wriggling and the toads, as it were, barked at him: he reached the top before the sun, seen from such a height, had quite set. "Oh, what a splendour!" The sea, the great majestic sea, which was rolling its long waves against the shore, stretched out before him, and the sun was standing like a large bright altar out there where sea and heaven met—all melted together in the most glowing colours; the wood was singing, and his heart too. The whole of nature was one large holy church, in which the trees and hovering clouds formed the pillars, the flowers and grass the woven velvet carpet, and heaven itself was the great cupola; up there the flame colour vanished as soon as the sun disappeared, but millions of stars were lighted; diamond lamps were shining, and the king's son stretched his arms out towards heaven, towards the sea, and towards the wood. Then suddenly the poor boy with the short-sleeved jacket and the wooden shoes appeared; he had arrived just as quickly on the road he had chosen. And they ran towards each other and took one another's hand, in the great cathedral of nature and poesy, and above them sounded the invisible holy bell; happy spirits surrounded them, singing hallelujahs and rejoicing.

The Girl who Trod on the Loaf of Bread

HE story of the girl who trod on a loaf of bread in order to avoid soiling her shoes, and how she was punished for it, is well known; it is written down—nay, even printed. Ingé was the girl's name; she was a poor child, but proud and haughty; there was a bad foundation in her, as the saying is. Already, when quite a small child, it amused her greatly to catch flies, pull their wings off, and to transform them into creeping things. Later on she took cockchafers and beetles, stuck them on a needle, and held a green leaf or a little piece of paper close to their feet. Then the poor animal seized it, and turned it over and over in its struggles to get free from the needle. "Now the cockchafer is reading," said Ingé, "look how it turns the leaf over." As years passed by she became rather worse than better, but she was beautiful, and that was her misfortune; otherwise something else might have happened to her than what really happened.

"Your bad disposition ought to be thoroughly rooted out," her own mother said to her. "As a child you have often trampled upon my apron, but I am afraid you will one day trample on my heart."

And that she really did.

She went into the country, and entered the service of some rich people who treated her like their own child, and dressed her accordingly; she looked very well, but her haughtiness increased.

When she had been there about a year, her mistress said to her: "Ingé, you ought to go for once to see your parents."

And Ingé went off, but only in order to show herself in her native place; she wished people to see how grand she had become. But when she came to the entrance of the village and saw the young men and girls chatting there, and her own mother

near them, resting on a stone, and having a bundle of sticks in
front of her which she had picked up in the wood, Ingé turned
back; she was ashamed to think that she, who was so well clad,

had a poor ragged woman for a mother, who picked up sticks in
the wood.   And she was not sorry that she returned; she was only
angry.

Again six months passed by, and her mistress said: "You
ought to go home again and visit your parents, Ingé.   I will give
you a large loaf of bread for them.   I am sure they will be
pleased to see you."

Ingé put her best dress and her new shoes on, raised her skirt,
and walked very carefully that she might be clean and neat about
the feet and for that no one could find fault with her.   But when

she came to the point where the path runs over the moor, where
it was muddy, and where many puddles had formed, she threw
the loaf down and trod on it, in order to keep her shoes clean;
but while she was thus standing with one foot on the loaf and the
other raised up in order to go on, the loaf sank down with her

AJG.

deeper and deeper, and she entirely disappeared. A large puddle
with bubbles on it was all that was left to show where she had
sunk. That is the story. But what became of Ingé? She sank
down into the ground, and came to the Marsh Woman below,
where she was brewing. The Marsh Woman is a sister of the
Elfin Girls, who are known well enough, for there are songs and
pictures of them; but of the Marsh Woman people only know
that when in the summer mists rise in the meadows, she is brewing below. Ingé sank down to the Marsh Woman's brewery, but
here nobody can bear to stay long. The dung hole is a splendid
drawing-room compared to the Marsh Woman's brewery. Every

vessel smells so disagreeably that one almost faints, and in addition the barrels are so closely packed that if there were a small opening between them through which one might creep, it would be impossible because of the wet toads and fat serpents which abide there. In this place Ingé arrived; all the horrible creeping things were so icy cold, that she shuddered all over, and then she became more and more rigid. She stuck fast to the loaf, which dragged her down as an amber button attracts a straw.

The Marsh Woman was at home. There were visitors at the brewery, for Old Bogey and his grandmother inspected it. And Old Bogey's grandmother is a wicked old woman, who is never idle; she never rode out on visits without having her needlework with her, and also here she had not forgotten it. She sewed little bits of leather to be attached to men's shoes, so that they continually wander about without being able to settle anywhere; she embroidered cobwebs of lies, and made crochet-work of foolish words which had fallen to the ground: all this was for men's disadvantage and destruction. Yes, indeed! She knew how to sew, to embroider, and to crochet—this old grandmother.

She saw Ingé, put her spectacles on, and looked at her again.

"That's a girl who possesses talents," she said; "and I request you to let me have the little one as a memento of my visit here. She will make a suitable statue in my grandson's ante-room."

And she was given to her, and thus Ingé came into still lower regions. People do not go there directly, but they can get there by a circuitous road, when they have the necessary talents. That was an endless ante-room; one felt quite dizzy if one looked forward or backward. A crowd of people, exhausted to death, were standing here and waiting for the gate of mercy to be opened to them. They had to wait a long time. Large, fat, waddling spiders spun cobwebs, which lasted thousands of years, over their feet, and cut like iron foot-traps and copper chains; besides this, every soul was filled with everlasting restlessness—a restlessness of misery. The miser was standing there, and had forgotten the key of his money-box; the key was in the keyhole, he knew that. It would lead us too far to enumerate all the tortures and misery which were seen there. Ingé felt inexpressible pain when she had to stand there as a statue; it was as if she had been tied to the loaf.

"That is the consequence of trying to keep one's feet clean and tidy," she said to herself. "Look how they stare at me!"

And indeed the eyes of all were fixed upon her; their wicked desires were looking out of their eyes and speaking out of their mouths, without a sound being heard. They were dreadful to look at.

"It must be a pleasure to look at me!" thought Ingé. "I have a pretty face and fine clothes." And then she turned her eyes, for she could not move her neck—it was too stiff. She had forgotten that she had been much soiled in the Marsh Woman's brewery. Her dress was covered with slime; a snake had fixed itself in her hair, and hung down her back; out of every fold of her dress a toad looked forth, croaking like a short-winded pug-dog. That was very disagreeable. "But the others down here look just as dreadful," she thought, and thus consoled herself.

The worst of all, however, was the terrible hunger she felt. Could she not stoop down and break off a piece from the loaf on which she was standing? No, her back was stiff, her arms and hands were rigid, her whole body was like a pillar of stone; she could only turn her eyes in her head, but right round, so she could also see behind her. It was an awful aspect. And then flies came and ran to and fro over her eyes. She blinked, but they did not fly away, for they could not, as their wings were torn off, and they were transformed into creeping things. It was a horrible pain, which was increased by hunger, and at last it seemed to her as if there was nothing left in her body. "If this is to last much longer," she said, "I shall not be able to bear it." But she had to bear it. Then a hot tear fell upon her head, and rolled over her face and her breast, down to the loaf upon which she stood; and another tear fell, and many others more. Who do you think was weeping for Ingé? Her mother was still alive! The tears of grief which a mother sheds over her child always reach it, but they do not redeem; they burn and augment the torture—this unbearable hunger, and not to be able to reach the loaf upon which she was standing with her feet! She had a feeling as if her whole interior had consumed itself. She was like a thin hollow reed which takes in every sound; she heard everything distinctly that was spoken about her on earth, but what she heard was hard and evil. Although her mother shed a great many tears over her, and was sad, she could not help saying, "Pride goes before a fall. That was your misfortune, Ingé. You have much grieved your mother."

Her mother and all on earth knew of the sin which she had committed; they knew that she had trod on the loaf, and that she had sunk and disappeared, for the cowherd had seen it from the slope near the marsh land.

"How you have grieved your mother, Ingé!" said the mother. "I had a sort of presentiment."

"I wish I had never been born!" thought Ingé; "it would have been much better. Of what use are my mother's tears now?"

She heard how her master and mistress, the good people who had taken care of her like parents, said that she was a sinful child who had despised God's gifts, and trod upon them with her feet. The gates of mercy would be very slowly opened to her!

"They ought to have chastised me, and driven out the whims, if I had any," thought Ingé.

She heard that a song was composed about her—the haughty girl who had trod on a loaf to keep her shoes clean—and that it was sung all over the country.

"That one must bear so much evil, and have to suffer so much!" thought Ingé. "Others ought to be punished too for their sins! But, of course, then there would be much to be punished. Alas! how I am tortured!"

Her mind now became harder than her exterior. "In such company," she said, "it is impossible to become better, and I don't wish to become better. Look how they stare at me!" Her mind was full of wrath and malice against all men. "At last those up there have something to talk about! Alas! how I am tortured!"

She also heard how her story was told to children, and how the little ones called her wicked Ingé. They said she was so ugly and wicked she ought to be severely punished. Again and again hard

words were uttered about her by children. Yet, one day, while
grief and hunger were gnawing her hollow body, she heard her
name pronounced and her story told to an innocent child—a little
girl—and she also heard that the little one burst into tears at the
story of the haughty, vain Ingé.

"But will Ingé never come up again?" asked the little girl.

"No, never," was the answer.

"But if she says 'please,' and asks pardon, and promises never
to do it again?"

"Then, yes; but she will not ask to be pardoned," they told the
child.

"I should like her so much to do it," said the little girl, and was
quite inconsolable. "I will give my doll and all my toys if she
may only come up. It is too terrible—poor Ingé."

These words touched Ingé to the depth of her heart; they did
her good. It was the first time any one had said, "Poor Ingé,"

and did not add anything about her faults. A young innocent child cried and asked mercy for her. She felt very strange; she would have much liked to cry herself, but she could not do it: she was unable to cry, and that was another torture.

While years passed on above, no change took place below. She more rarely heard words from above; she was less spoken of. Then suddenly one day a sigh reached her ear: "Ingé! Ingé! how sad you have made me. I have said it would be so!" It was the last sigh of her dying mother. Sometimes she heard her name mentioned by her former master and mistress, and these were pleasant words when the lady said: "Shall I ever see you again, Ingé? One does not know where one comes to!"

But Ingé was convinced that her kind mistress would never come to the place where she was.

Again a long while passed—a long bitter time. Then Ingé heard her name pronounced once more, and saw two stars sparkling above her. These were two kind eyes which had closed on earth. So many years had passed since the little girl had been inconsolable and had wept over "poor Ingé," that the child had become an old woman, whom God was calling back again, and in the hour when thoughts of various periods of her life came back to her mind she remembered how she had once as a little child cried bitterly when she heard the story of Ingé. And the old lady had such a lively recollection, in the hour of death, of the impression the story had made upon her that she exclaimed: "My God and Lord, have I not sometimes, like Ingé, trampled Thy blessings under my feet, without thinking it wrong? Have I not walked about with haughtiness? But in Thy mercy Thou hast not let me sink, but supported me. Oh, do not forsake me in my last hour!" The eyes of the old lady closed, and the eyes of her soul opened to see hidden things. She, whose last thoughts Ingé had so much occupied, saw now how deep she had sunk, and at this sight the pious woman burst into tears; in heaven she was standing like a child and crying for poor Ingé! And these tears and prayers resounded like an echo in the hollow outside shell that enclosed the fettered tortured soul; the never-dreamt-of love from above overwhelmed her; an angel of God was shedding tears over her. Why was this granted her? The tortured soul collected as it were in thought every action she had done on earth, and Ingé trembled in tears such as she had never wept. Grief at herself filled her, she felt as if the gates of mercy could never be thrown open to her; and while in contrition she recognised this, a beam of light rushed down to her in the precipice with a force much stronger than that of the sunbeam which melts the snowman that boys have put up, and much quicker than the snowflake melts that falls on the warm lips of a child, and becomes a drop of water; the petrified shape of Ingé dissolved into mist—a little bird flew up with the quickness of lightning into the upper world. But the bird was timid and shy towards all that surrounded it, it was ashamed of itself, ashamed to face the living creatures, and quickly concealed itself in a dark hole in an old weather-beaten wall. There it sat and cowered, trembling all over and unable to utter a single sound: it had no voice. It sat there a long time before it could see all the splendour around it; indeed it was very beautiful! The air was fresh and mild, the moon threw her silvery light over the earth; trees and bushes breathed forth fragrance, and the place where it sat was pleasant; its feathers were pure and fine. How love and brightness pervaded all creation! The bird wanted to burst into song, and to sing forth all that filled its breast, but was unable to do it; it would gladly have sung like the cuckoo and nightingale in spring. But God, who hears the soundless hymn of praise of the worm, also heard the notes of praise which filled its breast, as the psalms of David were heard before they were expressed in word and tune.

For weeks these soundless songs stirred in the bird's breast; a good deed had to be performed to make them burst forth!

Holy Christmastime approached. A peasant set up a pole near the wall and tied a bunch of oats to it, that the birds of the air might also have a pleasant Christmas and a good feed in this blissful time. When the sun rose on Christmas morn and shone upon the oats, the twittering birds flew in flocks round the pole. Then also a "tweet, tweet" sounded from a hole in the wall—the swelling thought became a sound, the weak "tweet, tweet," a whole song of joy, the thought of a good deed was called to life,

the bird left its hiding-place; in heaven it was known what sort of
bird this was!

The winter was hard, the water frozen over, and the birds and
the animals in the wood had little food.   Our little bird flew over
the highroad, and found a grain of corn here and there in the ruts
the sledges made, and a few crumbs at the halting-places; it ate
but few, but called all the other starving sparrows that they might
have some food.   It flew into the towns, looked all round, and
where a loving hand had strewn bread-crumbs on a window-sill
for the birds, it only ate a single crumb, leaving all to the other
birds.

In the course of the winter the bird had gathered so many
crumbs and given them to other birds, that altogether they
equalled the weight of the whole loaf on which Ingé had trodden
to keep her shoes clean.   And when the last bread-crumb was
found and given away, the grey wings of the bird turned white
and expanded.

"There flies a sea-swallow over the water," said the children
who saw the white bird; it dived down into the sea and
then rose up again into the bright sunshine; it glittered, and
it was impossible to see what became of it—they said it flew
into the sun.

The Shirt-Collar

HERE lived once a rich gentleman whose
whole goods and chattels consisted of a
boot-jack and a hair-brush, but he wore the
finest shirt-collar in the world, and it is about
this very shirt-collar that we shall hear
a story.   The shirt-collar had now become
so old that it thought of getting married;
and it happened that it was sent to the laundress together
with a garter.

"Truly," said the shirt-collar, "I have never seen anybody so slender and refined, so tender and nice before! May I ask for your name?"

"I shall not answer you," replied the garter.

"Where do you live?" continued the shirt-collar.

But the garter was somewhat shy, and thought it strange to be expected to answer such questions.

"I suppose you are a girdle," said the shirt-collar, "a sort of inside girdle. I see you are useful as well as ornamental, my little lady!"

"Do not speak to me," said the garter, "I think I have given you no encouragement to do so!"

"If one is as beautiful as you are," said the shirt-collar, "is this not encouragement enough?"

"Go away, and do not come too close to me!" said the garter, "you look exactly like a man."

"I am a gentleman, indeed," said the shirt-collar, "I possess a boot-jack and a hair-brush!"

But that was not true, for it was his master who possessed these articles.

"Do not come too near me!" said the garter, "I am not accustomed to that."

"Conceited thing!" said the shirt-collar.

Then they were taken out of the washing-tub, stretched and put on a chair in the sunshine to dry, and put on the ironing-board. And now came the hot iron.

"Mistress widow!" cried the shirt-collar, "little mistress widow, I am getting very warm! I am turning quite another being, all my creases are coming out; you are burning a hole in me! Ugh! I propose to you!"

"Wretch!" said the iron, proudly passing over the shirt-collar, for it imagined itself a steam-engine which was to run on metals and draw carriages. "Wretch!" it repeated.

As the edges of the shirt-collar were a little frayed, the scissors were brought to trim it. "I believe," said the shirt-collar, addressing the scissors, "you must be a first-class dancer. How you can throw your legs up! I have never seen anything more charming; no human being can do what you do."

"I know," replied the scissors.

"You deserve to be made a countess," continued the shirt-collar. "All I possess is a gentleman, a boot-jack, and a hair-brush. I wish, for your sake, that I had an earl's estate."

"What! He will propose to me!" said the scissors, and became so angry, that they cut too deeply into the shirt-collar, and it had to be turned out as useless.

"I shall have to propose to the hair-brush," thought the shirt-collar. One day it said, speaking to the hair-brush: "What remarkably beautiful hair you have, my little lady! Have you never thought of becoming engaged?"

"Of course! How could you have any doubt about this?" replied the hair-brush. "I am engaged to the boot-jack."

"Engaged?" said the shirt-collar. As there was now nobody left to propose to, the shirt-collar began to despise all love-makings.

A long time passed after this; the shirt-collar came at last into the bag of the paper-maker! There was a large company of rags, the fine ones lay apart from the coarse ones, as it ought to be. They had all a great deal to tell, but most of all the shirt-collar, for it was a wonderful bragger.

"I have had no end of love-affairs," said the shirt-collar; "they never left me alone; but, of course, I was a distinguished gentleman, and well starched. I possessed a boot-jack and a hair-brush, which I never used. You ought to have seen me—seen me when I was put aside! I shall never forget my first love! It was a girdle, and how fine, soft and nice it was! My first love threw itself, for my sake, into a large washing-tub. There was also a widow, which loved me very ardently, but I left it and it turned quite black! Then there was a first-class dancer, the very person which inflicted the wound upon me which you still see; it was a very excitable being. My own hair-brush was in love with me—and lost all its hairs because I disappointed it. I have seen a great deal of this sort of thing, but most of all I am sorry for the garter—girdle, I intended to say—which threw itself into a washing-tub. I have a great deal to answer for; it is time that I should be turned into white paper."

And to this the collar was transformed at last, the very same paper on which this story here is printed, because it had bragged so much and told things which were not true. And we ought to remember this, and never imitate the shirt-collar, for who knows if we may not one day also come into the rag-bag and be turned to white paper, upon which our whole story, even its most secret parts, might be printed, so that we should be obliged, like the shirt-collar, to run about and tell it ourselves.

The Happy Family

THE largest green leaf here in the country is certainly the burdock leaf: if you put it round your little waist it is like an apron; and if you lay it upon your head when it rains, it is almost as good as an umbrella, for it is extremely large. One burdock never grows alone; where one grows there are several more, making quite a splendid sight. And all this splendour is food for snails. Of these large white snails, which lived on burdock leaves, the grand people in olden times used to have fricassée made, and when they had eaten it they would say, "Dear me! how nice it is"; for they really believed it tasted excellent. And that is why burdocks were sown.

Now there was an old country-seat, where snails were no longer eaten. They had died out, but the burdocks had not died out. They grew and grew in all the paths, on all the beds; there was no stopping them any more—it was quite a forest of burdocks. Here and there stood an apple or plum tree; otherwise one would never have thought that it was a garden. Everything was burdock, and among it all lived the two last ancient snails.

They did not know themselves how old they were, but they could very well remember that there had been a great many more of them, that they came from a foreign family, and that the forest had been planted for them and theirs. They had never been out of it, but it was known to them that there was something in the world besides, which was called "the Castle"; there one was boiled, became black, and was laid upon a silver dish—but what happened after that they did not know. They could not imagine what it was like to be boiled and laid upon a silver dish, but it was said to be very fine and particularly grand. Neither the cockchafer, nor the toad, nor the earthworm, all of whom they questioned, could give them any information about it; for none of their kind had ever been boiled or laid upon a silver dish.

The old white snails were the grandest in the world: that they knew. The forest was there on their account, and the castle too, so that they might be boiled and laid upon a silver dish.

They lived very retired and happy, and as they themselves were childless, they had adopted a common little snail, which they brought up as their own child. But the little one would not grow, for it was only a common snail; the old people, however, particularly the mother-snail, declared that it was easy to see how it grew. And she said that if the father could not see that, he was only just to feel the little shell, and on doing so, he found that the mother was right.

One day it rained very hard.

"Listen how it drums upon the burdock-leaves—rum-a-dum-dum, rum-a-dum-dum !" said the father-snail.

"Those are what I call drops !" said the mother-snail. "It is running down the stalk. You see it will get wet here. I'm only glad that we have our good houses, and that the little one has his too. More has really been done for us than for other creatures; it is very plainly to be seen that we are the lords of the world. We have houses from our birth, and the burdock forest was planted for our sakes. I should like to know how far it extends, and what lies outside it."

"There is nothing," said the father-snail, "that could be better than it is with us: I have nothing to wish for."

"Yes!" said the mother. "I should like to be taken up to the Castle, boiled and laid upon a silver dish; that is what happened to all our ancestors, and you may believe that it is something uncommon."

"The Castle has perhaps fallen in," said the father-snail; "or the burdock forest has grown over it, so that the people cannot come out. But there's not the slightest hurry about it. You're always in too great a hurry, and the little one is beginning to be just the same. Has he not been crawling up that stalk for already three days? It really gives me a headache to look up at him."

"You must not scold him," said the mother-snail. "He crawls along very deliberately: we shall certainly live to have great joy of him, and we old ones have really nothing else to live for. But have you ever thought of where we shall get a wife for him? Don't you think that there are some of our kind still living farther in the burdock forest?"

"I daresay there are some black snails there," said the old man; "black snails without houses; but they are too vulgar, and yet they fancy themselves somebody. But we can give the ants the commission; they run to and fro, as though they had some business to do; they will certainly know of a wife for our little one."

"I certainly know the most beautiful one you could have," said one of the ants; "but I am afraid the proposal is of no use, for she is a queen."

"That doesn't matter!" said the old people. "Has she a house?"

"She has a castle," answered the ant; "a most beautiful ant-hill with seven hundred passages."

"Many thanks!" said the mother-snail. "Our son shall not go into an ant-hill. If you know of nothing better than that, we will give the white gnats the commission; they fly far around in rain and sunshine; they know the burdock forest in and out."

"We have a wife for him," said the gnats. "A hundred man's paces from here there is a little snail with a house sitting on a gooseberry-bush; she is all alone, and old enough to marry. It is only a hundred man's paces from here."

" Well, let her come to him," said the old people. " He has a burdock forest; she has only a bush."

And so they fetched the little maiden snail. She took eight days in coming; but that was the beauty of it, for by that one could see that she was of the right kind.

Then they had the wedding. Six glow-worms gave as much light as they could; for the rest, things went very quietly, for the old people could not bear much feasting and dissipation. A beautiful speech was, however, made by the mother-snail. The father could not speak; he was too deeply moved. Then they gave the young couple the whole burdock forest as an inheritance, and said what they had always said: that it was the best in the world, and that if they lived honest and upright lives, and multiplied, they and their children would one day be taken to the Castle, boiled black, and laid upon a silver dish. And after this speech had been made, the old people crept back into their houses and never came out again; they slept. The young couple now ruled in the forest and had a numerous progeny. But as they were never boiled and laid upon the silver dish, they concluded that the Castle must have fallen in, and that all the people in the world had died out. And as nobody contradicted them, they knew they were right. The rain fell upon the burdock leaves to play the drum for them, and the sun shone to colour the burdock forest for their sake. They were very happy, and the whole family was happy—infinitely happy!

Little Tuk

ELL, yes, that was little Tuk. That was not his name, but when he could not yet speak he called himself Tuk, which he meant for Charlie; and that does very well, but one must know it. He had to look after his little sister Gustava, who was much younger than himself, and at the same time he had to learn his lessons; these two things, however, would not go very well together. The poor boy sat there with his little sister on his knee, singing to her all the songs he knew, and glancing now and then into his geography book which lay open before him. The next morning he had to know all the towns of Zealand by heart, and all that any one can be expected to know about them.

Then his mother came home, who had been out, and took little Gustava herself. Tuk went as quickly as possible to the window, and read so zealously that he had almost read his eyes out; it became darker and darker, but the mother had no money to buy candles.

"There goes the old washerwoman from over the way," said the mother, looking out of the window. "The poor woman can hardly drag herself along, and has to carry a pail full of water from the well; be a good boy, Tuk, my child, run over and help the old woman. Will you?"

And Tuk ran quickly over and helped her; but when he came back to the room it had become quite dark, and as there could be no question about light, he was to go to bed; his bed was an old settle. He was lying upon it thinking of his geography lesson of Zealand, and of all the master had said. Of course he ought still to be learning, but that was impossible. He therefore put the geography book under his pillow, because he had heard that this helps one a great deal when one wants to learn a lesson; the only thing is, one can't depend upon it. There he was lying and thinking and thinking, and then it seemed to him suddenly as if some one kissed him on the eyes and mouth. He slept, and yet he did not sleep; he felt as if the old washerwoman looked at him with her kind eyes and said: "It would be a great pity if you did not know your lesson to-morrow! You have helped me; therefore I will now help you, as God always helps every one." And suddenly

the book under Tuk's pillow began to move. "Cluck, cluck!" It was a hen which came crawling out, and she was from Kjöge.[1] "I am a Kjöge-hen," she said, and then she told him how many inhabitants the town had, and of the battle that had taken place there, although this latter was not worth mentioning.

Then he heard a rattling noise and a plump—something fell down. It was a wooden bird, the parrot that was used at the shooting competition in Prästöe.[2] It said that there were as many inhabitants in that town as it had nails in its body; it was very

---

[1] Kjöge is a small town in the bay of the same name.
[2] Prästöe is a little town, only known because the Castle of Nysöe, where Thorwaldsen lived, is in its immediate neighbourhood.

proud too. "Thorwaldsen has been living quite close to me. Plump! here I am, quite comfortable!"

But now little Tuk was no longer lying in bed, but sat on horse-back, and went off at a gallop. A magnificently dressed knight, with a shining plume on his helmet, held Tuk before him on the saddle, and so they rode through the wood to the old town of Wordingborg,[1] and that was a large lively town ; on the king's castle were high towers, and light streamed from all the windows. Inside there was singing and dancing, for King Waldemar danced with the gaily-dressed Court ladies. Now it became morning, and as the sun rose, the whole city and the king's castle, tower after tower, sank down ; and at last one single tower stood on the hill where the castle had been standing. The town was very small and poor, and the boys came out of school with their books under their arms, and said: "Two thousand inhabitants ;" but that was not true, for there were not so many in the town.

And little Tuk was again in bed, and did not know if he was dreaming or not, but somebody stood close by his side. "Little Tuk, little Tuk," a voice said. It was a sailor who spoke, but he was as small as if he were a midshipman, although he was not one. "I have to greet you from Corsör; that's a rising town, and is very lively ; it has steamboats and mail-coaches—formerly they said that it was ugly, but that is no longer true."

"I am situated upon the sea," said Corsör ;[2] "I have high-roads and pleasure-grounds, and I am the birthplace of a poet who was witty and entertaining, qualities that not all poets possess. Once I wished to equip a ship that was to go all round the world ; but it did not do it, although it might have done it. In addition, I smell sweetly, for close by my gates grow the most splendid rose trees."

Little Tuk looked, but all was red and green before his eyes ; when the confusion of colours had passed by, he all at once saw a wooded slope near a bay, and high above it stood a beautiful old church with two high pointed spires. Springs of water flowed out of the slope in numerous jets, so that there was continual

---

[1] Wordingborg is known for the ruins of the old castle. Under King Waldemar it was a flourishing town.

[2] Corsör, a small town on the Great Belt.

splashing. Close by sat an old king with a golden crown on his long hair. He was King Hroar, near the springs, close by the city of Roeskilde,[1] as one now calls it. And over the slope went all the kings and queens of Denmark, hand in hand, with their golden crowns on their heads, up to the old church, and the organ was playing, and the springs rippled. Little Tuk saw and heard everything. "Don't forget the towns," said King Hroar.

All at once everything was gone again, but whither? It seemed to Tuk as if some one turned over the leaves of a book. And there stood an old peasant woman before him, who came from Soröe,[2] where the grass grows in the market-place. A grey linen apron was hanging over her head and back, and was very wet; it must have been raining. "Yes, it has," she said, and she could tell many amusing passages from Holberg's comedies and of Waldemar and Absolom. But all at once she shrank together and nodded her head as if she wanted to jump. "Croak," she said; "it is wet, it is wet; Soröe is as quiet as a grave!" Suddenly she became a frog. "Croak!" And then she turned an old woman again. "One must dress oneself according to the weather," she said. "It is wet! It is wet! My town is like a bottle—one has to go in at the neck, and come out at the neck again! Formerly I had most splendid fishes, and now I have fresh rosy-cheeked boys at the bottom of the bottle, who learn wisdom, Hebrew Greek. Croak!" That sounded as if the frogs croaked, or as if some one walked over the marshes with large boots—always the same sound, so monotonous and tiresome, that little Tuk fell asleep, and that could not do him any harm. But even in this sleep came a dream, or something of that kind. His little sister Gustava, with her blue eyes and golden curly hair, had suddenly become a tall slender girl, and could fly without having any wings; and then they flew right across Zealand, with its green woods and blue lakes.

"Do you hear the cock crow, little Tuk? 'Cock-a-doodle-doo!' The cocks fly up from Kjöge! You shall have a large farmyard

---

[1] Roeskilde was once the capital of Denmark.

[2] Soröe, a small beautifully-situated town; the Danish poet Holberg founded an academy here.

one day! You will never suffer want or hunger! And you will take the cake, as people say: you will become a rich and happy man. Your house will rise like the tower of King Waldemar, and will be richly adorned with marble statues like those at Prästöe. Understand me well: your name shall travel with glory all over the world, like the ship that was to sail off from Corsör, and at Roeskilde——"don't forget the towns!" said King Hroar—— "there you will speak well and cleverly, little Tuk; and when they place you at last in your grave you will sleep peacefully."

"As if I lay in Soröe," said little Tuk, and then he woke up.

It was broad daylight, and he could no longer remember his dream, but that was not necessary, for one must not know what is to come in future. He quickly jumped out of bed and read his book, and there, all at once, he knew his whole lesson.

The old washerwoman just then peeped in at the door, nodded kindly to him, and said: "Many thanks, you good child, for your assistance! May God realise your beautiful dream!"

Little Tuk did not remember what he had dreamt, but God knew it.

The Tinder-Box

 SOLDIER was marching along the high-road—left, right! left, right! He had a knapsack on his back and a sword at his side. He was returning from war, and now on his way home.

When he had gone some distance he met an old witch. She was dreadfully ugly, her underlip was hanging down upon her breast.

"Good evening, soldier," she said; "what a fine sword you have, and what a big knapsack! You are a true soldier, and now you shall have as much money as ever you wish for."

"Thank you, old witch," replied the soldier.

"Do you see yonder large tree?" asked the witch, pointing out a tree which stood not far from them. "It is hollow inside. You must climb right up to its summit, when you will see a hole; through this hole you can let yourself down and get deep into the tree. I shall tie a rope round your waist, so that I can pull you up when you call out to me."

"What shall I do down in the tree?" asked the soldier.

"Fetch money," said the witch. "You must know that you will find a spacious hall at the bottom of the tree; it is quite light, for there are no less than three hundred lamps burning down there. You will then see three doors; you can open them—the keys are in the locks. If you enter the first room you will find in the middle of the floor a large wooden chest and a dog sitting on it, which has a pair of eyes as large as tea-cups. Never mind him! I shall give you my blue checked apron; you can spread it on the floor; then go quickly, seize the dog and place him on my apron, open the chest, and take out of it as many coins as you like. They are of copper; if you prefer to have silver, you must go into the second room. There you will see a dog having eyes as large as mill-wheels. But do not be afraid; put him on my apron and take as much money as you like. If, however, you wish to have gold, you can have that too, and as much as you can carry, if you go into the third room. The dog which sits on the chest in this room has eyes as large as a church-steeple. He is a very wicked dog, I can assure you, but you need not fear him. If you put him on my apron he will not hurt you, and you can take as much gold as you like out of the chest."

"That is not at all bad," said the soldier. "But what do you expect me to give you in return, for surely you will not do all this for nothing?"

"Yes," replied the witch. "I shall not ask you for a single shilling. I only want you to bring up for me an old tinder-box which my grandmother forgot when she was down there for the last time."

"Well, then, tie the rope round my waist," said the soldier.

"Here it is," said the witch, "and here is also my blue checked apron."

The soldier then climbed up the tree, descended inside it by the rope, and arrived, as the witch had told him, in the great hall where the three hundred lamps were burning.

He opened the first door. Ugh! there the dog with the eyes as large as teacups was staring at him.

"You are a fine fellow," said the soldier, placed him on the apron of the witch, and took as many coppers as his pockets would hold. Then he locked the chest, put the dog upon it, and went to the second room. Really, there was the dog with the eyes as large as mill-wheels.

"You had better not look at me so hard," said the soldier, "you might strain your eyes," and put the dog on the witch's apron. When he saw the silver in the chest, he threw all the copper he had taken away, and filled his pockets and knapsack with silver. Then he went into the third room. That was dreadful to look at. The dog there had really two eyes as large as church steeples, which turned in his head like wheels.

"Good evening," said the soldier, and touched his cap, for he had never in his life seen a dog like this. When he had looked at him more closely, he thought "that is enough," lifted him down on the floor, and opened the chest. Good heavens! what a lot of gold there was! There was enough gold to buy the whole town, and all the sweets from all the sweetmeat stalls, in addition to all the tin soldiers, whips, and rocking-horses in the whole world. The soldier quickly threw away all the silver with which he had filled his pockets and knapsack, and replaced it by gold. He filled even his cap and his boots with gold, so that he could scarcely walk. Now he was rich.

He placed the dog again on the chest, shut the door, and called up through the tree.

"Now pull me up, old witch."

"Have you found the tinder-box?" asked the old witch.

"Upon my soul," said the soldier, "that I should really have forgotten." He returned and fetched it. The old witch pulled him up, and soon he was again in the high road, his pockets, boots, knapsack, and cap filled with gold.

"What will you do with the tinder-box?" asked the soldier.

"Do not trouble your mind about that," said the witch. "You have received your reward. Give me the tinder-box."

"Certainly not," replied the soldier. "Tell me quickly what you are going to do with it, or I shall draw my sword and cut your head off."

"No," said the witch.

Then the soldier cut her head off, so that she lay dead on the ground. He tied all his gold up in her apron, took it like a bundle on his shoulders, put the tinder-box into his pocket, and went straight to the nearest town.

It was a very pleasant town. He put up in the best inn, asked for the best rooms and for his favourite dishes; for he was rich, having so much gold.

The servant, who had to clean his boots, thought they were rather shabby old things for such a rich gentleman, for he had not yet bought a new pair. On the next day, however, he purchased decent boots and fine clothes. Thus the poor soldier had become a gentleman, and people talked to him about all the sights of their town, about the king, and about the beautiful princess his daughter.

"Where can one see her?" inquired the soldier.

"Nobody can see her," they all said, "she lives in a strong copper castle with many towers, surrounded by high walls. Nobody but the king himself can pass in and out, for there has been a prophecy that she would marry a private soldier, and the king will prevent that."

"I should very much like to see her," thought the soldier, but he could by no means obtain permission to do so.

He led a merry life, went to the theatre, drove in the Royal Gardens, and gave largely to the poor—that was very good of him; he remembered well of former days what it means to have not a single penny. He was now rich, had fine clothes, and soon found many friends, who all told him that he was a splendid fellow and a true gentleman; all this pleased the soldier greatly. As, however, he spent every day a good deal of money, without gaining anything, he had soon nothing left but two shillings; therefore he had to give up the elegant rooms which he occupied and live on the top of the house in a little garret; he had to black his own boots, and to mend them with a darning needle. None of his former friends came to see him, he lived so high up.

On one dark evening he could not even buy a candle. Then he remembered that there was a piece of candle in the tinder-box which he had fetched out of the hollow tree with the assistance of the witch. He took up the tinder-box and the little end of the candle, and was going to strike a light, when suddenly the door flew open, and the dog with a pair of eyes as large as tea-cups, which he had seen under the tree, made his appearance and asked: "Your lordship's commands?"

"What is this?" asked the soldier. "That is a capital tinder-box if I can get through it what I wish for. Get me some money," he said to the dog. The dog was gone like lightning; but in a moment he returned again, holding a large bag of coppers in his mouth.

Thus the soldier learnt what a wonderful tinder-box he had. If he struck once, the dog from the chest containing the copper appeared; two strokes made the dog who watched the silver come; and if he struck three times, the dog who sat on the chest containing the gold made his appearance. Now the soldier moved back into the elegant rooms, and appeared again well-dressed. All his former friends recognised him, and thought much of him.

One day the soldier thought: "It is very strange that nobody is allowed to see the princess. All agree in saying that she is so beautiful; but what is the use of her beauty if she is compelled to remain for ever in the big copper castle with its many towers? Is there no chance at all to see her?"

At this moment he thought of his tinder-box. He struck a light, and there the dog with a pair of eyes as large as tea-cups came.

"Although it is midnight," said the soldier, "I should very much like to see the princess for a moment."

No sooner had he pronounced his wish than the dog ran away, and returned in a few seconds with the princess. She was lying fast asleep on the dog's back; she was so lovely to look at, that nobody could help seeing at once that she was a princess. The soldier could not abstain from kissing her, for he was a true soldier.

Then the dog carried the princess back; but on the next morning, when she was at tea with the king and the queen, she told them that she had had a very strange dream of a dog and a soldier in the night; she had been riding on the dog and the soldier had kissed her.

"That would be a fine tale," said the queen.

Next night one of the Court ladies had to watch by the bed of the princess to see whether it was really a dream, or what else it could be.

The soldier felt a great longing to see the princess again, so he called the dog next night once more, who fetched her, running with her as fast as he could. But the old lady put on water-boots and followed him. When she saw that the dog disappeared with the

princess in a large house, she took a piece of chalk and made a
large white cross on the door, thinking that she would be able to
recognise the house again. Then she returned home and went
to bed. The dog soon brought the princess back; and when he
saw the white cross on the house where the soldier lived, he

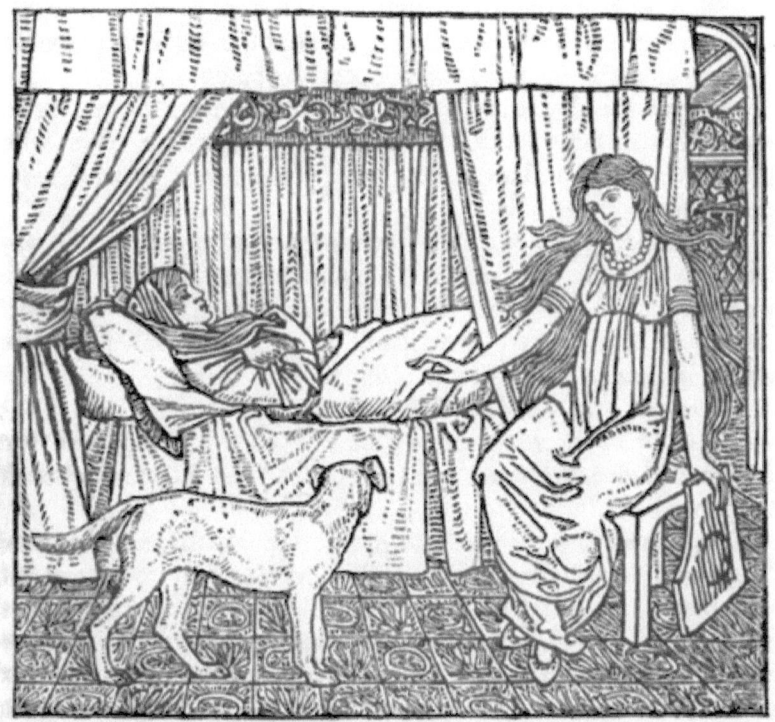

made white crosses on all the doors in the town, that the Court
lady might not be able to find it.

Early on the next morning, the king, the queen, the lady, and
many officers of the Court came to see where the princess had
been.

"There is the house," said the king when he saw the first door
with a white cross.

"No; there it is, my dear husband," said the queen, on seeing a
second door with a white cross.

"But there is one, and there is another," said all, and wherever they looked they saw white crosses on the doors. Then they understood that it would be useless to search any more.

The queen was a very clever woman; she could do more than merely ride in a carriage. She took her large golden scissors, cut a piece of silk in squares and made a nice little bag of it. This bag she filled with ground buckwheat, then tied it to the princess's back, and cut a little hole into it, so that the buckwheat could run out all along the road the princess was taken.

At night the dog came again, took the princess on his back, and ran with her to the soldier, who was deeply in love with her, and wished nothing more than to be a prince, that he might marry her.

The dog did not notice how the buckwheat strewed all the way from the castle up to the soldier's house, where he climbed up the wall to enter the soldier's window. Next morning the king and the queen knew where their daughter had been taken to: the soldier was at once arrested and thrown into prison.

There he sat, and found it awfully dark and dull. He was told, "To-morrow you will be hanged." All this was very unpleasant, and the worst was that he had left his tinder-box at the inn.

On the next morning he could see through the iron bars how the people were hurrying out of the town in order to witness his execution. He heard the noise of the drums and saw the soldiers march past. In the crowd he noticed a shoemaker's apprentice with a leather apron and wooden slippers on, who ran so fast that one of his slippers came off and flew against the wall, quite close to the window at which the soldier sat behind the iron bars.

"You need not hurry so, boy," cried the soldier, "they can't do anything until I arrive. If you would run to the place where I used to live and fetch me my tinder-box, I will give you four shillings."

The boy, who was very anxious to have so much money, fetched the tinder-box and handed it to the soldier. Now, let us see what happened.

Outside the town they had erected a high gibbet; soldiers and many thousands of people stood around it. The king and the queen were sitting on a magnificent throne opposite the judges and counsel.

The soldier was already standing on the top of the ladder, and they were just going to put the rope round his neck, when he said he knew that it was a custom to grant a last request to a poor criminal before he suffered death, and he should very much like to smoke a pipe—the last he would ever have a chance of smoking in this world.

The king would not refuse this favour, and the soldier took up his tinder-box and struck—" One, two, three." And lo ! there suddenly appeared the three dogs ; the first with eyes as large as tea-cups, the second with eyes as large as mill-wheels, and the third having eyes as large as church-steeples.

" Help me now, that they cannot hang me," said the soldier.

Then the dogs rushed at the judges and the counsel, took the one up by the legs, the other by the nose, and threw them high up into the air, so that they fell down and were smashed to pieces.

" Leave me alone," said the king ; but the largest of the dogs seized both him and the queen and threw them up after the others.

When the soldiers and all the people saw that, they had great fear, and cried : "Good soldier, you shall become our king and marry the beautiful princess."

They seated the soldier in the king's carriage, and the three dogs danced in front of it and cried " Hurrah ! " The boys whistled on their fingers, and the soldiers presented arms. The princess came out of the copper castle and became queen, and she liked it very much.

The wedding festivities lasted eight days ; the dogs sat at table and opened their eyes wide.

A Cheerful Temper

Y father left me the best inheritance any man can leave to his son—a cheerful temper. But who was my father? Why, that really has nothing to do with the cheerful temper. He was lively and quick, although somewhat stout and fat; in fact, he was in body and mind the very opposite to what one would expect from a man of his calling. But what was his position, what services did he render to the community? Why, if that were to be written down and printed at the very beginning of a book, some people in reading it would be likely to lay it aside and say there is something unpleasant about it; I don't like anything of that sort. And yet my father was neither a knacker nor a hangman; on the contrary, his office was such that it placed him at the head of the most distinguished citizens of the town, and he was fully entitled to be there, for it was his proper place. He must needs be the foremost of all—before the bishop, nay, even before princes of royal blood, because he was a hearse-driver.

There, now I have betrayed the secret! and I must confess that, when one saw my father sitting high up on the box of Death's bus, clad in his long wide black cloak, having a black-trimmed three-cornered hat on, and then looked into his face, which was as round and smiling as a picture of the sun, one could not think of mourning and the grave; for his face said: "It doesn't matter, never mind—it will go much better than one thinks."

So, you see, from him I have my cheerful temper and also the habit of often going to the churchyard: and that is quite amusing, if one goes thither in good spirits. I forgot to say that I also take in the *Advertiser*, as he used to do.

I am no longer young—I have neither wife nor child, nor a library, but I read, as I have mentioned, the *Advertiser*; that suffices me. It is my favourite newspaper, as it was my father's.

The *Advertiser* is a most useful paper, and contains really everything a man requires to know; therein you find who preaches in the churches and in new books; it tells you about charitable institutions, and contains many harmless poetical attempts. Marriages are desired, and meetings brought about. All is so simple and natural! One can indeed live very happily and be buried, if one reads the *Advertiser*—nay, at the end of one's life one has such a heap of paper that one can comfortably lie on it, if one does not care to rest on wood shavings.

The *Advertiser* and the churchyard were always the two things that most elevated my mind, and best nourished my good temper.

Everybody can peruse the *Advertiser* by himself, but let him go with me to the churchyard. Let us go there when the sun is shining and the trees are green; let us walk about between the graves. Every one of them is a closed book with its back turned up; one can read its title, which says all the book contains, and yet says nothing at all. But I know my way; I learnt much from my father, and something I know from my own experience. I have it all written down in a book, which I have made for use and pleasure; there is something written about them all, and about a few more.

Now we are at the churchyard.

Here, behind the railings, painted out in white, where one day a rose-tree stood—it is gone now, and only a little bush of ever green from the neighbour's grave stretches a few straggling branches in, lest it be quite bare—rests a very unfortunate man, and yet he was, as people call it, well-off when he was alive; he had sufficient to live comfortably, and something to spare, but the world—that is to say "art"—used him too badly. When he went in the evening to the theatre to enjoy a play thoroughly, he nearly went out of his mind when the machinist put too strong a light into one of the cheeks of the moon, or when the canvases representing the sky were hanging in front of the scene instead of behind, or if they made a palm appear in a garden at Copenhagen, or a cactus plant in Switzerland, or beech-trees in the northern regions of Norway. What does it matter to any one?

Who would trouble his mind about anything of that sort ? All is only a play which is intended to amuse people. Sometimes the people applauded too much in his opinion, sometimes not enough. "That is wet wood to-night," he used to say, "it will not catch fire ; " and when he looked round to see what sort of people were there, then he found that they laughed in the wrong places, when they were not expected to laugh at all. All this angered him, pained him, and made him miserable ; and now he rests in the grave.

Here rests a man who was very lucky in life; I mean to say that he was a nobleman of high birth, and that was his luck, for otherwise he would not have turned out anything at all. Nature orders all things so wisely that it is a pleasure to think of it ! He used to wear a coat richly embroidered with silk ; and one might very well have compared him with a precious bell-pull in a drawing-room. As such, a bell-pull generally has a good strong string behind it ; so he had a substitute to do his work for him, and he does it, in fact, still for some other man of that type. Yes, yes; all is so well arranged in this world, one has good reason to have a cheerful temper.

Now here rests—it is very sad indeed—a man who exercised his brains for sixty-seven years in perpetual search for a good idea ; at last, according to his own opinion, he had one, and was so pleased with himself that he died for joy. So his good idea was of no use to any-one, for nobody heard anything at all about it. I am inclined to think that this good idea will prevent him from resting quietly in the grave ; for suppose it was such that it could only be well explained at breakfast-time, and that, being a dead man, he can only rise about midnight—according to the common notion about ghosts—it is not suitable for the time ; nobody laughs at it, and the man must take his good idea again down with him into his grave.

Here rests a miser : in her lifetime this woman was so dreadfully stingy that she used to get up at night and mew in order to make people believe she kept a cat.

Here rests a young lady of good family, who liked immensely to sing in society : when she sang " Mi manca la voce," it was the only true thing she said in her life.

Here rests a maiden of another kind. Yes, indeed, love does not listen to reason! She was to be married; but that's an every-day story. Let the dead rest.

Here lies a widow who had a sweet voice, but bitterness in her heart. She used to visit the families in the neighbourhood and try to find out their shortcomings, and she was very zealous in this pursuit.

What you see here is a family grave. All the members of this family were so much of one opinion that when the whole world and all the newspapers said a certain thing was *so*, and the little boy came home from school and said it was *not so*, he was right, because he belonged to the family. And you can be sure, if it happened that the cock of this family crowed at midnight, they said it was morning, even if the watchman and all the clocks of the town were announcing the midnight hour.

The great poet Goethe concludes his " Faust " with the words: " May be continued "; we may say the same about our walk through the churchyard. I often come here; and when any of my friends or non-friends go too far, I go out to the churchyard, select a plot of ground, and consecrate it to him or to her, whom-soever I wish to bury; then I do bury them immediately, and they remain there dead and powerless until they return as new and better people. I write down their lives and deeds into my book in my own fashion; everybody ought to do so. Nobody should be vexed; if his friends do something foolish, let him bury them at once and keep his good temper. He can also read the *Advertiser*, which is a paper written by the people, although their hands are sometimes guided.

When the time comes that I myself and the story of my life are to be bound in the grave, I wish they may write upon it the epitaph:

A CHEERFUL TEMPER.

Little Ida's Flowers

"Y poor flowers are quite dead," said little Ida. "They were so beautiful last night, and now their leaves hang all withered on the stalks! Why do they do that?" she asked the student who was sitting on the sofa, and who liked her very much. He knew how to tell the most beautiful stories, and could cut the most amusing figures out of paper: hearts, with little ladies in them who danced, flowers, and large castles in which one could open the doors. He was a merry student. "Why do my flowers look so faded to-day?" she asked him again, and showed him the bunch, which was quite withered.

"Do you know what is the matter with them?" asked the student. "The flowers have been at a ball last night, and that is why they droop their heads so."

"But the flowers can't dance," said little Ida.

"Certainly," said the student. "When it grows dark, and we are asleep, they jump merrily about; they have a ball almost every night."

"Cannot children go to this ball?"

"Oh, yes!" said the student; "the little daisies and the snowdrops."

"Where are the beautiful flowers dancing?" asked little Ida.

"Have you not often been outside the town gate, near the large castle where the king lives in in the summer, where the beautiful garden is, with the many flowers? You have seen the swans which swim towards you when you give them bread-crumbs. Believe me, out there the great balls take place."

"I was out there in the garden yesterday with my mother," said Ida; "but all the leaves were off the trees, and there are no longer any flowers there. Where are they? In the summer I saw so many!"

"They are within the castle," said the student. "You must know that as soon as the king and his courtiers return to town the flowers immediately run into the castle and enjoy themselves. You ought to see that: the two most beautiful roses seat themselves on the throne, and then they are king and queen; all the red cockscombs come and place themselves on each side and bow —they are the chamberlains. Afterwards all the pretty flowers arrive, and a great ball takes place. The blue violets represent little naval cadets; they dance with hyacinths and crocuses, which they address as 'Miss'; the tulips and the large tiger-lilies are old ladies, who see that they all dance well, and behave themselves."

"But," asked little Ida, "is nobody there who hurts the flowers because they dance in the king's castle?"

"The truth is, nobody knows about it," said the student. "Sometimes, of course, the old steward of the castle, who has to watch out there, comes during the night; he has a big bunch of keys, but as soon as the flowers hear the keys rattle they are quiet, and hide themselves behind the curtains, and only peep out with their heads. 'I smell that there are flowers here,' says the old steward, but he cannot see them."

"That's splendid!" said little Ida, and clapped her hands. "But should I not be able to see the flowers either?"

"Yes," said the student; "only remember, when you go out again to look through the window—then you will see them. I looked in to-day, and saw a large yellow lily resting on the sofa and stretching herself. She was a lady-in-waiting."

"Can the flowers from the Botanical Gardens also go there? Can they go such a long distance?"

"Yes, certainly," said the student; "if they wish it, they can fly. Have you not seen the beautiful red, yellow, and white butterflies? They almost look like flowers, and that they have been. They have flown off their stalks high into the air, and have beaten it with their petals as if they had little wings, and then they flew. And because they behaved themselves well they obtained permission to fly about in the daytime too, and had not to return home and sit still on their stalks; and thus the petals became in the end real wings. That you have seen yourself. It is, however, very probable that the flowers in the Botanical Gardens have never been at the king's castle, or do not know that there is such merriment out there at night.   Therefore I will tell you how you can give a surprise to the Professor of Botany, who lives next door : you know him well, do you not ? When you go into his garden you must tell one of the flowers that a large ball takes place at the castle every night ; then the flower will tell all the others, and they will all fly away ; and if the professor comes into the garden he will not find a single flower there, and he will be unable to understand what has become of them."

" But how can one flower tell the others?   Flowers can't talk ! "

"Of course they can't," said the student, " but then they make signs.   Have you never seen that when the wind blows a little the flowers nod to one another and move all their green leaves ? That they understand as well as us when we talk together."

"Can the professor understand their signs ? " asked Ida.

"Certainly.   One morning he came into the garden and saw a large stinging-nettle making signs with its leaves to a beautiful red carnation.   It said : ' You are so pretty, and I love you with all my heart.'   But the professor can't stand things of that sort, and beat the nettle at once on its leaves, which are its fingers ; but then it stung him, and since that time he never dares touch a nettle again."

" That's amusing," said little Ida, laughing.

" How can one make a child believe such silly things ! " said a tiresome actuary, who had come to pay a visit and was also sitting on the sofa.   He could not bear the student, and always grumbled when he saw him cutting out the funny amusing figures : some times he cut out a man hanging on a gibbet and holding a heart in his hand, for he had been stealing hearts ; sometimes an old witch, who was riding on a broomstick, and carrying her husband on her nose.   But all this the old actuary could not stand, and then he generally said, as he did now : " How can one make a child believe such silly things ?   That is stupid fancy ! "

But to little Ida what the student told her about the flowers seemed very amusing, and she thought a great deal of it.

The flowers hung their heads because they were tired and had

danced all night; they were surely ill. Then she took them to
her other toys, which were placed on a nice little table, and the
whole drawer was full of beautiful things. In the doll's bed, her
doll Sophy was sleeping, but little Ida said to her: "You must
really get up now, Sophy, and be satisfied to lie in the drawer to-

night. The poor flowers are ill, and they must rest in your bed;
perhaps then they will recover!" And she took the doll out at
once, but Sophy looked displeased and did not say a single word,
for she was vexed that she could not keep her bed.

Then Ida placed the flowers in her doll's bed, pulled the little
counterpane over them, and bade them lie quietly; she would
make them some tea, so that they might get well again, and be able
to get up in the morning. She drew the little curtains round
the bed, lest the sun might shine into their eyes. She could not
help thinking the whole evening about all the student had told
her. And when she was going to bed herself, she first looked
behind the curtains, which were hanging before the window, on
which her mother's beautiful flowers stood, hyacinths and tulips,
and she whispered in a low voice: "I know where you are going
to-night—to the ball!" The flowers pretended not to understand
her, and did not stir a leaf, but little Ida was convinced it was so.

When she had gone to bed she lay for a long time thinking how delightful it would be to see the beautiful flowers dancing on the king's castle. "I wonder if my flowers have really been there?" Then she fell asleep. In the night she woke up again; she had been dreaming of the flowers and of the student whom the actuary had blamed. It was quiet in the bedroom where Ida slept; the night lamp was burning on the table, and father and mother were asleep.

"I wonder if my flowers are still resting in Sophy's bed?" she thought, "how much I should like to know that!" She raised herself a little and looked towards the door, which was ajar; in the room to which it led were her flowers and all her toys. She listened, and it seemed to her as if she heard some one in the room playing the piano, but quite softly, and she had never heard any one play so well before. "I am sure all my flowers are dancing in there," she thought. "How much I should like to see them!" But she dared not get up for fear of waking her father and mother.

"Oh! I wish they would come in here," she thought. But the flowers did not come, and the music continued to sound sweetly; at last she could no longer bear it—it was too beautiful; she crept out of her little bed, went softly towards the door and peeped into the adjoining room. What a splendid sight she saw there! There was no night lamp burning, and yet it was quite bright—the moon was shining on the floor; it was almost as light as day. All the hyacinths and tulips stood in two long rows in the room; not a single one remained on the window-sill, where only the empty pots were left. On the floor all the flowers danced very gracefully round one another, made figures, and held each other by their long green leaves while swinging round. At the piano sat a large yellow lily, which little Ida was certain she had seen in the summer, for she remembered distinctly that the student had said: "How much this lily resembles Miss Lina!" But then they had all laughed at him; but now it seemed to little Ida as if the flower was really like the young lady: she had the same peculiar manners when she played—sometimes she bent her yellow smiling face to one side, sometimes to the other, and

nodded in time to the sweet music! None of them noticed little
Ida. Then she saw a large blue crocus jump on the table, walk
straight to the doll's bed and draw away the curtains; there were
the sick flowers, but they got up at once and nodded to the others,
saying that they wished to dance with them. The old fumigator,
in the shape of a man whose underlip was broken off, got up and
bowed to the beautiful flowers; they looked by no means ill; they
leapt down to the others and enjoyed themselves very much.

Then it seemed as if something fell from the table. Ida looked
and saw the carnival birch-rod jump down, and it seemed as if it
was one of the flowers. It looked very pretty, and a little wax-
doll with a broad-brimmed hat, such as the actuary usually wore,
sat upon it. The carnival birch-rod hopped about among the
flowers on its three red stilts, and stamped on the ground, for it
was dancing a mazurka, a dance which the other flowers were
unable to manage, as they were too light and could not stamp on
the ground.

The wax doll on the carnival birch-rod suddenly grew up, and
raising itself over the paper flowers which were on the rod,
exclaimed: "How can one make a child believe such foolish
things? That is stupid fancy!" And the wax doll looked
exactly like the actuary—just as yellow and dissatisfied as he was.
But the paper flowers beat against his thin legs, and then he
shrank together again and became the little wax doll. All this
was very amusing to see, and little Ida could not help laughing.
The carnival birch-rod continued to dance, and the actuary had
to dance too. There was no getting out of it, whether he made
himself tall or long or remained the little yellow wax doll with the
broad-brimmed black hat. Then the other flowers, especially
those which had rested in the doll's bed, interceded in his favour,
and the carnival birch-rod gave in. At the same moment a loud
knock was heard in the drawer where Ida's doll Sophy lay with
many other toys; the fumigator in the shape of a man walked up
to the edge of the table, laid itself down at full length, and began
to open the drawer a little way. Sophy rose and glanced with
astonishment all round. "I suppose there is a ball here to-night,"
she said. "Why has nobody told me of it?"

"Will you dance with me?" asked the fumigator.

"You would be the right sort of fellow to dance with!" she said, and turned her back upon it.

Then she sat down on the edge of the drawer and thought that perhaps one of the flowers would ask her to dance, but none came. Then she coughed, "Hem, a-hem," but even in spite of this none appeared. Then the fumigator began to dance by itself—not so badly, after all! As none of the flowers seemed to notice Sophy, she let herself drop down from the drawer on the floor, to make a noise. All the flowers came running to her and inquired if she had hurt herself; they were all very polite to her, especially the flowers who had been in her bed. But she was not hurt, and Ida's flowers thanked her for the beautiful bed, and were very kind to her—took her into the centre of the room, where the moon was shining, and danced with her, while all the other flowers stood in a circle round them. Now Sophy was happy, and said they might keep her bed; she did not mind sleeping in the drawer.

But the flowers said: "You are very kind, but we cannot live any longer; we shall be dead by to-morrow. Tell little Ida to bury us in the garden, where she has buried the canary; then we shall wake up again next summer and be more beautiful than ever!"

"No, you must not die," said Sophy, and kissed them. Then the door flew open and many beautiful flowers came dancing in. Ida could not at all understand where they came from; surely they had come from the king's castle. Two beautiful roses with crowns on their heads walked in front; they were king and queen. Then came pretty stocks and carnations, bowing to all sides: they had brought music with them. Large poppies and peonies blew on pea-pods until they were quite red in the face. The blue hyacinths and the little white lilies of the valley tinkled as if they had bells. That was wonderful music! Then many other flowers came, and they all danced—blue violets, the red night daisies, and lilies of the valley. All the flowers kissed one another; it was very sweet to look at. At last the flowers said "Good-night" to one another, and then little Ida stole back into her bed again, and dreamt of all she had seen. When she got up in the morning she quickly went to the little table to see if her flowers were still there. She drew the curtains from the little bed, and there they lay, all withered—much more so than the day before. Sophy was lying in the drawer where she had placed her, but she looked very sleepy.

"Do you not remember what you have to tell me?" asked little Ida. But Sophy was dumb, and did not say a single word. "You are not good," said Ida; "have they not all danced with you?" Then she took a small paper box on which beautiful birds were painted, opened it, and placed the dead flowers inside. "This shall be your pretty coffin," she said, "and when my cousins come again they shall help me to bury you, out in the garden, that you may next summer grow again, and become more beautiful!"

The cousins were two bright boys called Jonas and Adolphe; their father had given them each a crossbow, which they had brought with them to show Ida. She told them about the poor flowers, and asked them to help her to bury them. The two boys walked in front with their crossbows on their shoulders, while little Ida followed, carrying the pretty box with the dead flowers. In the garden they dug a little grave. Ida first kissed the flowers and then laid them with the little box in the earth. Adolphe and Jonas shot with their crossbows over the grave, for they had neither guns nor cannons.

The Story of the Year

T was in the latter part of the month of January. A violent snowstorm was raging; the snow whirled along the streets and lanes and covered the outside of the window-panes all over, whilst it fell down in larger masses from the roofs of the houses.

All the people in the street were seized with a sudden haste; they hurried along, often jostling against one another or falling into one another's arms, holding on tightly, so as to be safe for a moment at least. Carriages and horses looked as if they were powdered all over with sugar; the footmen were standing with their backs to the carriages, in order to shelter their faces from the cutting wind; foot-passengers eagerly sought the protection of the vehicles which moved slowly forward through the deep snow. When at last the storm had abated, and narrow paths were cleared along the fronts of the houses, people nevertheless often came to a dead stop when they met, neither wishing to step aside into the deep snow to make room for the other to pass.

Still and silently they were standing face to face, till at last they mutually arrived at the tacit compromise of exposing each one foot to the snow-heaps.

Towards the evening the wind ceased to blow; the sky looked as if it had been swept, and became higher and more transparent; the stars seemed to be quite new, and some of them were shining marvellously bright and clear; it was freezing so much that the snow creaked, and soon it was covered with a crust strong enough to carry the sparrows at daybreak, when they hopped up and down, where the snow had been shovelled away; but there was very little food to be found, and it was bitterly cold.

"Twit," said one to another, "this is what they call a new year; it is much worse than the last, and we might just as well have kept the old one. I am very dissatisfied, and I think I have good cause to be so."

"Yes; people were running about and firing salutes in honour of the new year," said a little sparrow, shivering with cold. "They were throwing pots and dishes against the doors, and were nearly out of their minds for joy, because the old year was gone. I was glad of it too, for I hoped we should soon have warmer days again; but nothing of the sort has happened yet; on the contrary, it freezes much harder than before. I think they must have made a mistake in their calculation of the time."

"There is no doubt about it," said a third, an old grey-headed bird. "They have a thing they call a calendar, which is entirely their own invention, and that is why they wish to regulate everything according to it; but that can't be so easily done. When

Spring comes the new year begins; that is the course of nature—
I go by that."

"But when will Spring come?" asked the others.

"It will come when the stork comes back; but he is very
uncertain. Nobody here in town knows anything about him; they
are better informed in the country. Shall we fly thither and wait?
There we are certainly much nearer to Spring."

"That is all very well," said one of the sparrows, who had hopped
about and chirped for a long time, without really saying anything.
"I have found here in town comforts which I fear I should have
to go without in the country. Near here, in a courtyard, live
some people who had the happy thought of attaching two or
three flower-pots to their house, so that their open ends are close
to the wall, whilst the bottoms of the pots stand out; a hole is cut
into each of them large enough for me to fly in and out; there my
husband and I have built our nest, and there we have reared all
our young ones. These people have of course done all this to
have the pleasure of seeing us, otherwise I am sure they would
not have done it. For their own pleasure, also, they strew out
bread-crumbs, and thus we have food: we are, as it were, provided
for. Therefore I think my husband and I will stay, although we
are very discontented—yes, I think we shall stay."

"And we shall fly into the country to see if Spring is not yet
coming." And off they went.

In the country the winter was harder still, and the glass showed
a few degrees more cold than in town. The piercing wind swept
over the snow-covered fields. The peasant sat in his sledge, with
his hands wrapt in warm mittens, beating his arms across his
chest to get warm, whilst his whip was lying on his knees; the
lean horses ran so fast that they steamed; the snow creaked, and
the sparrows hopped about in the ruts and froze. "Twit! When
will Spring come? It takes a very long time."

"A very long time," resounded from the nearest snow-covered
hill far over the field; it might have been an echo which
one heard, or perhaps the language of the wonderful old man
who sat in wind and weather on the top of snow-heaps; he
was quite white, dressed like a peasant in a coarse white coat of

frieze; he had long white hair, was very pale, and had large clear eyes.

"Who is the old man yonder?" asked the sparrows.

"I know," said an old raven sitting on the post of a railing, who was condescending enough to acknowledge that we are all small birds in the sight of the Lord, and who was therefore ready to talk to the sparrows and to give them information. "I know who the old man is. It is Winter, the old man of last year: he is not dead, as the calendar says, but is guardian to the young prince Spring, who is coming. Yes, Winter is still swaying his sceptre. Ugh! the cold makes you shiver, you little ones, does it not?"

"Yes; but is it not as I said?" asked the sparrow. "The calendar is only the invention of men, it is not arranged according to nature. They ought to leave such things to us, who are more sensitive."

Week after week passed by; the frozen lake was motionless, and looked like molten lead; damp, icy mists were hanging heavily over the country; the large black crows flew about in long rows without making a noise; it was as if everything in nature was asleep. Then a sunbeam glided over the icy surface of the lake, and made it shine like polished tin. The snow covering the fields and the hill no longer glittered as before; but the white man, Winter himself, was still sitting there and looking unswervingly southward; he did not notice that the snowy carpet sunk, as it were, into the ground, and that here and there little green spots came forth, and on these spots the sparrows flocked together.

"Twit, twit! is Spring coming now?"

"Spring!" It sounded over field and meadow, and through the dark woods, where bright green moss was shining on the trunks of the trees; and the two first storks arrived from the south, carrying on their backs two lovely little children, a boy and a girl; they kissed the earth in greeting, and wherever they set their feet, white flowers sprang forth out of the snow; hand-in-hand they went to the old ice-man, Winter, and tenderly clung to his breast. In a moment they had all three disappeared, whilst the whole country round them was enveloped in a thick damp

mist, dense and heavy, which covered everything like a veil.
Gradually the wind began to blow, and rushed with a roar against
the mist and drove it away with violent blows; the sun shone
brightly.

Winter had disappeared, but Spring's lovely children had seated
themselves on the throne of the year.

"This is the new year!" cried the sparrows. "Now we shall
get our due, and damages in addition, for the severe winter."

Wherever the two children directed their steps, green buds
burst forth on the bushes and trees; the grass was shooting up;
the cornfields became day by day greener and more lovely to look
at. The little girl strewed flowers all around—there were no end
of them in her frock, which she held up; however jealously she
strewed them, they seemed to grow there. In her great zeal she
poured forth a snow of blossoms over apple and pear trees, so
that they stood there in all their splendour, before the green leaves
had time to grow forth.

And she clapped her hands, and the boy followed her example;
flocks of birds came flying, nobody knew where they came from,
and chirped and sang: "Spring has come!"

That was wonderful to see. Many an old woman came out of
her doorway into the sunshine, and basked in it, looking at the
yellow flowers, blooming everywhere in the fields, and thinking
that it was just like that in her young days; the world grew young
again to her. "It is a blessing to be out here to-day," she said.

The wood still wore its dark green garments, made of buds, but
the thyme had already come out, filling the air with sweet
fragrance, and there were plenty of violets, anemones and prim-
roses: every blade of grass was full of sap and strength. Truly
that was a marvellous carpet, on which one could not help wishing to rest. There the two Spring children sat down hand-in-
hand, singing and smiling, and continually growing. A mild rain
fell down from heaven; they did not notice it, the rain-drops
mingled with their own tears of joy.

The two lovers kissed each other, and in a moment the green
of the wood became alive. When the sun rose again all the
woods were green.

Hand-in-hand the betrothed wandered under the fresh hanging roof of leaves, wherever the sunbeams and shadows produced a change of colour in the green.

What delicate tints, what a sweet fragrance the new leaves had! The clear stream and brooks rippled merrily between the velvet-like rushes and over the coloured pebbles. "So it was for ever and shall ever remain so," said all Nature. The cuckoo sang, the lark flew up—it was a beautiful spring; but the willow trees wore woollen mittens over their blossoms; they were exceedingly careful, and that is tiresome.

Days and weeks passed by, and the heat came, as it were, rolling down ; hot waves of air passed through the corn and made it yellower from day to day. The white water-lily of the north spread its large green leaves over the surface of the streams and lakes, and the fishes sought shade beneath them. In a spot where the trees of the wood sheltered it stood a farmer's cottage ; the sun shone on its walls and warmed the unfolded roses, and the black juicy berries with which the cherry-trees were loaded. There sat the lovely wife of Summer, the same that we have seen as child and bride ; her glances were fixed on the rising dark clouds, which, like mountains, in wave-like outlines, dark blue and heavy, were rising higher and higher. From three sides they came, continually growing, and seemed very much like a petrified reversed ocean gradually settling down on the forest, where everything, as if by magic, had become quiet. Not a breath of air was stirring ; every bird was silent, there was an earnest expectation in the whole of Nature, but on the paths and roadways people in carriages, on horseback, and on foot, hastened to reach a shelter.

Suddenly there came a flash of light, as if the sun broke through the clouds again, flaming, dazzling, all-devouring ; and then again it became dark, and the thunder rolled. Rain came pouring down in torrents ; darkness and light, absolute silence and terrible noise, followed each other in quick succession. The wind moved the long, feather-like reeds on the moor like the waves of the sea ; the branches of the trees were concealed in watery mist. Grass and corn lay beaten down and swamped, looking as if they could never rise again. Then the rain gradually ceased, the sun burst forth, drops of water glittered on the stalks and leaves like pearls, the birds began to sing, the fishes darted out of the water, the gnats played in the sunshine; and out on a stone in the foaming water stood Summer himself, the strong man, with vigorous limbs, and wet, dripping hair, refreshed by the bath, basking in the sunshine.

All Nature seemed born anew, and stood forth in rich, strong, beautiful splendour; it was Summer, warm, sweet Summer.

Sweet and agreeable was the fragrance streaming forth from the rich clover field; the bees were humming yonder round the ruins of the old meeting-place; a bramble-bush wound itself round the stone altar, which, washed by the rain, was glittering in the sunshine, thither flew the queen with the whole swarm to prepare wax and honey. Only Summer saw it, and his vigorous spouse; for them the altar-table was covered with Nature's offerings.

The evening sky looked like gold; no church dome was ever so bright, and the moon was shining between the evening red and the dawn. It was Summer!

And days and weeks passed by. The shining scythes of the reapers glittered in the cornfields, the branches of the apple-trees were bending under the weight of the red and yellow fruit: the hops smelt sweetly and hung in large clusters, and under the hazel bushes, where the nuts grew in big bunches, sat Summer, with his serious wife.

"What a wealth!" she said; "blessings are spread everywhere. Wherever one turns it is pleasant to abide; and yet—I do not know why—I am longing for peace, rest; I cannot express what I feel. They are already ploughing again. Men are insatiable; they always wish to gain more and more. See, the storks come in flocks and follow at a little distance behind the ploughs; it is the bird of Egypt which carried us through the air. Do you still remember when we two came hither to this northern land? We brought with us flowers, lovely sunshine, and green woods. The wind has dealt very roughly with them; they are becoming brown and dark like the trees of the south, but they do not carry golden fruit like those."

"You would like to see the golden fruit?" asked Summer. "Look up, then." He lifted his arm, and the leaves of the trees became red and golden. A splendour of colour was spread over all the woods; the dog-rose hedge glittered with scarlet hips, the elder-trees were full of large bunches of dark-brown berries, the horse-chestnuts fell down out of their dark-green husks, and on the ground below violets were blooming for the second time.

But the queen of the year grew quieter and paler. "It is blowing very cold," she said; "the night brings damp mists. I am longing for the country where I passed my childhood."

And she saw the storks fly away. Not a single one remained; and she stretched out her hands after them, as if she wished to retain them. She looked up at the empty nests—in one a long-stalked cornflower, in another the yellow rape-seed were thriving, as if the nest was only intended to protect them and serve as a fence for them; and the sparrows flew up into the storks' nest.

"Twit! What has become of the master and his wife? They cannot bear it if the wind blows a little, and therefore they have left the country. I wish them a happy journey."

The leaves in the wood became more yellow day by day, and fell down one after another. The violent autumn winds were blowing; the year was far advanced, and on a couch of dry leaves rested the queen of the year, and looked with mild eyes at the sparkling stars, while her husband stood by her side. A gust of wind made the leaves rustle; a great many of them fell down, and suddenly she was gone; but a butterfly—the last of the year—flew through the cold air.

Damp fogs came, icy winds were blowing, and the dark long nights set in. The ruler of the year stood there, with white locks, but he was not aware of it; he thought snowflakes were falling from the clouds.

A thin layer of snow was spread over the green fields, and the church bells were pealing forth the Christmas chimes.

"The bells are telling of Christ's birth," said the ruler of the year. "Soon the new rulers will be born, and I shall go to rest, like my wife: to rest in the shining star."

And out in the green pinewood the Christmas angel consecrated the young trees which he selected to serve at his festival.

"May there be joy in the homes under the green branches," said the old ruler of the year: in a few weeks his hair had become as white as snow. "The time for my rest draws near, and the young couple of the year will receive my crown and sceptre."

"You are still in power," said the Christmas angel; "you must not yet go to rest. Let the snow still cover and warm the young seed. Learn to bear the thought that honour is done to another while you are still the ruler. Learn to be forgotten and yet to live. The hour of your deliverance approaches with Spring."

"When is Spring coming?" said Winter.

"He will come when the stork returns."

And Winter, ice-cold and broken down, with white locks and still whiter beard, was sitting on the top of the hill, where his predecessor had sat, and looked towards the south. The ice cracked, the snow creaked, the skaters enjoyed themselves on the smooth surface of the lake and the black of the ravens and crows stood in strong contrast to the white ground. Not a breath of air was stirring. Old Winter clenched his fists in the cold air, and the ice on the rivers and lakes was several feet thick.

Then the sparrows came out of town again and asked: "Who is the old man yonder?" And the raven was there again, or perhaps his son, which comes to the same thing, and replied to them: "It is Winter, the old man from last year. He is not dead, as the calendar says, but is the guardian of Spring, who is approaching."

"When will Spring come?" asked the sparrows; "then we shall have a better time and milder *régime;* the old one was good for nothing."

And Winter nodded pensively towards the dark leafless woods, where every tree showed the graceful outline of its branches, and during the long winter night icy fogs descended—the ruler dreamt of his young days, of his manhood, and at daybreak the whole forest was glittering with hoar-frost; that was Winter's summer dream, but the sunshine soon made the frost melt and drop down from the branches.

"When will Spring come ? " asked the sparrows

"Spring !" echoed the snow-covered hills : the sun shone more warmly, the snow melted, the birds chirped, "Spring is coming."

And the first stork came flying through the air, a second soon followed : each had a lovely child on his back.   They descended in an open field, kissed the ground and kissed the silent old man ; and as Moses disappeared on the mount, so he disappeared, carried away by the clouds.

The story of the year was ended.

"This is all very fine," said the sparrows ; "it is beautiful too ; but it is not according to the calendar, and therefore it must be wrong."

The Travelling Companion

OOR John was in great trouble, for his father was very ill and could not be cured. Besides these two there was no one at all in the little room : the lamp on the table was almost out, and it was late at night.

"You have been a good son, John," said the sick father; "the Lord will help you on in the world."   He looked at him with his grave loving eyes, took a deep breath, and died : it seemed as if he were asleep.   John wept; now he had no one in the world, neither father nor mother, neither sister nor brother.   Poor John!   He lay on his knees at the bedside, kissed his dead father's hand, and wept many bitter tears ; but at last his eyes closed, and he fell asleep with his head resting against the hard bedpost.

Then he dreamed a strange dream.   He saw the sun and moon bow down before him ; he saw his father alive and well again, and heard him laugh as he always laughed when he was right merry.

A beautiful girl, with a golden crown on her long shining hair, gave
him her hand, and his father said: "Do you see what a bride
you have obtained? She is the most beautiful maiden in the
world." Then he awoke, and all the joy was gone; his father lay
dead and cold upon the bed, and there was no one else in the
room. Poor John!

The next week the funeral took place. John walked close
behind the coffin; he could no longer see the kind father
who had loved him so dearly. He heard them throwing the
earth down upon the coffin, and gazed upon it till only the last
corner was to be seen; but with the next shovelful of earth that
too was hidden. Then he felt as if his heart must burst with
sorrow. Those around him were singing a psalm in beautiful
sacred tones that brought tears into his eyes; he wept, and that
did him good in his grief.

The sun shone beautifully upon the green trees, as if it would
say: "You must not give way to sorrow any longer, John! Do you
see how beautiful the sky is? Up yonder is your father, and he
is praying to the good Lord that it may always go well with
you."

"I will always be good," said John; "then I shall join my
father in heaven; and what joy it will be when we see each
other again! How much shall I then be able to tell him! And
he will show me so many things, and explain to me the glory of
heaven, just as he used to instruct me here upon earth. Oh!
what joy that will be!"

He saw it all so plainly that it made him smile, whilst the tears
were still running down his cheeks. The little birds sat up in the
chestnut-trees and twittered. They were joyous and cheerful,
although they too had been present at the funeral; but they knew
very well that the dead man was now in Heaven, and that he had
wings, larger and more beautiful than theirs. They knew that he
was happy now, because he had been good down here on earth,
and therefore they were pleased. John saw how they flew far out
into the world from the green trees, and he felt a desire to fly with
them. But first he cut a large wooden cross to place upon his
father's grave, and when he brought it there in the evening he

found the grave already strewn with sand and flowers. Strangers had done this, for all loved the good father who was now dead.

Early next morning John packed his little bundle, and carefully placed in his belt his whole inheritance, amounting to fifty dollars and a few silver pennies; with this he intended to start out into the world. But he first went to the churchyard to his father's grave, recited the Lord's Prayer, and said "Farewell!"

In the fields through which he passed all the flowers looked fresh and blooming in the warm sunshine; they nodded in the wind as if they wished to say, "Welcome to the green pastures! Is it not beautiful here?"

But John turned round once more to take a last look at the old church in which he had been baptized when a little child, and where he had gone to service with his father every Sunday, and where he had sung many a psalm. On looking back he saw the goblin of the church, with his little red pointed cap, standing high up in one of the openings of the steeple, shading his face with his bent arm to keep the sun out of his eyes. John nodded him farewell, and the goblin waved his red cap, laid his hand upon his heart, and threw him a great many kisses to show that he wished him well and hoped that he might have a right pleasant journey.

John thought of the many beautiful things he would now see in the great splendid world, and he went farther and farther—farther than he had ever been before. He did not know the places through which he passed nor the people whom he met; he was now in quite a strange land.

The first night he had to lie down to rest upon a haystack in the open fields; he had no other bed. But it was a very nice one, he thought; the king could have no better: the whole field, with the brook, the haystack, and then the blue sky above—what a fine bedroom it made! The green grass, with its little red and white flowers, was the carpet; the elder bushes and the wild roses were bouquets; and the whole brook, with its clear fresh water, in which the reeds bowed down and wished him good evening and good morning, served him as a wash-hand basin. The moon was really a splendid night-lamp high up under the blue canopy, and it would not set light to the bed-curtains—John could sleep in peace. And he did so too, not waking up till the sun rose and all the little birds round about were singing "Good morning! Good morning! Are you not up yet?"

The bells were ringing for church; it was Sunday. The people were going to hear the sermon, and John went in with them, sang a hymn and listened to the Word of God. He felt as if he were in his own church, in which he had been baptized and where he had sung hymns with his father.

Outside in the churchyard were many graves, and on some there grew long grass. Then he thought of his father's grave, which would one day look like these, for he would not be able to weed it and keep it trim. So he sat down, tearing up the weeds, setting upright the wooden crosses that had fallen down, and restoring to their places the wreaths which the wind had carried from the graves.

"Perhaps some one will do the same to my father's grave, since I cannot do so!" thought he.

At the churchyard gate stood an old beggar leaning on a crutch. John gave him the silver pennies he had, and then went farther on his way into the wide world, happy and contented.

Towards evening a dreadful storm came on. He hastened to get under shelter, but the dark night soon fell, and at last he reached a small church which stood alone upon a little hill.

"I will sit down in a corner here," he said, and went in. "I am tired, and must rest for a little while."

So he sat down, folded his hands, and said his evening prayer; and before he knew it he was asleep and dreaming, while outside it thundered and lightened.

When he awoke it was midnight; the storm was over and the moon was shining in through the windows. In the middle of the church stood an open coffin in which lay a dead man waiting to be buried. John was by no means afraid, for he had a clear conscience, and he knew that the dead hurt no one.

Only the living who do evil are wicked. Two of these living wicked people stood close by the corpse, which had been placed in the church before burial; they had come with the wicked intention of taking the poor man out of his coffin and of throwing him out before the church door.

"Why do you want to do that?" asked John. "That is wicked and bad; let him rest, in God's name."

"Fiddlesticks!" said the two evil-looking men. "He has deceived us. He owes us money which he could not pay; and now that he is dead into the bargain, we shall not get a penny of it: that's why we want revenge. He shall lie like a dog before the church-door."

"I have only fifty dollars," said John. "That is my whole inheritance; but I will gladly give it you, if you promise me, upon your honour, to leave the poor dead man in peace. I daresay I shall manage to get on without the money; I have strong healthy limbs, and the Lord will provide."

"Very well," said the men; "if you will pay his debts, we shall neither of us do him any harm, you may depend upon that." So they took the money that he gave them and went their way, laughing loudly at his simplicity. He then laid the body straight again in the coffin, folded its hands, and bidding it farewell went further into the wood with a light heart.

All around him, wherever the moon shone through the trees, he saw the pretty little elves playing merrily. They were not at all disturbed by him; they knew very well that he was good and innocent, and it is only bad people who never see the elves. Some of them were no taller than a finger's breadth, and had their long yellow hair fastened up with golden combs. Two by two they played at see-saw on the large dew-drops that lay upon the leaves and the tall grass; every now and then a drop rolled down, and then they fell among the long blades of grass, causing much laughter and noise among the rest of the little people. It was delightful! They sang, and John distinctly recognised the pretty songs which he had learnt when a little boy. Great gaily-coloured spiders, with silver crowns on their heads, were made to spin long suspension bridges from one hedge to another, and palaces that looked like glittering glass in the moonshine when the fine dew fell upon them. And so it went till sunrise. Then the little elves crept into the flower-beds, and the wind seized their bridges and castles, which flew through the air like spiders' webs.

John had just left the wood, when a strong manly voice called out after him: "Hallo, comrade, where are you going to?"

"Out into the wide world!" he replied. "I have neither father nor mother, I am only a poor fellow · but the Lord will help me."

"I am going out into the wide world, too," said the stranger. "Shall we keep each other company?"

"Certainly," replied John; and so they went together.

They soon grew very fond of each other, for they were both good men. But John perceived that the stranger was much wiser than himself. He had travelled almost all over the world and could speak of every possible thing that existed.

The sun was already high in the heavens when they sat down under a large tree to eat their breakfast. Just then an old woman came up. She was very old and lame, supporting herself on a crutch; on her back she carried a bundle of firewood that she had collected in the woods. Her apron was tied up, and John saw that she had three large bundles of ferns and willow-boughs in it. As she came near them, her foot slipped, and she fell with a loud cry, for she had broken her leg, poor old woman.

John at once suggested that they should carry the old woman to her home; but the stranger, opening his knapsack, took out a box, and said that he had a salve that would heal her leg, and make it strong immediately, so that she would be able to walk home herself, as if she had never broken her leg at all.

But he demanded that in return she should give him the three bundles she had in her apron.

"That would be well paid," said the old woman, shaking her head in a strange manner. She was very unwilling to give up the herbs, but it was certainly unpleasant to lie there with a broken leg. So she gave him the three bundles, and as soon as he had rubbed the salve into her leg she got up and walked much better than before. All this the salve could do. But it was not to be bought at the chemist's.

"What do you want the bundles for?" John asked his companion.

"They are three fine bundles of herbs," he replied. "I am very fond of them, for I am an odd kind of fellow."

They walked on some distance.

"Look how the clouds are gathering," said John, pointing straight before him. "How terribly black they are!"

"No," said his companion, "those are not clouds, they are mountains—the glorious high mountains by which one gets up amongst the clouds and into the fresh air. Believe me, it is delightful to be there. To-morrow we shall certainly be a good stretch on our way."

But they were not so near as they looked; they had to walk a whole day long before they reached the mountains, where the dark forests grew up towards the sky, and where there were stones almost as large as a whole town. It would certainly be a great exertion to cross them, so John and his companion turned into an inn to take a good rest, and recruit their strength for the morrow's march.

A great many people were assembled in the roomy bar of the inn, for there was a man giving a puppet-show. He had just put up his little theatre, and the people were sitting round in a circle to see the play. A fat butcher had taken the best seat in the first row, and by his side sat his big mastiff—a ferocious-looking animal—staring, like all the others, with all his might.

The show now began; it was a pretty little play, with a king and a queen in it. They sat upon a splendid throne, with golden crowns upon their heads, and long trains to their robes, for their means permitted it. The sweetest little wooden dolls, with glass eyes and great moustaches, stood at all the doors, opening and closing them, so that fresh air might come into the room. It was really a very pretty play. But when the queen got up and walked across the floor, the great mastiff—Heaven knows why !—not being held by the fat butcher, jumped right into the theatre, and seized the queen by the waist, making her crack. It was terrible !

The poor showman was very upset and grieved about his queen. She was the most beautiful doll he possessed, and now the ugly mastiff had bitten her head off. But when all the people had gone, the stranger who had come with John said that he would soon make it right again ; taking out his box, he rubbed some of the salve that he had used to heal the old woman's broken leg, into the doll. As soon as it had been applied, the doll was whole again ; indeed, it could even use all its limbs by itself; there was no longer any need to pull the string. The doll was just like a human being, except that it could not speak. The owner of the little show was delighted ; he no longer needed to hold this doll, for it could dance by itself. None of the others could do that.

Later in the night, when all the people in the inn were in bed, some one was heard groaning so terribly and so continuously that every one got up to see who it was. The showman went to his little theatre, for it was from that quarter that the groans came. All the wooden puppets, including the king and all the soldiers, lay scattered about ; they were groaning terribly, and looking most piteously out of their glass eyes, for they were all most anxious to be besmeared with the salve like the queen, so that they also might be able to move by themselves. The queen immediately fell upon her knees, and holding out her splendid crown, said in imploring tones: "Take this, but anoint my consort and my courtiers !" At this the poor showman could not refrain from weeping ; he really felt for her. He promised to give the stranger all the money he should receive for his play on the following evening, if he would only besmear four or five of his best dolls.

But the stranger said he desired nothing more than the sword that the showman carried at his side; on that being given him, he besmeared six puppets, which immediately began to dance, and so prettily, that all the young girls who were looking on soon began to dance too. The coachman and the cook, the waiter and the chambermaid, all the guests, and even the shovel and the tongs, joined in; the latter, however, fell over as soon as they had taken the first step. What a merry night it was!

Next morning John left the inn with his companion, ascending the lofty mountains, and going through the vast pine-forests. They got up so high that the church towers far beneath them looked like little blue berries amongst all the verdure; they could see very far, for many, many miles, places where they had never been. John had never before seen so much of the beauty of this fair world at once. The sun shone warm in the clear blue sky, and when he heard the sweet notes of the horn as it was blown by the huntsmen in the mountains, tears of joy came into his eyes, and he could not refrain from crying: "How good is God to have created so much beauty in the world, and to have given it us to enjoy!"

His comrade too stood there with his arms folded, gazing out over woods and towns, into the warm sunshine.

At that moment they heard a strange sweet sound over their heads, and looking up they saw a large white swan hovering in the air above them and singing as they had never heard a bird sing before. The song, however, grew fainter and fainter; with drooping head the bird slowly sank down at their feet, where the beautiful creature died.

"Two beautiful wings," said John's companion, "so white and large as those which this bird has, are worth money; I will take them with me. Do you see what a good thing it was that I had a sword?"

So he struck off both wings of the dead bird with one blow; he was going to keep them.

They now travelled many, many miles, far across the mountains, till at last they saw a great city before them, with hundreds of steeples that shone like silver in the sun. In the city was a splendid marble castle with a roof of pure gold. There lived the king. John and his companion did not wish to go into the town at once, but stopped at an inn just outside, in order to wash and dress themselves a bit, for they wanted to look neat when they went into the streets.

The landlord told them that the king was a very good man, who never did any one any harm; but as for his daughter—Heavens

preserve us!—she was a bad princess. She was beautiful enough; nobody was so pretty nor so dainty as she; but what was the use of that? She was a wicked sorceress, who was the cause of many handsome princes losing their lives. She had given everybody permission to woo her. Any one might come, were he prince or beggar; that was all one to her. He was only to guess three things that she happened to be thinking of when she asked him. If he could do so, she would marry him, and he would be king over the whole country when her father died; but if he could not guess the three things, she had him hanged or beheaded. Her father, the old king, was very grieved about it; but he could not prevent her from being so wicked, for he had once declared that he would never have anything to do with her lovers, and that she could do as she liked. Every time a prince came and tried to guess in order to have the princess, he failed, and then he was either hanged or beheaded. He had been warned in time; he might have gone away without guessing. The old king was so grieved at all the sorrow and misery she caused, that he and all his soldiers spend a whole day on their knees every year, praying that the princess might reform; but that she never would. The old women who drank brandy used to colour it black before they drank it—so deeply did they mourn. And more than that they really could not do.

"What a hateful princess!" said John. "She ought really to be flogged—that would do her good. If only I were the old king, she should soon be thrashed."

As they spoke they heard the people shouting "Hurrah" outside. The princess was passing; she was really so beautiful that all the people forgot how wicked she was, and so they shouted "Hurrah." Twelve fair maidens, all in white silk dresses, and each carrying a golden tulip in her hand, rode at her side on black horses. The princess herself was on a white horse adorned with diamonds and rubies. Her riding habit was of pure cloth of gold, and the whip which she held in her hand glittered like a sunbeam. The golden chain around her neck seemed as though composed of small heavenly stars, and her mantle had been made up from more than a thousand butterflies' wings. Nevertheless, she was still more beautiful than her attire.

When John beheld her, he got as red in the face as a drop of blood, and could not say a single word. The princess looked just like the beautiful maiden with the golden crown of whom he had dreamt the night his father died. He thought her so beautiful that he could not help loving her with all his heart. "It could not be true," he said to himself, "that she was a wicked sorceress, who had people hanged or beheaded if they could not guess what she asked them. Every one is free to woo her, even the poorest beggar. Then I will really go to the castle, for I feel that I must."

Every one told him not to go, and warned him that he would certainly share the fate of all the others. His companion, too, tried to dissuade him, but John was of opinion that it would be all right. He brushed his shoes and coat, washed his hands and face, combed his beautiful fair hair, and went into the town alone, and up to the castle.

"Come in," said the old king when John knocked at the door. John went in, and the old king, in his dressing-gown and slippers,

AJG.

came to meet him. He had his crown on his head and held the sceptre in one hand and the orb in the other.

"Wait a moment," he said, putting the orb under his arm in order to shake hands with John. But as soon as he heard that he was a suitor, he began to cry so bitterly that both the sceptre and the orb fell upon the floor, and he was obliged to dry his eyes on his dressing-gown. Poor old king!

"Pray, don't," he said. "You will share the fate of all the others. Well, you will see." Then he led him out into the princess's pleasure garden. What a terrible sight was there! In each tree there hung three or four princes who had wooed the princess, but had not been able to guess what she had asked them. Every time a gust of wind came, all the skeletons rattled, so that the little birds were startled and never ventured to comeinto the garden. All the flowers were tied up to human bones, and in the flower-pots were grinning skulls. It was really a strange garden for a princess.

"Now you see it," said the old king. "You will share the same fate. Therefore give up the idea. You will really make me very unhappy, for I take these things much to heart.'

John kissed the good old king's hand and said it would be all right, for he was charmed with the fair princess.

Then the princess herself came riding into the courtyard with all her ladies, so they went out to her and bade her "Good-day." She was marvellously fair to look at, and gave John her hand. He loved her still more passionately than before. She could certainly be no wicked sorceress, as all the people wanted to make out. Then they went into the hall and the little pages offered them preserves and ginger-nuts. But the old king was sad and could eat nothing. Besides, the ginger-nuts were too hard for him.

It was arranged that John was to come to the castle again on the following morning; then the judges and the whole council would be assembled to hear the guessing. If it turned out all right he would have to come twice more; but hitherto no one had yet guessed aright the first time, and had all lost their lives.

John was not much concerned about his fate. On the contrary, he was in good spirits, and thought only of the fair princess, feeling sure Heaven would help him—how, he did not know, and preferred not to think about it. He danced along the high-road as he went back to the inn, where his travelling companion was waiting for him.

John did not tire of telling how gracious the princess had been to him, and how beautiful she was. He already longed for the next day, when he was to go to the castle to try his luck at guessing.

But his companion shook his head and was very sad. "I am so fond of you," he said; "we might have stayed together a long while yet, and I am to lose you so soon. Poor dear John! I could weep, but I will not spoil your happiness on the last evening that we shall perhaps spend together. We will be merry, right merry; to-morrow, when you are gone, I will weep undisturbed."

All the people in the town had soon heard that a new suitor for the princess had arrived, and consequently there was great mourning. The theatre was closed; all the cake-women tied crape round their sugar-figures, and the king and the priests lay upon their knees in the churches. There was general mourning, for no other fate awaited John than that which had befallen all the other suitors.

Towards the evening John's companion made a large bowl of punch, and said to him: "Now let us be right merry, and drink to the health of the princess." But when John had drunk two glasses he became so sleepy that it was impossible for him to keep his eyes open; he sank into a deep slumber. His companion lifted him gently from the chair and laid him in the bed. When it had got quite dark he took the two large wings that he had cut off from the swan, and fastened them upon his own shoulders. He then put into his pocket the largest of the bundles which he had received from the old woman who had fallen and broken her leg, and, opening the window, flew over the town to the castle, where he sat down in a corner under the window that belonged to the princess's bedroom.

Stillness reigned throughout the city. As the clock struck a quarter to twelve the window opened, and the princess, with black wings and a long white mantle, flew away over the town to a high mountain. John's companion, making himself invisible, flew after her, and whipped her so with his rod that the blood came at every stroke. What a journey that was through the air! The wind caught her mantle, which spread itself out on all sides like a sail of a ship, and the moon shone through it.

"How it hails! how it hails!" said the princess at each blow she received from the rod; and it served her right. At last she arrived at the mountain and knocked. There was a noise like thunder as the mountain opened and she went in. John's companion followed her, for no one could see him: he was invisible. They went through a long wide passage where the walls shone strangely, for more than a thousand gleaming spiders were running up and down them, making them look as though illuminated with fire. Then they entered a great hall built of silver and gold. Red and blue flowers as large as sunflowers shone on the walls; but no one could pick them, for the stalks were hideous poisonous snakes, and the flowers were flames darting out of their jaws. The whole ceiling was covered with shining glow-worms and sky-blue bats flapping their flimsy wings.

The place looked quite horrible. In the middle of the floor was a throne, borne by four skeleton horses, whose harness had been made by the red fiery spiders. The throne itself was made of milk-white glass, and the cushions were little black mice, who were biting each other's tails. Over it was a canopy of rose-coloured spiders' webs studded with pretty little green flies that shone like precious stones. On the throne sat an old sorcerer, with a crown on his ugly head and a sceptre in his hand. He kissed the princess on the forehead, gave her a seat by his side on the splendid throne, and then the music began. Great black grasshoppers played on mouth-organs, and an owl beat the drum. It was a ridiculous concert. Little black goblins, each with a will-o'-the-wisp on its cap, danced around in the hall. But no one could see the travelling companion; he had placed himself behind the throne and could hear and see everything. The courtiers, who now entered, looked very noble and grand, but any one with common sense could see what they really were. They were nothing more than broomsticks with cabbages stuck upon them; the sorcerer had blown life into them and given them embroidered robes. But that made no difference; they were only used for show.

After there had been some dancing, the princess told the
sorcerer that she had a new suitor, and therefore asked him what
he was to think of for him to guess when he came to the castle
next morning.

"Listen," said the sorcerer; "I will tell you. You must choose
something very easy, for then he will not guess it at all. Think of
our shoes. He won't guess that. Have his head chopped off,
but don't forget to bring me his eyes when you come to-morrow
night, for I want to eat them."

The princess bowed low and said she would not forget the eyes.
The sorcerer then opened the mountain and she flew back again;
but the travelling companion followed her and whipped her so
with the rod that she groaned aloud at the severity of the hail-
storm, and made as much haste as she could to get back to her
bedroom through the window. The companion then flew back
to the inn where John was still asleep, took off his wings and lay
down on the bed, for he was naturally very tired.

It was early in the morning when John awoke. His companion got up too, and told that he had had a wonderful dream
at night of the princess and her shoe, and therefore begged him
ask her whether she had not thought of her shoe. For that
was what he had heard from the sorcerer in the mountain.

"I can just as well ask that as anything else," said John.
"Perhaps what you have dreamt is correct, for I trust in Heaven,
which I am sure will help me. But still I will bid you farewell,
for if I guess wrong I shall never see you again."

Then they embraced each other, and John went into the town
and to the castle. The hall was full of people; the judges sat in
their armchairs and had eider-down cushions upon which to rest
their heads, for they had a great deal to think of. The old king
got up and dried his eyes with a white pocket-handkerchief.

Now the princess entered. She was still more beautiful than
she had been on the previous day, and greeted every one in the
most gracious manner; but to John she gave her hand and said,
"Good morning to you."

Now, John was to guess of what she had thought. Heavens!
how kindly she looked at him. But as soon as she heard him

utter the word "shoe" she turned deathly pale and trembled all over. But that could not help her, for he had guessed aright.

Gracious! how pleased the old king was—he turned a somersault which it was a pleasure to see. And all the people clapped their hands in his honour and John's, who had guessed rightly the first time.

The travelling companion too was glad when he heard how successful John had been. But the latter folded his hands and thanked God, who he felt sure would also help him on the two other occasions. On the next day the guessing was again to take place.

The evening was passed like the preceding one. When John was asleep his companion flew after the princess to the mountain and flogged her more severely than the night before, for now he had taken two rods. No one could see him, and he heard everything. The princess was to think of her glove, and this he told John as if he had again heard it in a dream. He was therefore able to guess correctly, and it caused great joy at the castle. The whole Court turned somersaults, just as they had seen the king do on the first occasion. But the princess lay upon the sofa and would not say a single word. Now it depended whether John would be able to guess aright the third time. If he did, he would receive the fair princess's hand, and inherit the whole kingdom after the death of the old king. But if he guessed wrong, he would lose his life, and the sorcerer would eat his beautiful blue eyes.

The evening before the day John went to bed early, said his evening prayer, and slept peacefully. But his companion tied on his wings, hung his sword by his side, took all the three rods, and flew to the castle.

The night was dark and it was so stormy that the tiles flew from off the houses, and the trees in the garden, with the skeletons on them, bent like reeds before the wind. The lightning flashed every moment, and the thunder rolled as though it were one continuous peal all night. The window opened, and the princess flew out. She was as pale as death, but she laughed at the storm and

hought it was not bad enough. Her white mantle fluttered in
he air like the great sail of a ship, and John's travelling companion
vhipped her with his three rods till the blood ran down upon the
round and she could scarcely fly any farther. At last, however,
he reached the mountain.

"What a terrible hail-storm!" she said; "I have never been
ut in such weather."

"One can have too much of a good thing," said the sorcerer.
Then she told him that John had guessed aright the second time
oo, and if he did the same the next morning he would have won,
nd she would never be able to come to the mountain again, or
ractice such magic arts as she had formerly done; therefore she
vas very grieved.

"He will not be able to guess it this time," said the sorcerer.
I will think of something for you that he has never thought of,
nless he be a greater magician than I. But now let us be
nerry."

And then he took the princess by both hands, and they danced
round with all the little goblins and will-o'-the-wisps in the
oom. The red spiders ran up and down the walls quite as
errily; and it seemed as if the fiery flowers were throwing out
arks. The owl beat the drum, the crickets whistled, and the
ack grasshoppers played on mouth-organs. It was a merry
ll.

When they had danced enough the princess had to go home,
t she might be missed at the castle. The sorcerer said he
uld accompany her; they would thus still be together on
e way.

Then they flew away through the storm, and the travelling
mpanion broke his three rods across their backs. Never had
e sorcerer been out in such a hail-storm. Just outside the
stle he bade the princess good-bye, and whispered to her:
Think of my head!" But the companion had heard it, and
t as the princess slipped through the window into her bedroom,
d the magician was about to turn back, he seized him by his
g beard and with his sword struck off his hideous head just at
shoulders, so that the sorcerer did not even see him. He

threw the body into the sea to the fishes, but the head he only dipped in the water, and then tying it up in his silk handkerchief he took it with him to the inn and lay down to sleep.

The next morning he gave John the handkerchief and told him not to untie it before the princess asked him what she had thought of.

There were so many people in the great hall of the castle that they stood as close as radishes tied together in a bundle. The councillors sat upon their chairs with the soft cushions, and the old king had new clothes on ; his golden crown and the sceptre had been polished up, and he looked quite stately. But the princess was pale and wore a black gown, as though she were going to a funeral.

" What have I thought of ? " she asked John.

He immediately untied the handkerchief, and was himself startled when he beheld the hideous head of the sorcerer. All the people shuddered, for it was horrible to look at ; but the princess sat there like a marble statue, and could not utter a single word. At last she rose and gave John her hand, for he had guessed aright. She looked at no one, but sighed deeply and said " You are my master now ; the wedding shall take place this evening."

" Well, I am pleased," said the old king. " That's just what I wished."

All the people shouted "Hurrah," the band played in the streets the bells rang, and the cake-women took the black crape off thei sugar figures, for now there reigned great joy. Three roast oxer stuffed with ducks and chickens were put in the middle of th market-place, and every one could help himself to a slice. Th fountains ran with the finest wines, and if you asked for a penn roll at the baker's, you got six large buns as a present—and wit raisins, too.

In the evening the whole town was illuminated ; the soldiers le off cannons, and the boys crackers ; there were eating and drinking toasting and dancing, up at the castle. All the grand lords an ladies danced together; at a great distance they could be hear singing :

Here are many maidens fair
Dancing all so gladly,
Turning like a spinning-wheel
In the maze so madly;
Dance and jump the whole night through,
Till the sole falls from your shoe.

But the princess was still a witch, and did not care for John at
l. His travelling companion had thought of that, and he there-
re gave John three feathers from the swan's wings, and a little
ottle containing a few drops. He then told him to have a large
b full of water placed before the princess's bed, and when she was
out to retire, he must give her a little push, so that she might fall
to the water in which he was to dip her under three times, after
ving first thrown the feathers and the drops into it. This would
spel the charm under which she was, and she would love him
arly.

John did everything that his companion told him. The
incess shrieked when he dipped her under the water, and
uggled in his hands in the form of a great black swan with
arkling eyes. When she came out of the water for the
cond time, the swan was white, with the exception of a black
g round its neck. John prayed devoutly to Heaven, and
the water close a third time over the bird's head, and
the same moment it was changed into the most beautiful
ncess. She was more beautiful than before, and thanked
n with tears in her glorious eyes for having dispelled the
arm.

The next morning the old king came with his whole Court, and
ere were congratulations till late in the day. Last of all came
hn's travelling companion; John embraced him many times, and
d him he must not go away, but must remain with him, for he
s the cause of his good fortune. But the other shook his head
d said quietly and kindly: "No, my time is up. I have only
d my debt. Do you remember the dead man whom the
cked men wanted to ill-treat? You gave everything you
ssessed, so that he might rest in his grave. I am that dead
n!"

Saying this, he vanished.

The wedding lasted a whole month. John and the princess loved each other dearly, and the old king lived to see many happy days, and used to let his little grandchildren ride on his knee and play with his sceptre.

And in time John became king over the whole land.

"There is no Doubt about It."

" HAT was a terrible affair ! " said a hen, and in a quarter of the town, too, where it had not taken place. "That was a terrible affair in a hen-roost. I cannot sleep alone to-night. It is a good thing that many of us sit on the roost together." And then she told a story that made the feathers on the other hens bristle up, and the cock's comb fall. There was no doubt about it.

But we will begin at the beginning, and that is to be found in a hen-roost in another part of the town. The sun was setting, and the fowls were flying on to their roost; one hen, with white feathers and short legs, used to lay her eggs according to the regulations, and was, as a hen, respectable in every way. As she was flying upon the roost, she plucked herself with her beak, and a little feather came out.

"There it goes," she said; "the more I pluck, the more beautiful do I get." She said this merrily, for she was the best of the hens, and, moreover, as has been said, very respectable. With that she went to sleep.

It was dark all around, and hen sat close to hen, but the one who sat nearest to her merry neighbour did not sleep. She had heard and yet not heard, as we are often obliged to do in this world, in order to live at peace; but she could not keep it from her neighbour on the other side any longer. "Did you hear what was said ? I mention no names, but there is a hen here who intends to pluck herself in order to look well. If I were a cock, I should despise her."

Just over the fowls sat the owl, with father owl and the little owls. The family has sharp ears, and they all heard every word that their neighbour hen had said. They rolled their eyes, and mother owl, beating her wings, said: "Don't listen to her! But I suppose you heard what was said? I heard it with my own ears, and one has to hear a great deal before they fall off. There is one among the fowls who has so far forgotten what is becoming to a hen that she plucks out all her feathers and lets the cock see it."

"*Prenez garde aux enfants!*" said father owl; "children should not hear such things."

"But I must tell our neighbour owl about it; she is such an estimable owl to talk to." And with that she flew away."

"Too-whoo! Too-whoo!" they both hooted into the neighbour's dove-cot to the doves inside. "Have you heard? Have you heard? Too-whoo! There is a hen who has plucked out all her feathers for the sake of the cock; she will freeze to death, if she is not frozen already. Too-whoo!"

"Where? where?" cooed the doves.

"In the neighbour's yard. I have as good as seen it myself. It is almost unbecoming to tell the story, but there is no doubt about it."

"Believe every word of what we tell you," said the doves, and cooed down into their poultry-yard. "There is a hen—nay, some say that there are two—who have plucked out all their feathers, in order not to look like the others, and to attract the attention of the cock. It is a dangerous game, for one can easily catch cold and die from fever, and both of these are dead already."

"Wake up! wake up!" crowed the cock, and flew upon his board. Sleep was still in his eyes, but yet he crowed out: "Three hens have died of their unfortunate love for a cock. They had plucked out all their feathers. It is a horrible story; I will not keep it to myself, but let it go farther."

"Let it go farther," shrieked the bats, and the hens clucked and the cocks crowed, "Let it go farther! Let it go farther!" In this way the story travelled from poultry-yard to poultry-yard, and at last came back to the place from which it had really started.

"Five hens," it now ran, "have plucked out all their feathers to show which of them had grown leanest for love of the cock, and then they all pecked at each other till the blood ran down and they fell down dead, to the derision and shame of their family, and to the great loss of their owner."

The hen who had lost the loose little feather naturally did not recognise her own story, and being a respectable hen, said: "I despise those fowls; but there are more of that kind. Such things ought not to be concealed, and I will do my best to get the story into the papers, so that it becomes known throughout the land; the hens have richly deserved it, and their family too."

It got into the papers, it was printed; and there is no doubt about it, one little feather may easily grow into five hens.

Soup from a Sausage-Peg

HAT was an excellent dinner yesterday," said an old mouse of the female sex to another who had not been present at the festive meal. " I sat number twenty-one from the old mouse-king; that was not such a bad place ! Would you like to hear the *menu* ? The courses were very well arranged : mouldy bread, bacon rind, tallow candles, and sausage—and then the same things over again. It was just as good as having two banquets. Everything went on as jovially and as good-humouredly as at a family gathering. There was absolutely nothing left but the sausage-pegs ; the conversation turned upon these, and at last the expression ' soup from sausage skins,' or, as the proverb runs in the neighbouring country, ' soup from a sausage-peg,' was mentioned. Now every one had heard of this, but no one had tasted such soup, much less prepared it. A very pretty toast to the inventor was drunk ; it was said that he deserved to be made an overseer of the poor. That was very witty, wasn't it ? And the old mouse king rose and promised that the young female mouse who could prepare the said soup in the most tasty way should be his queen ; he gave her a year and a day for the trial."

"That wasn't bad !" said the other mouse ; "but how is the soup prepared ? "

" Ah ! how is it prepared ? " That was just what all the other female mice, both young and old, were asking. They would all have liked to be queen, but they did not want to take the trouble to go out into the wide world to learn how to prepare the soup, and yet that was what would have to be done. But every one is not ready to leave home and family ; and out in the world cheese-rinds are not to be had for the asking, nor is bacon to be smelt every day. No, one must suffer hunger, perhaps even be eaten up alive by a cat.

Such were probably the considerations by which the majority

allowed themselves to be deterred from going out into the world in search of information. Only four mice gave in their names as being ready to start. They were young and active, but poor; each of them intended to proceed to one of the four quarters of the globe, and it would then be seen to which of them fortune was favourable. Each of the four took a sausage-peg with her, so that she might be mindful of her object in travelling; the sausage-peg was to be her pilgrim's staff.

They set out at the beginning of May, and not till the May of the following year did they return, and then only three of them; the fourth did not report herself, nor did she send any word or sign, notwithstanding that the day of trial had arrived.

"Yes, every pleasure has its drawback," said the mouse-king; then he gave orders that all the mice for many miles round should be invited. They were to assemble in the kitchen, and the three travelled mice should stand in a row alone; a sausage-peg, hung with black crape, was erected in memory of the fourth, who was missing. No one was to give his opinion before the mouse-king had said what was to be said.

Now, we shall hear!

II.

What the First Little Mouse had Seen and Learnt on her Travels.

"When I went out into the wide world," said the little mouse, "I thought, as a great many do at my age, that I already knew all there was to be known. But that was not so; years must pass before one gets as far as that. I went straight to the sea. I went in a ship that sailed to the north. I had been told that a ship's cook must know how to make the best of things at sea, but it is easy to make the best of things if one has plenty of sides of bacon and great tubs of salt pork and mouldy flour; one has delicate living there, but one does not learn how to make soup from a sausage-peg. We sailed on for many days and nights; the ship rocked fearfully, and we did not get off without a wetting either. When we at last reached our destination I left the vessel; it was up in the far north.

"It is a strange thing to leave one's own corner at home, to sail in a ship which is only a kind of corner too, and then to suddenly find oneself more than a hundred miles away in a strange land. I saw great trackless forests of pines and birches, that smelt so strong that I sneezed and thought of sausages. There were great lakes there too. The waters when looked at quite close were clear, but from a distance they appeared black as ink. White swans lay upon them ; they lay so still I thought they were foam, but when I saw them fly and walk I recognised them. They belong to the same race as the geese ; one can easily see that by their walk—no one can deny his descent. I kept to my own kind. I associated with the forest and field mice, who by the way know very little, especially as regards cooking, and yet that was just what I had gone abroad for. The idea that soup might be made from a sausage-peg seemed to them so extraordinary that it at once spread from mouth to mouth through the whole wood. That the problem could ever be solved they thought an impossibility, and least of all did I think that there, and the very first night too, should I be initiated into the manner of preparing it. It was the height of summer, and that, said the mice, was why the forest smelt so strongly, why the herbs were so fragrant, the lakes so clear and yet so dark, with the swans floating upon them.

"On the edge of the wood, surrounded by three or four houses, a pole as high as the mainmast of a ship had been set up, and from the top of it hung wreaths and fluttering ribbons—it was a may-pole. Lads and lasses danced around the tree, and sang as loudly as they could to the music of the fiddler. All went merrily in the sunset and by moonlight, but I took no part in it—what has a little mouse to do with a May-dance? I sat in the soft moss and held my sausage-peg fast. The moon threw its rays just upon a spot where stood a tree covered with such exceedingly fine moss that I may almost say it was as fine and soft as the mouse-king's fur ; but it was green, and that is good for the eyes.

"All at once the most charming little people came marching out. They did not reach higher than my knee, and though they looked like human beings they were better proportioned. They called themselves elves, and wore fine clothes of flower-leaves trimmed with the wings of flies and gnats, which did not look at all bad. Directly they appeared they seemed to be looking for something—I did not know what; but at last some of them came up to me, the chief among them pointing to my sausage-peg, and saying: 'That is just the kind of one we want! It is pointed—it is excellent!' And the more he looked at my pilgrim's staff the more delighted he became.

"'To lend,' I said, 'but not to keep.'

"'Not to keep!' they all cried; then they seized the sausage-peg, which I let go, and danced off with it to the spot with the fine moss, where they set it up in the midst of the green. They wanted to have a maypole too, and that which they now had seemed cut out for them. Then it was decorated; what a sight that was!

"Little spiders spun golden threads round it, and hung it with fluttering veils and flags, so finely woven and bleached so snowy white in the moonshine that it dazzled my eyes. They took the colours from the butterflies' wings and strewed these over the white linen, and flowers and diamonds gleamed upon it so that I did not know my sausage-peg again; there was certainly not another maypole in the whole world like that which had been made out of it. And now only came the real great party of elves. They wore no clothes at all—it could not have been more genteel. I was invited to witness the festivities, but only at a certain distance, for I was too big for them.

"Then began a wonderful music! It seemed as if thousands of glass bells were ringing, so full, so rich that I thought it was the singing of the swans; I even thought I heard the voice of the cuckoo and the blackbird, and at last the whole wood seemed to join in. There were children's voices, the sound of bells, and the song of birds; the most glorious melodies and all that was lovely came out of the elves' maypole—it was a whole peal of bells, and yet it was my sausage-peg. That so much could have been got out of it I should never have believed, but it no doubt depends upon what hands it gets into. I was deeply moved; I wept, as a little mouse can weep, for pure joy.

"The night was far too short, but up yonder they are not any longer about that time of year. In the morning dawn the light breezes sprang up, the surface of the woodland lake became ruffled, and all the dainty floating veils and flags floated in the air. The wavy garlands of spiders' web, the hanging bridges and balustrades, or whatever they are called, vanished as if they were nothing; six elves carried my sausage-peg back to me, asking me at the same time whether I had any wish that they could fulfil. So I begged them to tell me how to make soup from a sausage-peg.

"'How we do it?' asked the chief of the elves, smiling. 'Why, you have just seen it. You hardly knew your own sausage-peg again.'

"'They only mean that for a joke,' I thought, and I told them straight away the object of my journey and what hopes were entertained at home respecting this brew. 'What advantage,' I asked, 'can accrue to the mouse-king and to the whole of our mighty kingdom by my having witnessed this splendour? I can't shake it out of the sausage-peg and say: "Look, here is the sausage-peg; now comes the soup!" That would be a kind of dish that could only be served up when people had had enough.'

"Then the elf dipped his little finger in the cup of a blue violet and said to me: 'Pay attention! Here I anoint your pilgrim's staff, and when you return home and enter the mouse-king's castle, touch the warm breast of your king with it, and violets will spring forth and cover the whole of the staff, even in the coldest winter time. And with that I think I have given you something to take home with you, and even a little more!'"

But before the little mouse said what this "a little more" was, she touched the king's breast with her staff, and in truth the most beautiful bunch of violets burst forth. They smelt so strongly that the mouse-king immediately ordered the mice who stood nearest the chimney to put their tails into the fire to make a smell of burning, for the scent of the violets was not to be borne, and was not of the kind they liked.

"But what was the 'more' of which you spoke?" asked the mouse-king.

"Well," said the little mouse, "that is, I think, what is called 'effect.'" And thereupon she turned the sausage-peg round, and behold, there was no longer a single flower to be seen upon it: she held only the naked peg, and this she lifted like a conductor's baton.

"'Violets,' the elf told me, 'are to look at, to smell, and to touch. Hearing and taste, therefore, still remain to be considered.'" Then the little mouse beat time, and music was heard —not such as rang through the forest at the elves' party, but such as is to be heard in the kitchen. What a sound of cooking and roasting there was! It came suddenly, as if the wind were rushing through all the victuals, and as if the pots and kettles were boiling over. The fire-shovel hammered upon the brass kettle, and then —suddenly all was quiet again. The low subdued singing of the tea-kettle was heard, and it was wonderful to listen to: they could not quite tell whether the kettle was beginning to boil or leaving off. The little pot bubbled up and the big pot bubbled up; the one did not care for the other, and it seemed as if there were no rhyme or reason in the pots. Then the little mouse waved her baton more and more wildly—the pots foamed, threw up large bubbles, boiled over; the wind roared and whistled through the chimney—ugh! it became so terrible that the little mouse even lost her stick.

"That was a heavy soup!" said the mouse-king.

"Isn't the dish coming soon?"

"That is all," answered the little mouse, with a bow.

"All! Well, then let us hear what the next has to say!" said the king.

III.

WHAT THE SECOND LITTLE MOUSE HAD TO TELL.

"I was born in the castle library," said the second mouse. "I and several members of our family have never had the good fortune to get into the dining-room, let alone the larder; it was only on my travels and here to-day that I saw a kitchen. Indeed we often had to suffer hunger in the library, but we acquired much knowledge. The rumour of the royal prize offered to those who could make soup from a sausage-peg reached our ears, and then my old grandmother brought out a manuscript that she could not read herself, but which she had heard read out, and in which was written: 'If one is a poet, one can make soup from a sausage-peg.'

She asked me whether I was a poet. I felt that I was innocent
in that respect, and she said that then I must go out and manage
to become one. I again asked what I was to do, for it was
quite as difficult for me to find that out as to make the soup.
But my grandmother had heard a good deal read out, and she said
three things above all were necessary : 'Understanding, imagination, and feeling. If you can manage to attain these three, you
are a poet, and then the matter of the sausage-peg will be an easy
one for you.'

" I departed and marched towards the west, out into the wide
world, to become a poet.

" Understanding is of the most importance in everything—that I
knew ; the other two qualities are held in much less esteem, and
I therefore went in quest of understanding first. Yes, where does
it dwell ? 'Go to the ant and learn wisdom,' said a great king of
the Jews ; that I had learnt in the library, so I did not stop till I
came to the first great ant-hill, and there I lay upon the watch to
become wise.

" The ants are a very respectable little people ; they are understanding all over. Everything with them is like a well-worked sum
in arithmetic that comes right. To work and to lay eggs, they say,
means both to live and to provide for posterity, and so that is
what they do. They divide themselves into clean and dirty ants ;
the ant-queen is number one, and her opinion the only correct one.
She contains the wisdom of all the world, and it was important for
me to know that. She spoke so much, and it was so clever, that
it seemed to me like nonsense. She said that her ant-hill was the
highest thing in the world, though close beside it stood a tree
which was higher, much higher—that was not to be denied, and
so nothing was said of it. One evening an ant had lost herself on
the tree and had crawled up the trunk—not so far up as the
crown, but still higher than any ant had reached till then ; and
when she turned round and came home again she told of something far higher that she had come across out in the world. But
this all the ants thought an insult to the community, and the ant
was therefore condemned to be muzzled and to be kept in solitary
confinement for life. But shortly afterwards another ant came

across the same tree and made the same journey and the same discovery. She spoke about it with deliberation, but unintelligibly, as they called it; and as she was, besides, a much-respected ant and one of the clean ones, she was believed; and when she died an egg shell was erected to her memory, for they had a great respect for the sciences. I saw," continued the little mouse, "that the ants always ran about with their eggs on their backs. One of them once dropped her egg, and though she took great pains to pick it up again, she did not succeed; just then two others came up who helped her with all their might, so that they nearly dropped their own eggs in doing so. But then they immediately stopped in their efforts, for one must think of one's self first—and the ant-queen declared that in this case both heart and understanding had been shown. 'These two qualities,' she said, 'give us ants a place in the first rank among all reasoning beings; we all possess understanding in a high degree, and I have the most of all.' And with that she raised herself on her hind legs, so that she could not fail to be recognised. I could not be mistaken: I swallowed her. 'Go to the ants to learn wisdom'—now I had the queen!

"I now went closer to the large tree I have already mentioned several times. It was an oak, with a tall trunk and a full wide-spreading crown, and was very old. I knew that here dwelt a living being, a woman called a Dryad, who is born with the tree and dies with it. I had heard of this in the library; now I beheld such a tree, and one of these oak maidens. She uttered a terrible cry when she saw me so close to her. Like all women, she was very much afraid of mice; but she had more cause to be so than others, for I could have gnawed the tree through, on which her life depended. I spoke to the maiden in a friendly cordial way, and inspired her with courage; she took me in her dainty hand, and when I had told her why I had gone out into the wide world, she promised me that very evening I should probably have one of the two treasures of which I was still in quest. She told me that Phantasy was her intimate friend, that he was as handsome as the God of Love, and that he rested many an hour under the leafy branches of the tree, which then rustled more strongly than ever over the two. He called her his Dryad, she said, and the tree his

ree; the beautiful gnarled oak was just to his taste, the roots
spread themselves deeply and firmly in the ground, and the trunk
and the crown rose high up into the fresh air; they knew the driving
snow, the keen winds, and the warm sunshine, as these should be
known. 'Yes,' continued the Dryad, 'the birds up there in the
crown sing and tell of foreign countries they have visited, and on
he only dead bough the stork has built his nest—that is very
ornamental, and one hears a little too about the land of the
pyramids. All this pleases Phantasy, but it is not enough for him;
o I myself have to tell him about the life in the woods, and have
o go back to my childhood's days when I was young and the tree
as frail, so frail that a stinging-nettle overshadowed it; and I
ave to tell everything till now that the tree has grown big and
rong. Now sit you down under the green thyme yonder and
ay attention; and when Phantasy comes I'll find some oppor-
nity to pinch his wings and to pull out a little feather; take the
ather—no better one has been given a poet for a pen—and it
ill suffice you!'

"And when Phantasy came, the feather was pulled out, and I
ized it," said the little mouse. "I put it in water and held it
ere till it got soft. It was very hard to digest even then, but
ill I nibbled it up at last. It is very easy to gnaw one's self into
ing a poet, though there are many things that one has to
allow. Now I had two—understanding and imagination—and
rough these two I knew that the third was to be found in the
rary; for a great man has said and written that there are novels
nich exist purely and solely to relieve people of their superfluous
rs, and are therefore a kind of sponge to suck up the feelings.
remembered a few of those books which had always looked
rticularly appetising, and were well thumbed and greasy; they
ust have absorbed an infinite deal of emotion.

"I betook myself back to the library, and devoured, so to
eak, a whole novel—that is, the soft or essential part of it; but
t crust, the binding, I left. When I had digested it, and
other one besides, I noticed what a stirring there was inside me,
a I devoured a piece of a third novel. And now I was a poet.
I aid so to myself and told it to others too. I had headache and

stomach-ache, and I don't know what aches I didn't have. Then I began to think what stories might be made to refer to a sausage-peg, and a great many pegs and sticks and staves and splinters came into my thoughts—the ant-queen had possessed an extra-ordinary understanding. I remembered the man who put a white stick into his mouth by which he could make both himself and the stick invisible. I thought of wooden hobby-horses, of stock rhymes, of breaking the staff over any one, and of goodness knows how many expressions of that kind concerning staves, sticks, and pegs. All my thoughts ran upon pegs, sticks, and staves, and if one is a poet—and that I am, for I have tortured myself till I have become one—one must be able to make poetry on these things too. I will therefore be able to serve you up a peg—that is, a story—every day in the week; yes, that is my soup!"

"Let us hear what the third one has to say!" ordered the mouse-king.

"Peep! peep!" was heard at the kitchen door, and a little mouse—it was the fourth of the mice who had competed for the prize, the one whom the others believed to be dead—shot in like an arrow. She threw the sausage-peg with the crape right over. She had been running day and night, had travelled on the railway by goods train, having watched her opportunity, and yet she had arrived almost too late. She pressed forward, looking very crumpled; she had lost her sausage-peg, but not her voice, for she began to speak at once, as if they had been waiting only for her and wanted to hear her only—as if everything else in the world were of no consequence whatever. She spoke at once and went on till she had said all she had to say. She appeared so un-expectedly that no one had time to object to her speech while she was speaking. Let us hear what she said.

IV.

What the Fourth Mouse had to Tell, before the Third One had Spoken.

"I immediately betook myself to the largest town," she said "the name has escaped me—I have a bad memory for names

From the railway station I was taken with some confiscated goods
to the town-hall, and when I arrived there, I ran into the gaoler's
dwelling. The gaoler was talking of his prisoners, especially of one
who had uttered some hasty words. About these words other words
had been spoken, and then again others, and these again had
been written down and recorded.

" The whole thing is soup from a sausage-peg," said the gaoler ;
' but the soup may cost him his neck ! "

" Now this gave me some interest in the prisoner," said the
little mouse, " so I seized an opportunity and slipped in to him ;
there is a mouse-hole behind every locked door ! The prisoner
looked very pale, and had a long beard and large sparkling eyes.
The lamp flickered and smoked, and the walls were so used to
that, that they grew no blacker for it. The prisoner was scratch-
ing pictures and verses in white upon black, but I did not read
them. I believe he felt very dull, and I was a welcome guest.
He lured me with bread-crumbs, with whistling, and with gentle
words. He was very glad to see me : I gradually began to trust him,
and we became friends. He shared his bread-and-water with me,
gave me cheese and sausage, and I lived well ; but I must say that
after all it was principally the good company that kept me there.
He let me run about in his hand, on his arm, and right up his
sleeve ; he let me creep about in his beard, and called me his
little friend. I really began to like him—such things are mutual !
I forgot what I had gone out into the wide world to seek, and left
my sausage-peg in a crack in the floor ; it lies there still. I
wanted to stay where I was ; if I went away, the poor prisoner
would have no one at all, and that is too little in this world. I
stayed, but he did not. He spoke to me very sadly the last time,
gave me twice as much bread-and-cheese as usual, and threw me
kisses ; he went and never came back. I don't know his history.
' Soup from a sausage-peg ! ' the gaoler had said, and to him I
now went. He certainly took me in his hand, but he put me into
a cage, into a tread-mill. That's awful ! One runs and runs and
gets no farther, and is only laughed at.

The gaoler's daughter was a most charming little girl with a
head of curls like the finest gold, and such joyous eyes and such

a smiling mouth! 'You poor little mouse,' she said; and peeping
into my hateful cage she drew out the iron pin, and I sprang down
upon the window-sill and so out upon the gutter of the roof.
Free! free! I thought only of that, and not of the object of my
travels.

"It was dark—night was drawing near. I took up my lodgings
in an old tower where a watchman and an owl dwelt. I trusted
neither, and least of the two the owl. That animal is like a cat,
and possesses the great failing of eating mice; but one may be
mistaken, and that I was. She was a respectable, highly-educated
old owl; she knew more than the watchman, and quite as much
as I. The owl children made a fuss about everything. 'Don't
make soup from a sausage-peg,' the old one would say; those
were the harshest words she could bring herself to utter, such
tender affection did she cherish for her own family. Her behaviour
inspired me with such confidence that I sent her a 'peep'! from
the crack where I sat; this confidence pleased her very much,
and she assured me that I should be under her protection,
and that no animal would be allowed to do me harm. She
would eat me herself in winter, she declared, when food got
scarce.

"She was in every way a clever woman; she explained to me
that the watchman could only shriek through the horn that hung
loose at his side, saying, 'He is terribly conceited about it, and
thinks he is an owl in the tower. He wants to look big, but is
very little! Soup from a sausage-peg!'

"I begged the owl to give me the recipe for the soup, and then
she explained it to me: 'Soup from a sausage-peg,' she said, 'is
only a human expression, and can be used in different ways.
Every one thinks his own way is the most correct, but the whole
thing really means nothing.'

"Nothing!" I exclaimed. I was struck. The truth is not
always agreeable, but truth is above everything, and the old owl
said so too. So I thought it over, and soon perceived that if I
brought home that which is above everything, I should bring far
more than soup from a sausage-peg. And thereupon I hastened
away, so that I might get home in time and bring the highest and

best, that which is above everything—the truth. The mice are an enlightened little people, and the mouse-king is above them all. He is capable of making me queen—for the sake of truth!"

"Your truth is a lie!" said the mouse who had not yet spoken. "I can prepare the soup, and I will prepare it too."

V.

HOW IT WAS PREPARED.

"I didn't travel," said the third mouse; "I remained in the country, and that's the right thing to do. There is no necessity to travel—one can get everything just as good here. I remained; I did not get my information from supernatural beings, did not gobble it up, nor yet learn it from owls. I have evolved mine from my own thoughts. Now just you get the kettle put upon the fire. That's it. Now some water poured into it! Quite full—up to the brim! So—now more fuel! Let it burn up, so that the water boils—it must boil over and over! That's it! Now throw the peg in. Will the king now be pleased to dip his tail into the boiling water and stir it with that tail? The longer the king stirs, the stronger the soup will become. It costs nothing. It requires no other ingredients—only stirring!"

"Can't any one else do that?" asked the king.

"No," said the mouse, "it is only the king's tail that contains the power."

And the water boiled and spluttered, and the mouse-king placed himself close to the kettle—there was almost danger attached to it—he put out his tail, as the mice do in the dairy when they skim a pan of milk, and then lick their creamy tails; but he only put his tail in as far as the hot steam, then he quickly sprang down from the hearth.

"It's understood, of course, that you are to be my queen!" he cried; "but we'll leave the soup till our golden wedding; in this way the poor of my kingdom, who will have to be fed then, will have something to look forward to with pleasure, and for a long time,

Then they held the wedding. But several of the mice said as they were returning home, "that was really not to be called soup from a sausage-peg after all, but rather soup from a mouse's tail." This and that of what had been told they thought very good ; but the whole thing might have been different. "Now I would have told it so—and so—and so——!"

These were the critics, and they are always so wise—afterwards.

This story went out all over the wide world, and opinions differed about it, but the story itself remained as it was. And that is the best thing in both great things and small, even with regard to soup from a sausage-peg—not to expect any thanks for it

The Beetle

HE emperor's favourite horse was shod with gold ; he had a golden horseshoe on each foot.

But why was that?

He was a beautiful creature, with slender legs, bright intelligent eyes, and a mane that hung down like a veil over his neck. He had carried his master through the smoke of powder and the rain of bullets, and had heard the balls whistling past ; he had bitten, kicked, and taken part in the fight when the enemy pressed forward, and leaping with the emperor across the fallen horse of one of the foe, had saved the bright golden crown and the life of the emperor—and that was worth more than all the bright gold. And that is why the emperor's horse had golden horseshoes.

A beetle came creeping out. "First the great, then the small," said he ; "but size is not everything." And with that he stretched out his thin legs.

"Well, what do you want?" asked the smith.

"Golden shoes," replied the beetle.

"Why, you must be out of your senses!" cried the smith. "You want golden shoes too?"

"Certainly—golden shoes!" said the beetle. "Am I not as good as that creature there, that is waited on, and brushed, and has food and drink put before him? Don't I belong to the imperial stables too?"

"But why has the horse golden shoes?" asked the smith. "Don't you understand that?"

"Understand? I understand that it is a personal slight for me," said the beetle. "It is done to vex me, and I will therefore go out into the wide world."

"Go along!" said the smith.

"You rude fellow!" said the beetle; and then he went out of the stable, flew a short distance, and soon afterwards found himself in a beautiful flower garden, fragrant with roses and lavender.

"Isn't it beautiful here?" asked one of the little lady-birds that were flying about with their red shield-shaped black-spotted wings. "How sweet it is here, and how lovely!"

"I have been used to better than that," said the beetle. "You call this beautiful? Why, there's not even a dunghill."

Then he went on, under the shadow of a big gilliflower, where a caterpillar was creeping along.

"How beautiful the world is!" said the caterpillar; "the sun is so warm, and everything so happy! And when I one day fall asleep and die, as they call it, I shall awake as a butterfly."

"What things you do fancy!" said the beetle. "To fly about as a butterfly! I come from the emperor's stable, but no one there—not even the emperor's favourite horse, that wears my cast-off golden shoes—fancies anything like that. Get wings! Fly! Well, we'll fly now!" And away flew the beetle. "I don't want to be vexed, but I am all the same," he said, as he flew off.

Soon afterwards he fell upon a great lawn; here he lay awhile, and pretended to be asleep, but at last he really dozed off.

Suddenly a heavy shower of rain fell from the clouds. The noise awoke the beetle, and he wanted to creep into the earth, but could not, for he was being turned over and over. First he was swimming on his stomach, then on his back, and flying was not to be thought of; he despaired of getting away from the place alive. So he lay where he lay, and remained there. When the rain had left off a little, and the beetle had blinked the water out of his eyes, he saw the gleam of something white; it was linen laid out to bleach. He reached it and crept into a fold of the damp linen. It was certainly not so comfortable here as in the warm dunghill in the stable, but nothing better happened to be at hand, and so he stayed where he was—stayed a whole day and a whole night, and the rain stayed too. Towards morning he crept out; he was greatly annoyed at the climate.

On the linen sat two frogs, their bright eyes sparkling with pure joy.

"This is glorious weather," said one. "How refreshing! And the linen keeps the water together so beautifully. My hind legs are itching to swim."

"I should like to know," said the other, "whether the swallow which flies about so far has ever found a better climate than ours in her many travels abroad. So nice and damp! It is really like lying in a wet ditch. Whoever doesn't like this can't be said to love his native country."

"Have you then never been in the emperor's stable?" asked the beetle. "There the dampness is warm and fragrant: that's the climate for me! But you can't take it with you when you travel. Is there no dung-heap in the garden here, where people of rank, like myself, can feel at home and take up their quarters?"

The frogs either could not or would not understand him.

"I never ask twice!" exclaimed the beetle, after he had already asked three times and received no answer.

Thereupon he went a little further, and came across a piece of broken pottery which should certainly not have been lying there, but which, as it lay, afforded a good shelter against wind and weather. Here lived several families of earwigs; they did not require much—only company. The females are full of tenderest maternal love, and every mother therefore praised her child as the most beautiful and cleverest.

"Our little son is engaged to be married!" said one mother. "Sweet innocence! It is his sole ambition to get into a parson's ear some day. He is so artless and loveable; his engagement will keep him steady. What joy for a mother!"

"Our son," said another mother, "had hardly crept out of the egg, when he was off on his travels. He's all life and spirits; he'll run his horns off. What joy for a mother! Isn't it so, Mr. Beetle?" They recognised the stranger by the cut of his wings.

"You are both right!" said the beetle, and then they begged him to enter the room; that is to say, to come as far as he could under the piece of pottery.

"Now you see my little earwig too," cried a third and a fourth mother. "They are the sweetest children, and very playful. They are never naughty, except when they occasionally have pains in their inside; unfortunately, one gets those only too easily at their age."

In this manner every mother spoke of her baby, and the babies joined in too, and used the little nippers that they have in their tails to pull the beetle by his beard.

"Yes, they're always up to something, the little rogues!" said the mothers, boiling over with maternal affection. But this bored the beetle, and so he asked whether it was much farther to the dunghill.

"Why, that's out in the wide world, on the other side of the ditch," answered an earwig; "I hope none of my children will go so far—it would be the death of me."

"I'll try to get as far anyhow," said the beetle; and he went off without saying good-bye, for that is considered the most polite way. By the ditch he met several of his kind—all beetles.

"We live here!" they said. "We are very comfortable. May we ask you to step down into the rich mud? The journey has no doubt been very fatiguing for you?"

"Very," said the beetle. "I have been exposed to the rain, and have had to lie on linen, and cleanliness always weakens me very much. I have pain too in one wing through having stood in the draught under a broken piece of pottery.

It is really quite a comfort to get once more among one's own kindred."

" Perhaps you come from the dung-heap ? " asked the eldest.

"Oho ! from higher places !" cried the beetle. " I come from the emperor's stable, where I was born with golden shoes on my feet. I am travelling on a secret mission, but you must not ask me any questions about it, for I won't betray the secret."

With that the beetle stepped down into the rich mud. There sat three young beetle maidens ; they giggled, because they did not know what to say.

"They are all three still disengaged," said the mother ; and the young beetle maidens giggled again, this time from bashfulness.

" I have not seen greater beauties in the imperial stables," said the beetle, taking a rest.

" Don't you spoil my girls for me, and don't speak to them unless you have serious intentions. But about that I have no doubt, and so I give you my blessing ! "

" Hurrah ! " cried all the other beetles, and our beetle was now engaged. The engagement was immediately followed by the wedding, for there was no reason for delay.

The following day passed very pleasantly, and the one after that fairly so ; but on the third day the time had come to think of food for the wife, and perhaps even for the children.

"I have allowed myself to be taken in," thought the beetle ; "nothing is therefore left for me but to take others in, in return."

So said, so done. Away he went, and stayed out the whole day and the whole night—and his wife sat there, a lonely widow.

" Oh ! " said the other beetles, "that fellow whom we received into our family is a thorough vagabond ; he went away and left his wife sitting there, to be a burden upon us."

" Well, then she must be passed off as unmarried again, and stay here as my child," said the mother. " Fie on the villain who deserted her ! "

In the meantime the beetle had gone on travelling, and had sailed across the watery ditch on a cabbage-leaf. In the morning two people came to the ditch; when they spied him, they picked him up, turned him over and over, and looked very wise, especially one of them—a boy. " Allah sees the black beetle in the black stone and in the black rock. Isn't it written so in the Koran?" Then he translated the beetle's name into Latin, and enlarged upon its species and nature. The second person, an older scholar, was for taking him home with them. But the other said that they had specimens quite as good as that, and this, our beetle thought, was not a polite thing to say—so he suddenly flew out of the speaker's hand. His wings being now dry, he flew a pretty long distance and reached a hotbed, where, one of the windows of the glass-house being ajar, he slipped in comfortably and buried himself in the fresh manure.

" How delightful it is here ! " he said.

Soon after, he fell asleep and dreamed that the emperor's favourite horse had fallen and had given him his golden horseshoes, with the promise to have two more made for him.

That was very acceptable. When the beetle awoke, he crept out and looked about him. What splendour there was in the hothouse ! In the background were palm trees, growing to a great height ; the sun made them look transparent, and under them what a wealth of verdure and bright flowers, red as fire, yellow as amber, and white as driven snow !

"There is an incomparable splendour in these plants," said the beetle; "how fine they will taste when they decay ! This is a good larder ! There must certainly be relatives of mine living here. I'll have a look round to see if I can find any one to associate with. Proud I am, and that is my pride." And now he strolled about in the hothouse, and thought of his beautiful dream of the dead horse, and the golden horseshoes he had inherited.

Suddenly a hand seized the beetle, pressed him, and turned him over and over.

The gardener's son and a little girl who played with him had come up to the hotbed, had spied the beetle, and wanted to have some fun with him. First he was wrapped up in a vine-leaf, and then put into a warm trousers-pocket. There he cribbled and crabbled about with all his might; but for this he got a squeeze from the boy's hand, and that taught him to be quiet. Then the boy ran off to the great lake at the end of the garden. Here the beetle was put into an old half-broken wooden shoe, in which a little stick was placed for a mast, and to this mast the beetle was bound by a woollen thread. Now he was a sailor and had to sail. The lake was very large, and to the beetle it seemed an ocean; he was so terrified by it that he fell on his back and kicked out with his feet. The little ship sailed away, and the current of the water seized it. But when it went too far from the shore, the little boy would turn up his trousers, go into the water, and fetch it back to the land. But at last, just as it was setting out to sea again in full sail, the children were called away for something important; they hastened to obey, and running away from the lake, left the little ship to its fate. This drifted farther and farther away from the shore, and farther out into the open sea; it was terrible for the beetle, for he could not get away, being bound to the mast. Then a fly paid him a visit. "What lovely weather!" said the fly. "I'll rest here and bask in the sun; it's very pleasant for you here."

"You talk of what you don't understand! Don't you see that I'm tied fast?"

"But I'm not," said the fly, and flew off.

"Well, now I know the world," said the beetle. "It's a base world. I'm the only honest one in it. First, they refuse me golden shoes; then I have to lie on wet linen and stand in a draught; and, to cap all, they fasten a wife on to me. Then, when I have taken a quick step out into the world, and learn how comfortable one can be there, and how I ought to have it, up comes a human boy, binds me fast, and leaves me to the wild waves, while the emperor's favourite horse prances about in golden shoes. That vexes me most of all! But one must not count on sympathy in this world. My career is very interesting; but what's the use of that if nobody knows it? The world doesn't deserve to be made acquainted with my story, for it ought to have given me golden shoes in the emperor's stable when the emperor's favourite horse was being shod, and I stretched out my legs too. If I had received golden shoes I should have been an ornament to the stable; now the stable has lost me, the world has lost me—all is over!"

But all was not over yet. A boat, in which there were some young girls, came rowing up.

"Look, there's an old wooden shoe sailing along," said one of the girls.

"There's a little creature tied up in it!" cried another.

The boat came quite close to our beetle's little ship, and the young girls fished it up out of the water. One of them drew a small pair of scissors out of her pocket, cut the woollen thread without hurting the beetle, and when she got to the shore placed him in the grass.

"Creep, creep. Fly, fly—if you can," she said. "Freedom is a glorious thing."

The beetle flew up and went through the open window of a large building; there he sank down, tired and exhausted, upon the fine, soft, long mane of the emperor's horse that was standing in the stables where both he and the beetle were at home. The beetle clung fast to the mane, sat there quite still for a short time, and recovered.

"Here I sit on the emperor's favourite horse—sit on him just like an emperor. But what was I going to say? Ah, yes! I remember. It's a good idea, and quite correct. Why does the emperor's horse have golden shoes? That's what the smith asked me. Now the answer is clear to me. The horse had golden horseshoes on my account!"

And now the beetle was in a good temper. "Travelling opens one's brains," he said.

The sun's rays came streaming into the stable upon him, and made things bright and pleasant.

"The world is not so bad after all, when you come to examine it," said the beetle, "but you must know how to take it."

Yes, the world was beautiful, because the emperor's favourite horse had only received golden shoes so that the beetle might become his rider. " Now I will go down to the other beetles and tell them how much has been done for me. I will relate to them all the disagreeable things I went through in my travels abroad, and tell them that I shall now remain at home till the horse has worn out his golden shoes."

Printed by BALLANTYNE, HANSON & Co.
London & Edinburgh